STO

THE MATRUSHKA DOLL

THE
MATRUSHKA DOLL

A NOVEL BY
BARBARA FISCHMAN TRAUB

RICHARD MAREK PUBLISHERS
NEW YORK

First printing

Library of Congress Cataloging in Publication Data

Traub, Barbara Fischman.
   The matrushka doll.
   1.   Holocaust, Jewish (1939–1945)—Fiction.
I.   Title.
PZ4.T776Mat   [PS3570.R338]   813'.5'4   79-9807

ISBN 0-399-90044-6

Printed in the United States of America

Acknowledgments

My gratitude and love
to Bella and Francis Rézmüves for remembering;
to Ada Truppin for causing a spark;
to Milton Fisher for his faith in me;
to Lenora DeSio, Shirley and Carl Bakal, Ron Fredricks, Zsuzsi
    and Bandi Gál, Monique and Dan Goldwasser, Stanislaw Jo-
    nas, Giszella Perl, Dorothy and Ivor Schapiro, Nellie Dermer
    Schnur, Elga and Steve Stulman, and Ollie Turner, for caring;
and to Deborah Zaitchik, my editor, for understanding.

I dedicate this book to the memory of my parents, Regina and Nandor Fischman, to my husband Herman and son Ralph, and to my great friend Sol Yurick.

PRELUDE

Weisswasser (Germany? Czechoslovakia?), spring 1945

The large poster on the wall depicts a huge finger vertically across an enormous mouth. The lips are tightly pressed together, the finger has a squarely filed nail and a neatly manicured cuticle. Underneath the mouth and finger a slogan warns: PST! FEIND HÖRT MIT! "Pst! The enemy is listening!"

Lisa Engler takes her eyes off the poster, then reaches to a shelf and removes a small box, shaped like a canister, studded with bolts and screws and wire connections.

She wonders what day it is. It must be Saturday morning, she concludes, because work at the factory began later than it did yesterday. Standing at a worktable, she tests the canister with two prods attached to a small box.

If the meter needle swings left of center, the canister she is testing is defective and needs to be repaired. She is supposed to put each defective canister on a special table, then walk away. A French "volunteer worker" would then go to that table, take the canister to his own worktable and do the required repair. The Frenchman is forbidden to walk to the special table while she is still there. Should that happen, her head would be shaven and his mail or food parcels from home would be confiscated.

When the needle swings to the right, the canister is perfect.

Yes, Lisa Engler thinks, right is good, left is bad. Right is life, left is death. *Links, rechts, links. Links. Links. Links.* It was always left.

She has been testing since early February. Maybe it was January. She is not sure. January, February, what does it matter? All she knows for sure is that the day after she had arrived at this camp, she was assigned to work in the testing section at the factory. She has no idea what the canister-shaped boxes she is testing are, though she suspects they are airplane parts.

She routinely tests another canister. She never puts a defective canister on the special table, only perfectly good ones. The defective ones she places on the shelf marked IN ORDNUNG, "in order." The defective ones will be used as good ones, she thinks. The thought that she passes on defective canisters as good ones makes her pulse quicken. Right is life, left is death; and she switches left for right. She envisions a Stuka suddenly exploding in the air, Nazis blown to bits. Good!

She goes on testing. The needle swings to the left. The canister is damaged but she puts it on the shelf marked IN ORDNUNG. She tests another: the needle now swings to the right. Perfect. She brings the canister to the special table. The Frenchman understands. He pretends to fix whatever she places on the table. Volunteer indeed! *Comme un pion du jeu d'échecs,* he had whispered to her once. A pawn in a chess game.

She notices the man in the white smock staring at her, and she wonders if today she ought to place an authentically defective canister on the special table. She knows the man wears an SS uniform under the smock. He is the factory SS supervisor.

Her hands tremble, she can barely steady the testing prods.

Someone approaches her table. She dares not look up, merely steals a glance at eye level. She sees white in front of her.

The SS supervisor has discovered the sabotage, she thinks. And closes her eyes.

"Der Krieg ist heute zu Ende," he says. She opens her eyes, sees him place something on her table, then quickly walk away. She is shaking all over. The war came to an end today, he said. What did he mean? Who won? She cannot control her jitters and looks at the small parcel wrapped in brown paper the SS left on the table. She knows, without touching it, it's a slice of bread.

Der Krieg ist heute . . . She reaches for the parcel, then abruptly pulls her hand back, as if burned. No, she must not believe him. He is an SS. She must not touch the parcel. It is a trap, the parcel, the *Krieg* . . .

The SS wants to trick her. Accuse her of stealing bread, then shave her head again.

The Ukraine, spring 1944

The evening the Romanian guards disappeared, two hundred Jews were still alive in the ghetto at Bershad. The *Wehrmacht* had cleared out earlier that day.

The Transnistrian village of Bershad was liberated next dawn. A Russian captain entered the ghetto with a platoon of soldiers and asked to speak with the *oscina*, as the council of Jews was called. Two old men, one limping and one toothless, came forth. The captain asked to be shown at once where the mass grave was. The toothless old man pointed to the end of the ghetto where the ravine had been. Last January the Nazis had filled it up with two thousand five hundred men after having mowed them down with machine guns in less than an hour. The men were murdered because some of them had hidden a few Russian partisans. Two thousand among those men were Jews.

The soldiers began to pile earth on top of the mass grave till it grew into a big mound. By the time the mass grave looked more like a hill, all the villagers had come into the ghetto. The Jews did not mingle with them.

A soldier raised a bugle to his lips and the captain unfurled a red flag. He planted it in the ground along with a freshly made wooden marker bearing the inscription: "In memory of two thousand five hundred martyrs brutally slain by imperialist-fascist forces during the great patriotic war." The captain's eyes lingered briefly over the marker, then he shook his head lightly, a look of pain on his face.

His name was Leonid Yashenko.

Weisswasser (Germany? Czechoslovakia?), same morning

The whistle blows to signal the Jewish women inmates to file up for the latrine. But the SS *Aufseherin* is not taking them there. She marches out with them, back to camp.

There are no guards at the entrance. A few civilians dart out from the SS quarters.

The realization suddenly hits the women: there are no SS at all in the camp!

"They're hiding outside the wires, I bet," someone yells. "They want us to think the war is over and leave camp, so they can shoot us down for target practice."

"*Zählappel!*" someone else yells. "Roll call! Let's have it with or without them. If we don't follow regulations, they'll kill us."

Women stand in rows of five waiting to be counted. A few hang around for a while, then leave the rows, get closer to the wire fence. The camp is high on a hill and down the road, outside the camp there is commotion, people dash back and forth. Nobodys wear Nazi uniforms. They all seem to be civilians.

Lisa Engler suddenly screams:

"There he goes! The *Kommandant!*"

Everyone now runs to the wire fence and looks at him from inside the camp. The commandant is dressed in a gray suit, white shirt and a blue tie, a soft hat pulled down over his forehead.

"Let's kill the bastard!" someone yells.

"Shoot him!"

Nobody moves.

The commandant is flanked by three men dressed in civilian clothes. From the hill, inside the camp, the inmates look down on the scurrying civilians. They look like little dots frantically running about, ants gone berserk after a farmer's boot had smashed an anthill.

"There they run, the whole bunch of *verfluchte* SS!"

"Let's go after them!"

"Let's!"

Nobody moves.

"There are guns, explosives buried in bunkers. I've seen them—"

"So let's shoot the *Schweinhunde!*"

". . . the SS *Dreck!*"

"After the *dreckige Bande!* Now!"

Nobody moves.

"It's over, the war is over, don't you see? We are free! Free!"

"After the SS *Dreck*, I tell you! Now is the time to get the SS shit," a tall woman yells.

Nobody moves.

Then someone screams at the civilians below:

"Kaput! Verfluchte, Schweinhunde, Dreck you called us. Now you are *kaput! Kaput* Nazis! Nazis *kaput!"*

"Nazi *Dreck! Kaput! Kaput!"* the chorus echoes.

The civilians keep hurrying by. They don't look up.

"Let's go after them!" the tall woman yells again. "Now, before they run away. Come on! Now!"

But the women don't move. They can't. All they can do is scream:

"Kaput, Nazi *Dreck, kaput! Kaput!* . . ."

The Ukraine, spring 1944, same morning

After the ceremony, Captain Yashenko walked over to the group of Jews.

"Show me the ghetto records," he told the Jew who limped.

The man shrugged his shoulders.

"Before the Nazis murdered the two thousand five hundred men, they destroyed everything. The records too. Set them on fire."

"Were there any Jews from Iasi in the ghetto?" the captain then asked.

The limping Jew turned to the toothless old man.

"Moshe," he said, "you've been with the *oscina* longer than I. Were there any Jews from Iasi in Bershad?"

The old man looked at the captain, sighed. His eyes were watering. He wiped them with the cuff of his sleeve, sighed again.

"Come on, old man." The captain's voice broke for a moment, then he cleared his throat. "Any Jews from Iasi?"

The old man nodded.

"What happened to them?" the captain asked thickly.

"Dispersed to other ghettos. Pevomaisk, Bobrinets, Voznosensk . . . who knows. Gone."

The captain gave the old man a pack of cigarettes.

"Take it," he said, then lit the old man's cigarette and lit one for himself. They smoked in silence for a while.

"Yashenberg," the captain said slowly. "Did you know anyone by that name? Nachum and Rifka Yashenberg? Middle-aged? Were they here?"

The old man took a last drag of the cigarette, dropped it on the ground, then slowly crushed it with his foot.

"There were so many," he said apologetically. "Maybe they

were here. Maybe not. Maybe they were here, then taken somewhere else. Who knows . . . I am sorry."

Weisswasser, same day, later

"A man wants to see you," an inmate tells Lisa Engler.

It is Papa, Lisa thinks, and runs outside the camp. It must be Papa, my Papa has found me. Papa is here. The nightmare—over. . . .

"Come with me." Dressed in civilian clothes, the SS supervisor looks shabby. "The Russians will be here tomorrow," he says. "They are brutes, these Russians. Pigs. They may harm you . . . rape . . . The Americans are not far from here. Come, I'll take you there, save you from the Russian pigs. You'll tell the Americans I saved you. Wait! Don't run away . . . Wait!"

Poland, Lublin, June 1944

"It's not a ghetto; it's not a work camp," the sergeant told Captain Yashenko. "I've seen nothing like it before . . ." He shuddered, spat on the floor. "They look like cadavers. *Ver—Vernichtungslager*, one of them mumbled. What's a *Ver*—you know what I mean, comrade captain."

The captain was leafing through a file on his desk. He did not look at the sergeant.

"*Vernichtung*: nullification, annihilation. Extermination. As if it never was. *Nicht*: none, nothing, negative." He quickly flipped pages to steady his hand. "What's the name of the camp, comrade?"

"Treblinka."

Captain Yashenko drove to Treblinka. It was a short trip, only three kilometers from Lublin. He walked through the camp, spoke to a few survivors. His face glistened. His cheeks were bathed in a moist filmy glow, as though he was weeping. But then, it was very hot that day in Treblinka. The captain may have been simply perspiring.

"Any Jews from Iasi?" he asked a man. The man stared at him out of deep black sockets. A fly was stuck in the ooze of his lower lip. The captain saw the man's skin and bones through the torn shirt.

Another man trudged closer.

14

"He can't hear you anymore," he said pointing his chin to the man in the torn shirt. "He is like in a trance. Succumbed to visions of food. That's all he can think of. He is a goner. They are all goners once they give in . . . we call them *Muselmans.* He'll die in a day or two . . . What was your question, captain?"

"Any Jews here from Iasi?" the captain repeated, and gave the man a pack of cigarettes. "Yashenberg," he went on, "did you know anyone by that name? Rifka and Nachum Yashenberg? From Iasi?"

"Let me think." The veins at his temple throbbed, he was breathing fast. "Sorry," he said, touching his head. "I can't think. It hurts. And it's hard to remember. There were so many."

Somewhere in Germany, early spring 1945

The snow is frozen. Their feet are wrapped in rags. Blankets hanging round their shoulders are soggy. They had been marching through forests, without a pause, for days. Maybe weeks. Or months.

Miklos Engler vaguely remembers the SS feverishly blowing up installations in Auschwitz. The factory at Buna, the crematoria in Birkenau. Then came the selections. Some were put in trains, others in columns. Others . . . But he was lucky.

He marches beside Dr. Rausk, a man from his town. Since evacuation they have eaten only roots, frozen grass, a few acorns and berries.

Once in a while Dr. Rausk says something.

"My son, he plays the violin."

Miklos Engler nods. He remembers the doctor's son. The boy is his sister's friend. Then Miklos thinks of his own little boy and tears well up in his eyes. He wants to wipe them off but has no strength to lift his hands. He looks at them. They are dead white, the skin is peeling. He tries to move his fingers. He cannot. It is just as well, he thinks, they would fall off. The peeling skin is like foam or ash. If he does not move his fingers, he is sure they will stay stuck to his hands. He lets the tears flow down his frozen cheeks.

A man quietly lies down in the snow, closes his eyes, sighs. It is over in a minute.

"We must hold out," Dr. Rausk whispers.

15

Miklos wants to reply, say something. Speak of his love for his little son and for his wife Naomi. Speak of the garden in his house. He wants to remind the doctor of old familiar streets. Of poetry recitals the doctor's wife had sponsored. Hum a few bars of the Schubert Quintet in C Major. Speak of good books. Of strolling by the river, looking at mountain peaks.

"I can't," Miklos says feebly. "Bread . . . Bread."

Auschwitz, January 27, 1945

When the Russians liberated Auschwitz, all they found were 2,819 survivors.

Captain Yashenko looked at the rubble before him. He was in the women's camp in Birkenau, Lager C. The road was dotted with crouching figures. He went over to one, gently tapped her shoulder. She keeled over. He discovered women hiding under damp barrack floors, someone buried in a hole.

"You are free," he said, helping her out of the hole. The woman shielded her face from daylight in the crook of her arm.

"What took you so long?" another woman said. Her voice was hoarse. A death rattle. "What good is it now?"

The captain's eyes teared.

"I'm sorry," he said. "we should have come sooner. Much sooner."

He took off his scarf and fur hat.

"Put it on." He wrapped the scarf around her neck. "Have you met any Jews from Iasi?" he asked her softly. "Have you come across a woman named Rifka Yashenberg?"

"No," she said. "But who knows. There were so many. How can I remember all of them. . . ."

Gelsenkirchen, North Westphalia, Germany, early spring 1945

The sound of airplanes splitting the air and the shrilling of sirens are simultaneous. First, the SS run to the underground shelter, then the Gelsenkirchen factory supervising staff, and then the workers. The Jewish inmates go last. Their shelter is not underground but in the large courtyard, off the main factory building. It is an open shed policed by dogs.

As she runs to the shed, Naomi Engler looks at the sky. Bombs rain around her. The factory is wrecked in no time. She feels like cheering, but some of the women were hit. There is crying and

16

shouting. She looks again to the sky. Open umbrellas float under the sky. Myriads of them.

"Parachutes!" she yells.

Even the wounded women now shout:

"Tommies, Americans! Come on! Give it to the Nazis! Hurray! Give it to them! More! More!"

But as soon as the planes are gone, the SS fan out in great number. Aided by dogs, they swiftly collect the Jewish inmates, then divide them into two groups.

"To recuperate in Bergen-Belsen," they tell the group at the left, and whip them into marching columns. They jam the group on the right into open cattle cars:

"To work in Somerda."

Buchenwald, April 11, 1945

American troops liberate Buchenwald. Naftuli Kahn walks out of camp, looks at the electrified fence he leaves behind. He is not sure whether to go to the left or to the right. Buchenwald is north of Weimar, that much he knows. But how can one be sure which way is north and which way is south?

He turns right, walks a few yards, then changes his mind and turns left. An American army truck picks him up. The soldiers empty their pockets and give the contents to him.

Back in camp, Naftuli discovers dollar bills among the items the soldiers had given him. He goes to his former block *Kapo* and talks him into trading a dollar bill for a carton of American cigarettes the *Kapo* had somehow come by.

Then Naftuli Kahn walks out of camp again.

Weisswasser, same day

The kitchen is a mess. Women eat lard and honey.

"*Zählappel!*" someone yells. A few stiffen.

"Idiot. Some joke . . ."

Thuringia, Germany, April 1945

The left group marched on foot for six weeks, maybe four, but maybe eight. At the end of the march they arrive in Somerda. The SS told them Bergen-Belsen, but it is Somerda, after all. Where is Somerda, anyway?

Naomi Engler is assigned to work in the munitions factory.

Each time Jewish inmates arrive or leave the factory, an SS walks ahead of them ringing a bell and carrying a sign ACHTUNG! JÜDEN KOMMEN!

Weisswasser, next day

"I am gong to Grosswasser," someone says. "It's another camp, close by. I've heard it's a concentration camp. Not an extermination camp. Only a concentration camp. Maybe my mother is there. Or my sister. I am going to look for them. For someone—"

"I'll go with you."

"Me too."

"Where is Grosswasser!" someone asks.

"I don't know. But I'll find it. Somehow."

A group of women run down the hill. Which way is Grosswasser? they ask. A man points to the right. Another points to the left.

Half the group goes to the right, half to the left.

Somerda, early May 1945

Is Somerda in Bohemia or Moravia? they still wonder. Maybe it's in Thuringia, after all. Or Schleswig-Holstein. Certainly not in Bavaria. But who knows . . .

After work, they return to camp. There is no *Zählappel.* The SS herd them brusquely into a windowless wooden barn. The door is bolted tight from the outside.

The women become hysterical.

"They'll set us aflame, explode the barn!"

"They'll butcher us! Help! Please, help! Help . . ."

There is a rapid burst of fire. It comes from far away.

"Maybe . . . maybe." Naomi is incapable of finishing the thought.

They hear commotion on the outside. The women jostle each other, put their ears to the walls. Some peer through narrow plank slits.

"I see shadows. They move fast, back and forth."

"They'll gun us down—"

"Let's not panic!"

"Panic? Who is panicking?"

"Maybe," Naomi says again, but someone shrieks:

"They'll kill us, why do you think they shut us up? They'll kill us, butcher us—"

"Shut up!"

"They'll kill us—"

"Don't panic, I tell you!"

"Supper, what about supper?"

"They'll murder us—"

"I am hungry—"

"How long have we been locked up?"

"Supper—"

". . . kill us."

"Don't panic!"

Days go by, or maybe just hours. The bolt is pulled away. The doors abruptly swing open, daylight inundates the barn.

"La guerre est finie!" French prisoners of war stand at the door. They smile.

Somerda, first day of liberation, May 1945

The Russians sweep through the camp in the morning, rape several women. They are done before noon.

"Enjoy the freedom," they say in leaving.

Naomi has hidden in the cellar. She appears after the ravaging and runs away from camp.

"Is the war over for everyone?" she asks a civilian. He rushes by without responding.

"Is the war really over? Everywhere?" she keeps asking whomever she encounters on the road. Nobody has time to answer. The road teems with people, carts, Russian soldiers.

She returns to camp. Some women cry, others have broken into the food storeroom. They devour chunks of meat and butter, swallow raw eggs mixed with marmalade, bite into onions as though they were apples, and gorge themselves with granulated sugar by the spoonful.

A woman vomits.

Another woman rummages in the SS quarters.

"I am going," Naomi says. "I won't spend another night here."

"Where are you going?" Sarah asks.

"Vee ahin sol ich gehen," Naomi broods. Then her face lights up: "I'll go home . . . Home, of course. Home, home . . ."

19

"How?"

"I don't know. But I know I am going home. To my husband. My little boy."

She goes back to the town of Somerda the way she came and walks till she comes to a train station. A train stands at the platform. People push and claw to get on it. Naomi too is pushing. When the train begins to move, she is inside it.

"Where does it go?" she asks.

"To Weimar."

"No. To Gdynia," another voice says.

The following evening the train comes to a halt in the middle of an open field. Noami gets off, walks on the road. A cart comes by.

"Want a lift?"

She climbs in and falls asleep. When she wakes up, she is back in Somerda.

Weisswasser, same day

The group which went to the left passes by the factory again. The *Herr Direktor*'s mansion is next to it. The women go in. The house swarms with people. Villagers, liberated prisoners of war, a few Russian soldiers.

"Look!" one of the women yells, holding up a four-branched silver candelabrum. She points to Hebrew letters engraved in its base. "Stolen from us!"

Their eyes narrow, frothing spit specks the corners of their mouths.

"Jewish silver," they scream, and yank open drawers, closets, cabinets. "Pilfered Jewish silver the Nazis looted, robbed," they scream, and grab silver knives and spoons, forks. Silver candelabra. "It's ours! Let's take it back!"

Somerda, late May 1945

Groups organize themselves. Some want to go north, others south. Others are not quite sure where. But they all keep moving about.

Naomi and two other women take to the road again. They hitchhike, sleep in open fields, huddle on filthy floors in small railroad stations. They wait for trains and board any train which comes along. When the train stops, they descend and pile into carts. On their way, they encounter other survivors coming from opposite directions looking for relatives in other liberated camps.

Yet somehow, a few days later, or maybe a month later, they all meet again, a few miles farther east or farther west.

Poland, June 1945

In four weeks the group of three women will have grown to ten. They will finally arrive somewhere. Not home, but somewhere. It will be Poland, in a place called Glatz or Klodzko. Maybe both names will designate the same location. The women will never be certain of that.

They will then need documents to move around. The Russians will start to check on refugees because word will have gotten around that many Nazis run to the Allies disguised as Jewish survivors. The Russians will want to catch all war criminals. So they will say.

In Glatz or Klodzko there will be a center for Jewish survivors. The men in charge will give Naomi Engler a stamped safe-conduct for twenty Jews, although her group at that time will number only ten. But one never knows.

Maybe Yankel Schwartz, whom the Americans liberated in Dachau, will join a group going west; then in Augsburg or Nurnberg or Stuttgart he will switch to another group claiming to know of a shortcut to America by going through Gmunden. Yankel Schwartz, who will want to go to America, finds himself in Gmunden, which is in Austria. He will then find another group heading to America through Kosice, Czechoslovakia, and again Yankel Schwartz will find himself somewhere else. In Kladanj, Yugoslavia, or Krupnik, Bulgaria. Yet somehow, Yankel Schwartz will end up in Glatz or Klodzko, although all along he will want to go to America. For at one time or another everybody will end up in Glatz or Klodzko, or a place like Glatz or Klodzko.

Glatz or Klodzko will be a long way from home. Nobody will be certain how far north or south, east or west they will be from home. But whatever the distance, and wherever their home was, they will be determined to get there. Even Yankel Schwartz will now want to go home. He will join the group of women.

They will leave Glatz or Klodzko and go searching for a way to get there. Where? Home. As they will leave, two men will approach them. The two strangers will speak the women's native language.

"We are Jews," they will say. "We ran away from a work camp two months ago. Escaped. Were fugitives. We got ourselves some money. Don't ask how. In fact, we have quite a lot of money. But we don't have safe-conducts. You have safe-conducts, but don't have money. Let's make a deal: you include us in your safe-conducts, we buy a car in Ostrava. We'll all get home. In a motorcar!"

Naomi will be slightly troubled, but they will all agree at the end. At Krnov the Russians will check papers. Krnov will be the border town between Poland and Czechoslovakia.

"All Jews?" the Russian patrol will ask the women.

"Yes," they will say.

"And you?" the patrol will ask the three men.

"Yes," they will say, but the involuntary head shake of the two strangers will contradict them.

The two men will be arrested and the women sent back to Glatz or Kodzko. Yankel Schwartz may or may not return with them. In Glatz or Klodzko the women will have to wait till the Russian authorities will issue them formal identification papers.

The papers will eventually arrive. Another four weeks, maybe six, if they are lucky. Then the head of the Center for Jewish Survivors will find a Russian soldier who will be willing to drive the women to the Hungarian border in return for a couple of bottles of Polish vodka. When they will reach Zakopane, a lovely ski resort at the foot of the Polish side of the Tatra Mountains, the Russian soldier will be dead drunk, quite incapable of driving through the winding mountain passes. Naomi and her companions may or may not cross into Czechoslovakia by foot through the Tatra Pass, and they may or may not arrive at Lomnicky, which is or was or will be on the Czech side of the Tatra Mountains. Lomnicky is or will be, maybe it was, a lovely ski resort in the winter. Then again, maybe Naomi will return to Glatz or Klodzko.

On their way home, some survivors ate themselves to death and others acquired candelabra, and a number of them arrived in Sweden though they had wished to go to another country—to France, or Greece, or Hungary, or Belgium, or Poland, or Holland, or Romania, or Czechoslovakia.

The survivors traveled north and south, dashed to east and west, returned in a chaotic swirl to reorient themselves and kept going to reach their destination.

Only sometimes the survivors wondered whether the day was today or yesterday, whether tomorrow had already passed and whether what was to come would again be what had been.

BOOK I

"And God said: This is the token of the covenant which I make between Me and you . . . for perpetual generations: I do set my bow in the cloud . . . the waters shall no more become a flood to destroy all flesh."
—Genesis 9:12, 13, 15

1

Lisa asked if her father was dead. Her voice was dry, without timbre.

"My father went to the right, isn't that so, Naftuli?"

The question took him by surprise. He hesitated, then shook his head.

"Left," he muttered, "not right."

"That's what I mean. He went to the right." She reached for a chair, drew it near her. "Right?" she repeated then began to finger the chair.

we are dragged out of cattle cars, vomited into an impenetrable black night. suddenly torches brighten up a black sky and i clearly see the night: it engulfs a square drenched in searing brilliance by powerful floodlights

in the illuminated square, under the lit up black sky, we stand in rows of five. my throat is parched. i haven't had a drop of water in four days. i want to ask for water but the words burn away in my throat. i begin to gulp air as if it were water which would put out the fire in my throat but the air i breathe stinks. i retch

then screams knife the air and i cover my ears with my hands. torches keep licking the sky like rainbows, flaming rainbows, and i quickly close my eyes but still i see the flames through my closed lids and the screams slash through my hands, into my ears. then a horrible stench hits my nostrils. i gasp for air but i choke. i am terrified. i don't know what to do. i grip mamma's shoulder with my right arm, clinging to her. she'll know how to make the nightmare go away

an ss man reeking of perfume, a long thin whip in his gloved hand, his shiny black patent leather boots mirroring the flaming rainbows, glares hard at mamma and me. his pale blue eyes dart from side to side like a metronome, his bloodless lips twist into a smile, and as he keeps glaring at us he seems to expand, spread till his head touches the red sky, his body and limbs becoming one with it, and i know i see *malach-hamoves*, a perfumed angel of death whose crooked smile promises what? what?

he flips the whip with jerky little motions

playfully

then the whip abruptly taps mamma's right shoulder, whipping my hand briskly and sharply

says to mamma **links!**

smiling the crooked smile he tears us apart

pushes mamma to the left

my right arm hurts

She continued to finger the chair, her palms sliding back and forth over the curvature of the backrest. She tilted her head, looked with half closed eyes at the chair, then smiled barely perceptibly, though the smile could have been just a passing facial twitch. She gripped the chair firmly, felt the texture of polished wood in her hands and sighed with relief.

Naftuli said *right*. She heard him. It was the moment she had been waiting for. She knew this moment would come the instant she touched contours of familiar objects: a bed, a table. Or a chair, as she was doing now. There would be instant magic in touching familiar objects, she had always known. It would immediately dissolve the nightmare; and once again she would belong. If she could only touch other familiar objects right away. The book on mythology bound in dark blue linen hard covers, embossed with patterns of tiny semicircles, or the wooden base of the grandfather clock inlaid with brass and tortoiseshell. Or the heart-shaped mirror with the gilded frame.

Yes, she would soon find all those familiar objects, touch

them, and then everything would be the way it had always been. Almost. She would not question Naftuli again; let it remain as it was. She had fashioned weapons against the night.

"My father went to the right, Naftuli; didn't he?" She only asked to hear him say *yes* once more, she thought, holding on to the chair, and then the nightmare would be no more. All would be the way it always was, or at least if not all, some things.

Naftuli looked up. He straightened out wearily, got up from the chair and walked around the table, avoiding the corner of the sofa where Lisa sat. Damp wisps of hair ringed his head and beads of perspiration glistened on his forehead. He smoothed his crumpled jacket and tugged at his shirt collar as if to adjust a tie which was not there, then pulled out a handkerchief from his pocket and wiped the top of his head.

Lisa's eyes followed Naftuli's every move. It will happen now, at last. The nightmare will be over before long; wasn't she touching the chair?

Naftuli sat down next to Lisa. He reached towards her, then stopped midway and began to twist the handkerchief still in his hands. He opened his mouth and made a hoarse inarticulate sound, wiped the top of his head again, then cleared his throat.

"No," he said. "No. Your father didn't go to the right; he was sent to the left."

She let go quickly of the chair and spat three times to the left, as they used to do *there* when certain words were uttered. Then she shook her head slowly, turning it from side to side, forming soundless words with her lips, keeping her eyes fixed on Naftuli. She thrust forward abruptly, as if a heavy blow had struck the back of her head. He thought, she will scream. But she only winced.

"I am sorry," Naftuli said. "I thought you knew."

"I knew," she said flatly and continued to turn her head from side to side. "Of course I knew. I alone knew. It was a bakery, but no one believed me."

where is mamma, i ask the first day, and no one answers me. where is mamma, when will i see her? the second day, the third day. they just look at me and shake their heads. they are strange creatures, these oldtimers. they look like women, have breasts, but there is a crazed look in their eyes and their voices do not sound human. when they say something they don't speak: they bellow like animals. bark, snort, roar, howl. they have festering sores on their arms and feet, their teeth are missing. there is wildness on their faces.

where is mamma? i ask one of them the fifth day. on the square they told us we'll be reunited with our parents. i want to be with mamma.

can you please kindly tell me, won't you please be so kind and tell me: when will i see my mamma? where?

she lets out a shriek, it's like a neigh. maybe she thinks it's a laugh.

you want to know where your mamma is, you stupid hungarian idiot, you really want to know where your mamma is?

i nod eagerly. this one here, her arms full of abscesses, under her eye a gash which healed in an ugly way leaving little pussy ridges under her skin, this oldtimer seems kinder than the others. at least she speaks to me.

so you want to know where your mamma is, she yells again. idiot, she says, but i don't mind it. all the oldtimers call us hungarian idiots.

idiot, she repeats, what were you doing while we were burning here, hah? you went on sleeping under silk comforters, that's what you did while we burned; you had sweet girlish dreams under nice down silk comforters while we slept in puddles of filth and were covered with lice and fleas. and all that time hungarian idiots still slept under silk comforters.

mamma, i say, please, won't you please be kind enough and tell me, please tell me, when will i see mamma. where. they promised us on the square.

idiot, she yells again but i know that's the only way she can speak so i don't mind. look! she screams and grabs my head and turns it toward the big brick building with tall chimneys belching smoke.

look idiot! that's where your mamma is, was. look at the chimneys, that's where she went out and up, up

up

up in the sky,

your mamma and all the mammas. you idiot. now you know where your mamma is, was. so you'll stop pestering me with questions. idiot.

the poor wretch is demented, i know. she is demented after being in this vile, mad place for so many years. she is demented, she lost her mind. that's why she speaks of burning. the red brick building is a bakery, everyone can see that. the tall chimneys are bakery chimneys, everyone knows that. the smoke is from bread, everyone can smell that. they bake bread every day in the brick building, day in and day out, all night long, every night.

they bake bread.

i can smell bread. it's a bit scorched the smell, but it *is* from bread. those poor demented creatures can't even smell anymore. i can.

the shooting flames are from bakery chimneys.

i can smell bread baking.

they all lost their minds to speak of burning. i won't let them infect mine.

i turn to another oldtimer.

won't you please kindly tell me when can i see mamma. my mamma. they promised us on the square

idiot! look! she yells, look at the chimneys. that's where your mamma is, was

Naftuli watched her sitting on the corner of the sofa, her arms dangling at her sides. She was mumbling to herself, shaking her head from left to right and right to left. She looked wilted and fragile, worn out, like a little old woman. One could not tell from her looks she was not quite eighteen, he reflected. She kept blinking. Something was stuck under her eyelids, he was certain, and he imagined he heard faint scratching of sand against dry stone. His own eyes began to smart.

She was staring at him, or perhaps beyond him, and he stifled a sob. Her drawn features, the thin neck and shoulder blades sticking through her dress, reminded him how beautiful she used to be. Lisa Engler, the pretty girl with her freckled face and large green eyes, wavy red hair framing her face. He would steal glances at her firm springy breasts when she passed him by on the street. His penis stirred and he blushed; the vacant look on her face, dazed and dulled and exhausted, was that of a sick animal.

"I dreaded this," he said. "Listen, your father, he was in my transport. We were all together, in the same cattle car, Miklos

31

and Naomi, your father and I. When we arrived *there,* the doors of the cattle cars were yanked open and we saw flames. Then your father began to recite the *shema* and *kaddish.*"

"And after that he was sent to the right," she said.

"No," Naftuli replied softly. "I told you: no. He was sent to the left. But he finished *davening* just in time. He got through with the whole *shema* and *kaddish.*"

She looked at him with disgust and tried to figure out why he told lies. What was in it for him? She concluded he lost his mind to speak of her Papa *davening* the prayers for the dead. Surely only a madman would confuse the *kaddish* and the *shema* with lullabies. It was a lullaby her Papa must have sung in his sweet voice to soothe everybody. Her Papa did not chant prayers for the dead, his own *kaddish.*

With a short, sharp wail, she got up.

"Go away," she said blinking. "Go."

Naftuli sighed. After a long silence he said:

"I want you to come and stay in my house. Right away. I am your only relative now. When your brother Miklos comes back I'd want him to find you with his brother-in-law. That's me. I don't want him to find you with strangers."

"I am not with strangers. I am with friends. And sometimes strangers are friends." She did not look at him.

"Yes." Naftuli sounded troubled. "I mean . . . I feel responsible for you until Miklos returns." He added, as an inducement: "My house is in good condition. I've been back since April, you know."

when the ss said the end is coming it was april. april 12. i remember because we all cried when he said roosevelt the jew died at last. the war was going to be over now, finished. the *herrenrasse* shall win the war with the new weapon, the v-2. he said fau zwo. grand weapons which will devastate whole countries in one fell swoop and if you won't be killed you'll be a slave, he said with a sneer and pinched my breast and quickly looked whether someone saw him. yes, the *kommandant saw him, and then the ss kicked me and said, you swine jew shit, move, come on, move, move*

"I am not going to move!" she exclaimed. "You can't make me."

She felt confused and wished she could sort out her thoughts that crowded her mind, pressing in. Why should Naftuli bid her come to his house? Her sole link to him was his sister Naomi whom Miklos had married five years ago. Why should Naftuli now claim her as a family member? They were never that close.

Didn't he say he was back in town since April, she mused, and looked suspiciously at him. But the war was over only in early May. It must be a ruse, a trick, maybe he is one of *them*, she thought. Naftuli the sly one, that's what they used to call him. Yes, he could be one of *them*. One can never tell. After all, he denies that Papa went to the right, although it is well known it was a bakery.

"Of course I am not going to make you," he said. "But I am sure they will be back soon, Naomi and Miklos," he pushed on. "Someone saw their names posted on one of the Red Cross or JOINT lists, I am not sure which. It's going to be a matter of days, at the most two weeks; they'll be soon home, you'll see." Naftuli pleaded with her: "Meanwhile your place is with me. I am certain Miklos would wish it that way. Please come."

Lisa looked at Naftuli and again tried to think this through. She sensed he wanted something only she could give him, otherwise why would he be so concerned where she stayed? She felt brittle, crumbling, as if the marrow of her bones had been siphoned off, sucked out. Fatigue overcame her.

"I am tired now. Come back tomorrow." The process of thinking was too demanding. Smells, sounds, sights, were all that had mattered *there,* and all her responses had been automatic. This was too complicated. She could not hold onto a thought for more than a fraction of a second. The tiniest thought evaporated like mist. She ached and wished for sleep.

"Come back after tomorrow," she added.

"Please come," he insisted. "It's important."

"I'l try to think about it."

"Good. Then I'll come back soon."

Naftuli got up and walked towards the door. He stopped and fumbled for the handkerchief, then patted his cheeks with it.

"Oh yes," he said as an afterthought. "There is a man who holds some of your things. I mean your family's things. Like jewels and such. The man says he'll return everything only to an Engler. You are an Engler."

He looked inquisitively at her, a coaxing glint creased the corners of his eyes. "Will you go and get back the jewelry from him? Will you?"

She stared at him. With an effort, she replied:

"I don't know yet. I'll see."

2

She did not sleep that first night. She lay on a cot with her eyes open, gazing into the dark. Rozika and Bozsi, her two friends, slept in the same room in a double bed. The three of them had arrived in town that morning and had come directly to Rozika's house.

Lisa got off the cot, walked to the window and opened it wide. The scent of acacia and jasmine flooded the air. Greedily, she inhaled the fragrance of the June night and, breathing fast, she shut her eyes tight to savor the soothing familiar scent. Instantly, the sweet smell of acacia and jasmine turned to a sour, singed odor, and she retched, fighting nausea.

Then the cadence of marching steps disrupted the muted night. Her body stiffened at once. The rhythm too was familiar: *vier, drei, zwei, LINKS;* four, three, two, left. *LINKS, RECHTS, LINKS.* Left, right, left. *vier, drei zwei, zero; zero, zero, RECHTS.* She shuddered, listened again. Her fingers involuntarily tapped the window sill, keeping time with that rhythm. She strained for a while listening till she clearly heard the words *odin, dva, tree, chotiri.*

One, two, three, four, she counted out loud, with relief. Her fingers stopped tapping, her hand relaxed. The Russians; they are ubiquitous but invisible, she thought, and recalled a recent encounter with them. It was a week ago.

3

She was on a train. She had lost count how many days she had been on it, how many stops the train had made. What kept her going since the middle of May was an indomitable stark drive to get home at once, touch familiar objects. Then everything, almost everything, would be the way it had always been.

The train stops seemed endless. They grated away her stamina and, at the same time, increased the urgency to reach her destination. Each stop, like a shower of small arrows, pricked and pierced at something inside her. Beware. Keep alert. Watch out. Do you know where you are going?

Yes, she calmed herself, she knew where she was going. Once the train had crossed into Hungary it would take her to Budapest. The train could lead nowhere else. Budapest. That was her initial destination. From there she would get home soon, very soon. Wouldn't she?

Through the jammed compartment, she pushed her way to the window. There were no people working or plowing the rolling fields. The countryside was empty, colorless. Where was everybody, she began to wonder, where does this train lead? Frantically, she grabbed the handle of the window and tried to open it.

"Help me," she cried out to the passengers in the compartment, "I want to get out. Quick, help me open the window! *Raus!* I want out, out! *Raus* before I reach the square . . . Help! *Raus!* The square. . . ."

they squeeze us into cattle cars and say destination camp *kenyérmező*. from their ghettos that's where the jews will be relocated, temporarily, to await the end of the war. lucky jews, the magyars say to us, to be whisked off to a nice camp like that in a fine spot in hungary. even the name of the camp is nice: camp breadfield, that's what *kenyérmező* means. there the jews won't have a worry in the world, so the magyars say; and although no jew has ever heard of such a camp or of such a name before, we are all convinced, heart and soul, such a place exists. we are being transported to western hungary, to nice camp breadfield, we reassure each other.

and we stay cooped up in the stink of the cattle cars, dreaming that the end of the war will find us in camp breadfield. we are hungry and thirsty but the end of the war will end that too. we dream.

i dream of water, clear and cool water i shall drink in camp *kenyérmező*. my dream is disrupted by mrs. katzenbogen, who offers me a walnut from a huge sack full of walnuts. it is her only possession, the sack full of walnuts, and she sits on it as if she were sitting on a throne of gold. i wonder why she dragged along from the ghetto into the cattle car a sack of walnuts, of all things. nothing else.

i am hungry and tempted to take the walnut she offers me with the air of a dowager bestowing an heirloom on a not quite worthy heir. thirst has deadened my throat and i can barely swallow. i shake my head and mrs. katzenbogen stuffs the walnut back into the sack with a sigh of relief.

we go on dreaming.

then one night a gust of air blows in through the little window,

and those who can still move push to the window to draw in a breath of fresh air rippling into the thick of stink. the thin lashes of cold air paw my face.

then suddenly mr. weinfeld jumps up screaming and yelling

yidn, listen, he yells, listen jews! yadwiga the child says it smells like home. yadwiga the child thinks she is going home, her home is in poland

why is now everybody shrieking, tearing their hair?

gewalt, yidn! the train has left the soil of hungary, mr. weinfeld continues to yell, we'll never reach camp *kenyérmezö*. we are all dead though we think we are alive. i tell you, *yidn,* it's over for us! the fresh air is the tatra air, that's what the child smells.

we've crossed from hungary into poland.

we'll never reach camp *kenyérmezö*. there was never such a camp;

gewalt, yidn, we are lost, it's over, we've been betrayed, sold to *malach-hamoves*, the angel of death, which even now breathes through the window.

they'll kill us, butcher us, i know. that's what they did with the child's parents. we are helpless, we have no weapons, where is god

yidn, yidn, gewalt!

and i wish mr. weinfeld would stop wailing

see, the train came to a halt, the doors are blasted open.

mr. weinfeld is quiet.

everyone is quiet

and pajama-clad strange creatures grab us

raus! raus! they scream

and we are dragged out from the cattle cars, vomited into a square

that's our destination, the square

". . . there is no other destination!" Lisa was screaming at the startled passengers as the train came to a halt.

It was the railroad station of a small village. Throngs of people swarming on the platform tried to wedge themselves into the packed compartments. They bumped into descending passengers, who surged towards the back of the station where three farmers stood, holding baskets of food.

Lisa got jostled off the train by disembarking passengers and was swept towards the station. She found herself before a woman holding a basket full of fresh loaves of bread and bottles of milk. The woman measured Lisa with a quick, expert glance, then picked a bottle of milk from the basket, held it up and swayed it before Lisa's eyes. The motion of the milk, undulating, enticing, left a translucent film of moisture, thinned out and whitish, inside the slim bottle neck and Lisa, as if in a trance, began to sway along with the bottle.

* * *

the train comes to a halt. i climb on top of a valise and look out through the small opening in the upper left corner of the cattle car. i always do that when the train stops: i check for signs reading "camp kenyérmezö." i see no such sign yet, but i see a woman running towards the train, cradling two bottles in her arms. as she approaches the window i see the bottles contain water and i want to swallow to wet my throat and palate. i can't, i have no saliva. i think i'll die of thirst any minute. then i see the water in the bottles she holds up to me. the water is clear, undulating, enticing; i reach through the barred window with my hands. then she says

a diamond ring, a nice fat jewish diamond ring if you want a bottle of water, two nice big diamond rings for two bottles of water,

or a beautiful ruby bracelet, the kind you filthy jews wear.

and i turn to the people in the cattle car and say

she wants diamond rings for water, she wants ruby bracelets for water.

some of the people can't even hear me anymore, they are half dead or dead all the way. they died of hunger and thirst. and then someone, i think it's mamma, gives me a diamond ring and i hold it between my fingers and the woman sees the ring and asks

where is the other? oh hell, you jews always cheat. i'll take it anyway because the train will be soon moving along and we'll get rid of you jewish swine once and for all. then we'll get all of it.

she climbs on a small wooden stepping stool she brought along with the two bottles of water, and her gnarled fingers and calloused hands shoot up towards the barred window; she says

the ring first

and i drop the ring in her palm and then she holds up one bottle of water and i grip it by its neck

and then the ss springs forward and knocks the bottle out of my hand.

i watch the bottle crash to the ground and see the water spill, clear drops of water sparkling like clusters of diamonds

and the train starts to move again

"Ten *pengö*," the woman said, rubbing her forefinger and thumb against each other. "Only ten *pengö*, and it's fresh. I milked the cow myself this morning."

Lisa's eyes were still glued to the bottle.

"You have no money, I can see that. But you have something, I bet," the woman grinned. "You people always do. A ring, a bracelet, what do you have?"

Lisa opened her satchel. Inside, there was a tin bowl and a tin spoon. The woman sternly pursed her lips, wagged her finger. Lisa then remembered a flowered kerchief someone had given her. She touched her head and felt the ends of her short-cropped hair bristle through the kerchief. She looked again at the bottle of milk the woman now rocked in the crook of her arm. Resolutely, Lisa pulled the kerchief off her head.

"Take it. It's all I have."

A Russian soldier suddenly pounced forward. He grabbed the bottle of milk from the woman's arm, seized a loaf of bread from the basket.

"*Pazsaluszta!*" He placed the milk and bread in Lisa's hands. "Please." He pointed to the kerchief still in her hand, then to her head and repeated the motion.

He shoved the woman with the butt of his rifle.

"*Davai!*" he barked, "move on!"

4

The train brought Lisa the same afternoon to the Budapest eastern terminal station.

"Go to the Clearinghouse for Refugees," a man advised her.

"I've been to many. I have just come back from one . . . and I don't want to go to another one."

"Suit yourself." He shrugged his shoulders. "But there won't be any more trains today coming or going, I'll tell you that."

". . . I want to go home." She sat down on a bench, folded her arms.

"They all refuse to go at first," the man said. "Then they go anyway. When they become hungry."

"I'll wait here."

It was late in the afternoon, almost dusk, when she became hungry. Reluctantly, she started to walk in the direction of the Clearinghouse for Refugees. There was merely a handful of civilians on the streets. They strutted a bit, swung their left arms lightly. A veiled *heilhitler* salute, she thought in a panic, and ran for cover in a doorway. She peered at the civilians, then noticed red hammer-and-sickle bands wrapped around their swinging arms. Cautiously, she stepped out into the street again.

From the Clearinghouse for Refugees she was sent to the Jewish Shelter. It was housed in the Jewish Gymnasium, a building Lisa knew well: she had gone to school there.

Approaching the familiar wrought-iron gate, she quickened her steps, then dashed up the path leading from the gate to the entrance door. She should not be late for class, not today, she thought.

The man in charge at the shelter spoke gently. As soon as there were enough people wanting to go in the direction of her hometown, he would organize them into a group, then make arrangements for their safe arrival there. Lisa was not sure whether she heard *Kommando* or group, *transport* or organize, *solution* or arrangement. She nodded wearily, placed her satchel on a bed assigned to her in a large dormitory and began marking time.

She waited. Sometimes with patience and hope, sometimes with apprehension of what the next day might bring. But she waited with undaunted determination to get home—where all would be the way it always was or if not all, at least some of the few remaining important things.

To avoid the strutting civilians flaunting their new arm bands, she never left the shelter. She liked walking through the familiar halls and classrooms or sitting on a bench in the garden under a blue sky and watching the arrival of other survivors.

They kept coming daily, the survivors, from morning till late at night. Some staggered in singly, others came in groups. She watched reunions of relatives, of friends. When there were no relatives to be found nor friends, strangers became relatives or friends. A huddle of entwining bodies desperately clinging to each other for hours on end. Some raised their arms against the sky, pounded their chests with their fists. Others tore their hair or clawed the flesh on their faces.

She saw all that, heard cries and wails of agony and listened to the sounds of sorrow and sometimes of relief. She witnessed the gluing together of what was left, but each scene registered in her mind only.

Her heart was not yet thawed.

5

One day, standing at the entrance door, she saw a group of survivors come through the gate. Someone cried out her name, and all at once there were arms around her shoulders. She recognized the voice instantly. Though everything was blurred in front of her by pressing bodies, she knew the arms holding her were those of Rozika. She expected another pair of arms, those of Mariko, Rozika's sister, to hug her next.

she fusses over my swiss pinafore with embroidered daisies and tiny pleats. at last *fräulein* trude ties the ends of the waist band in a big bow at the small of my back. i make believe the bow is a pair of wings, i flap my arms.

i am a butterfly, i can fly, i can fly, i say laughing to my governess. *fräulein* trude frowns. she smells of talcum powder and her white starched uniform is stiff. i imagine it would crackle if i pinched her. in truth, i want to pinch her.

what's this foolishness about flying? she looks at me critically up and down, gives a last smoothing to a rebellious pleat.

we are going to be a well-behaved little lady today, *ja*? she informs me. don't forget to *puckerl* when you are introduced to the *maman* of the little young ladies, *ja*?

suddenly the butterfly is in my stomach. will the sisters like me?

43

after all, one of them is a year older than i. she is five years old. her name is mariko.

* * *

ballet school. little girls are picked for a *corps de ballet*. they shall wear pink tutus and angel wings. why wasn't i picked as my friends rozika and mariko were? what's wrong with me? is it because angels don't have freckles and red hair? i am ashamed of myself but i don't want to cry. i turn to the wall.

someone takes my hand. it's mariko.

don't feel bad, she whispers, there'll be another year. i know a story. it's called the ugly duckling . . .

* * *

we play together, rozika, mariko and i.

they'll grow up into young ladies worthy of young men with eyes for beauty, someone says.

or sought-after plums for young men in quest of big dowries, someone else adds.

whatever the case, another one says, these are three lucky little girls. yes indeed.

* * *

mariko is a grade higher than rozika and i. the three of us go to the same school, wear the same style uniforms: black poplin smocks, immaculate white pique collars tied with enormous floppy bows of white silk and black polka dots. i seem to be always wearing bows of some sort: on my back, under my chin, in my hair. will i ever grow up?

the three of us are good students. we love our country and our king. we are appalled when we learn that Tatar hordes have nasty designs to steal parts of our land.

then one day teachers, subjects, and language change. we are instructed to extol the wisdom of regent admiral horthy miklós. wherever i turn i see posters or framed photographs of an admiral wearing a resplendent uniform pinned with medals and ribbons. the admiral is atop a horse. it seems awfully funny to me.

a horse instead of a ship's prow, i tell a classmate. i am expelled from school for a whole week.

now we sit in special sections in the classroom. we don't wear bows anymore, nor uniforms. it's all right, after all we are older. or growing up.

neither do we receive prizes at the end of the school year.

44

during an intermission a classmate says that jews should be grateful for being permitted to attend school. i open my mouth but mariko pulls me away.

let them talk, she says. it's empty hollow bombast. though she is only a year older than rozika and i, mariko knows more about the ways of the world than we do. so we both listen to her.

after all, mariko continues, what about the league of nations? i've heard my parents speak of a sacred trust of civilization the members of the league of nations are honor-bound to uphold. they'll do it any day now, you'll see

"Rozika," Lisa whispered, "where is Mariko?"

Rozika slowly withdrew her arms. They looked at each other in silence, then Lisa turned to the wall, near the door. She opened her mouth to say something, curse or scream, but her vocal cords seemed paralyzed. She bit her lips and felt no pain. Her lips too seemed paralyzed. She kept staring at the wall, biting her lips till her tongue tasted blood.

Then she put her arms around Rozika's shoulders.

6

A young girl named Bozsi began trailing after them the day she arrived at the shelter. Lisa and Rozika took her in their midst without asking her any questions. Thereafter, Bozsi made herself useful in many little ways. She straightened out their beds, stood in line to pick up their food rations, held their seats free till they could come to the dining hall.

The morning Drifter met Lisa she was by herself at the shelter. Rozika and Bozsi had gone to the city. The man's name was Zoltan Feldman though no one called him by that name. Everyone knew him as Drifter. He came daily to the shelter, several times during the day, to look for his wife and child, and stayed only long enough to question every newly arrived survivor about the camps.

He had short dark hair, flat cheeks and a square chin, sunken brown eyes. He was thirty-one years old, seemed tough and seasoned, a sinewy man with a grainy voice, strong arms and a sorrowful look on a gaunt face. A thin pale scar ran from behind his earlobe down his left jaw, then curved in under his chin, like a long white thread lost in the folds of a hem.

There were many rumors of the scar's origin, as there were many rumors of his deeds. In the opinion of those who knew him, and even of those who only heard of him, Drifter was shipped to Russia early in 1940, with the very first Jewish forced labor unit. It was the only fact about him on which there was complete agreement. From that point on, those who spoke of Drifter appeared to speak of several men, heroes or demigods, all embodied in him.

One set of rumors had Drifter working with the Russian partisans. He was a leading secret Russian agent, someone maintained, a high official of the GPU. It was the NKVD, someone else countered. Not quite, another insisted: he had learned from a special source that Drifter was in the hospital at Doroschitzin when the Nazis set it ablaze with all the sick inside; no GPU or NKVD member was in the hospital when the Nazis burned it down, only Jews from the Hungarian forced labor unit. Everyone perished in the Doroschitzin fire, except Drifter. He alone escaped, then joined the partisans. Maybe, they said, but no one knows with Drifter; he may have been the one and only NKVD or GPU member in the Doroschitzin hospital. Maybe he went there on purpose, part of a plan. One never knows with Drifter, not with Drifter. . . .

According to another version, he had been a runner between the Underground and the Warsaw ghetto. No: he stole arms from the Nazis and smuggled the weapons into the besieged ghetto. Not quite: during the uprising he pinned down single-handedly a platoon of Nazis in the sewers of Warsaw, held the bastards at Katyusha point for a whole hour, thus giving many Jews a chance to flee from the burning ghetto into the forest, where they joined the partisans. Drifter alone had saved dozens of Jews. Yes, indeed, someone nodded knowingly, and that was when he got the scar. Oh no, he was scarred another time: when he participated in the revolt of the *Sonderkommando* which blew up the crematoria in Auschwitz. Drifter was the *Kommando's* sole survivor. How could that be, someone else pointed out, the Auschwitz revolt occurred at the end of 1944, in December, don't you remember? We could hear the rataplan of machine gun fire and the big bang when one of the chimneys exploded, oh my God . . . anyway, Drifter was there of course, but the scar does not seem that fresh.

Sure, he got it in the south of France when he was with the *Maquis* and ambushed a battalion of Nazis. Perhaps it was in North Africa, El Alamein, Tobruk . . .

He was with Tito and his partisans. Knew Tito personally.

Was kissed on each cheek by De Gaulle.

Someone waved his hand: what do you all know? Nothing! Listen, Drifter was, and is, a secret agent of the Jewish Agency. He is Moshe Shertok's kid brother. For sure.

When they spoke of Drifter stars became planets. Weeks, days, months, were compressed into moments or expanded into eons. Evil was rooted out by fearless and noble men like Drifter. He was all that which their human weakness precluded them from being, and what in fact he himself was not. But he had to be what he was in their imagination, for he was them—every man who dreams of justice and honor, of courage, humanity, and manhood.

Drifter had heard of Lisa's family, he told her that morning, and had met her brother Miklos at a Zionist congress some years before.

"You need someone," he said gruffly. "You are all alone. A child. You need a guardian, someone. I'll be it, if you want. I'll get you home safely, as soon as I have news of my wife and child. We are all heading in the same direction."

"I have two friends——"

"Then I'll take care of the three of you," he said promptly. "I can handle it. You'll all be soon home."

But when, Lisa thought, and again nodded her head in agreement. She did not ask his real name, it mattered not to her. What alone mattered was his promise to take care of her for a while and to bring her home.

7

Drifter, who spoke Russian fluently, was an interpreter at the *kommandatura* in Budapest. The Russians paid him with weekly food rations and cigarettes and with a permit to drive a motor vehicle.

Two weeks after he had met Lisa, someone at the shelter informed Drifter his wife had been spotted with a group of survivors heading east. Apparently the group had bypassed Budapest and was hitchhiking its way homeward.

Without wasting any time, Drifter got hold of a truck that had only one headlight working and no spare tires at all, loaded the rickety vehicle with Russian rations and boxes of food provided by the shelter.

"The time has come," he then told the girls. "Be ready tomorrow at dawn. We are going home."

The long-awaited words have been spoken at last; *we are going home for real*, Lisa wanted to shout but she only stared at him.

The ability to speak of feelings, to express the joy of deliverance, now eluded her. She then wanted to sink to her knees, thank Drifter for uttering the words, *we are going home*. But she could not stir. The burning desire to hear those very words, which had fueled her all this time, and the vision of her dream becoming reality now immobilized her muscles, deadened her nerves. Her inability to find words diminished her. She was scared out of her wits and kept staring at him and at the other two girls in numbness and emptiness. She forgot how to name feelings.

Drifter walked out of the room. After a while, he returned.

"Don't be frightened." His grainy voice was soft, almost smooth. "We'll face *them*, there is no other way. We've come back; we won't hide anymore. For no one's sake." He looked at them thoughtfully. "One should celebrate on the eve of a special dawn. So let's celebrate. I'll take you out tonight for dinner."

The girls stopped staring at him, then exchanged glances. Something moved in Lisa.

"Of course! We've come back!" she exclaimed. "We've made it—and nobody can unmake it!" She turned to Rozika and Bozsi: "Listen, we are going home; tomorrow morning, we are going home! Home!" She became elated, her eyes lit up with hungry wanting, impatient and compelling. "Let's go, Drifter. Why not? Let's celebrate."

8

They chose the Emke Restaurant, a well-known dining place. Electricity had not yet been fully restored to the city. When they entered the restaurant the lights were dim, flickering now and then, casting strangely shaped shadows on the patina of old frescoes.

The elegance of the once fashionable restaurant was otherwise unmarred. The waiters wore colorful uniforms, tight black breeches tucked in slim boots, red vests over hand-embroidered white shirts. Round-bellied little vases, filled with fresh field flowers, were on each table. White damask tablecloths were starched and spotless. On an elevated platform, in the middle of the dining room, a musician struck the strings of a zither, a fixed, empty smile on his face.

The headwaiter subtly maneuvered Drifter and the girls towards a table in the back of the dining room.

"Who would have believed it," Drifter muttered under his breath looking at the diners, "the black-market barons, the manipulators, and the Hungarian aristocracy! What an alliance. . . ."

As they made their way to their table, every pair of eyes in the restaurant followed them. The busboys poured water on the immaculate tablecloths instead of in the goblets, and the zither player struck a string off-key. Then the waiters started to dash from table to table, zealously brushing away imaginary crumbs or wiping away undiscernible spots on glasses and silverware. A few diners took their eyes off Drifter and the girls and pretended not to have noticed their shuffling walk, their striped garments. The diners with cigars between their fingers suddenly became immersed in the delicate operation of depositing intact blobs of ashes in the ashtrays. This activity required their full concentration, for it was not a simple matter to accomplish a perfect separation of cigar from ash. There were certain strategic areas on the cigar, as small as the head of a pin, which had to be tapped skillfully, ever so lightly and at proper degrees of thrust, to make the ball of ashes fall in the ash'tray in one single lump. A hasty or a misplaced tap might produce ashes crumbled to dust, a most embarrassing sign of one's unsteady hand.

Nonsmoking diners gyrated big brandy snifters in their hands, intently contemplating the slight agitation of the amber-colored liquid. Ladies accompanying them seemed to be hypnotized by the swirling motion of the brandy inside the snifters. Their heads gyrated along with the snifters and their eyes were glassy, while the female companions of men engaged in cigar tapping merely gaped with admiration at the neat little ash blobs in the ashtrays.

Drifter and the girls had become invisible.

Dining continued elegantly, with style and decorum.

The waiter held a covered dish in front of Lisa. He removed the lid and a steamy fragrance rushed into her nostrils. She took the silver serving fork the waiter gave her to help herself to the meat and potatoes shimmering in sauce.

hey, stupid! don't be fancy on a garbage dump! stop picking with your fork, irma says mockingly, dig with your fancy fingers! where do you think you are, at your mother's dining table?

her jeering doesn't bother me there on the garbage dump, behind the kitchen, where the smell of rotten turnips and putrid cabbage weds the smell of burnt flesh belching from chimneys and the smoke spells across the ugly sky in gothic script

food is life

food is morality

food is power

stop it, irma, can't you see i dig with my fingers? who is finicky? i dig till my nails break, i must dig quickly before the ss sees me rummaging in the garbage dump. chunks of mushy potatoes. i grab it before irma does. no, not with my fork, and i stick my fork in my shoe, i grab it with my fingers, stuff the potato peels in my mouth quickly and spit out the maggots. irma yells again

hey, princess, quick! before we are caught! leave that shitty fork in your shoe, dig with your little fingers, stupid, not with the fork, how many times must i tell you. and they called you smart, you stupid.

my heart beats fast, faster now because i hear dogs barking and ss curse

shitty jews, they eat garbage

and i keep filling my mouth with shit from the garbage

Lisa had flung the silver fork to the marble floor. The diners looked up again, with marked annoyance this time. Their otherwise pleasant evening was now irretrievably ruined by creatures that should have stayed invisible.

They watched Lisa reach into the dish held by the waiter, scoop out chunks of meat and potatoes dripping with sauce with her hands and stuff her mouth full.

i must chew quickly, i must compete with my heartbeat which slows me down. my heart is one big drum pounding wildly. i must be quicker than my heart, chew fast, quick, before the ss comes and beats me for eating garbage, quick

"How disgusting," a dainty voice exclaimed in the elegant dining room. "I always said these Jews have no manners!"

9

Odin, dva, tree, chotiri . . .

It was dawning, and the Russians still marched.

The previous dawn, when the truck driven by Drifter rolled into town, there was a pale rainbow in the mauve sky. But Lisa did not notice the rainbow in the sky. She looked straight ahead at the town and was aware of only one thing: Drifter had kept his promise. He had brought her home.

BOOK II

God went on creating worlds and
destroying them till He created this
world and said "it was very good"
—Gen. 1.3./Abbahu. Gen. R., 3.7.

1

Transylvania is not the land of make-believe where Count Dracula rises from his coffin at the stroke of midnight. Transylvania is a place where several million people live and die, or get killed, on twenty-two thousand square miles of land rimmed by a gigantic natural coliseum of soaring peaks and crescents and fog-topped mountain ranges. The Carpathian Mountains.

The physical beauty of the land is generously matched by its inherent wealth. The Transylvanian plain bounded by the Carpathians is rich in forests of pine, spruce and beech, tall oaks and elms. Its hills are covered with pear and apple orchards, its rivers and lakes teem with fish. Vast fields of barley and wheat bear heavy crops, and the land's brown soil contains deposits of natural gas, oil and coal, and metals.

Yet instead of a blessing, Transylvania's bounty became its curse: the land's opulence provoked greed, and for centuries Transylvania was the grand prize Eastern rulers claimed by hook or crook.

In the first century of the Christian era, Transylvania had been the nucleus of the Dacian kingdom ruled by Decebalus. At the beginning of the second century the emperor Trajan colonized it with Roman legionnaires. The descendants of the Dacians and the Romans ultimately became the Romanian people.

A succession of barbaric tribes, Germanic, Ural-Altaic and Slavic, kept sacking Transylvania until the ninth century. Then, *via* Turkey, a tribe of Tatars from Central Asia overran and conquered the Romanians of Transylvania. They were the Magyars, the people that other nations call Hungarian.

For the next thousand years battles and violent disputes among the Magyar princelings, the Romanian *voivods*, the Ottoman Empire and the House of Hapsburg plagued the Transylvanian natives. Their bloody history culminated in the disastrous 1848 revolution, when Transylvania lost its autonomy and became essentially subject to Austrian rule, later under the guise of the "dual monarchy" of the Austro-Hungarian Empire.

From that time on, the enmity seething for centuries between the Romanians and the Magyars of Transylvania intensified into fanatical hatred. Each people blamed the other for the 1848 defeat, accused the other of abject cowardice or treason, and vowed to wipe out the ethnic shame with the other's blood. They each kept their promise. Transylvanian blood moistened the soil of the land for generations. In school, the children were given little flags to wave and taught to sing patriotic songs. Sometimes the children waved the red-white-and-green Hungarian flag and sang in shrill voices:

> The Carpathian snowy peaks
> We claim, we claim, we claim.
> We aim, we aim, we aim
> To keep that lovely plain
> For it is the land, the land, the land
> The sacred Magyar land
> Our ancestors always had.
> And we swear, we swear, we swear
> The Romanians won't steal it again!

At other times, since regimes changed swiftly and brutally overnight, the same children were given the blue-yellow-and-red Romanian flag and taught another patriotic song:

King and Country, beloved and great,
I am yours, it is my fate.
The Tisza, the Danube, the Nistru
Shall stay Romanian borders for ever!
My life in its defense I pledge,
Every Tatar brute to catch
Till peace and justice reign supreme
Under King Carol's great regime.

The natives of Transylvania knew that one regime would follow the other only to be toppled by the former, which would again be replaced by the latter. The rhythm of power changed incessantly. What never changed was what was in their hearts.

When Austria-Hungary was defeated in World War I, the Romanian natives of Transylvania declared the land united with the Romanian kingdom. In 1920 the Treaty of Trianon ratified that union.

2

In the northern part of Transylvania, where the peaks of the Carpathians are speckled with edelweiss and the snow never melts, there is a town at the foot of one of the mountain ranges. It is hugged by two rivers: the Tisza on the west and the Iza on the east, like moats winding around a castle. It was an island, a *sziget*, the Magyars had said when they first settled on that tongue of land which was really a peninsula. The Magyars named the town Sziget. When the Romanians took over, they continued calling it by that name, but they spelled it Sighet.

The town like an island, Sighet, was the town where Lisa Engler was born.

"The world has eight continents: Europe, Asia, Africa, Australia, North America, South America, Antarctica. That's seven. The eighth continent is Sighet."

Although this was said in derision by out-of-towners, Sighet's enormous stature in the world was a matter of staunch belief by its natives. They never doubted Sighet's decisive role in the shaping of cosmic events and were convinced that without Sighet's dynamism the world would have difficulty spinning on its axis. While there were a few who did question Sighet's global significance, there was wholehearted unanimity in viewing the town as an impregnable citadel of safety and peace. Was there any other purpose in Nature's having created mountain peaks like the Solovan and the Prislop, great rivers like the Tisza and the Iza, than to protect the thirty thousand people living in Sighet?

Indubitably, Sighet was a receptacle for things good and bad, graceful and vulgar, brave and ignoble, vital and trivial, for it contained within its confines beauty and homeliness, wealth and squalor, knowledge and virtue, Hungarians and Romanians. And Jews.

The snowcapped mountaintops touched the blue skies, rows of chestnut trees lined wide streets, and in spring and summer the town was saturated with scents of acacia, jasmine or lilac spilling from gardens. Canopied horse-drawn carriages, painted in gay colors, looked charming when they passed by. The clop of hooves on cobblestones, the tintinnabulation of bells dangling from horses' necks sounded pleasant.

Yet a breath of doubt, camouflaged by sweet sights and smells, lingered somewhere. Why did the Jews always lower their voices when they walked past the Protestant, Catholic, or Greek Orthodox churches dominating Main Street? Why did the tolling of church bells and the heavy smell of incense, seeping through church portals, perturb the Jews of Sighet?

There were many synagogues and houses of study as well. Of course. But a Jewish visitor, in town for the first time, could not find them easily. One of the two main synagogues, the Orthodox, was slightly behind Main Street. The other, the Neulogue Synagogue, was close to the Market Place, on a side street far from the center of town. One had to ask for directions to find either of these synagogues.

The rest of the Jewish houses of worship were at the edge of town in the Jewish Section, which was near the Gypsy Quarter. It was simply not true, as some troublemakers insisted, that the Section and Quarter were back to back! One look at the empty strip of land running between the Section and the Quarter was sufficient to make it instantly apparent how far apart one was from the other. That strip of land, which was owned by the Jewish Community and would never be for sale, was a demarcation line creating a distance as great between Section and Quarter as the distance the Red Sea had created between Israelites and

Egyptians. The Jewish visitor would not have to fear straying into strange regions. He could also easily find many houses of worship in the Section, *Talmud Torahs*, *stibels*, even the great *tzadik's* temple, without asking for directions. All he would have to do was to look and listen.

Sighet was not an ordinary little town, a village, God forbid. Sighet was a city! The capital of Judetul Maramures, indeed one of Transylvania's finest regions. Sighet was particularly proud of its smoothly run city administration and of its brilliant judiciary. There were always cynics who maintained the smoothly running administrative and judicial wheels were the result of a copiously greased baksheesh system. If that was so, was it not proof of an inherent goodwill in people, a reliable patron-client relationship guaranteeing stability? And was it not stability everyone sought, never mind the jaundiced view of a few cynics?

At any rate, it was a lively town for sure. Its fashionable stores along Main Street were full of customers, the big Crown Hotel, in the center of town, was full of tourists and businessmen, and residents and out-of-towners jammed the Crown Gambling Casino at night.

The Astra Palace, an impressive old stone building with cone-shaped turrets and a marble staircase of regal proportions winding up from a marble-columned entrance hall, was the town's cultural center. It had a music conservatory whose students performed at the annual Benefit Gala Concert in June, when the large concert hall was packed to capacity by the performers' relatives and friends.

That Sighet was a great place of learning was evidenced by the quantity and quality of its schools. Elementary school was compulsory, of course, but matriculation in secondary and high school depended on merit and the ability to pay tuition. Mostly on the ability to pay tuition. There were many high schools to choose from: the Catholic Convent School, the Liceul Domnita Ileana for girls, the Liceul Dragos Voda for boys, and, the apex of scholastic establishments, the Training School, which was a branch of the famous Transylvanian Teachers' Institute. What in part made the Training School more sought after than any other in town was indeed the fact that the girls looked adorable in their black poplin uniforms, black polka-dotted white silk bows under their chins and white piqué starched collars around their necks—even the boys looked dashing wearing silver or gold-braided school caps. But the school's attraction lay mainly in the fact that a special entrance examination was required. By some quirk of nature, children of the intelligentsia and/or of the rich never failed to achieve the required entrance marks. Even so, those who were turned away could always find a place in a trade school or business school. Then there were also private dancing schools, cooking schools and petit point schools, bridge clubs and chess clubs, writing clubs and reading clubs, poetry clubs, an endless array of intellectual and artistic avenues to please even the most finicky culture lover.

In the Jewish Section there were lots of schools too: several Talmudic schools of various theological nuances, a couple of *Bet Yaakov* Hebrew day schools attended by the children of the comfortable and lots of *heders* with an open admission for the children of the poor. Children of wealthy Jews were tutored in their own homes by needy Talmudic students. There were also two Zionist clubs in Sighet: one was called Barissia, the other Habonim.

But the most precious jewel in Sighet's treasure chest, the shiniest of tiaras envied by other towns, was the one and only Grand Corso.

Between the prefecture and the Vigado Cinema, in the middle of Main Street, there was a park about two blocks long and one block wide. In spring and summer it bloomed at various times with red tulips, anemones and lilies, purple and yellow mums, jasmine and azalia and delicate pink roses. Criss-crossed by wooden benches, the park had in its center a pavilion where, during summer evenings, the town's military brass band played a medley drawn from Lehár operettas, Strauss waltzes, tangos and fox-trots.

Only inclement weather kept Sigheters from promenading on the Grand Corso every evening and weekend mornings. Young maidens, decked out in *couturier* creations copied by local dressmakers from French fashion magazines, walked arm-in-arm up and down the Corso, on the sidewalk and in the middle of the street, careful not to take one step below nor above the confines of the Corso, such a trespass placing them on plain Main Street; and for *that*, one did not have to spruce up. One spruced up, after all, to impress the twirlers and puffers, bachelors who seemed to have made a career of holding up buildings along the Corso by leaning against them to flirt in a state of repose with the promenading maidens. The twirlers twirled canes and tipped their fedoras or straw hats when a particularly pretty maiden passed by. The puffers—who were more difficult to please—puffed long Turkish cigarettes while inspecting the feminine parade from under half closed eyelids, and if certain maidens caught their fancy they blew elaborate curlicues of smoke to indicate that the next time around the chosen ladies would be addressed by them.

There was another park, the Malom Kert, huge and dense with oak trees and weeping willows, at the foot of Solovan Mountain, along the bank of the Iza. At a good distance from town, the Malom Kert was a hideout for students cutting classes and a haven for lovers seeking privacy. Near the river was the Strand, an Olympic-size swimming pool amidst small wooden dressing cabins, Ping-Pong tables and canvas lounging chairs. There was a small admission charge for the use of the Strand, though it was a public facility. But the clay tennis court adjacent to the Strand belonged to a private club. Its club house was shielded by weeping willows, the tennis court fenced in behind thick hedges. Jews were politely but unequivocally refused membership at the club. Then the Jews got a permit to build their own tennis court a little farther down on the bank of the Iza, near a small bridge which led to Vad, a hamlet across the river. The Jews built two tennis courts instead of one and erected a soccer stadium next to them. They also chartered their own club and called it The Samson Sports Club. So there.

3

There were twelve thousand Jews in Sighet. The rest of the population was Romanian and Hungarian. Penalties were meted out in school if students were caught speaking Hungarian. One *lei* for every Hungarian word. It became quite expensive to speak Hungarian. But the children of the rich could afford to be bilingual. The adults kept up their ethnic feud with renewed vigor, their sole common link being the Jews—whom both groups despised. The Romanians seemed to lack the Hungarians' gut hatred of Jews. The idea of being bested on any issue by their enemy prodded the Romanians to summon up, on occasions, anti-Semitic sentiments of such magnitude that they soon became experts at hating Jews.

The Jews called both the Romanians and the Hungarians *goyim*, meaning non-Jews. The Jews kept to themselves, sometimes by choice but mostly for lack of alternatives.

The Jewish community was called the *Kehilla* and its yearly elected president the *roshokol*. He was an important man in town, usually a wealthy merchant. Maintaining a truce between the Jewish and *goyish* communities was among his heaviest responsibilities. He lined administrative and judicial pockets with hefty contributions from the *Kehilla's* treasury and achieved truce. The Jews' contributions, euphemistically called "voluntary," filled up the treasury with bulging money belts always kept in readiness for emergencies. Funds from the treasury were also used to maintain free kosher kitchens in the City Hospital and Insane Asylum, to fully subsidize *heders*, and to provide dowries for pious poor maidens before they succumbed to spinsterhood.

The deepest dip into the treasury was, of course, the baksheesh. Still, everyone agreed it was better to give than to receive—as the Jews in Kishinev and Iasi had learned during pogroms.

The *roshokol* and his council of elders met once a year to deliberate fiscal matters, then taxed every Jew commensurate with his financial circumstances. Some were excused from contributing, others were taxed heavily. A few fretted silently or complained bitterly, but no one doubted the *roshokol* and his council of elders made just assessments although without the benefit of auditors' statements. Each Jew knew exactly the other Jew's business. It was no use denying one's prosperity: the members of the Jewish Community knew their obligations and paid their dues. And the *roshokol*, who also knew his obligations, dutifully paid the baksheesh to assure peace. Peace was everything. As was written in the Great Book of Zohar: "God is peace, His name is peace, and all is bound together in peace." And where there is peace there is prosperity. So there!

4

The Jews lived unmolested in Sighet, it was true. They were even allowed to thrive. The Romanian *goyim* had a vested interest in their well-being. As long as Jews had money, the baksheesh system secured many a Romanian official and his family a grand vacation at one of the Black Sea resorts at Mamaia or Carmen Sylva, or at an elegant hotel high up in the mountains. The Romanians had no reason to crack the whip yet. The Jews appreciated that being a *Jewish* minority, religious and economic freedom, social equality, were beyond their reach. Such rights belonged only to *goyim*. The Jews fomented no trouble; they were grateful not to be given trouble. Some *goyim*, very few indeed, looked upon the Jews with patronizing benevolence, even taking under their wing certain members of the Jewish intelligentsia who also happened to be professionals. A bunch of interesting people, these Jews of the elite, the *goyim* said behind their backs. A sort of crossing between *couleur locale* and dynamite. To be watched constantly, of course.

Some *goyim* genuinely liked Jews, as handsome Judge Barcescu did. He had political aspirations early in his career. He also had serious gambling habits and an eye for pretty women. He married Luisa, the pretty Jewess, who was also rich. The lion did lie down with the lamb, after all.

School started at nine in the morning and was over at one o'clock in the afternoon, six days a week. Jewish children were accepted in school. But they were given the choice of either attending Sabbath morning classes or being suspended. The school board, however, in its generosity, allowed Jewish students to refrain from writing, thus avoiding a direct transgression of the Sabbath. So Jewish children went to school on the Sabbath. If truth be told, their elders were grateful that the children were not forced to write on Sabbath mornings. That would have been truly a sin. And what could they have done about it? Deprive their children of learning? After all, didn't the great Hillel say that he who does not learn forfeits his life?

Yet, the Jews were too reticent, perhaps too superstitious, to speak freely of suppression and anti-Semitism. By evoking the specter of pogroms one may hasten their coming.

Pinched *goyish* mouths and eyes flashing hate, sudden explosions of vile anti-Semitic curses and the mushrooming of obnoxious graffiti, were the behavior of a very small, inconsequential, though troublesome, element. Just like the perverts standing in alleys near the girls' school watching the students walk by in the mornings and afternoons, leering and making lewd remarks while they opened their flies and exposed their penises or silently masturbated in doorways. One did not speak of such depravity in decent circles.

Besides, if one did not look one did not see ominous signs. If one did not listen, one did not hear sounds of hate. All was transient. Or, as the Baal Shem-Tov said: "Evil is only a throne for good."

The Jews of Sighet were not too reticent to boast about their town though, their place of birth where the huge Jewish cemetery contained thousands and thousands of their ancestors. The Jews boasted about the town's vigor, the incomparable Grand Corso, the Malom Kert. About the world-famous Jewish violinist who even called himself after his natal town. About its plain folk who were smart enough to outsmart even a Litvak Jew, admittedly the shrewdest trader in the East. They boasted about Sighet's businessmen who were not merely astute: they were giants of trade, tycoons of commerce. Sighet's Jewish women were not merely pretty: they were exquisite fusions of Mona Lisas and

68

Esthers. Their sages and rabbis were not merely paradigms of wisdom and piety: they were, in all likelihood, among the Thirty-Six Just Men.

The Jews also boasted of Sighet's poetic soul, became its troubadours and created original lyrics praising the town's idyllic spirit to the tune of *Popeye the Sailorman* or *Stormy Weather*. In moments of hyperbolic bragging, they proclaimed the town almost as chic as Bucharest. They even named Sighet "mini-Paris" the instant the one big neon sign was put up.

It was a belated though admittedly resolute step on the ladder of technological progress, for sure. The sign was installed only in 1938, but when it finally came, it was fireworks! The neon tubes cast the Corso in splendiferous streams of blue, green, red, yellow fluorescent lights. What a spectacle that was, the huge sign on top of the Engler store in the center of Main Street! It read THE HOUSE OF ENGLER AND SONS. The first year the sign was up, it caused traffic jams on the Corso. The people could not take their eyes off the sign; they stopped and gazed at it in wonder. Each letter fluoresced in alternating blue, yellow, and green lights. Only the name ENGLER blazed in solid red. The sign became a landmark. Every Sigheter, Jew and *goy* alike, took great pride in it, particularly since the sign stayed lit from seven o'clock in the evening till midnight, come rain or shine.

The post-Versailles and Trianon decades brought to the country a strong Francophile attitude. In Sighet, France was the symbol of liberalism and culture, the French language the expression of refinement and elegance. The hallmark of a young woman's matrimonial eligibility *par excellence* was not just her dowry and the dexterity with which she played the piano: what tipped the scale was her facility in rolling the letter *r* under her tongue.

Perhaps Sighet was also called "mini-Paris" because of the big house at the edge of town, near the City Hospital and Insane Asylum. The house was in the Bandzalgo Section. It had pink awnings, mirrored walls glimmering through sheer curtains, and at night prurient laughter filtered through half open French windows. That house was the bordello, the only licensed whorehouse in Judetul Maramures. The bordello's French flavor was obvious: it was called *Le Jardin*, only French champagne was served on its premises, and the mattresses were directly imported from Paris. Even the exotic whores were supposedly French.

One could see the whores once a month sweep through town in horse-drawn carriages or striding arm-in-arm, three abreast, going to the health department at City Hall for the mandatory monthly medical checkups and whore-license renewals. The day of their official business in town was the first Wednesday of each month. The whores wore tight dresses, flaunted deep décolletages and high side slits, had thickly rouged cheeks and vermilion red lips. They laughed loudly and left trails of cheap perfume as they breezed through town in the morning, then breezed back to the Bandzalgo Section around noon.

It was the same Wednesday morning Jewish beggars came to Sighet from nearby hamlets and villages to collect alms from the town's *oishers*, the prosperous Jewish merchants. Other days of the week the beggars worked other towns. But Wednesday was reserved for Sighet. It was an old custom.

At the time the whores trooped down south to City Hall, the beggars plodded their way up north towards Main Street, stopping at every Jewish store to pick up their alms. Whores and beggars met midway, in the center of the Grand Corso, each scornfully eyeing the other. The whores thumbed their noses, opened dress buttons so their breasts popped out and taunted the beggars. The beggars shook their fists, cursed and spat at them, then covered their eyes with their hands and turned their heads away, but not before they took a good look.

The Jews also kept up with matters outside their world, beyond the familiar rivers and mountains. They knew all about the *goldene medina*, America the Golden, where Jews had unlimited freedom to worship any way they chose despite their being a minority, where trains ran on rooftops, and where buildings rose to a height of 381 meters.

"Who would want to walk up 102 stories anyway," they said. "One could get dizzy and fall, God forbid . . ."

Then they looked at the mountains and rivers holding their world, their Sighet, and knew it was good.

"*Ki tov*," they said. "It is good here."

5

Lisa Engler's immediate ancestors originated in Sighet. Her father's parents had died when she was an infant, and her mother's father, Shlomo Dankenberg, died many years before that. Family reminiscences kept his memory alive, depicting him as a fiery red-bearded Hasid with long side curls, wearing a fur-trimmed velvet hat, a hardy man who threw his weight about, but who also sat at the rabbi's feet, a pious man poring over sacred texts all day, forsaking them to knock down any man who wronged him, a stubborn, stern man who was feared or respected and envied for his vigor and independence.

When Shlomo married Miriam, Lisa's grandmother, he was fifty years old and Miriam was eighteen. When Lisa's mother Rachel was born, he was seventy-two. The Jews who questioned Shlomo's ability to sire a child at that age knew little or nothing of Mendelian theory, or did not notice that he and Miriam and their children had blue eyes. Perhaps the Jews were jealous of Shlomo's sudden burst of virility and of his pretty wife Miriam. They began to rehash past events and pointed out with a mean wink that Miriam was thirty-two years his junior *and* his second wife. While still arguing which one had been the lesser or greater disgrace—his divorce in middle age or marrying an eighteen-year-old virgin—the Jews dubbed Shlomo "the Hasidic Sex Maniac" and "Haman of the Apple Orchards."

Indeed, it was a grave matter for a Jew to seek a *get*, a religious divorce. A *get* sought by a Hasid was grave *and* shocking. But a fifty-year-old Hasid had to be either mad or bewitched by the Devil to go through the ordeal. The Jews knew Shlomo was not mad. They also knew that certain special circumstances called for the granting of a *get*. But they refused to look upon Shlomo's motive for seeking the *get*—his concupiscence, no doubt—as a special circumstance. When Rebbe Shaye, whose disciple Shlomo was, granted the *get* at once, the Jews were first stunned, then outraged. They also envied Shlomo's nerve, begrudged him the instant divorce and the young new bride, and muttered about loose living unbecoming a Hasid.

What the Jews did not know at the time, and Rebbe Shaye did, was that Malka, Shlomo's first wife, was a dipsomaniac, a lush who consumed staggering quantities of slivovitz and tzuika, powerful local mountain dews for which Sighet was famous.

Though Shlomo had been a devoted disciple of Rebbe Shaye even before he had married Malka and had zealously studied the Scriptures under his tutelage, Shlomo also was a prosperous man. At the time of his marriage to Malka he owned seven apple orchards and a pub. Thenceforth Malka ran the pub and managed the apple orchards and Shlomo engaged in every pious married Jew's occupation: study. Study of the Bible, of the Cabala, study, study . . . and let the wife run the business. Eager to help, or having no options, Malka relieved Shlomo of secular daily cares. Eventually she took to drink, first as a friendly gesture to humor the customers at the pub, then dutifully to taste the brandy they made at the stills in the orchards to be sure of its quality. And once she got the hang of it, she began drinking in earnest.

Rebbe Shaye understood Shlomo's predicament: a pious Jew and an *oisher* to boot, as Shlomo was, should not be burdened with the problems of a tippling wife. Shlomo had suffered enough. His condition was deemed a "special circumstance."

When Shlomo married Miriam, the eight children from his previous marriage also were married and living near Sighet. He had three children with Miriam: Haskell, David and Rachel.

Because Miriam saw her function only as a wife and mother,

Shlomo now attended to all business matters and went to the rabbi just once a week. It was on Sabbath afternoons he went to Rebbe Shaye, when the Rebbe's lunch leftovers were divided among his disciples. To eat the Rebbe's leftovers was one of the great honors that befell only worthy disciples; therefore, they fought over every morsel and crumb of food left on the Rebbe's table. Shlomo, not being the timid type, always got himself the lion's share. Slowly, his fellow disciples ceased begrudging his luck as they began appreciating his pretty wife Miriam, who made the best *kugel* in town, a potato-honey-and-raisin pudding. Every Sabbath afternoon Shlomo brought to Rebbe Shaye's table a *kugel* which he proudly carried on top of his fur-trimmed velvet hat.

"From my wife Miriam," he said each time he placed the *kugel* on the Rebbe's table, "a *kugel* from Miriam."

The Jews began calling him "Shlomo Kugel" till he reached eighty-five. It was then that he died.

Haskell, Shlomo's and Miriam's eldest son, was now the head of the family. He also became rich, very rich. Unacquainted with the subtleties of ancient Greek and Mideastern history, people said Haskell was born lucky—like Croesus. The shooting star racing across the sky that a neighbor claimed to have seen the night Haskell was born supported that theory. Others maintained that the bleating black sheep that roamed in Shlomo's orchards for seven days after the boy's birth brought him luck.

At the age of twenty-five, when he married Hannah, Haskell was already on his way to wealth. Although greatly impressed by Talmudic knowledge in others, he had no time nor inclination to refine his own mind with theological intricacies. He had to support the family and that, he said, took up all his time.

A keen sense of trading made him sell the apple orchards and pub at a time when he could reap the highest profits. The choice of a new trade proved equally fortunate.

He began dealing in handwoven rugs and carpets. Symmetrical geometric patterns, rich red, dark blue and green, hues of yellow and gold, may have attracted Haskell. Or the thick, sturdy texture of the rugs may have given him a sense of permanence, of endurance. Had he have known that the famous Transylvanian rugs, which made him a wealthy man, were copies of seventeenth-century Turkish prayer rugs used in Christian churches, he probably would not have gone into that business at all. Haskell was a pious Jew in spite of his Talmudic ignorance. He never walked by a church without murmuring *Shema Israel, Adonai Elohenu, Adonai Echad:* Hear O Israel, the Lord our God, the Lord is one. As it was, to the great benefit of a few and the general good of many, Haskell was also ignorant of the cultural and religious significance of his wares.

He bought herds and herds of sheep. Their wool was shorn, washed, bleached, then worked by peasant women skilled in the arts of spinning, dyeing, and hand looming. Haskell became an authority on rug patterns, knew all about inner field and border designs, inner and outer guard stripes, allover patterns, panel compositions, and medallions. He knew everything about yarns, about warps, woofs and piles of various strength and thickness, about looms, about vegetable and mineral dyes. Most of all he knew how to pool scattered home industries into one great commercial enterprise with markets reaching beyond the borders of Transylvania. He revitalized a static local commerce, brought employment to many and wealth to himself.

Haskell's repute as the number one wholesale rug dealer was firmly established by the end of World War I. The two-story house on Main Street, the beaver-lined winter coat with shiny black astrakhan fur lapels, and the first-row-center seat in the Orthodox synagogue were the only exterior marks of his wealth. Otherwise he was frugal, drank a dram of schnapps only once a week—on Sabbath evenings after lighting of the *havdalah* candles—and never took seconds at mealtimes. He never owned more than two suits at a time, a sturdy serge drab gray for business and a navy blue with a vest for synagogue attendance. He never took holidays, and never gave presents.

The Jews treated him with deference, but not with love. He was the wealthy Haskell, and they spoke of him as commanding, not bossy. He was tenacious, not stubborn. A true son of Shlomo Kugel, they said, no doubt about that. They considered him a wise man holding on to his fortune with care, not with obsession. A cultivator, not a dissipator. They never called him stingy or tightwad to his face. Haskell was the *Kehilla's* highest taxpayer, and a man of substance deserved extra consideration.

The Jews' tolerance faced a severe test when Haskell was elected *roshokol*. He bluntly refused to pay the baksheesh that year on the simple ground that he considered bribing immoral. Instead of giving bribes, he gave instructions to the Jewish Community to live strictly by the letter of the law. No smuggling into Sighet of textiles from Slatina, the Czech town across the Tisza, nor dealing with any other contraband commodities. Everyone fumed. Custom officials threatened reprisals. The Jews complained of low profits. Still, Haskell stuck to his principles and refused to pay the baksheesh. For one year Sighet was law-abiding. And never again was Haskell elected *roshokol*.

Yet, some of his habits made people smile or wink. Like his habit of sitting on money.

The lower level of his two-story building was a huge store, stacked to capacity with hundreds of rugs and carpets arranged on shelves according to size and use—some rugs were hung on walls to decorate or to keep a house warm, others were used as floor covering. In the back of the store there was a small room in which there were a plain table, a bare electric bulb hanging from the ceiling, a chair and two steel safes. Every evening, before locking up the store, Haskell brought to this room the cash register with the daily intake and emptied the drawer full of paper money on the center of the table, directly under the light. He then sat down, moistened his fingertips with saliva and began smoothing out, one by one, the crumpled edges of banknotes with infinite patience and tender care. Then he pressed each banknote against the flat of the table and again smoothed out every crease with his wet fingertips, sometimes hastening the process with a few well-directed sprays of spit. He made several packets of smoothed-out banknotes, got up from the chair and neatly padded its seat with the packets. He placed over the money a cardboard cut out to the shape of the seat, then sat down on the chair purposefully, like a hen laying eggs. So as not to idle while sitting erect on the money, he went on smoothing out other piles, till an inner timer signaled to him that the previous batch of packets had reached its maximum compression. He exchanged the compressed packets for yet uncompressed but smoothed-out money, deftly squeezed the compressed packets into one of the safes, already stuffed with rows of compressed money, and sat down on the next batch of money.

The Jews called this practice "Dankenberg money hatching"

or "Dankenberg money ironing" and attributed bizarre reasons to it. It never occurred to them that Haskell stuffed his safes full of cash because he did not trust banks, and that the counting of money, the touching, fondling, and rearranging of the banknotes at his own will, gave him the feeling of independence and of freedom. Also, Haskell loved the feel of money.

He built his wealth with vigor and a tight hand, and Hannah gave part of it away behind his back. She gave to the poor, gave loans to Jews whom Haskell had refused, gave dowries to girls whom the *Kehilla* had turned down. She gave and gave, and Haskell did not notice. Or did not want to notice.

Miriam, the matriarch, lived with them. They called her "Miriam the Peacemaker." She soothed feelings hurt by Haskell's peremptory decisions and made *sholom* between quarreling parties.

David, the younger brother, lived with Haskell till he turned twenty-one. He then left Haskell's house and the job in his store and went out on his own. Wearing white spats and beige glacé leather gloves and brandishing an ivory-handled cane, David took to loose living, even smoked on the Sabbath. Haskell cut off his salary at once, but Hannah secretly made up part of it.

One day David underwent a religious conversion prompted by a dream or a vision, no one knew for sure which. He sprouted floating side curls and a long fiery red beard. He swallowed a horse, the children teased him, but left the tail hanging out of his mouth. Eventually someone ferreted out David's reason for turning to God so suddenly: it was the clap he had caught at Le Jardin. In return for God's curing him, the rumormonger said, David vowed to devote the rest of his life to studying the Almighty's laws. Apparently God was a great and speedy physician, for David became soon a disciple of Rebbe Gedaliah, the son of Rebbe Shaye. Haskell approved of David's conversion and reinstated his salary. The sincerity of David's repentance must have been indeed impressive: he married Reisl, an uncomely, taciturn old maid, fat and short, whose attributes kept David at Rebbe Gedaliah's feet from morning till late at night. The Rebbe called him Dovedl, the favorite disciple, even though Reisl refused to bake *kugels*.

Hannah and Haskell had no children. They loved Rachel as if she were their own daughter. Hannah taught her how to run a house with modesty but with authority, and Miriam taught her to read Hebrew and chant prayers. Rachel's curiosity about the world induced Miriam to permit her to read newspapers, even though she was only a girl. Rachel was even allowed to read a novel now and then. Haskell took the young girl to the store twice a week, after school, taught her the rudiments of rug design and rug manufacturing and showed her how to keep a ledger.

After David's forsaking the world of trade, his job was filled by a young man named Andras Engler. He soon knew almost as much as Haskell about warps and yarns and knots. Andras had a pleasing manner and was handsome. A charmer. He was tall and slim, had dark hair and a beautifully tended mustache ending in jaunty little twirls, an aquiline nose and a sweet smile. Andras was a worldly man with more than two suits, all cut to the latest fashion, wore a gold chain across his breast linked to a gold watch he kept in his vest pocket, and knew all the new dance steps and songs. Humorous stories poured out of his mouth, but not quotations from the Scriptures. Haskell wished his manager, which Andras had become, would be less involved in worldly frivolities and more aware of Jewish piety. It would have added to Haskell's prestige to have a learned manager, a *Talmud-hacham*. With great restraint, Haskell only dropped hints as to what a Dankenberg manager ought to be and continued to hatch more money.

When Rachel fell in love with Andras, she was sixteen years old, he twenty-three. The prospect of her marrying a man ignorant of Talmudic writings inordinately upset Haskell.

"A man lax in traditional observance, an *apikoros,* is not for our Rachel," he decreed.

Still, Haskell's good sense prevailed: he did not fire Andras who was too good a manager to let go. But he strictly forbade Rachel to set foot in the store where she could meet Andras. They met, nonetheless, behind bales, in the storeroom, while Haskell hatched money, or saw each other briefly in the mornings in the Malom Kert. When she reached eighteen, Rachel asked Haskell's permission to marry Andras, after she had already obtained Miriam's and Hannah's.

"No," Haskell said. "You must marry this other fellow, Shmuel Schwartz who is a *Talmud-hacham* and an *oisher*. Reb Schwartz is a *sheiner Yid*, a fine Jew. You must give up Andras, the song-and-dance man. That's final."

Next morning Rachel was not in her room, but Miriam found a letter from her there. It said she would roam the world, if need be forever, till Haskell agreed to her marrying Andras. Miriam and Hannah found her in David's house, sitting on her valise before a silent Reisl. Giving in to Miriam's wish, Haskell now consented to the marriage and, strange man that he was, gave Rachel the finest dowry a girl in those parts could have wished for: he made Andras a partner in his rugdom.

6

Meanwhile, World War I had broken out and run its course. Count István Tisza, prime minister of Hungary and archsupporter of Austria-Hungary's alliance with Germany, was blamed for the Hungarian defeat. Magyar patriots assassinated him at the end of 1918. Transylvanian-born Béla Kun, who had been taken prisoner by the Russians in 1915 and had joined the Bolsheviks, returned to Hungary in November 1918, and recruited a red army. The Hungarian red revolution was on its way. In March 1919, Kun ousted Mihály Károlyi, the provisional president of the newly declared independent Hungarian republic. The *coup* brought a reign of terror to Hungary and Transylvania, for Kun reconquered some of the Transylvanian territory that had been awarded to Romania by the Allies. Romanian troops then reconquered that territory and marched into Budapest in August 1919. Eventually they let the Allies persuade them to retire east across the Tisza River, the border between Transylvania and Hungary. A counterrevolution put an end to Kun's regime and its reign of terror, brought another reign of terror of its own, and, in March 1920, Admiral Horthy Miklós rode into Budapest on a white stallion. He was hailed as the savior of the monarchy and proclaimed Regent of Hungary.

During the convulsions of revolution and counterrevolution,

the people of Transylvania fled back and forth. Escaping Kun's red terror, they encountered Magyar terror. Escaping that, they faced Romanian revenge. Atrocities were committed by all sides. People could not tell the difference between red plunder, Magyar brutality, or Romanian marauding.

Before the final implementation of the Treaty of Trianon in June 1920, a Magyar unit of revolutionaries or counterrevolutionaries was scattered around town. To vent their sentiments about the Versailles and Trianon treaties and to repay the humiliation of having had the streets of Budapest desecrated by Romanian boots, one night the Magyars attacked the defenseless inhabitants of Vad, the hamlet across the Iza. They beat up a few peasants and raped a couple of women. The Magyars then took to the mountains to avoid the wrath of the Romanian army that was to occupy Sighet at dawn. They barricaded themselves in a cave, but a Romanian platoon soon discovered them and blocked the entrance. After five days of starvation, the Magyars shoved a white rag through the mouth of the cave. The Romanians responded with pistol shots, a wild stream of curses, threats of murder, and vivid descriptions of dismemberment methods so that certain parts of Magyar anatomy could be sent to Béla Kun in Russia—where he had found asylum after his red debacle—or to the Kaiser in Dutch exile. The Hungarian units remained trapped in the mountain cave.

Until Haskell rescued them. It puzzled everyone in Sighet, Jew and *goy* alike. What moved him to action seemed an unsettling mystery. But Miriam had quietly spoken of suffering, ordinary suffering. She spoke of humanity and the value of life, of punishment fitting a crime, and of how everybody was his brother's keeper.

Haskell commissioned all the bakers in town to make extra supplies of bread. He paid them in smoothly pressed money and loaded two ox-drawn carts filled with bread. Alone, at night, he guided the carts through unused old mountain paths he knew from the days of the orchards and reached the besieged cave, undetected by the Romanians. Some people said Haskell had paid off the Romanians; others saw God's hand protecting Haskell while he smuggled the Magyars out of the cave. Only a few conceded that his success was due to sheer pluck and shrewd strategy.

Haskell was decorated *in absentia* by the Hungarian royal government. He was awarded the Double Special Gold Cross, made an honorary citizen of Hungary and given a special charter which declared him a privileged person to whom the people of God-fearing Magyarország would be eternally grateful.

7

In 1927, when Lisa was born, the astute observer of political trends could have easily detected portents of danger in the rumblings of post-Versailles Germany. The Jews of Sighet, at the time, were steeped in theological tracts or absorbed in intellectual pursuits, or were too wrapped up in building and holding on to their fortunes to hear discordant political notes.

During the next fifteen years, their otherwise nimble minds turned to putty when reading that the German Nazi Party gained 107 seats in the 1930 elections; that in 1933 the appointment of Adolf Hitler, the author of *Mein Kampf,* as chancellor of Germany was followed by the burning of the Reichstag building; that a 1934 plebiscite had voted Hitler Führer of Germany; that in 1935 the Nurnberg racial laws were promulgated; that the Führer remilitarized the Rhineland in 1936 after he had already won a plebiscite and reincorporated the Saarland into his Reich; that there were ugly riots by the Sudeten Germans living in Czechoslovakia; and that in 1938 there was the *Kristallnacht.* The Jews of Sighet unaccountably gave up interpreting what they clearly read. It was as if a spell had taken hold of them—and breaking that spell meant a complete upheaval of their lives. For this they were not prepared.

8

Lisa was the youngest of the three Engler children, and the only girl. Miklos was fourteen years old and Laszlo ten when she was born. To them she was a plaything they patted possessively, sometimes tenderly. Miriam taught her the names of flowers and trees, and taught her to count and read by the time she was four. When she entered first grade, Lisa wrote readily in capital letters. Miklos gave her a diary for her seventh birthday, a gold-edged red leather-bound book, with a lock and key. Her name was printed on the face of the book in large gold letters.

"Jot down what you don't want to forget," Miklos said to her. She held on to her diary for many years.

Laszlo played ball with her, performed stunning cartwheels and chin-ups for her amusement, delighted her with magic card tricks. When he felt particularly affectionate, he allowed her to kick his soccer ball.

Her earliest memories were of people who loved her. She was indulged by the family perhaps because of her rosy, freckled cheeks, the titian red hair primped up with a taffeta bow, and the twinkling green eyes in a dimpled face. Maybe. But maybe the family loved the little girl simply because she was the granddaughter Haskell and Hannah wished they could have had, or maybe because the thrust of her chin and the color of her hair reminded them of Shlomo Kugel. Then again, they may have loved her for no special reason, but because—in the words of the old Gypsy song Andras adapted for her—to them she was:

> The one and only girl to love,
> Is Lisa, the sweet little dove.
> God Almighty made me elect
> My Lisa to love and always protect.

The Englers had become rich. Not extremely rich like Haskell, only very rich. They owned a large house in a section where the streets were lined with chestnut and acacia trees and where Jews and *goyim* greeted each other with reserve but smilingly in the most civilized way. The house had a terrace which overlooked a garden full of jasmine and lilacs, of daffodils, daisies and lilies of the valley. In the back of the house there was a grove with apple, plum and peach trees and a thick ancient walnut tree. Rachel had furnished her home with traditional pieces, oak tables and rosewood dressers and commodes, and covered the floors and walls with beautiful rugs. She hand-embroidered a silk piano cover with golden threads and crocheted lacy antimacassars for the plump wing chairs. A cook prepared the meals, a maid cleaned, and Anna, the peasant washerwoman, came to the house twice a month to do the heavy laundry. Rachel went to the Market Place on Tuesday and Friday mornings, followed by the cook, who carried two straw baskets. When the governess took Lisa for her morning and afternoon walks, there was not much left for Rachel to do. Other women like her joined bridge clubs, or pursued a social life in a whirl of afternoon teas and gossip. Rachel had no taste for such activities. Instead, she read newspapers: the daily *Sighet News,* the biweekly Zionist *New Dawn* published in Cluj, the largest city in Transylvania, and, on Sunday mornings, the national paper *Romania.* On Sunday she also read books by Stefan Zweig, Arthur Schnitzler and Emile Zola. She still had time left to visit Miriam and Hannah daily. When Lisa entered first grade, Rachel took to going to the family store every morning.

Rachel did not pamper Lisa. There were so many others who did that. Perhaps too many, Rachel feared. Hannah showered the little girl with gifts, gold pins and necklaces with tiny pearls, rings with little rubies, and dainty gold bracelets.

"Wait till you grow up," she told Lisa, "you'll get more, much more." Meanwhile, she bought her walking dolls and speaking dolls, ordered a special doll carriage from Bucharest, even a porcelain chamber potty with handpainted flowers and her name on its rim.

Someone must teach Lisa about limits and moderation, Rachel decided, about the difference between material and spiritual needs, between temporal and eternal values. She became that someone.

Rachel spoke to Lisa of responsibility, of self-reliance and self-discipline, of a social system where there were not always clearly defined areas of good and bad. The ability to distinguish between these areas, then choosing the good path simply because it was morally right to do so constituted the essence of ethical behavior. And *that,* Rachel held, was the way people should conduct themselves. Certainly it was the way she hoped Lisa would conduct herself.

"The right path is easy to find if you honestly look for it," often she told Lisa. "Anything you set your mind to do you can do. I have great trust in you." Lisa sensed enormous strength and conviction in those words. Her mother was like a mountain, a natural force. Lisa felt invulnerable and indomitable in her presence. She embraced Rachel with her right arm.

"Yes Mamma, I can do it." She did not know what exactly it was she could do, but Rachel's confidence gave her self-confidence too. "I'll just have to set my mind to it. . . ."

Rachel's standards for her were not debatable, that Lisa knew. She was expected to study well, and she did. A young Talmudic scholar came to the house twice a week to instruct her in Hebrew. She did not chafe at being the only girl among her friends to be taught Hebrew. She practiced at the piano daily, and after she finished her school assignment generous praise came from her mother.

Respect was another measure of Rachel's standards. When Haskell heard that Lisa was to be enrolled in a children's ski class, he came over to the Englers at once.

"The child mustn't go." He was agitated. "Whoever heard of a six-year-old girl skiing?" he asked Rachel. "And what's the good

of going up a mountain only to slide down? It's foolish, dangerous! And bitter cold out there. A crazy sport. Not for Jews. The
child mustn't go. That's final."

Before Rachel could answer, Lisa piped up: "Mamma lets me
go. You can't boss me around, Uncle Haskell! So I'll go!"

She did not go that year.

"You need time to appreciate Uncle Haskell's concern," Rachel said. "Maybe next winter you'll even understand something
about respect. We'll see . . ."

Miss Duncan, a spinster who lived next door to the Englers,
read fairy tales to Lisa and gave her licorice. Baroness von Te-
nick sent word to the Englers that she would welcome monthly
visits from Lisa. At first Lisa balked at going.

"The baroness is lonely," Rachel told Lisa. "We must learn not
to be selfish. It will do you good. You'll go. It's the right thing to
do."

The baroness's husband, daughter and granddaughter many
years before had drowned in Lake Balaton. After the tragedy, she
lived in solitude, behind tall windows overhung by awnings.
Her mansion was on the same street as the Englers' house. The
first time Lisa visited the baroness, she felt lost among the rococo
furniture and the Biedermeier overstuffed sofas and footstools.
Then the baroness treated Lisa to hot chocolate and whipped
cream, opened the concert grand Bösendorfer piano and played
Chopin nocturnes and Mozart sonatas. Lisa relaxed, sat on a foot-
stool near the piano, and gravely listened.

"To do the right thing," Rachel reminded her each time Lisa
came from the baroness, "is its own reward."

9

Andras lavished love on Lisa. It was limitless and unequivo-cal.

He brought her sweets, chocolates, nougats and caramels every evening, put her to sleep with old Gypsy songs about nightingales and lovers. He sang to her softly, holding her small hands in his, till she fell asleep, a smile on her face way into the night—for her dream world was not much different from her real one. They both held the promise that nothing would change except that someday a handsome man like Papa would appear in her life and be entirely her own.

But until her own man would arrive, Papa was her Prince Charming. Papa took care of everything. He knew how to protect her and show her his love.

She was left alone in front of the stage, the curtain had been lowered behind her. She must have stood apart from the rest of the children when they all bowed and curtsied at the end of their ballet performance. It was at the Astra Palace. She was six years old. She stood alone before a full house, between the curtain and the orchestra pit. She wore her pink tutu and angel wings and was bathed in the illumination of the footlights. Standing there alone, she was frightened. There was no way to join the children behind the curtain, but she could hear them snigger. The audience began to chuckle. Her lips curved down. Then she saw Papa come down the aisle, a big warm smile on his face, tall and handsome, his gold chain swinging and shimmering across his chest. He walked into the orchestra pit, climbed a chair and reached for her. She was safe in his arms as he lifted her down the front of the stage, and the audience burst into applause.

Miriam died at the age of eighty-two, at the time the great depression caught up with Sighet. It was in 1933. The rug trade held its own for a while, then the volume began to drop. Haskell started to manufacture *halina,* a sturdy thick grayish-white wool cloth Romanian peasants used for winter coats and jackets. Haskell set up a *halina* mill downtown, at a good distance from the rug store, and spent most of his time at the mill. The business was reorganized. Haskell stayed with the mill, and the Englers continued the rug trade. A new firm was formed, THE HOUSE OF ENGLER AND SONS, where Miklos now worked full time. Laszlo was still in school, involved in sports. He was the young soccer star of the Samson Sports Club; but once he would finish school, star or no star, he was expected to work in the firm. The time would come, with God's help, when both sons would be partners with Andras.

As for Lisa, the world was open. She could even go study at the University when she grew up, though the Englers couldn't really see why a girl should spend years in studying instead of getting married. Particularly when she was pretty and had a huge dowry as Lisa had.

10

"February 8, 1936.

"We played the Abyssinian War again. I know where Abyssinia is, I looked it up in the atlas. It is in Africa. Melanica Popescu said because I am class president I should be Haile Selassie. He is the king of the Abyssinians. She was Mussolini and called her group fascisti. Mussolini is the king of the Italians. Not king, but something like that. Mamma thinks the game is silly. Anyway. Melanica named all the Jewish kids Abyssinians. So they are in my group. I am glad. Melanica said they are my partners, the Abyssinians, and laughed in a funny way.

"Anyway. We play the game during recess. Melanica draws two big squares on the ground with a stick."

"February, next day.

"She draws the squares. All right. Then she and I stand with our soldiers inside our squares. We want to win ground from the other, that's why we play the game. Mamma says it's a silly game, surely, she says, it's not for girls. ? Then we throw our ball. The ball which rolls furthest wins the mostest square. There are two girls who judge whose ball is furthest. The color of my ball is red, Melanica's white.

"P.S. I forgot: the judges are Maria Sandriu and Viorica Ionescu. I wanted Rozika to be one of the judges, Melanica said, oh no. She doesn't want to play without Maria and Viorica. She said. And would tell everyone I am a coward. So I let it be. I am not a coward."

"March 12, 1936.

"They always win. Even when they lose. Today my ball went further then hers, but Viorica and Maria didn't say so. They said it was her ball, the white one. They lied. They kicked it further away from mine. I saw that. They cheat. I told them that. It's a crooked game, I told them. It's not fun.

"Anyway. Aunt Hannah brought me a present. A beautiful book called *Mythology—Stories of Gods and Heroes of Ancient Greece and Rome.* The pages are smooth and shiny like Aunt Hannah's satin blouse. There are lots of pictures in the book of naked men and ladies.

"P.S. I want to stop playing the Abyssinian War. Something funny is happening. I don't mean funny, I mean bad. I don't understand what. But when I play the game I always get angry. Angry. I want to scream. But nothing hurts but something hurts. They call themselves fascisti and laugh."

"April 19, 1936.

"Tonight I overheard Mamma calling Papa POPPILY. He is my Papa, why does she call him POPPILY? He is my Papa, how can he be hers too. He is my Papa. He is not hers. He is not."

"May 14, 1936.

"I don't care if I don't get first prize at the end of the year. Who cares? I don't care I don't care I don't. Melanica tore up my composition and called me dirty Jew. I tore up her composition and called her dirty Christian. They play crooked awfully. So I refused to play. She said ha ha, coward, you lost the war, and tore up my composition. So I tore up hers then the teacher said I won't get first prize this year. Who cares? I don't care.

"P.S. I forgot: when I called Melanica dirty Christian she kicked me. That's when I kicked her back. Anyway."

"Kicking? Is that what a well-brought-up girl does?" Rachel asked Lisa.

90

"Must a well-brought-up girl let herself be kicked? Must she, Mamma?"

Rachel tried to suppress a smile.

"There are times——"

"Then I don't want to be a well-brought-up girl!" Lisa burst out. "If someone kicks me, I'll kick back, Mamma, I will . . . I don't care. . . ."

"Hush my child, hush. Listen to me." Dear God, let her be a child a little longer, she is too young to understand, Rachel thought, watching Lisa sob in her lap. She is too young, dear God, to juggle values and keep her morality intact; give her time to grow up and understand. . . .

"Listen, please," Rachel said, softly brushing Lisa's hair with her hand. "Sometimes we must overlook things. Pretend we don't see certain things. And that's all right, as long as you know that *your* conduct is proper. If you know in *your* heart that what you did was right, it will have to suffice sometimes. You always must do the right thing, even if others don't." Rachel stopped briefly, then continued slowly, slowly: "But you must learn to overlook things. You must."

11

When Lisa performed at the music conservatory she was eleven years old. It was the year-end gala concert of June 1938. She played *Für Elise* on the piano, a piece she had been practicing assiduously for six months.

The whole family came to the concert, even Haskell. The Englers and Dankenbergs sat in the first row center, and Hannah was beaming even before Lisa's turn came to perform. Wearing laces and ruffles, her diamond earrings fluttered slightly each time Hannah turned her head to gauge the reaction of the audience to what was being presented on stage. Wait till you hear ours, she mused after each number, our Lisa is a real *artiste,* wait till you hear real music! Rachel was fingering her double strand of pearls and watched Andras reach into his vest pocket for his gold watch, then check the printed program. Miklos and Laszlo sat dutifully in their seats, pretending not to be bored. Only Haskell seemed ill at ease.

She played *Für Elise* without a mistake. The long and loud applause came from the first row. Lisa curtsied the way she had been taught by Mademoiselle Lucille, her dancing teacher, demurely keeping her eyes on the ground. The applause coming from the first row would not stop and she straightened up.

"Look at our young lady," Miklos whispered to Laszlo, and

continued to applaud out of love for her. He suddenly realized she was not a little girl anymore. She was growing into a self-assured, poised young lady. Rachel signaled him to stop applauding.

But Hannah was carried away.

"Such talent!" she said. "The child should have the finest instrument to play on. A Bösendorfer. I've made inquiries; it's the best. I'll get her a Bösendorfer. Such talent!"

"She can still play on our old piano, Hannah dear." Rachel did not want a Bösendorfer. Why stir up envy? People will talk, they always do.

Since Hannah could not get Lisa a Bösendorfer, she ordered a bicycle from Bucharest. It was the first girl's bicycle in Sighet. All shiny chrome, except the seat and tires, it glittered and threw sparkles in the sun. The upper part of the back wheel was covered with red netting to prevent skirts from catching in the spokes.

The bell rang out clearly and distinctly as Lisa pedaled through the town on her bicycle. Nobody resented her too much, the young girl in the navy blue culotte skirt, white blouse and white beret, jingling the bell while riding on her bicycle in the middle of the Grand Corso. It was the only girl's bike in town after all, even if it belonged to a Jewish kid. The Sigheters smiled and called the bicycle "the silver bike." So there!

BOOK III

"This makes madmen who have made man mad
By their contagion, Conquerors and Kings,
Founders of sects and systems to whom add
Sophists, Bards, Statesmen, all unique things
Which stir too strongly the soul's secret springs,
And are themselves the fools to those they fool."
—Lord Byron, "Childe Harold III," xliii

BOOK III

1

After the Munich Pact, in September 1938, there was a sigh of relief in town. The Jews hummed the Lambeth Walk, some even knew how to dance it. Each day brought new jokes about Chamberlain's bow tie and umbrella. A four-leafed clover appeared on the front cover of the national magazine *Libertate* showing a picture of each of the Munich Pact signatories in one of the clover leaves. Hitler and Mussolini, Chamberlain and Daladier. At last there will be peace, they said, look at Daladier, the French premier: judging by his forehead, he must be Jewish. Don't you think so? Yes, he *is* Jewish; it is a good sign, no? Surely it means peace. So you give a little; a little of Moravia, a little of Bohemia. All Hitler wants is the Sudetenland. What's a little soil compared to peace?

Peace.

And to maintain peace, the Allies stood still while Germany occupied Czechoslovakia on March 15, 1939 and split it into a German protectorate and a puppet Slovak state. The Nazis made Father Josef Tiso, a Catholic priest, prime minister of Slovakia; together with the right-wing Catholic nationalist Hlinka party, he ran the newly formed state.

The Jews in Sighet stopped humming or dancing the Lambeth

Walk. They still joked about Chamberlain, but the laughter was a bit shrill and sometimes the jokes were stale.

Then in May they stopped telling jokes altogether. A group of Slovak refugees, Jews and Protestants, arrived in town. They spoke of restrictions, exclusions and persecutions, of anti-Semitic violence.

The refugees found temporary haven within hours. Their hosts called them "guests" and treated them gingerly till they found ways to flee to the West—or to the East.

The Englers' guest hardly spoke and barely ate. He stayed most of the time in his room by himself.

One afternoon Lisa went to his room carrying a bowl of fruit. She knocked at the door. Receiving no answer, she entered the room and left the bowl of fruit on the table.

Then she saw him. Wearing the same Czech lieutenant's uniform he wore the day he arrived at Sighet, their guest stood with his back to the door, facing a map on the opposite wall. It was the map of Europe. The lieutenant did not turn when she entered the room. There was a small valise on a chair, a framed photo on top of the valise. She picked up the photo and saw the picture of a young woman holding a little girl.

She tiptoed over to him.

"Are they going to join you soon?" she asked, pointing to the photograph.

He did not answer. His right hand was on the map. Like a lover caressing his beloved he was caressing Czechoslovakia slowly, tenderly. After each caress his shoulders quivered as if in a spasm. In fact, the Czech lieutenant was sobbing while caressing Czechoslovakia.

Miklos later said the Czechs should have hoisted the red flag over Hradcany Castle in Prague before March 15 and then declared Czechoslovakia a Soviet republic. The Germans would not have dared invade Soviet territory; or if they would have been foolish enough to do so, Stalin would have retaliated instantly. Teach the Nazis a good lesson.

The lieutenant did not answer immediately.

"Ah," he sighed and shook his head sadly, "*that* would have been ideal. But *Realpolitik* is business—even in the Union of Soviet Socialist Republics."

98

* * *

The double-petaled purple lilac bush in the Englers' garden bloomed with excessive richness. The fragrance of lilac permeated other gardens as well. Rachel sent lilac bouquets to all her neighbors, including Miss Duncan and the baroness.

That summer the Englers did not go to Karlsbad or to Piestany to take the baths. Next summer, they said, there will be total peace, may God grant it sooner, next summer we will go again.

Lisa rode on her bicycle to the Malom Kert everyday to meet Rozika and Mariko. They played tennis in the morning on the Samson tennis courts and in the afternoon they swam in the pool at the Strand, or climbed on rafts made of large logs that were floating down the Iza River, towards the lumber mills.

There were weekly soccer games in Sighet that summer. The Bar Kokhba team from Satu-Mare arrived every Sunday to play the Sighet Samson team. Although Satu-Mare was a town with a larger Jewish population than that of Sighet, the Bar Kokhbas were no match for the Samsons. The Samsons had an overwhelming lead by the end of the summer. After the final game, Laszlo, the Samson fullback who had executed dazzling passes throughout the games and crashed through every defense formation, was carried three times around the soccer field on the shoulders of a cheering crowd.

2

During that summer, the putty that clogged the Jews' minds wore off miraculously. The Jews rediscovered their old knack of interpreting events, mostly contemporary political events, and they went at it with boundless gusto. Suddenly possessed with uncanny insights, they offered rational explanations for everything. The conclusion that all would end well appeared irrefutable.

They trusted Romanian political craftsmanship, for one thing. They pointed out that Romanian politicians were old hands in the high art of political meteorology. Had not Romanian statesmen accurately predicted the political climate during World War I and changed sides with perfect timing and aplomb, thus winding up with Transylvania? Was that not a masterstroke of Romanian *Realpolitik*?

For another thing, King Carol's state visit to England in January of 1936 now took on added significance. Although the Romanian king's visit was made ostensibly to attend the funeral of King George V, the important question had always been why he had taken along his handsome son and heir to the throne, Prince Mihai, *a gezund an sein kepele*. At last, *now*, the Jews of Sighet decoded the *true* purpose of the Romanian royal visit: father and son had gone not merely to a royal funeral, but on a royal *bekook*

100

as well. A looking-over before choosing and concluding a future *shedach* with one of the two lovely daughters of King George VI. Official announcements, from the Windsor and the Hohenzollern houses, of royal nuptial preparations were in the air. . . .

Having convinced themselves of the Romanian king's brilliant strategy that would utilize powerful allies to keep the country out of any imbroglio, the Jews went beyond the obvious, into the sphere of the occult, to reason themselves into safety:

First, the king got rid of the head of the Iron Guard, that *mashumed* Corneliu Codreanu, evil incarnate and Jew hater. He was no more. Second, Prime Minister Octavian Goga, another *mashumed* and archenemy of the Jews, suddenly died a natural death. No assassination, no garroting, none of that. He died in his bed of an ordinary heart attack one month after he had ordered big swastikas to be installed on top of city halls in all major cities. Was not that ordinary heart attack a clear omen that the Almighty was looking out for the Jews? And a fair warning to all *mashumeds* . . . ?

And then came the ultimate proof: the king's true love—who was indeed the king's true love—bless the heart of a king with such fine taste. Who was the king's one and only love? Magda Lupescu, that's who, the beautiful red-haired Magda, the *yiddishe medele* née Miriam Wolff. So there!

On September 1, 1939, the Jews of Sighet were jolted into a reality they no longer could ignore: war had broken out. The explosion was on. No amount of interpretation of signs or omens, terrestrial or celestial, could explain away Hitler's Panzer divisions sweeping into Poland. The Jews reluctantly added a new word to their vocabulary: *Blitzkrieg*.

Even so, once France and England declared war on Germany on September 3, it took the Jews merely a few days to pull themselves together and interpret events again.

The British battleships *Athenia* and *Royal Oak* were sunk by the Germans, in quick succession, at the outset of the war. The various theories the Jews concocted as to why the British should have permitted such capital vessels to undergo destruction made little sense. They then endowed the British naval staff with a brilliance in tactical maneuvers that even the Sighet Jews could not figure out. They gave up interpreting that event and turned their attention to a new leader called Winston Churchill. With each passing day, the Jews' obdurate belief that Hitler would soon be destroyed by the Allies firmed into dogma. With Roosevelt and Churchill on earth and God Almighty in Heaven, could there by any doubt that good would triumph over evil, righteousness over wickedness? Besides, Hitler was a farce, a humbug. The laughingstock of the intelligentsia. Cultured and civilized people like the Germans could not be misled indefinitely by a funny-mustached raving maniac. Nor would they stand for ersatz coffee and synthetic butter for long. . . .

With their confidence recharged, the Jews went about their business, surreptitiously flashing the two-finger victory sign and imitating a cigar-smoking individual. They reevaluated the Evian Conference in Switzerland convoked by Roosevelt in July 1938, and attended by thirty-two democratic nations. The Jews came to the conclusion that the conference was additional proof of the Allies' intention to protect the European Jews. For some reason, the minds of the Jews in Sighet temporarily turned to putty again. They failed to notice that the Evian Conference had deteriorated into doing nothing beyond uttering banal pieties about humanity. Had the putty not clogged their minds at the time, they might have even realized that the attitude of the thirty-two nations at that conference was merely a reflection of the world's lack of intention, or inclination, to help the tens of thousands of Jews already fleeing from the Nazis.

When even before the invasion of Poland Hitler had concluded the nonaggression pact with Stalin on August 23, the Jews were appalled. They were vociferous in expressing outrage at betrayed socialist and *verbrente* radical sentiments.

But when Hitler and Stalin divided Poland between them in the second half of September all the Jews were heartsick. They began praying to God at once for the extra strength the Allies needed to take on the two *mashumeds*.

"On the other hand," they said, "maybe now the *mashumeds* have had it. They've gobbled up more than they can chew and they will have to stop to digest it. That's when the Allies will strike. . . ."

3

While Europe quaked, Judge Barcescu divorced his Jewish wife Luisa—just before Christmas. Then in January 1940, he eloped with the eighteen-year-old Mady Dekler, another Jewish girl. It happened during her last year in school, before she was to receive her baccalaureate. The day she eloped, she walked out of school and into a black limousine the judge drove to Satu-Mare. There they were married in the chambers of another judge, an old friend of the Barcescu family.

Mady was not just pretty. She was gorgeous—no wonder the Judge fell in love with her. And of course she was young, much younger than Luisa. Mady's crown of curly red hair, large dark eyes and slim waist were the talk of the town for weeks. It took the Jews' minds off weighty world events. Sometimes Mady's twin brother Mano was also mentioned: the young man seemed to have taken Mady's elopment too much to heart, they said.

The Barcescu-Dekler affair briefly eclipsed the German invasion of Norway and Denmark, Holland, Belgium and Luxembourg. By the time the Jews faced up to it, all they could do was to thank God that the raving madman didn't hanker after their country, to pray and hope that he never would, and to go about their business. Which they did.

4

Lisa's circle of friends now included Nellie and Edit, Dolly, Zsuzsi and Eva, though Rozika and Mariko remained the closest to her. Some of the girls, along with Pista Braun, Paul Manheim and other boys of Lisa's age, often met in the afternoons to play "post office." They drew by lot for the job of mailman, who delivered a letter to a pair of players. The letter was a handkerchief the mailman held between the faces of a boy and a girl. While the recipients read the invisible message nose to nose, they were permitted to kiss discreetly through the handkerchief. If the kissing exceeded the bounds of propriety, was too loud or lasted too long, the mailman could call a halt to the letter reading.

"Post office is not bad but I feel nothing special when I touch lips with one of the boys through the handkerchief," Lisa wrote in her diary. "I read in a book about love and kissing and . . . It said love is a great feeling. But puckering lips with the boys doesn't make me feel great. I want to feel great. But when? I am already thirteen years and I am menstruating. Mamma explained things to me. I let her. She doesn't know I have books on these things. I read them at night and keep them under my pillow. Some books have naughty stories and funny drawings and I read them with Rozika and Mariko during afternoons Mamma is at the store. Mariko knows everything. This whole thing about love I don't quite understand and I keep wondering. Does it hurt when . . . Anyway. But I so wish to know what love is."

"You'll know what it is when it happens to you," Miklos said to her one day, early in the spring. He was in the habit of coming into her room before dinner to chat and never spoke to her with the condescension of grown-ups. "Love is like a *coup de foudre*," he continued, "a thunderbolt."

Miklos knew what he was talking about: he was in love with Naomi Kahn whom he had met at one of the many Zionist meetings he lately attended. She was tall and slim, with large hazel-brown eyes and natural blond hair bobbed in countless ringlets. The tip of her nose was flat but this minor flaw merely set off her smooth, glowing skin on which there never was any makeup, not even lipstick. She had the stride of a queen, majestic and aloof. She was justified to walk boldly, the Jews of Sighet said, for Naomi had proved herself to be a true daughter of Zion: the previous June she had refused to take the written finals for the baccalaureate because the test was held on the Sabbath. Her stand had cost her the forfeiture of the oral test, which she had passed the day before, and earned her the respect of the Jews.

"It was a matter of principle to refuse to write on the Sabbath," Miklos had explained to Lisa. "Naomi isn't that religious. But she saw it in terms of identity. Jewish identity."

Then one spring afternoon Miklos went to the Malom Kert with a group of friends to go boating on the Iza. Naomi was among them. They moored the boat and walked towards a willow to picnic. He and Naomi found themselves trailing behind. On an impulse, Miklos kissed her.

"The expression on her face," he now told Lisa, "I'll remember it as long as I live. The surprise; the delight. And the pure joy which overcame me. It was a *coup de foudre*. It took me only a moment to know I loved Naomi. And would love her forever."

Mr. Zalmen Kahn, Naomi's father, balked at giving Naomi a dowry. Yes, it was customary to do so, he agreed. But Miklos Engler does not need a dowry at all. The son of a wealthy father and partner in a prosperous business, what does he need a dowry for? The Kahns, on the other hand, still had two unmarried daughters. Dowries had to be kept ready for them in case they married poor men. Old man Kahn had explained all this to Andras very cleverly and peppered his arguments with ample quotations from the Talmud and the Midrash that Naftuli, his eldest son, had researched in advance. Andras had been completely swamped by the avalanche of scholarly arguments. He agreed there was no need for Naomi to get her dowry.

But Rachel was shocked and objected to the marriage. It was not because of the money, she explained to Miklos. It was the corruption of a tradition that she resented. What mattered to her was to do the honorable thing simply because it was right, without being cajoled or forced. To do one's duty as a matter of principle. Like giving a daughter a proper dowry—when one is available, Rachel emphasized. To do the right thing. The Englers would have done it: they would have declined the dowry after an initial offer. Mr. Zalmen Kahn had no right to preempt the Englers.

Though passionately in love with Naomi, Miklos left town. He went to Bucharest, from where he wrote a letter that he would return to Sighet only if the Englers and Kahns found a solution to their conflict so that he could marry Naomi.

Although Mr. Kahn's penury had soured the relationship between the two families beyond repair, Rachel was moved by echoes of the past Andras invoked. She consented to Miklos marrying Naomi without a dowry and asked him to come back home. He returned at the end of August and had the wedding just in time. . . .

5

. . . just in time for Miklos to become a Hungarian subject
overnight, along with a hundred fifty thousand Jews in Northern
Transylvania.

It happened on August 30, 1940, under the gilded ceilings of
the Schönbrunn Palace in Vienna, where Hitler and Mussolini
had summoned Hungarian and Romanian representatives to witness the carving up of Transylvania.

The deed may have been executed after a stroll in the re-
nowned Schönbrunn gardens. Then, in one of the exquisite palace chambers a Romanian limb was chopped off and thrown to
Hungary as a reward for having agreed to toe the Nazi line. The
famous Maria Theresia yellow walls may have numbed Romanian pairt and the suturing of Romania's stump with formal signatures may have left blotches of ink-blood on the dainty rococo
operating table.

As a result of that day in Schönbrunn Palace, Northern Transylvania became Magyar, and Sighet changed again to Sziget.

6

The Jews of Sziget now stopped ridiculing Hitler or calling him a raving maniac. Pretending, or predicting, all would turn out well had become slightly tenuous. The Magyar Nazi party, the Crossed Arrows, was continuously publishing articles on Jewish turpitude in its official gazette, *Awake*. Ferencz Szálasi, the head of the Crossed Arrows, ranted daily on the national radio against Jewish power running the world. He vowed to cleanse the sacred soil of Magyarország by getting rid of the Jews. How should he get rid of the Jews? Szálasi boomed the question at mass meetings. The Magyar Nazis roared back the answer with a song:

> Bring the fuse, one, two, three!
> To blow up the Jews, Szálasi.
> This is the cue:
> Hang the top Jew, one, two, three!
> Szálasi, hail Szálasi!

The Jews cringed at the mention of his name. Another *mashumed* who, with God's help, will come to the same end as Goga and Codreanu did. It occurred to them that by now God was burdened with a motley collection of *mashumeds* and while

He was devising their nemesis, the Jews ceased listening to the radio at certain hours. They also stopped reading certain newspapers.

Now and then, a few Jews fleeing from Germany, or from annexed Austria or from conquered Poland, passed through Sziget on their way to Constanta, the Romanian port on the Black Sea.

"Run," the refugees bluntly told their fellow Jews. "Escape while you can."

"It will pass," they replied. "God will help us. God, America and England."

"We too have waited for that sort of a help. Now look at us."

The Sziget Jews looked at their bewildered faces, at their meager valises.

". . . and we are the lucky ones," the refugees noted.

"Our roots are here," the Sziget Jews said. "Our homes. This is Sziget, our island."

"Your lives, you fools!" the refugees pleaded. "Your lives are at stake, not your homes."

7

Dr. Abraham Ried, one of Sziget's prominent attorneys, was an ardent Zionist since his youth. In 1941 he became the chairman of the Zionist movement in Transylvania. A year later he traveled clandestinely to the Jewish Agency headquarters in Istanbul. When he returned to Sziget he went at once to see Chief Rabbi Rosenbaum.

"I will not mince words," Dr. Ried said. "There is a Nazi plan called the FINAL SOLUTION, to kill European Jewry. Unless we take immediate steps, we'll be exterminated by the Nazis."

Chief Rabbi Rosenbaum lifted his heavy-lidded eyes from the sacred text he was studying. Through the filmy haze caused by age and thousands of hours of straining over minuscule ancient writing he looked into Dr. Ried's face and began to shake, his lips moving without uttering a sound.

"I have seen irrefutable proof," Dr. Ried continued, "smuggled-out copies of German documents. The Nazis have set up huge ovens in certain parts of Poland. They have been burning Jews since 1941."

The rabbi stood up to his full six-foot height, his white beard reaching to his waist. He covered his eyes with one hand, stretched out the other as if attempting to dispel the abominable image evoked by Dr. Ried.

"Yes, rabbi, the Nazis are burning our brothers. They will burn us too if we don't act in time." He grabbed the rabbi's extended arm: "You must tell the Jews to leave Sziget at once! They will do what the chief rabbi, their spiritual leader, tells them to do. Only you can save them."

"Nur der Rebonoshelolom kan rateven die kinder," the rabbi now cried out, "only the Almighty can save the children. Where would they go, *Rebonoshelolom?"* he asked. And it was Dr. Ried who quickly replied:

"To Zion. I received money to charter a boat from Constanta to sail there. It's all arranged. The wholesale granting of twelve thousand exit visas by the Hungarian government can also be arranged for a big sum of money. But this money I do not have. Each Jew would have to contribute according to his means. The ransom is high, but it can be managed if you give the word, rabbi, to go. *To go now* while Sziget's Jewry can be saved. Twelve thousand Jews, rabbi, your flock. . . ."

Dr. Ried was told to come back for the answer the following morning.

The chief rabbi wept all afternoon in his chambers. At night he did not sleep.

Did the rabbi seek signs of divine guidance? An oracular revelation? Or did he earnestly believe, as all ultraorthodox Jews must, that only when Messiah comes can the Jews of the Diaspora be admitted to their Holy Land. Perhaps the rabbi prayed for the Messiah to come that very night, for he could hardly conceive of a secularized Holy Land—as undoubtedly it would become, God forbid, should these young hotheaded Zionists have their way.

Dr. Ried listened in silence to Chief Rabbi Rosenbaum's words the next morning:

"If *Rebonoshelolom,* may His name always shine, wanted the Jews of Sziget to be in Yerushalaim at this time, surely He, in His infinite goodness and wisdom, would have already found a way to take them there. But since my children are here, and not in the Holy Land, it is His will, blessed be He, that we stay here."

The Jews of Sziget did not leave when they could have. Instead, they held on to their beliefs and candlesticks and waited for God, America and England to deliver them from the *mashumeds.*

111

8

They met during the summer of 1942; Lisa was fifteen and Mano nineteen years old.

It was the summer the British stopped Rommel at El Alamein and began the battle to recapture Tobruk. The German *Wehrmacht* reached Stalingrad, and two hit songs from America, *It's a Big, Wide Wonderful World* and *Bewitched, Bothered and Bewildered*, reached Sziget.

"I know what a *coup de foudre* is," Lisa wrote in her diary. "I think I am in love. I AM IN LOVE, I don't think, I know I AM IN LOVE, I think. His name is Mano Dekler. The most handsomest man in the world! We walk in the evening on the Grand Corso. He touches my hand. Oh! That's all! I melt . . .

"He is a head taller than I, has straight jet-black hair. Big forehead. Wears eyeglasses. He is very handsome. The heavy dark-rimmed eyeglasses don't make him look like an owl, as some of my dear friends tease me. Rather it makes him look *distingué!* He shaves, his face is smooth and cool. A man. Not a boy, like the kids hanging around my friends. Well . . . Mano is the handsomest man I ever met. Except Papa. But Papa is Papa.

"P.S. It's rumored Mano has been at . . . well . . . at Le Jardin. Rozika and Mariko say he is a ladies' man. Well. I am a lady, no? But he has had many dates with me. For the past month I saw him every day, almost."

Mano was the young man who the Szigeters thought had taken his twin sister's elopement with Judge Barcescu too much to heart. It was true. Mano and Mady had always been very close, as twins usually are. The year Mady eloped, Mano dropped out of school and looked for solace in poker and at the whorehouse. His parents were too distraught to notice. Mr. Dekler resigned from his job at the bank, and Mrs. Dekler hardly left the house. In the tradition of the Orthodox, they mourned their daughter as one dead.

Mano pulled himself together sufficiently in 1941 to enroll again in the eighth grade of the lyceum, and in June 1942, he received his baccalaureate.

He was relaxed that summer, more relaxed than he had been for the last two years. Young men and women did not stop talking when he joined them, nor did they give him that special look. A few of them frankly asked about Mady. Has he heard from her? No, he would reply, he did not hear from her, he did not know how she was, let's speak of something else.

Of course he knew very well how she was. She wrote to him once a month *poste restante*. She was happy, Mady wrote, gloriously happy with the judge, who had been appointed chief justice at Timisoara, the capital of Judetul Banat, in southwestern Romania. They visited Bucharest monthly, attended the opera and gambled at the casino in Sinaia. What a life, he thought with a touch of yearning and reproach. Why did she do it, why . . . and to conceal his secret grief, he posed as hard-boiled and blase.

Except with Lisa. That summer, seeing her in the Malom Kert, he wanted to run after her, catch her before she would fly away on that shiny bike.

"Red, hey, Red," he called after her on an impulse. "Stop. I want to tell you something."

She wheeled around.

"You don't even know my name, but you want to tell me something." She laughed. He stared at her face, the tiny freckles, the green eyes. She was beautiful, he thought.

113

"My name is Lisa Engler." She got off the bike, shook hands with him. "Now you can tell me."

"I want to tell you . . ." What did he want to tell her? He collected himself. *"My* name is Mano Dekler. I would like to meet with you this evening on the Grand Corso. At six o'clock. I would like very much to walk with you. Will you meet me?"

She looked at him thoughtfully. She had heard the name.

"Yes," she said. "I'll meet you on the Grand Corso this evening."

By the end of the summer Lisa and Mano were going steady. When school started, he waited for her daily at the school entrance and carried her books with the pride of an Olympic champion walking off with a gold medal.

He went to her house in the afternoons she told him Rachel would be in the store. They held hands, listened to records by Katalin Karády, the famous *chanteuse,* singing in her husky voice *Embers of My Cigarette.* They also spoke of how things would be once the war was over. She told him she wanted to study law at the University in Kolozsvár, the town the Romanians called Cluj. Mano noted it was not customary for a girl to go to graduate school. She should get married, he said; after receiving her baccalaureate a girl should get married.

They stood in front of the fireplace one afternoon, holding hands. They forgot to turn on the light. He took her in his arms and kissed her. Kissed her eyes first, then her cheeks; tasted the smoothness of her forehead with his lips, the warmth of her mouth with his tongue. He touched her breasts and felt the firm roundness of her nipples.

At first, a slight embarrassment prevented Lisa from even acknowledging he was fondling her. Rachel had been intimating that till the proper time to wed arrives, sexual stirrings were to be overcome by the purity of spiritual love or, if that was impossible, by sheer willpower. A young lady must elicit respect from her young man, she had told Lisa, and she could never achieve that if she becomes intimate with him. Her chastity was her intrinsic treasure, a precious jewel to be guarded intact till bestowed upon a worthy someone when the time was ripe. And in Rachel's set of sexual mores there was only one event which made the time ripe: the wedding night.

114

But Mano's touch sparked curiosity and wonder in Lisa and aroused her first sexual sensation. Still, she was apprehensive all along that someone might surprise them, that Rachel might materialize through the window, scattering real jewels as a warning. Fear and excitement clouded her senses and her inner turmoil grew into a tremendous urge to touch him, to feel him. She took his hands and placed them inside her blouse, over her breasts, then unbuttoned his trousers and touched his penis.

But they did not sleep together.

"October 7, 1942.

"Mano kissed me on the mouth, he touched my tongue with his, and put his hands on my breasts. Everywhere. All begins to tingle inside me, I must touch him too. The same way, everywhere. I touched his . . . Anyway. At first I got scared. It was big and hot, pulsating like a living thing. I held it in my hands and liked holding it. My heart beat fast, I felt thirsty and hot all of a sudden, and the lower part of my tummy ached. Cramps down there. I thought I was going to menstruate but nothing happened. Still, it was a great feeling, the best I've ever had. Or nothing like I've ever had.

"I know I should not have let him touch me all over. What about respect and pride and my jewel, all the things Mamma has been telling me. But I couldn't help myself, my mind was sluggish, it couldn't order me around.

"I think of my darling all the time. And how it feels when we touch."

A few days later she wrote him a note:

"My darling I love you. But I don't think it's proper to kiss that way. It's not that I don't like it: it's that kissing that way shakes me up in strange ways and I don't know what to do about it.

"I love you but we mustn't kiss that way anymore. It's not proper. Please understand. Let's hold hands."

Mano promised he would not kiss her *that way* anymore. He knew "love" and "esteem" went hand-in-hand in their society. There were certain girls one did not do certain things with. Lisa Engler was such a certain girl, she surely was. He solemnly agreed to stay within the conventional rules of courtship.

But such a promise could not be kept. Each attempt to quell

115

desire brought forth more desire, stronger and sharper than before. Clamoring for fulfillment, bursting with heat.

They went on kissing with passion and sustained their long-
ing, guiltily petted but remained unsatisfied and waited impatiently for the proper time to marry.

Meanwhile, they became a familiar sight on the Grand Corso
and at the Zionist Habonim meetings on Saturday afternoons.
There they listened to speeches about Theodor Herzl and his vision of a Jewish Homeland. "A dream willed into reality," the
speaker quoted Herzl. Lisa and Mano linked fingers, interpreted
the slogan in personal terms and blood rushed to their heads.

They danced the *hora* and sang Hebrew songs with the rest of
the Habonim members. The small hall was crowded, the chairs
were hard and the windows had no shades. The shabby sur-
roundings did not matter. What mattered was that the Habonim
members gradually danced the *hora* less timidly and sang *Hatik-
va* with increasing conviction. In the dingy Habonim hall the
Jewish youth of Sziget reforged its heritage, awakened by the urgency of Jewish national aspirations while fire was gutting Europe. Yet they believed they could, somehow, implement those
aspirations before it was too late.

Lisa and Mano knew there were great odds to overcome to
fulfill the Jewish dream, just as there were great odds to overcome to fulfill their personal dream. But the most formidable
odds to overcome, once they would reach marriageable age, they
knew would be Rachel.

She did not like Mano.

"Tell me why, Mamma," Lisa wanted to know.

That was precisely the problem. Rachel could not state specific
reasons. The young man walked into the house, a cigarette dangling from his mouth, and asked to see Lisa without going
through polite small talk customary on such occasions. This was
not a good reason to dislike him, naturally. It was merely reason
to assume the boy lacked manners or was shy. With time, his behavior would improve. What disturbed Rachel was a weakness
she sensed in him, an emotional flaw she herself did not understand nor know how to define. The fierceness of Mano's attach-
ment to Lisa outstripped a young man's infatuation with a pretty
girl, Rachel was sure of that. He frightened her a little. All her in-

stincts warned her to keep Lisa away from him. How could she convince a young girl in love to heed a mother's intuition . . . ?

"Whether I like him or not is of secondary importance," she said calmly. "The main reason I wish you'd stop seeing him is that you are too young, much too young to have a steady beau. You are only sixteen."

"How old were you when you fell in love with Papa?" Lisa asked sheepishly.

Rachel sighed and let it go for the time being. But she resolved to persuade Lisa in the near future to stop seeing Mano, even forbid her to see him, if Lisa proved obstinate.

9

At the moment Rachel was busy with Naomi, who was pregnant. Rachel walked with her the daily mile prescribed by the obstetrician, planned and shopped for the nursery, knitted wool coverlets for the baby carriage and embroidered dozens of bibs. In the middle of October, Naomi gave birth to a boy. He was named Shlomo, but everyone called him Sonny. The child had a flat nose, curly red hair and hazel-brown eyes. A replica of old Shlomo, Haskell declared, the spitting image of Shlomo Kugel, may he rest in peace. Look at the color of the child's hair, not of his eyes, Haskell urged everyone. And don't pay attention to his flat little nose. . . .

The high regard Naomi had earned from the Jews for having refused to write on the Sabbath had slowly vanished after she had married Miklos.

"She dusts with silk rags, wearing silver slippers," they said, "and she hardly cares to know some of us any longer." Her life as Naomi Engler revolved around bridge playing and tea parties. The Jews joked about her collection of shoes, twenty-seven pairs, and the snakeskin pumps she had custom-made to match her ostentatious snakeskin luggage was the talk of the town.

So was Dr. Ried's decision to remain in Sziget with his family. It was God's subtle way of showing that redemption was just around the corner, the Jews concluded; otherwise, why would the Almighty keep Dr. Ried in Sziget with valid exit permits in his pocket for himself and his family? It was God's will—not Yolanda Ried's adamant refusal to leave town unless her Bösendorfer concert grand piano went along with them. Dr. Ried tried to convince his wife they would not need a piano where they would be going, at least not for a while. Then he asked the authorities to grant him permission to ship the piano out of the country. He failed in both of his attempts. He stayed in Sziget with his wife and daughters, listened in the evenings to Yolanda playing on the Bösendorfer Schubert *Lieder,* Mendelssohn barcaroles and Mozart rondos, while he perused documents permitting him and his family to leave the country by December 1943.

And life went on. The Jews sneered at Naomi's shoe collection or took heart in Dr. Ried's presence among them. Life went on as if things were normal. Almost normal. As if war was on another continent, in another world. The war never touched them directly.

Dim echoes of ugly stories about brothels the Germans had set up somewhere on the Russian front reached them periodically. Stories the trickle of refugees brought along of how Jewish girls from Poland, Slovakia, the Czech Protectorate, were being transported to those brothels to service Nazi soldiers. Such odious stories, hallucinations born out of much suffering, were too repugnant even to be repeated.

In early 1943 nearly every Jew in Sziget was still innocent. They could not grasp the idea that there might be some truth in the stories filtering down to them. They did not even bother to interpret them. The less said the better. Such baseness could simply not occur among human beings. Enemies or no enemies, in the final analysis everyone is a human being, they maintained. And that was what counted in the final analysis: the basic bond of humanity.

While they waited stalwartly for God, America and England to bring an end to the war, the Hungarian government forbade Jews to travel abroad and annulled all exit permits it had issued to them. The government then began harassing Jewish merchants with decrees and regulations designed to make earning a living practically impossible. The solution was either to give up one's business or accept an Aryan business partner the government readily supplied from the membership of the Crossed Arrows Party. Jewish merchants were reluctant to give up their businesses, of course. Each accepted the government-designated partner and transferred to him three-fourths of the business, lock, stock, barrel, and profits, as decreed.

One could still live comfortably on one-fourth. And besides, the Allies would soon win the war.

10

Because Hungary had taken the bait in Vienna on August 30, 1940, she paid for it when the time came, as she knew she would.

After Germany's attack on Russia in 1941, Hungary was pressed into sending a token force to assist the *Wehrmacht.* Since Germany could not *blitzkrieg* her way through Russia and was sustaining heavy losses even before the battle of Stalingrad, additional manpower was demanded. In early 1942 a general mobilization was put in effect in Hungary, and a special Jewish labor force was created, actually a Jewish forced-labor army, into which Jewish men between eighteen and forty were conscripted to be sent to the Russian front. They had no weapons or uniforms. Their only distinction was a yellow band with the Star of David on their left sleeve.

None of the conscripted men had yet come back from Russia to tell what was happening to them, though the Jewish male population was thinning out. The Jews in Sziget became apprehensive. In their anxiety, they held on even tighter to their heavy silver candelabra and to the concert grand pianos. They also renewed their determination to wait faithfully, fanatically, wait for God, America and England to come to their rescue.

* * *

In 1943 Laszlo was conscripted into the labor force. Each day his unit was still in Hungary was proof the Almighty looked out for him. If God Almighty was too busy, at times, to look out for him, there was a Jewish lad in his outfit who did so. His name was Himy Lieber, a sturdy chap with a nose for units that were not designated "destination Russia." Lieber's skill in detecting such units, and then having himself and Laszlo transferred to them, depended on the amount of money he had for payoffs. The Englers were generous with the money and Himy Lieber was a clever *macher*. Little wonder God Almighty took good care of Laszlo.

11

One night early in May, a certain Mr. Weinfeld heard strange noises in his garden. He found a whimpering little girl sitting by herself under a tree. He took her into the house, then read the note written in Yiddish that had been pinned on to her dress: "We escaped from the Warsaw ghetto. Are on our way to Constanta. Uncertain of making it. Lost our papers. The child Yadwiga is the daughter of Feiga Ziegenblum. Feiga is dead. Save the child." The last sentence, *ratevet das kind,* was twice underlined.

In their shock and grief, the Weinfelds made Yadwiga lie down, put cool compresses on the child's feverish forehead and cried the whole night through. In the morning they offered Yadwiga food, but she would not eat. They questioned her about Mr. Weinfeld's sister, Feiga. The child's sentences were unintelligible, a mixture of Yiddish and Polish punctuated by little screams and abrupt silences followed by a melody reminiscent of *Ani Maamin.* The Weinfelds fetched Smuel Grynspan, the only Jew in town who spoke Polish fluently.

He took the little girl's hand. "Don't be afraid," he said in Polish. "You sing beautifully, Yadwiga."

"Bronca Kowalska, that's my name. I am eight years old, Catholic . . ."

"Tak, tak," Smuel said. "Yes. Where are your parents?"

She began to scream:

"Mamushka, Mamushka! . . . Mamushka! Look, look! Tanks! . . . Ach!"

"Wszystko bedzie dobrze," he tried to calm her. "Everything will be all right . . . You are safe here——"

"They promised me candy. No, marmalade. Candy, marmalade. Just go to the Umschlag Platz. Mamushka, I want to go . . . let me go! I am hungry . . ."

Yadwiga was shaking and Mr. Weinfeld gave her warm milk and honey. She fell asleep and slept a whole day. In the evening Smuel Grynspan came again. He stayed alone with her for a couple of hours. When he emerged from her room, his eyes were red, his cheeks wet.

"Poor child. She is hallucinating. Or maybe just a little girl with a vivid imagination. One can't believe everything. . . ."

He wiped his eyes, coughed.

"They had been shot, she said, her mother had been shot with the others. In sewers. They ran to the sewers from cellars . . . There was an uprising yesterday, but maybe it was last month; or last year, the child doesn't remember. She says Jews were throwing sticks and stones and bottleflames . . . and that Nazi tanks were burning. But mostly Jews, dead Jews everywhere, hundreds, thousands of them, she says everywhere she looked she saw dead Jews, in the gutter, in the cellars, in the attics. In the sewers . . ."

Smuel Grynspan could not continue. Mrs. Weinfeld made tea, each held a cube of sugar in his mouth and sipped tea in silence.

Then Yadwiga came out of her room and sat in Smuel's lap.

"Ratevet das kind," she whispered. "He said to save the child. Did you? . . . He pulled me out from under Mamushka, she was so heavy . . . and warm. All wet. Then he pulled me out and began to run with me. He held me in his arms tight, but the cold air made me shiver. Like this." Smuel Grynspan held the shivering little body in his arms. "The man keeps running. Mamushka, Mamushka, I shout. He puts his hand over my mouth. There were two others. They'll be your Mamushka and Tatushka till you get home, the man said. But my house burned down. Home in Eretz Ysroel, the man said. . . ."

She looked up to Smuel Grynspan.

"Is this Eretz Ysroel?"

The men were crying and Mrs. Weinfeld asked:

"Who was the man who saved you . . . do you know?"

Her eyes lit up, a faint smile crossed her face.

"I know," she said. "He was tall as a mountain and strong as a hurricane. I called him Lion." She thought for an instant. "Scar-faced Lion."

The Weinfelds looked at Smuel Grynspan. All nodded in agreement: the child was still hallucinating. After she went back to her room, they pledged to each other not to spread Yadwiga's tales. Why alarm people? It only creates confusion. A lion with a scar . . . indeed.

12

A couple of Jews wondered why Miklos was not conscripted into the Jewish labor force. The rich always had a way out, they said. Haskell the miser was not such a miser when it came to his own. It must have cost him thousands of *pengö* to get Miklos an exemption from the labor force.

True, Haskell did try to get an exemption—but for Laszlo, not Miklos. Haskell had put on his navy blue suit on a Wednesday morning and went to the Office of Jewish Affairs. He showed the chief the special charter and the Double Special Gold Cross he received from a grateful Magyar nation back in 1920. All he asked now was that the conscription of his nephew Laszlo Engler be postponed for six months. That was not much to ask from a grateful Magyar nation after he had saved an entire Magyar unit from starvation, was it?

The chief laughed in Haskell's face.

"Go home, you old Jew turd," he said. "If you bother us again, we'll take you *and* your shitty nephew; and we'll use your charter for wiping our asses."

Miklos did have a six-months exemption from the labor force but it had nothing to do with Haskell. The Jews could not have known that his exemption was arranged by the Aryan who had become an Engler three-fourths partner by fiat. This man was slightly better educated than the average Crossed Arrows Party member and slightly more greedy. Merely pocketing profits was not his style. He wanted to own THE HOUSE OF ENGLER AND SONS in its totality, but first he needed Miklos to teach him how to run the business. The man reckoned it could be done in six months' time.

In September 1943, the Hungarian government decreed that only two accredited schools in the entire country, the Jewish gymnasiums in Budapest and in Kolozsvár, Cluj to the Romanians, would be permitted to matriculate Jewish students. The rest of the schools were to be closed to them. Though the Englers believed in Maimonides' teaching that "the advancement of learning is the highest commandment," Rachel also saw a chance of getting Lisa away from Mano. She was sent to the Jewish Gymnasium in Budapest to continue school.

And life went on in Sziget. Why not? The Jews led limited lives, it was true, but who was in the mood to travel these days anyway? The *Kehilla* was practically intact, war was still somewhere else—although one had to admit with a sinking feeling that the sound of war seemed to be coming closer and closer at times. Still, nothing really touched the Jews, for nothing was irremediably ripped asunder.

Yadwiga's stories began to get around. While flashing the two-finger victory sign with a trace of embarrassment, the Jews began to speak of Babylonia, Torquemada and Chmielnicki, analyzed the Exile, the Inquisition and the cossack boot, then synthesized Jewish history. They came to the conclusion the present storm would be weathered too: have they not survived those terrible tempests of the past? However, overcome by a religious urge, the majority of Jewish men went to the synagogue twice a day to pray and gave up smoking on the Sabbath. Pious women reread the story of Exodus from Egypt, wept at the suffering of the Israelites at the hands of the Egyptians, and found solace in God's causing the enemies of Israel to drown in the Red Sea.

David Dankenberg sent word he was coming to visit the Englers. At once Rachel pushed apart the twin beds in her bedroom and placed a night table between them to conform, temporarily, to religious marital rules.

His face framed in his red beard and impressive side curls, David arrived at the Englers and walked straight into the bedroom. He nodded approvingly at the sight of the separated beds, then went to the kitchen to check if the separation of meat and dairy utensils and dishes conformed to the laws of *kashrut*. Finding no obvious transgression in that area either, he sat down in the living room with Rachel, Andras and Miklos.

"We are all sinners," he said. The blue in his eyes was faded, he looked tired and drained, as if he had not eaten for days. "The Almighty would not try us otherwise. We are sinners because we've turned away from the path of righteousness and allowed the *goyish* world to seduce us. Jewish children went to *goyish* schools, Jews wore *goyish* clothes and speak the *goyish* language. We've forsaken the ways of the Torah, we've given up *Yiddishkeit*. I've been fasting and praying, fasting and praying. My vision cleared. Time is running out, I tell you. Repent before it's too late. Return to *Yiddishkeit;* God may still save us. Only He, in His infinite goodness can deliver us."

David's proposal to arrest or appease the overwhelming forces of hostility and hate by a sudden religious conversion perplexed the Englers.

"Repent before it's too late," David continued. *"Daven, daven.* Pray as you never prayed before. Atone for your sins. Turn back to God. The King of the Universe may save us."

He looked at Rachel and chided her for not wearing a ritual wig.

"You should wear a *sheitl* to keep temptation away from you and others." To Andras he said: "A *Yarmulka* on your head, as befits a Jew." "And you," he told Miklos, "you must put on *tefilin* every morning for your prayers. It's God's law. Now, let us all *daven.*"

The Englers did not change their way of life, and Rachel did not cut her hair to wear a wig. She merely had her hair trimmed.

It seemed that the end of the darkness was near, at last. The Allies had landed in Southern Europe, a Jew who had listened to a secret radio said. Italy had declared war on Germany, the links of the Axis chain were falling apart. The Russians had begun their push to the West: they had reconquered Smolensk and Kiev. God has tamed Stalin the *mashumed* who was now conferring with Churchill and Roosevelt in Teheran. Laszlo was in another unit, still in Hungary. There were omens again: French and English movies were being shown, even American films. Hardly any German-made UFA films. Early in 1944, the Vigado Cinema showed *Modern Times* and because Hannah liked Charlie Chaplin, the whole family went to the movies. Even Haskell.

Lisa went to the movies in Budapest with Mano to see *Gone with the Wind.* He had showed up one morning in front of the school. It was the week Andras was also in Budapest.

He invited Mano to have dinner with them.

"But not a word to Mamma," he said.

They dined in style at the Emke Restaurant and from there Andras took them to the Arizona, the newest nightclub with a revolving dance floor and *intime* booths for romantic couples.

Dancing with Papa, with Mano, she tasted pure joy. She was the luckiest girl in the world, she thought. She was happy and knew it was good.

13

On March 19, 1944, the German army marched into Hungary.

The sacred soil of Magyarország was not raped—unlike Poland, Czechoslovakia, France, Holland, Belgium, Norway, Greece, Yugoslavia. Magyarország rejoiced at the sound of German goose steps and cheered at the sight of the swastika.

Two weeks later all Jewish stores were ordered to be closed. Labels reading CONFISCATED BY ORDER OF THE HUNGARIAN GOVERNMENT were plastered on the steel shutters. Jewish doctors and lawyers were forbidden to practice. Any Jew holding a job anywhere was summarily dismissed.

The dragnet was on.

Individual units, each consisting of a Crossed Arrows Party member, two secret policemen and three gendarmes whose shakos were bedecked with long, slender yellow and red plumes, dispersed throughout town with utmost speed. They had in their hands lists with names and addresses and columns and columns of figures and itemized articles. The units burst into every Jewish house, demanded at gunpoint cash, gold, and jewelry, then expropriated everything of value the Jews were unable to hide in time.

Under penalty of death, the Jews were ordered to wear a yellow Star of David on their garments "over their hearts." A six p.m. to ten a.m. curfew was imposed. Any Jew disobeying either of these orders would be shot on sight, the Hungarian authorities warned.

School examinations in Budapest took place in the middle of April, two months ahead of schedule. Lisa returned to Sziget on the last train Jews were permitted to ride.

14

"It's all set," Miklos said. "There is no other way. Anna the washerwoman is willing to hide her. She is waiting."

They sat around the lovely oval oak table, Rachel, Andras, Miklos, Haskell and Hannah, whispering to one another. On March 19 the local Hungarian authorities had requisitioned the Engler's house, allowed them to use two rooms and billeted five SS officers in the rest of the house. Loud German words now came through the walls and the *Horst Wessel Lied* blared from the radio.

"She is waiting," Miklos repeated. He glanced at Lisa and his chest tightened. There she sat, the plaything he and Laszlo had once patted possessively, protectively. She sat without stirring, her large intelligent eyes taking in every word without blinking, her shoulders straight, her head high, a solemn face that would make a stone weep. He pictured her hiding in a hut, a haystack or a sty, walking barefoot, disguised as a peasant girl, milking cows, shoveling manure. No matter. The child Yadwiga had not been hallucinating, after all. And God, America and England were not around the corner just yet. But the prospect of Jewish girls servicing Nazi soldiers was.

"We mustn't let it happen . . . We must protect her." Miklos ·read the faces around the table and knew their minds were still beclouded. "She is in danger, don't you see . . . Nazi soldiers . . . security measures . . ."

"Yes." Hannah's words were barely audible. "We'll protect her." Her lips trembled and she imagined yards and yards of gauzy silk and satin being rolled back into bolts.

"Anna?" Haskell said, "Anna the washerwoman? Never heard of her." He looked suddenly old and broken, the steel in his eyes was dulled, his jowls hung. "The child is ours. Our responsibility. Not Anna the washerwoman's." Of the entire Dankenberg-Engler clan Lisa was closest to his heart at that moment. She reminded him of Shlomo, the thrust of her chin, the sharp, penetrating look in her eyes. And her red hair.

"Let's pray to God that He be her main protector." She shall be Lisa the Matriarch one day, as his mother Miriam had been. Keep alive the Dankenberg lineage . . . mother of a son called Haskell. "Anna the washerwoman," he said again, and sighed long and heavily. "Who is she? . . . The child is ours. Who would love her as we do? The child mustn't go."

Rachel heard their words; she also heard the unspoken words as to why they wanted Lisa to go or to stay. Hurting all over, Rachel was Rachel and she was Lisa too. Flesh of her own flesh in her own flesh. She had nurtured the seed, carried it nine months under her heart and Rachel now remembered the exquisite fulfillment. She wished she could keep her daughter forever, put her back in her womb. A stab in her heart conveyed to her that even in her womb Lisa could find no safety any longer. To keep her, Rachel must send her away. The fierce pain of her love told Rachel clearly what needed to be done and she knew she could do it—even though Rachel would have to cut into her own flesh.

"*Ratevet das kind,*" she appealed. Her voice was steady, very gentle. A prayer. "We must let her go. Don't cling to her, I beg of you. Let my child go . . ."

Then Andras slowly pulled Lisa up by her hand and embraced her.

"She is my child too . . . and I can't let go." He was sobbing. "My one and only little girl. Forgive me."

He rocked her in his arms as he did when she was a little girl. He softly sang between sobs, softly:

The one and only girl to love
Is Lisa, the sweet little dove.
God Almighty made me elect
My Lisa to love and always protect.

The next day members of the Crossed Arrows Party rounded up all Jewish men between eighteen and twenty-two. They were to be sent to the Ukraine with a Jewish labor force detachment.

Mano was among them.

Lisa went to the station.

"I love you," he shouted from the slowly moving train. "I'll always love you, Red, don't you ever forget it. I'll come back, I promise. Wait for me."

15

At the end of April ten tall Magyar gendarmes, gay bright plumes fluttering in their shakos, smiles on their faces and rifles in their hands, barged into twenty prominent Jewish homes and arrested the head of each household.

When the gendarmes came for Andras Engler, Rachel ran to the baroness to beg her to save him. But the baroness was not receiving that morning. Haskell again showed the gendarmes his special charter—the Double Special Gold Cross medal had already been confiscated—but the gendarmes were not in the mood to read special charters. They tore it up, urinated on it and said:

"Stuff it up your asshole."

Amidst Yolanda Ried's shrieks, the Bösendorfer concert grand piano was hoisted out of her house and delivered to the Crossed Arrows party chief. Then Dr. Ried was arrested with the rest of the Jews.

The twenty-one Jews arrested were thrown in jail like common criminals. No one knew the reason. Confusion and fear gripped the rest of the Jews. They stayed in their homes and continued to pray.

Some wailed, poured ashes over their heads, rent the lapels of their garments, and promised to give half their fortunes to the poor, should their fortunes be restituted. Others swore to mend their ways and never sin again if only God would deliver them before it was too late.

Maybe Chief Rabbi Rosenbaum believed the Messiah would come presently. Maybe he prayed for his instant appearance, which would facilitate the transport of his children to the Holy Land. But maybe the chief rabbi was able to see in the Messiah's reluctance to appear on cue God's infinite wisdom (may His name be blessed!) in testing, testing, testing . . . in testing His children's love for Him.

The Jews continued to pray to God to speed the arrival of the liberators who were now a stone's throw away from Sziget. They were not the British or the Americans, but the Russians. The Jews in Sziget could hear cannons boom in the mountains, on the other side of the Solovan. It was not far away—only fifty kilometers from Sziget, at the Uzok Pass, where the Red Army had stopped.

While the Jews prayed to God to hasten the Russians' crossing of the mountain, the gendarmes acted first. They relocated the Gypsies in the Bandzalgo Section; then, with the help of an unprecedentedly large body of local volunteers, one night the gendarmes separately circled the Jewish Section and the Gypsy Quarter with barbed wire. By dawn, the existence of two ghettos was a *fait accompli*. Next, tens of squads of gendarmes evicted all the Jews from their homes, whipped them into columns and drove them through Sziget's shiniest jewel, the Grand Corso, all in record time. The removal of twelve thousand Jews from their homes into the ghettos took only one day, from dawn to evening.

By some strange coincidence, Rachel, Lisa and Hannah were placed in one ghetto and Miklos, Naomi and Sonny in the other.

By the evening it became clear that the twenty-one Jews were hostages to insure the orderly deportment of the ghetto populations. The Magyars had learned from the Nazis that *Ordnung muss sein*, and the Nazis had learned their lesson in the Warsaw ghetto that Jews do resist.

At night in the ghettos the Jews did not sleep. They listened to the cannons boom in the mountain as though they were listening to heavenly music. It sounded as if it were coming from the street adjacent to the ghettos, not fifty kilometers away. Their conviction that they would be liberated in the nick of time had become an obsession.

16

The gendarmes whipped the Jews into columns once again: this time to drive them out of the ghettos, towards the railway station. It was the morning of May 14, 1944. The gendarmes shouted, cursed, and grinned. They used rubber sticks, rifle butts, their fists, on women and children, on men, young and old. The gendarmes were hitting haphazardly, whomever they could reach. They were not discriminating at all—they were merely grinning. They grinned throughout the day.

The Jews plodded through Sziget, their island. Their cradle. They were a tormented mob, surrounded and defenseless, eviscerated, stunned, crazed.

The impossible had become possible.

Some murmured prayers, others had incoherent thoughts about God, America, England, and now Russia too. A few wondered where the Messiah was.

It was the time of the year Sziget was most beautiful. But wasn't it always beautiful?

As she marched in her column, Lisa looked around and saw jasmine in bloom and a nightingale perched on a tree branch. She saw dainty lace curtains move slightly, then smiling faces peering out of window niches to watch the columns of Jews.

Under a bright blue sky, forty empty cattle cars were lined up in the freight yard.

SS shoved Jews into the cattle cars.

And from tree-lined streets the scent of acacia subtly permeated Sziget.

BOOK IV

"After the end of the world
after my death
I found myself in the middle of life
I created myself
constructed life
people animals landscape"
—Tadeusz Rözewicz, *In the Middle of Life*

1

That first night back in her hometown, Lisa did not budge from the open window. She was certain the smell engulfing her was that of baking bread but in fact it was the smell of acacia, the same scent as the one which had subtly permeated the town one year ago. Just as the town was the same town too, except that a year ago its name was spelled Sziget. Now it was Sighet again.

. . . *tree, chotiri. Odin, dva.* . . .

The sound of marching Russians faded away.

It was dawning.

A pale rainbow again appeared in the mauve sky but again she failed to notice it. From the window, she was staring straight ahead, beyond the row of houses across the street. Then the image of a large house with tall French windows floated before her eyes.

Two of the windows are open. The room behind them is the dining room. She walks in, passes by the rosewood breakfront, the blue settee and tea table, the oak oval dining table covered with a lace table cloth. There is a vase of flowers in the center of the table, clusters of double-petalled purple lilac from the garden. She hesitates for a moment, then buries her face in the flowers. Their sweet aroma makes her smile and, sighing softly, she leaves the flowers, then stops between the two windows, before the grandfather clock. It is her favorite piece. It stands on the wood base inlaid with tortoiseshell and brass and its long case has a glass door that reveals cylindrical weights attached to chains, and a pendulum with a shiny disk. The enameled white clock face has Roman numerals and two small holes, one near III and the other near IX, for winding. The key is kept at the bottom of the case, inside the glass door.

The clock had originally been in the foyer till Uncle David pointed out it ought to be in a vital part of a Jewish home, for instance in the dining room, where one utters daily prayers. He then lectured on the value of time. God Almightly takes no account of time as such, he said; it was the nature of one's deeds within the time allotted to him that mattered. What did it profit Adam that he lived nine hundred and thirty years and transgressed? Uncle David asked. On the other hand, did Moses lose anything by living only one hundred and twenty years? Not at all! Uncle David stressed, for within that time Moses delivered the Ten Commandments to the world in the name of the Jewish People. Time never stops, Uncle David concluded, and a clock must always be wound to remind us how little time there is to accomplish much.

Lisa was glad when the clock had been moved because from her room she could clearly hear the chimes strike. Their mellow sound would keep her awake at night. She would count the chimes, one, two, *drei, vier,* then wait for them to strike again.

It was then, during the intervals of chiming, that she played the secret game. She knew the game was childish and often thought of how embarrassed she would have been if her friends found her out. She couldn't imagine anyone else playing the silly games of *a wish fulfilled for a contract fulfilled,* as she called the game. Its rules, which she had devised, were simple: a wish of hers, stated at the onset of the game, would be fulfilled *if* she could tick off as many lines from a poem, or names of famous people, of mountains, of rivers, or cities, as were equal to the number of chimes struck. Her wishes were plain—they revolved around school marks and school activities—routinely realized in the ordinary course of events—but she attributed their fulfillment to mysterious powers which she alone, through the ritual of the game, could bring forth. She was playing with magic to make good things happen to her . . . a sort of insurance against adversity.

She must play the game again. But the pendulum is at a standstill. The clock must be wound at once, how else would she hear the chimes? They key is behind the glass door.

Her fingers now searched for the key on the window sill. She turned around and saw Drifter. She stretched out her hands to him:

"The key. I can't wind the clock without the key. Give me the key."

"What key?"

"It was behind the glass door . . . the grandfather clock . . . game. It's important. The foyer, no, the dining room . . . at home. I want the key."

He took her hand:

"Let's go and look for the key. In your house. Let's go together. . . ."

She blinked rapidly, as if she had not realized he was there, then pulled away her hand.

"Hello, Drifter. What is it?"

"Let's go over to your house. I'll go with you."

"No. Rozika's brother Moritz said the house is kaput. Ransacked." She thought for a while. "Maybe I'll go tomorrow, I promise. But not today. Tomorrow."

"Sure I understand," he said. "You are a little scared. It's not easy . . . But you must go just the same, you know." The pupils in her eyes grew large till the irises formed a narrow circle around them. She looked as if she were in a trance. He knew that look and wished he could help clear her mind, bring her out of the fog. Compensate for the Emke Restaurant incident. He still felt responsible for what had happened and blamed himself for having misjudged her readiness to face the ordinary world.

"I'll help you confront it." He reached for her trembling hands again. They felt like crushed little birds with delicate little bones. She was not listening to him, her pupils were dilated. It hurt him to see her like that. "Don't let go," he said, softly pressing her hands. "Listen, to me, girl. Do something; you must do something."

Was it his pain or hers he felt? He was not sure anymore. It mattered not whose pain it was, it felt the same.

"If I had pondered, tried to make sense out of things instead of doing something about them, I wouldn't be here today," he said, and her prostration made him see how it was then, the Jewish labor force unit, and he part of it. The group of men with yellow arm bands, reduced to human mine sweepers, inching along Russian mine fields to spare Magyar and German soldiers and materiel; the hail of fire and bullets from planes and tanks and machine guns while they dug entrenchments in open fields and the Magyar and German warriors hid in deep bunkers. The Jews were systematically shot, starved, or burned by the *Soldaten* of the New Order, or left to rot from disease once they outlived their usefulness.

No, he had had no time to figure out what went wrong with the world's psyche. Time never waited for those who stopped to indulge in *Weltschmertz* in the middle of a jungle, or to bemoan the vileness of the beasts attacking them. One fought the beasts in whatever way one could and if one wanted to live, there was no respite for anything else.

"I'd be rotting in a hole or on a dump in Doroschitzin in the Ukraine if I'd taken time for an accurate reading of what was happening to us. I'd have had to conclude that it was hopeless to keep going, that in the end we would all be dead and that to save myself a great deal of pain I should put myself out of misery before the beasts got me. No rational man could have believed otherwise. To keep going, one had to be irrational, a little mad. We were that, of course. And that's what saved us. The madness. Reasoning, deliberating, was for later."

They called her *Piroshka*; why did they call her Ginger, he now wondered, the child was blond, his little girl was an angel with blond hair. Why should she have been called *Piroshka?* Yes, Zoltan Feldman had promised *Piroshka*, he would come back. She had kissed him several times, then said "I'll wait for you, Papush." He had also promised Elsa, his wife, he would return. He had betrayed them, let them down, had he not? and now he could never explain to them how things were, but Zoltan Feldman was another man. *He* was someone else. He could see this someone else step out of Zoltan Feldman, detach himself and become Drifter who could now speak of Zoltan Feldman as a person he once knew intimately but with whom he had nothing in common anymore. Zoltan Feldman was a different man, not at all like Drifter. . . .

"Feldman crawled out under a burning hospital in Doroschitzin," he continued. "When the Nazis caught him, they dumped him into a cattle car with hundreds of others. And Feldman squeezed through two rotting floor boards, lowered himself to the ground between the tracks, and lay flat under the moving train till . . ."

He was breathing fast, his voice was grating. He searched in his pockets, found a white pill and chewed it up quickly, then swallowed. He cleared his throat.

"Feldman made it. He didn't give in and he didn't deliberate. He didn't even feel sorry for himself. There was time for none of that, if he wanted to stay alive. And he did want to stay alive." Drifter lit a cigarette, inhaled several times. "The war is over. You are alive and I . . . at least I kept one promise: I brought you home. Don't turn inward now. You must remember how much you wanted to come home, to your house. . . ."

She should interrupt him, tell him she had come back to wait for Papa. For her brothers and Papa. And Mano . . . For the house too, to touch the contours of familiar objects.

But she said nothing.

"Please do what has to be done and be done with it. You'll start breathing again. It hurts badly, I know. Get angry, and say so. Scream. Scream and curse and get it out of your system. I'll hold you while you vomit up the poison. You'll feel better, you'll see."

He put his arm around her:

"Come, I'll go to your house with you."

"I can't, Drifter," she said faintly, "I just can't. Please . . ."

2

Later in the morning Drifter went with Rozika, Bozi and Lisa to register at the American Joint Distribution Committee. The headquarters of JOINT, as it was simply called, was in the building of a knitting factory whose Jewish owner had been deported the previous May. The factory building had been closed till JOINT moved in. That was in April. The knitting machines were stored in the basement and the workrooms transformed into reception, dining and sleeping halls.

Loaded with food parcels they received from JOINT, the group walked towards Main Street.

It was all there, intact. The park. The Grand Corso. The tall spire of the Protestant church seemed now of a peculiar shape, like an upside-down exclamation mark, or an oddly shaped chimney. Perhaps it was an oddly shaped bakery chimney, Lisa thought, then quickly told herself to stop thinking of *that*, at least not here, not now when at long last she was stepping, for real, on the cobblestones, *eins, zwei, drei,* of her dream island, her Sighet. She had rehearsed that encounter over and over, how its beat would wake her up, extricate her from the grip of the nightmare, *links, rechts, links,* and the breath of Sighet would thaw her heart. All she would have to do would be to touch familiar objects, buildings. The earth of Sighet.

She crouched and flattened her palms against the ground. The soft spring earth felt warm to the touch, warm and soft like sand, crumbling sand, a shower of silky sand.

night is day, bright and red. red. red. like the sky. the red sky.

An open truck full of people comes by. They wave good-bye hello. an old man waves to me, his long beard trails from the truck like a white, silky train. there is a red cloud, lots of red clouds and the truck seems to go in the direction of the red clouds, step onto them, ascend to the red sky. if i run fast after the truck i could hold on to the old man's white silky train. ascend to the sky up, up, up where mamma is

meet mamma

i run after the truck and i hear songs, songs and cries and gurgles of little voices. they all come from the truck. children's voices.

the old man beckons to me. i run, run

to meet mamma up, up there in the red sky

but the truck slows down. it doesn't ascend to the sky

mamma, mamma

the truck comes to a stop. it tilts, its sides drop. the old man and lots of children, lots of little children, children, children, are being dumped dumped dumped in a huge pit; slide, tumble into the pit, the children. wiggle wiggle the children like fish dumped from a net to the bottom of a boat.

another truck

standing near the pit

tilts and dumps sand in the pit

dumps sand dumps sand

fine silky sand, a curtain of fine black sand

over the children over the old man with a white beard.

there is nothing but darkness

there is nothing but stillness

and i am scared

children, gurgles, little voices, old man

where are you

up up up i want to go to meet mamma, mamma, mamma

the world tilts and you'll fall in the pit they all scream, the little voices, children, gurgles, old man

you'll fall in the pit, you'll fall in the pit and i run, run in the darkness in the stillness i run keep running and then i crash into something, a huge something, enormous like a mountain

a quaking, rumbling, crumbling mountain
the prislop the solovan
no. this mountain is the world
it falls apart it disintegrates this mountain
the world falls on me. it punishes me, for what, for what
help. help.
the mountain is falling on me in little bits is falling on me. a mountain of shoes is falling on me.
thousands of shoes. tens of thousands of shoes.
they are not my shoes. they want to belong where they belong, with the children, children, children, with the old men and women, the young men and women, with the people of the world, people, people, people
they are not mine, the mountain of shoes, solovan prislop such mountains

Her eyes were focused on the mountains in the background and a foul-tasting lump filled her mouth. She wanted to get up from the crouching position, but before she could straighten up she vomited.

Why did she throw up? she wondered, and wiped her mouth with the back of her hand while Drifter helped her get up. She was in Sighet, the town she saw during sleepless nights in the bunk where lice and cockroaches crawled on her and hunger made her drool like a mad dog. To keep herself sane she had hung on to an image, sometimes blurred, sometimes ethereal, but always the same image: Sighet, the sacred, damned island. She saw herself walk on the Grand Corso, in her prettiest dress, or riding her silver bike. She brushed cockroaches off her body and dreamed of how someday she would be in Sighet again, and the whiff of acacia would soothe her, wash away the stink of the cesspool; that Sighet would help make her whole again, someday. That there would be rejoicing at seeing her come back.

She looked around, defiantly. There was the park, neglected and full of litter instead of flowers and there was the Grand Corso full of marching Russians instead of promenading maidens. But still, it was Sighet. The dream will become reality any moment now, Lisa thought, as soon as one among the civilians walking on the Grand Corso at a fast clip, tight lips and eyes fixed on some distant point, would welcome her.

People she dimly recognized as townsfolk passed her by. In a flash she understood that reality never matches dreams and she also understood she must not allow reality to destroy her dreams.

"Where are the trumpets, the flowers?" she cried out in the middle of the Grand Corso, desperately trying to force reality to match her dreams. "They are here somewhere, they must be here. . . ."

A civilian walked by.

"Look at me!" She ran after him. "I am back. I made it! I am a survivor. You are glad to see me, aren't you?"

The man looked at her, then coughed:

"Sorry," he said. "I don't know you. I don't even know what you are talking about. . . ."

Drifter quickly took her by the arm:

"Wake up, Lisa, and listen well. I am not going to repeat it." He spoke fast, the threadlike scar turned red on his pale face and the grip on her arm intensified.

"The fact is *they* are not glad we are back. To the contrary. Our return merely points up their guilt. The fact is one half of the civilized world was exterminating us like vermin while the other half allowed it to happen. Or didn't know it was happening. I don't really know which is worse. Meanwhile, the survivors bleed, and I wonder if our bleeding can be stopped at all . . . It's going to be hell, this our survival, that's for sure. But even if our wounds are permanent, we ourselves must stop the bleeding. We must do it, never mind *them*. Anything we set our minds to do we can do."

"Someone once said this to me," she suddenly remembered. "Who?"

He shrugged his shoulder, began walking briskly with her to catch up with the others.

"You don't need their hosannas for having come back. We are back, period." He broke into a smile. "But *I* am glad you are alive, my girl, I really am. Would that do for a while?"

"Miss Engler!" Two men and a woman were running towards them. Lisa noticed the woman's long blond hair. "Remember me?" The voice was close and Lisa took her eyes off the woman's blond hair. The man speaking to her wore a double-breasted

151

beige linen suit. The wide-lapelled jacket was pinched at the waist, had two side flaps and reached to the middle of his thighs. The shirt he wore was a light green and the tie was red. A wide smile on his face almost concealed his small eyes in their sockets. His complexion was ruddy, his prominent nose dotted with open pores.

"Remember me, yes?" He grabbed her hand, pumping it frantically. "I am Himy Lieber. Remember me? Your brother Laszlo and I were together in the Jewish labor force. I was Laszlo's best friend." He continued to pump her hand. "Nice outfit, what?" He pointed to his suit, chuckled. "From America. The latest model. I wish Laszlo could see it."

"Have you heard anything about Laszlo?" she asked in a whisper.

"Lisa. May I call you Lisa? Thank you, miss. Well Miss Lisa, let's talk later. Now is welcome time. Welcome, welcome!" He pressed her hand to his heart, then abruptly dropped it to wave to a Russian officer walking by. He grabbed her hand again, twirling her around. "Let me look at you."

"My name is Ilona," the woman with the blond hair now said. "I work for Mr. Lieber." She turned to Drifter and the girls. "You wouldn't know me, none of you would. I am a Gentile, you see. Before the war . . . well." A dimple appeared on her left cheek. "But I remember you," she said smiling at Lisa. "You had a silver-colored bicycle and used to ride it on the sidewalk. I remember——"

"No more talk, I say." Himy motioned to the other fellow standing near him. "Lunchtime. Go tell them I'm bringing company. And what company!" he exclaimed. "I want the best! Tell them the Mogul said so." He turned to Lisa. "That's what they call me now, you know. Himy the Mogul," he said proudly. He slapped his forehead. "That I should be the first to greet Lisa Engler and her friends! An honor, I tell you, a real honor. . . ."

He whisked them along to the Crown Hotel. The restaurant too, like the park, was neglected. The tablecloths were crumpled and stained, the floor dirty. A waiter shuffled to their table, brushed crumbs off its top with his hands. Another waiter, holding a bottle of wine under one arm and a bottle of soda under the other, deferentially approached their table.

"My best wine for you, Mr. Mogul," he said bowing. "The *gulyas* is already cooking. It's the last morsel of meat we have. But for you . . ." He bowed again. "They took away everything," he said pointing with his thumb in the direction of Main Street. "Those damn Bolsheviks."

"Stop whining. You didn't begrudge the Nazis when they took things from you, did you?" Himy reached in his pocket, took out a wad of banknotes and threw it on the table. "This should pay for your pains. And bring more wine and soda. *Davai!*"

"What a prince, that Laszlo," he said sighing. "A real prince. You thought all he knew was how to play soccer." He smacked his lips and sighed again. "You should have seen him play poker. Ah! There was no one like him. A real genius, Laszlo. He would sit at the poker table all night and play, getting up only to go to the toilet—you should excuse me, Miss Lisa. Otherwise, Laszlo sits up straight all night, holds the cards, spreading them barely, barely." He reached in his pockets for two banknotes, aligned them, then slightly lowered the one on top. "Like this," he said. "Laszlo called it 'card teasing.' 'Light me,' he says and I light cigarettes for him while he plays. Even the sergeant, that bastard—excuse me, Miss Lisa—even the sergeant admired Laszlo's poker playing. Who wouldn't? I ask you." He finished his drink. "Ah, what nerve, what bearing! A prince, that's all. Doesn't blink an eye. He doubles, triples the pot. Not a muscle moves on his face. He was beautiful, I tell you. And his bluffing!" He rolled his eyes, pursed his lips. "Ah! Sheer poetry, believe me, sheer poetry."

He refilled the glasses and got up. His eyes were bloodshot, his face red and shiny. He held his glass in one hand, the other hand over his heart:

"To Laszlo, my friend. To the Poker Prince." He drank the wine in one long swig, then slapped his forehead again. "I talk, talk. And look at you . . . you still wear that horrible striped thing. You, the sister of the Prince." He leaned over and embraced her. "Permit me. I, Himy the Mogul, shall buy your first new dress." He turned to Ilona. "After we finish eating you go to the store with Miss Lisa. She gets everything. The best, the most expensive. Whatever she wants. Tell the storekeeper I said so. Let him put it on my account. On Himy the Mogul's account."

Lisa began to fidget and Himy firmly put a hand on her shoulder:

"Please, Miss Engler," he said, tears brimming in his eyes. "For Laszlo's sake. Do it for him. Please."

3

The survivors who had returned to Sighet during the previous weeks and months came to Rozika's house that evening. They came to find relief in common grief, but they said they came to greet the new arrivals.

Erno the engineer, who had been hidden in a hayloft by a Romanian peasant for six months, came. So did Motke and Ezra. Along with a group of Jewish socialists they went underground in 1941 and joined the partisans, then surfaced to help rout the Nazis when the Russians had broken through the Uzok Pass in early September 1944. Huna the Butcher was there, and so were Beila and Esther, Naftuli, all former inmates of liberated extermination camps. Himy the Mogul brought along bottles of slivovitz and vodka, cigarettes, cans of food, and a batch of American K rations.

Yosl and Abe, who had feigned madness to avoid conscription in the Jewish labor force, came too. They had defecated in the park at noontime, the day after the twenty-one prominent Jews had been arrested, got undressed, put a match to their clothes and ran naked through the streets, yelling and screaming that the Second Coming was here, the imminent salvation of mankind by the new Messiah, whom they called *Malach-Hamoves*, Homunculus or Siegfried, was a matter of days. They urged everyone to follow their example and burn their clothes to receive the new Messiah unburdened by worldly paraphernalia. "Be born again," they screamed, "be as innocent as a naked child." The two men were stark raving mad, the authorities declared, and promptly put them away in the Insane Asylum. Then the mass deportations took priority over everything else and the authorities forgot about them, or forgot that they were Jews.

Gyuri the law student, Imre, Otto, and Sandor the Handsome arrived at the same time. All of them, including Rozika's brother, Moritz, had been back in Sighet since September 1944.

He will show up any minute, Lisa thought, Mano was in the same Jewish labor force unit with Imre and the rest. She kept her eyes on the door.

They hardly spoke to each other at first. Their eyes were dulled, their movements awkward. They kept passing the bottles from mouth to mouth in silence, mechanically.

"Too much gloom," someone muttered. "Talk, speak . . . let's hear life."

"I am not from Sighet," Bozsi said, "and neither is Drifter."

"Drifter." Motke became agitated. "Did you say Drifter? Where is he?"

Drifter cleared his throat, raised a finger. Motke ran over to him.

"Let me shake your hand, *chaver*. Hey Ezra, that's Drifter, you hear? Listen," he said to the people in the room, "this man here that they call Drifter someday will have a place of honor among the heroes of our people. He sure deserves it, Drifter does."

"Please," Drifter said, "please. You exaggerate."

"Exaggerate?" Motke exlaimed. "How can you exaggerate the value of life, I ask you. This man here," he said, pointing at Drifter with awe, "this man here smuggled arms into the besieged Warsaw ghetto and smuggled Jews out. Saved eighteen children. Eighteen, that's *chai*, the number for life, remember that. I tell you, Drifter was our David. His fame reached us in the mountains. It reached the *goyim* too. Saving lives, Jewish lives. Eighteen children. Eighteen . . ."

Drifter kept a bottle at his mouth for a long time. He saved children's lives but couldn't save his own child. He banged the empty bottle on the table.

"Come now," he said, "cut it out. This eighteen business. You

156

exaggerate, I told you. I did what anyone else would have done in my position." What would someone else in his position have done? he now wondered. Damn it, he thought, he had no choice, none whatsoever. There was always something else to do, always a last foray, a last fucking foray before he would go save his own. Or go die with his own. Indeed, what else could he have done?

He kicked the foot of the table.

"Drifter, don't," Lisa said, and slid her hand over the foot of the table where he kicked it, gently smoothed it. He was hurting it. Drifter was hurting the contours of familiar things.

"Mano will be here soon," Otto said.

Lisa ran to the door.

"I mean, he'll be here in a few days," Otto continued. "When he left Sighet, Mano asked me to send him a telegram the minute you arrived. I've done that. He'll be here soon, you'll see."

"Sure," she said, "he'll be here soon. I know."

"He was here till last week," Imre said, "waiting for you. Then his sister wrote him he'd have to go enroll at once at the university in Cluj if he wanted to matriculate this year." Imre killed his cigarette in a saucer. "Barcescu is a big shot now, you know. He's the chief justice in Cluj."

The taste of gall was in her mouth, she felt queasy again, just like in the morning. She must not vomit though. The queasiness must be pushed back where it came from, down, deep down in her stomach and kept there. She reached for a bottle.

"We were stationed near the Szamos River, two hundred kilometers south of Sighet. The six of us, including Mano," Imre said, pointing to Gyuri, Otto, Sandor and Moritz. "Buddies in the same labor unit, waiting to be shipped to Russia any minute . . . Then, late in August, we heard that the Ruskies had finally crossed the Uzok Pass. One night, the guard at the compound gate got dead drunk. His gun and gun belt lay on the ground. I grabbed the gun, stuffed it in my shirt and got the five other guys. We made a dash for the gate and didn't stop till we reached the foot of the Carpathians. Now Mano pulls out your photograph. He had been looking at your picture all the months in the labor unit. The picture was creased, almost discolored from all that looking. There wasn't a guy in the unit who hadn't seen it. Before we get ready to start running again, Mano kisses

157

your picture. 'I'll see you yet, Red,' he says. Each time we stopped to rest and each time we were ready to start again, he kisses your picture. And the same chant: 'I'll see you yet.'" He took a long swig from the bottle. "For six days we just kept walking through the mountains and for six days he kept kissing your picture. Then we reached Sighet."

"The Nazi and Hungarian units had evacuated the city in the first week of September," Moritz said. No one was listening to him. Each one had retreated behind glassy eyes, buffered by liquor and smoke. But Moritz did not want to stop; he wanted to say it over and over, repeat it until it would stop hurting, until the pain in his gut would disappear. "Radio Budapest and Radio Berlin blared day and night: 'tactical retreat' and other crap. The bastards were finished, kaput, of course; they knew it too. Everyone knew it." He turned to Rozika: "Only you didn't know it there . . . Even so, it wouldn't have done you much good anymore. For you it was too late. Too late . . . " He embraced her and began to cry.

"Before they evacuated, the Nazis blew up the bridges over the Tisza and Iza," Otto said. "The Magyars blew up the electrical plant and then set fire to the Orthodox synagogue which had been converted into a warehouse after the Jews were deported. The synagogue was packed with food and clothing when the pigs burned it down. It stunk all over town. The food was gone, so was electricity——"

"Tell 'em about the buttons and the clouds of feathers," Sandor said.

Otto chuckled. "The epic of 'War and Feathers,' by Sighet's leading citizens. All right. Pillows, comforters, eiderdowns the Hungarian regime expropriated from Jewish homes, had been meticulously sorted and stored in warehouses, then officially sealed, waiting to be shipped to the front. But when the Nazis and Magyars beat it out, the townspeople broke the seals. They pulled and grabbed, scratched and kicked, to get a pillow or a comforter—and they blanketed the city with feathers and buttons."

"Yeah, they fucked themselves sick with Jewish pillows and sunk their Aryan asses in Jewish comforters," Huna the Butcher grumbled. "Then they hit the Jewish stores. They hammered the

158

locks off and picked them clean. Like locusts . . ." He spat and crushed a package of cigarettes with his fingers: "One of these days . . ."

"There was no resistance when the Ruskies marched in next day," Otto said, "because the looting heroes were hiding in cellars and attics, shaking in their boots——"

"But not you, Sandor the Handsome," Abe razzed him. "You and the *shiksa,* what's her name, shook with something else, eh?"

"Shut up," Himy said. He had been drinking all night long, listening with eyes closed, nodding his head once in a while. "There are acts and there are acts, Abe. Don't be a fool. And you," he called to Sandor who was walking towards the door, "don't be so sensitive. Ilona gave you shelter and she is a *shiksa.* *Nu?* Face up to it, man. Where are you running? Sit down and have a drink. It will clear your mind. *Lechaim!"*

Motke picked up the story: "A small detachment of Russian officers entered town during the night, and next day Sziget was occupied by the Russian Red Army. 'Liberated,' that is."

"So it was the Ruskies' turn to loot," Imre said. "They were crazy for watches, the Ruskies. Ripped watches from wrists like they were plucking apples from trees. It was *davai ciassi* or else. . . . A Rusky had found a big wall clock; he brought it to the watchmaker, slammed it down on his worktable and ordered him at gunpoint to make at least three wristwatches out of the big clock. Crazy for watches——"

"And women," Gyuri said, "don't forget women."

"About women they were quite democratic," Otto quipped, "let's grant them that. Raped every woman regardless of shape or vintage——"

"Toothless old Marcsa could tell you about that. . . ."

"What about Dr. Bocskay who was forced at gunpoint to watch his wife being raped?"

Otto pushed away an empty bottle:

"All that *goyish* suffering could have been avoided, the *goyim* said, if some Jews, a small group only, had been kept in prison instead of being deported. The Russians would have had somebody else to celebrate their victories on. The Jews who, after all, were used to pogroms, knew how to cope with *gewalt.* . . ."

After a long silence, Motke said:

"But it was a Jew who brought the town out of darkness, right, Erno?"

"No one else could have fixed the electric plant," Erno shrugged.

"And the filth . . . unbelievable," Ezra said. "The *goyim* were infected with lice, there was no soap, no detergents. There was the specter of a typhoid epidemic. The Ruskies distributed a few ounces of delousing powder——"

"Which could make you rich," Yosl chimed in. "An ounce of delousing powder could make you an *oisher*. . . ."

It was way into the night but no one showed any signs of leaving. They had settled down for the remainder of the night, it seemed, as if being together, whether talking, listening, drinking, or dozing, would dilute their pain, ease their loneliness.

". . . and for a few days we were part of the Ukraine," someone said. "Our capital was Munkacsevo."

At the mention of that name Drifter drained the remains of a bottle of liquor in one long gulp. Lisa reached for his hands, intertwined her fingers with his.

"That's your town," she whispered. "Munkacsevo is your Sighet. . . ."

"It was a *fait accompli,*" Gyuri said. "A few weeks after the occupation the Russians simply announced that Sighet and all Maramures was an integral part of the Ukraine! Well. The farmers of Maramures, Romanian peasants all, were outraged——"

"Did they expect to be consulted?" Erno sneered. "The poor fools must have believed all that propaganda about peoplehood——"

Gyuri continued: "The peasants got together from the surrounding countryside, hundreds of them, and started to march towards the city. They were unarmed. They waved flags and placards with slogans about freedom and demanded elections."

"The peasants were approaching Sighet from the other bank of the Iza. They went through Vad. The one bridge the Nazis had forgotten to blow up was the one from Vad to Sighet. A platoon of Russian soldiers waited with guns cocked at the Sighet end of the bridge. The first group of peasants who came across the bridge, about thirty of them, were shot in cold blood. Then the

160

annexation was called off, canceled. Oops sorry, we made a mistake. It didn't really happen."

"And after that," Moritz said wearily, "a civilian ad hoc committee was formed. Imre and I and Gyuri were on the committee. Till the Romanians assumed civilian control of Transylvania, in around mid-January 1945, our committee was the only link between the Russian occupying forces and the civilian population."

"There's a young Russian captain in town," Gyuri said. "His name is Leonid Yashenko. Comes to JOINT once in a while like he's looking for something, or somebody. I don't know. Anyway, Captain Yashenko keeps dropping hints: 'The borders are open; what are you waiting for.' Very strange . . . Even so, four fellows already left." Gyuri looked around: "What are *we* waiting for? . . ."

"My sister," Beila said. "I'm waiting for her to come back——"

"So will my brother, you'll see . . ."

". . . and my sweetheart."

"Where else could we go after what we went through?" Esther asked. "Haven't we wandered enough? You have to come back to the source, everyone else does. I mean, this is our island. Sighet."

"On revient toujours à son premier amour." Otto took another drink. "Why the hell must we always return to our first love, particularly when that love betrayed us? We're tied to Sighet like embryonic creatures to a womb. The umbilical cord is accursed, I tell you, it's going to strangle us——"

"Don't be a pessimist," Imre said. "Have a little faith, for God's sake. So far the Romanian provisional government has maintained its independence, right? Why, it even promised elections in the near future. The Peasant, the Liberal, the Nationalist parties have become active again——"

"Yeah," Otto grinned, "these parties are squeezed in in the so-called Democratic Party Bloc, which *de facto* is run by the Romanian Communist Party. All government posts, city administration jobs, are controlled by the Party. The DPB is nothing but a front for the Romanian commies, a *'poudre aux yeux'* for the simpletons. . . ."

"You're a pessimist and a cynic, Otto. A cynical pessimist. So there are a few communists in the Democratic Party Bloc. So

161

what? Haven't the communists liberated us? Or have you forgotten how we cheered when we saw the red troops marching in? And remember another thing: there was a war going on, not a mardi gras. The motto is 'reconstruction.' In good time we'll function without the communist element; but right now we need them. To show good faith . . . can't you see?" Imre asked, turning up his palms.

"Yeah . . . to show good faith we reconstruct Mother Russia with lumber from thousands and thousands of acres from this land. The forests are left bare, despoiled——"

"War compensation!" Imre became slightly irritated. "What did you expect? Manna from heaven?"

". . . and the wheat from the fields, Russia needs that too," Otto droned on, "never mind the starving population. Or haven't you noticed? The Ruskies also requisitioned farm machinery, livestock. The quota must be met, they say, so many chickens, so many horses . . . Mother Russia is sure big. Insatiable."

"Back to politics," Ezra mumbled. "Where did it lead us, ha?" He closed his eyes, slumped on the floor.

"Yeah. How the hell can you care what happens here?" Yosl asked Imre.

"I have nothing left to care for . . . If I don't find something to fill up my thoughts I'll go around bashing in heads. Would that be better?"

"Maybe, maybe . . ." Huna said.

"Besides," Imre continued without paying attention to Huna, "I love this land, goddammit! It's my home; the 'source,' as Esther said. Don't let's be idiots: it's the people who did us in, not the land. The system was rotten, don't you see? That system is changing now. That's why I'll stay. Also, I'll be a reminder, not afraid to yell and scream, kick up a fuss if they try so much as to touch us again——"

Otto opened another bottle: "You do that, brother Imre! I'll tell you this much though: when that happens, I won't be around to join the chorus. *Lechaim!*"

"Argue, argue," Yosl commented, "look at them! Just like . . ." His voice trailed off.

Ezra opened his eyes:

"A loaf of bread two million *lei*. We are millionaires, did you know?"

". . . and Sighet is the capital for black-market salt," Yosl laughed. "Himy's its leader."

Yosl's laughter alerted Himy. He too began to laugh:

"Who else saw the potential, ha? A gambler, that's who . . . like Himy the Mogul. *Nu,* I organized the retired miners, got them mules and shovels. *Davai, davai.* We go down in the old salt mines in Sugatag, in Rona, a couple of miles from Sighet. The mines have been closed for years but there is a fortune there waiting to be dug out. Just waiting . . . for Himy the Mogul. So I reopen the mines, pack sacks and sacks full of salt. It's poetry, I tell you, digging out this fortune . . ."

He wiped his mouth, rubbed his eyes.

"I have salt, lots of salt, Comrade *Balaboos* Officer. A few Russians were ready to listen." The words tumbled out of Himy's mouth, half formed. "Gimme trucks and I'll make you rich, I said to the Ruskies. You can have lots of *ciassi* and lots of *devushki,* I said to them, after all, what else is there besides women and wristwatches, ha? So now they listen. Ah! We must get salt to Budapest, I tell them, that's where the money is. *Da, da.* How do we get to Budapest? In Rusky trucks pretending we are Rusky soldiers, that's how. Ah, they say, ah, well . . . Well, I say, we take the risks, not you, right? *Da, da* . . . But, I say, if the fine alert Rusky patrols stop our salt convoy . . ." Drunk, his speech slurred, Himy the Mogul pressed his finger against his temple and made a popping sound. "Risks, great risks, I tell the Ruskies. *Da, da.* So, I say, fair is fair and we must split the profits fairly too: twenty-five percent for the Comrade *Balaboos* officers and seventy-five percent for Himy the Mogul, his old miners and *the convoychiks. Harasho,* the Ruskies said, *davai, davai* . . ."

"He transports the salt in Studebaker trucks that the Americans lent the Russians during the war," Otto said. "The black market prospers and so does Himy's salt empire. At least American trucks are put to good capitalist use——"

"But I don't keep it for myself, not all of it. You want some, brothers? Here . . ." Himy swept the empty bottles off the table and put a pile of money there. He reached for a liquor bottle, opened it slowly then held it to his mouth for a long time.

"Little sister," he then said to Lisa, banging the now half-empty bottle on the table. "The time has come. Truth time is here. I weep that I, Himy, must do it." He kicked the dozing

Motke and Huna. "Wake up you guys, up! It must be told." He smashed the bottle against the wall. "Help me, brothers. I can't do it alone; help me . . ."

He began yelling at the ceiling as if an invisible figure had materialized there just for his benefit:

"I begged him to hold out till evening, you know. I said, 'Prince, wait till dark, wait.' 'No, buddy. I'm hungry now. I am very hungry. I can't wait,' he says. 'Let's finish the card game then,' I beg him, 'it's noon, all the *mashumeds* are out. Don't go . . . Prince, wait . . .'" Sobs shook his body.

Ezra put his hand on Lisa's shoulder. "Your brother left his hiding place to get food. He hadn't eaten for five days. He was hungry."

"It was December. Both he and Himy were hiding in Budapest," Yosl said slowly.

"It was the worst time: the Nazis and the Crossed Arrows bandits were rounding up Jews everywhere—even from foreign consulates. At night the pigs drove the Jews into the Danube and shot them. The river was crimson. Dead bodies floated for days," Ezra added.

"It was an old classmate of Laszlo's who denounced him," Sandor the Handsome said. "One György Strimbely. A big wheel in the Crossed Arrows Party."

"Laszlo begged that son of a bitch to let him go," Gyuri said quietly. "But Strimbely had to have a war trophy. . . . It was Laszlo Engler. Strimbely took him to the Danube."

4

Thereafter, Lisa lay for several days on the cot in her room. Rozika came in a couple of times during the day, stayed for a few minutes and left without saying a word. Voices Lisa recognized as those of Himy and Drifter seeped in to her. In her numbness, she did not know what was happening outside her room nor did she care to know. Drifter stayed with her, sometimes for hours, trying to snap her out of her lethargy by making her talk.

"I am tired," she kept saying. "I want to sleep. Please . . . let me sleep."

Each time she opened her eyes, Drifter was there. He gave up his attempt to make her talk. Instead, he made sure she would eat. He brought her food, a candy bar or a fresh apple, and sat near the cot till she finished eating.

The third morning Lisa got off the cot, combed her short hair. She reached for her head kerchief and contemplated its daisy pattern as though she saw the kerchief for the first time. Then she carefully folded it, slipped it into a drawer.

"I am ready," she said to Drifter. "Ready to go home."

He got up.

She put her hand on his arm and gently said, "Thank you, Drifter, but no. I want to face it alone."

* * *

She was sitting in her garden, on a tree stump. It was all that was left of the old walnut tree. Who would have wanted to cut it down, reduce a living tree to a piece of dead wood? she wondered bitterly. Whom did it harm?

A heavy tranquility, lazy and quiet, was all around her. Only the lulling hum of tiny insects, invisible to the naked eye, gently filtered through the morning air as if to remind her of her purpose in being there.

She looked around again. The moon-shaped flower beds were wrecked. Hundreds of uniform small stones painted white that had embellished the flower-bed borders lay scattered about. Hedges along the path leading from the gate to the main entrance were crushed, the trellises on the terrace broken and the vines ripped off. The grass was brown and burnt, the fountain well jammed with debris. The double-petalled lilac bush alone was intact, though the clusters of blossom were discolored and dead.

Almost the entire wooden fence alongside the Duncan garden was gone, just a few planks stood aslant in the ground.

She stared at the lush green tree crowns in the Duncan garden, at slender-stemmed irises and dainty moss rose shrubs. After a while, her head began to pound. She got up from the tree stump, turned her back to the Duncan garden and faced the house in front of her.

A large hole, dark and menacing, yawned before her. It was what had been left of her bedroom window which had overlooked the garden. Sashes, glass panes, even the window frame were gone. Her window was no more. Only the dark ugly hole, like the open mouth of a gargoyle, was there to remind her of what had been.

The massive wooden front door to the house was gone too. It was of solid oak, no man could have carried it on his back alone. She bent down, scooped up a handful of earth; it crumbled in her fingers, abrasive dry black dust.

She looked at the void where the door had been and panicked. The shed, she thought suddenly, there was the shed behind the flower garden. Maybe she ought to go there first. She wanted to turn her head to look for the shed but her legs, independent of her will, moved towards the house.

At first she thought the heavy smell was that of baking bread and walked directly into the kitchen. The cooking stove, shelves, cupboards, copper pans hanging from hooks, the big chopping board, were gone. The sink and pump were gone too.

She crossed the center hall, went through all the rooms of her house to touch the contours of familiar objects, a bed, a table, a chair . . . But there was nothing to touch.

The house was empty, completely empty, not a stick of furniture, not a door or a window was to be found. The walls were full of holes and gashes, the plaster hacked away as if someone had wrecked the walls with an ax in a fit of rage. Yanked-out wires and electric switches dangled from walls and ceilings like the rotted innards of butchered animals. The floor boards were pried loose. Mounds of dank dirt and animal droppings littered the floors.

There was one undamaged wall in the entire house: it was the dining room wall where the rosewood breakfront had been. On that wall someone had smeared in dung brown DEATH TO YOU—FUCK SWINE JEW under crudely sketched gallows. The den was empty too, except for the map of Europe on which someone, perhaps the same artist, had painted a red swastika across the continent.

In the middle of another room there was a hand-painted pink porcelain chamber pot full of feces.

The source of the stench.

It was her room.

She ran out and stopped before a wall showing the marks of a picture frame.

She traced the marks with her fingers.

"Mamma," she whispered, "my lovely Mamma."

Rachel's blue eyes in the portrait had a warm look, her high cheeks glowed and a sweet smile lingered at the corners of her mouth. Her brown hair was parted in the middle and rolled in a thick pompadour. She wore a high collar of beige lace with tiny pearl buttons and her hand rested on a double-string of pearls hanging from her neck. There was a plain gold wedding band on her finger.

Lisa now touched Rachel's eyes lightly, as if wishing to wipe off a few teardrops that clung to her lashes like drops of dew on lilac petals. Rachel moved her lips almost imperceptibly.

"Mamma," Lisa murmured, caressing the empty wall space enclosed by the frame marks, "my Mamma . . ."

Softly, she started to cry.

"Mamma, tell me: why?" she asked stroking the wall. "Why? Why did they do this to us? . . . Why?"

She flattened against the wall, spread her arms on it.

"Mamma," she sobbed, "what am I to do? How can I go on? How? . . . I am alone. Help me, Mamma, help me . . ."

Hugging the wall, she clung to it as though it were alive. She stayed that way for a long time.

"Love me back, Mamma!" she suddenly cried out. "Just love me please . . . I am so frightened! And I hurt all over, I hurt, Mamma. I hurt day and night, all the time. I hurt! I don't know what to do. . . . Help me, Mamma, please help me. . . ."

She began pounding the wall, banging at it with her fists:

"Do you hear me, Mamma? Help me, Mamma . . . Mamma . . ."

When she came out of the house the sun was at its zenith. It was warm and the blue sky was clear, not even a small cloud marred its perfection. It was a beautiful spring day in Sighet, after all.

The sun bathed her chalk-colored face, but she walked stiffly towards the shed without blinking.

Then she saw the stripped bunker.

The night the Nazis had marched into Hungary, Andras Engler dug a bunker in the shed, about four feet wide, three yards long and a yard deep. In the bunker the Englers concealed silver candlesticks and menorahs, silver tea sets, trays and bowls, and other valuables.

"It's a grave," Lisa had said, helping Andras and Rachel fill the bunker with boxes and parcels wrapped in canvas, "the end."

"No, *mein kind,*" Rachel replied. "It's not the end. It's only a horrible episode in our lives. But not the end. We believe in a tomorrow, that's why we do this," she said pointing to the bunker. Silk nightgowns and hand-embroidered clothes were carefully placed next to lace curtains and monogrammed linen. "You must never give up. Never. Promise me you'll do what needs to be done to live out your days. It's your right. . . . It's everyone's right."

They had covered the bunker with earth, stacked logs on top and made sure they left no telltale signs.

The empty bunker in the dark shed brought back the memory of the open grave. She walked out quickly into daylight.

She picked up a few stones, began throwing them one by one against the wall, slowly at first, waiting for each sound to die down before throwing another stone.

"The tables, the chairs, the beds, the chandeliers," she said louder and louder as she hurled each stone at the wall. "The rugs, the paintings, the books," she screamed, "the pots and the pans, the plates and the cups. The candlesticks. The mirrors. The bathtub, the faucets, the pump. The flowers."

"Quiet!" A thin, sharp voice intruded in the clatter. "Quiet!"

Lisa ran to the end of the garden. A small stooped figure dressed in black was coming through the broken fence and ran after her.

"Lisa," the figure squealed, "stop! Wait, it's me, your neighbor, Miss Duncan. Stop the fuss, you hear? You are disturbing the neighborhood." She wagged her finger. "This is a quiet neighborhood, have you forgotten? Besides, we are in mourning. The baroness died last week. Please, a little respect for the dead, you hear?"

Lisa was shaking, her teeth were chattering. She continued to pick up stones, pebbles, aiming them savagely at the concrete.

"My clock, my desk, my books, my window, the doors . . . the walls, *eins, zwei, drei, vier,* the garden . . . kaput, kaput; the world, the bunker, the vase, the flowers, the walnut tree."

Freeing the seething anger left her light, strangely satisfied. There was no more retching, no more queasiness in her. With each throw of a pebble or a stone she only felt release and nothing mattered beyond that.

"The clock, the bicycle, *eins, zwei, drei, Links,* the piano . . ."

"I have the piano," Miss Duncan shouted, "I do."

Lisa let go of a stone she was ready to hurl at the wall. The stone rolled away and stopped at Miss Duncan's feet. Lisa stared at the quilted slippers Miss Duncan wore over black stockings, then raised her eyes and stared at her face, noting each wrinkle, the lashless lids rapidly blinking over small beady eyes, the stretched yellow skin on her nose and the flat narrow tongue licking pink toothless gums.

She touched Miss Duncan's shoulders and parodying her younger self, she curtsied, saying in a small, childish voice:

"Good morning, Miss Duncan. May I sit in your lap again while you read me a fairy tale?"

"Tsk, tsk," Miss Duncan rebuked, shaking her head, "what's happened to you, Lisa? . . . About the piano: someone would have taken it. So why not me?"

Drifter refilled the glass with vodka, pushed it across the table.

"Another one," he urged Lisa.

She shook her head and slowly raised her arms, perhaps to reach out to him. Then, as if the weight of her arms was too heavy a burden for her, she dropped them on the table and buried her face in them.

When her sobs came at last, Drifter himself shivered. He felt her agony as if it were his own, as if the dozens of sharp needles scraping through her insides were tormenting his own guts. He wished he could be alone somewhere to howl from the agony her pain caused him. If he could scream till his vocal cords snapped, or his brain exploded into smithereens, or his heart burst, surely then, he thought, the pain would cease.

He closed his eyes, nervously searched through his pockets till he found several pills. He swallowed them without chewing, waited a few minutes, then opened his eyes. She was still slumped over the table. He put his hand on her back.

A mauled cub, he thought watching his hand quiver on her back. A mauled cub with wounds beyond healing perhaps.

"It's bad, very bad. I know," he said. "But it's over; you've come through it! You've done it. You went there."

If only he too could sob; it might help him too.

"Let me help you. Tell me what happened, please. . . . Let it come out," he said louder, "it will hurt less." He patted her head gently. "Come on, speak. Tell me what you feel."

"I can't." Her voice was hoarse. "I can't, Drifter. . . ."

"Try. Please. Get it out of your system——"

"But I can't, I can't," she repeated. "I can't——"

"Why not?"

There was no answer. Her head was still on her arm and she had stopped sobbing.

"Why can't you, Lisa? Tell me: Why can't you talk to me of your feelings?"

"Because," she murmured, "because . . ."

"Because of what? why?"

"Because I am . . . so ashamed," she moaned.

"Ashamed? You?"

"Yes, I." She raised her head, looked at him. "I am ashamed of what they have done to me. To us. As if . . ."

She dropped her head back on her arm. Drifter waited a few seconds, then took hold of her shoulders and made her sit up straight.

"As if what, Lisa?"

"As if I was . . ."

"Say it!" He held her face between his hands. "Say it!"

"As if I was raped in broad daylight," she whispered, "in the middle of the Grand Corso while the *goyim* watched. Leered . . .

". . . if just one of them would walk up to me and say 'sorry.' Acknowledge that something has happened. That's all," she said. "As it is, they pretend nothing has happened. They saw nothing, they did nothing. So what's this fuss all about?" She became agitated, the veins pounded in her temples. "We were murdered, maimed, robbed. But nobody did it! Where must I turn, whom must I confront? There is no one—no one to even acknowledge witnessing the rape. It didn't happen, they say. And I am left with the shame. And the pain."

He could not bear her stare. He looked away, touched his scar, then took her hands and riveted his eyes on her slim fingers.

"Listen," she said, "do you know what Lisa Engler did the day after she was liberated?"

A queer intensity in her voice made him look up. He ought to stop her from telling him, he told himself, she has gone through enough agony for one day; but seeing her contorted face he realized it was too late for that.

". . . nothing! Lisa Engler did absolutely nothing the day after she was liberated. Was she embarrassed to do what others did? Too crude? Or . . . or what? Or was she simply a coward? Then again, maybe she was stupid enough to think of right and wrong in the middle of the jungle. . . ."

171

Her words were shooting forth like bullets filled with self-loathing, he thought; their peculiar trajectory would bring the bullets back to their source where they would explode. He was familiar with the ravage such blasts cause.

He held her hands tighter.

". . . but maybe I did nothing because I was nothing!" she exclaimed. "*Dreck,* the Nazis called us. Shit. So maybe we believed them, that we were *Dreck,* what do you think? Let me tell you something, Drifter. Listen: even before the Russians liberated us the Nazis had already fled the coop. The *Herr Direktor*'s mansion was near the camp. One of the Krupp mansions, someone said. Anyway. We were afraid to step out of the camp even though the Russians assured us we were free. I mean, it took a long time to penetrate. We couldn't believe it. Afraid of another trap. The gates were wide open and we still didn't dare go out. But the next day a few girls went to the mansion to look for food, shoes, clothes. I went along with them. The *Herr Direktor,* the staff, were all gone. Maybe they had fled the previous day, maybe a few days before. Who knows? A beautiful crystal vase, filled with long-stemmed yellow roses, stood on a gilt table in the hallway. Lots of people milled around, opening closets and drawers and carting things away. Russian soldiers, drinking brandy and cognac from bottles, looked on. I ran to the vase ready to smash it. I lifted the lovely vase, held it in my hands—sometimes I still feel the cool crystal against my palms—then I put the vase gingerly back on the table. Next I went into a room where there were several glass cabinets filled with *objets d'art.* Meissen pieces, Nymphenburg porcelain figurines. Each time I picked up a piece to smash it or break it, I put it back. Then I went to the *salon* and saw these paintings. I took my time reading the brass labels: a Rubens, a Tintoretto, a Holbein. A small Vermeer. I was going to rip one of them up; I think I even reached for the Holbein, when I saw the piano. A big concert grand piano. A shiny black Bösendorfer. And do you know what I did?"

"I went to the piano and opened it," she said without waiting for his answer. "Then I sat down and played *Für Elise.* That was all I wanted to do then, Drifter. If I would have only——"

"Smashed, destroyed something. Tasted revenge."

"Yes! I wouldn't hurt so much now. I wouldn't be ashamed——"

172

"I don't know." Drifter said thoughtfully. "I really don't know. Maybe . . ."

"Why couldn't I bring myself to smash something, Drifter?" she asked plaintively. "What's wrong with me?"

She rested her head on his chest.

"Drifter," she whispered shuddering, "I wish I could have killed at least one Nazi . . . killed a Nazi."

He rocked her as a mother rocks a sick, feverish child. He was not aware he was kissing her face, gently wiping her tears away.

"My girl . . . my aching little girl." His voice was tender. "You feel the way you should feel, and that adds to the pain. Still, you mustn't feel different. You can't. But to go on living the score must be settled first within ourselves. Then we can figure out what to do with our hate, with our conscience. With the urge to revenge. Learn how to balance powerful emotions. And meanwhile, there is the raw pain." He sighed. "I know . . ."

He too ached, he thought, he too must settle the score, wrestle with his pain. And guilt.

"Where does one draw the line," he said, "and when. I wish I knew. For a while I pretended my wife and child were alive somewhere. Yet it was no use. Denying their loss did not bring them back. But I couldn't mourn them either. I still can't. As if my mourning would seal their death." He bit his lips, then went through his pockets till he found another pill.

"Munkacsevo," he said after swallowing the pill, "yes, it is my hometown but I'll never go back there. I want no part of it. My house or your house, they are the same: mocked, plundered. Raped. All of us have been raped."

He held her tight, stroking her short hair which was already growing smooth and silky to the touch.

"There is much to sort out," he said. "But this I know already: we must learn to mourn, if we are to go on living; and we must learn to act against evil without fear or compromise."

5

One morning a week later Lisa walked through the Market Place. She saw Anna the washerwoman stand in front of a cart holding a pair of chickens in one hand and a basket of eggs in the other.

"The finest chickens," Anna was shouting, dangling the birds upside down before shoppers. "The freshest eggs! The best in the market!" She wore a loose peasant blouse which bulged like a tent around her middle. During the many years Anna had done the washing at the Englers her stomach always protruded, whether she was pregnant or not.

Lisa walked over to her.

"Anna, going to have a baby?"

Anna turned, stared at Lisa, then slowly put down the chickens and basket. She crossed herself.

"*Sfanta Maria*," she said, "Saint Mary, Mother of God." She reached out to Lisa, pulled her impulsively to her chest. A warm whiff of sweat, milk and garlic rose from her bosom.

"What did they do to you?" she lamented, holding Lisa in her embrace, "*ai, ai*, what did they do to you, my pretty miss? *Ai, ai*. For pity's sake, what did they do to you? I am sorry, sorry, my precious little miss." She let go of Lisa, took Lisa's hands and buried her face in them and began to cry quietly. Each sob caused Anna's stomach to heave like a balloon in which air was being pumped in and out, in and out.

Lisa blinked several times.

"Anna. You cry? *They* don't cry for me. No one does . . . Don't cry," she said but wanted Anna to go on crying.

Anna released Lisa's hands and turned her leathery face to the girl. She wiped her eyes with the hem of her skirt, then straightened up.

"Thank the good Lord you are back already, Miss. He was good to you, the Lord." She touched Lisa's face gently, almost tentatively, as if it might disappear at the touch. "I thought of you and your parents often. I prayed for all of you. When will your parents come back?"

Lisa quickly grabbed an egg from the basket and began to roll it between her palms.

. . . *drei, vier links!*

. . . my right arm is cold. it hurts, mamma, where is she . . .

i should ask the man reeking of perfume where he sent mamma. he stands on a stool, or a ladder, he seems so tall, his head touches the red sky

where do you think you are going? another ss asks

to mamma, i say, and point to the left

aber fräulein

. . . he calls me *fräulein,* the ss does

aber fräulein, you'll see your *mutter* later, i assure you you'll meet her——

now, now

we've put them on trucks, the elderly folk need special consideration after the long journey, *ja?*

i nod

we are not savages, after all, *fräulein*——

he calls me *fräulein* again

we have *sonderkommandos* to take special care of the elderly. they'll have special showers, then perhaps recuperate in a nice green forest

when will i be together with mamma

ach, fräulein, fear not. on my word as an ss officer, you'll be together with your *mutter* soon, we'll see to it. we are not savages, not savages, not savages

175

Lisa was rolling the egg up and down along her right inner arm, then slid it into the crook of her arm. Her eyes were closed, her face ash gray.

Anna looked on. She suddenly crumpled like a puppet and sank to her knees. She began to pray.

Horses neighed in the Market Place, poultry cackled, vendors and bargain hunters shouted—Anna the washerwoman was praying.

Lisa opened her eyes. She saw Anna kneel, sway back and forth, touch the earth with her forehead, then raise her eyes to the sky. Her lips moved feverishly, emitting at rhythmic intervals piercing little cries of anguish—or of propitiation.

She mourns, Lisa thought, she knows how to mourn. Anna was mourning Lisa's dead just as she would have mourned her own dead, accepted their death as God's unquestionable will, then go on with the business of living because that too was God's will. She knew of no other.

Anna finished praying and crossed herself. She got up, adjusted her kerchief, then scratched her nose.

"It's like this, miss," she said looking in Lisa's eyes. "Before those devils took you away your Mamma gave me things to hide from them." She spat and crossed herself again. "She gave me a big bundle. Furs and coats and suits. Plenty of clothing. Even your ski boots. Lots of your clothes. Then she gave me some presents for having been willing to hide you . . . She said something about courage and a lady baroness, and that we are all each other's keepers. I didn't quite understand what she meant. Your Mamma gave me shoes and clothes, and she gave me enough money to buy two cows."

Anna sniffled, pulled the two ends of the kerchief tighter under her chin.

"She was a fine lady, your Mamma, may her soul rest in peace, she was . . . Now I'll tell it to you the way it happened. I swear to you I don't lie. See miss, last summer that good-for-nothing husband of mine, drinking tzuika all day he drinks, last summer that drunken oaf blubbers and boasts at the pub that we are rich, we have fancy clothes. Then the village headman comes and threatens to put me in jail for hiding Jews, he says. What could I do? It was no use arguing. I had to give him the clothes, you see.

But not all of it. I had promised your Mamma that I'd hold on to your things no matter what happens. You'll use them again some day, she had said. 'Anna,' she said, 'you must keep them for Lisa.' *Ai, ai* . . . So I gave the headman everything—I had to. But not your things. They were buried in the ground. I am sorry I couldn't save everything, miss, I am so sorry. . . ."

"But you did save some things . . . something," Lisa said. "You saved more than you know. Thank you."

She kissed Anna quickly and hurried away.

6

JOINT had become a home-substitute for most survivors. They went there at least once every day. It was the world, humanity atoning, the survivors said of JOINT. In the desolation of that *other* world, it was what they dreamed the outside world would do for them, should they survive the slaughter: the world would then devise unheard-of remedies, discover new balms intended especially to heal them, as JOINT tried to heal them. Though it was common knowledge that JOINT was an organization sponsored by American Jewry which drew forth from its financial resources enormous amounts of money to underwrite their rehabilitation, still the survivors made believe JOINT was the symbol of universal goodness, a nondenominational contrition and goodwill towards them.

No questions were asked at JOINT. Those in charge knew how things were. A glance at a tattooed number on an arm, or a look into glazed eyes and frigid faces, was enough. Words were unnecessary. They were also inadequate. The Romanian authorities, the mayor's office, the police department, were cooperative. It also helped that Gyuri had been appointed acting chief of police and that Dr. Barka, a socialist from way back, was now the mayor.

Lisa went to JOINT every day. She craved for something—not

for a Hershey bar or for the sugar-coated cereal flakes in small boxes, the standard treats JOINT offered each time survivors stopped by. She craved for a slip of paper tacked on the bulletin board, a tiny bit of paper with her name on it. A sliver of hope, a brief message: "Lisa Engler to contact so-and-so" or "attention Engler, so-and-so is coming home." She checked and cross-checked lists of names looking for Miklos's. It was not there. Nor were there messages awaiting her.

She began lighting three small candles every Friday night, as the sun was setting.

"I want to light candles," she told Rozika after being rebuked by her because only married women were supposed to light Friday night candles. "God broke the rules; it's time someone made new rules. . . ."

There had been strain between Rozika and Lisa ever since Lisa had finally inquired about Mariko.

"She went out one morning with a field *Kommando*. They brought her back dead," Rozika had answered tight-lipped. "Stop badgering me with questions. . . ."

At night, Lisa heard Rozika moan and cry in her sleep, thrash about in her bed.

"Let's talk," Lisa suggested one evening, "as we used to. . . ."

"Leave me alone," Rozika snapped, "go talk to your Drifter."

Drifter worked at JOINT. He accompanied the survivors when they went to identify and reclaim their property from townspeople who refused to return it to them. His mere presence lent moral support to the survivors. He was a troubleshooter, someone to whom everyone turned with trust. Leave it to Drifter, the survivors said, he knows how to settle matters; Drifter understands; Drifter is strong.

The Russian occupying forces had taken over the telephone network and granted JOINT one private line. The mail was delivered irregularly, making it safer to rely on messages received or sent through JOINT. The Russians were also in full control of the railroad, and train schedules were uncertain. Most civilians traveled by road. However, the bus from Cluj came to Sighet regularly, twice a week.

Twice a week Lisa was at the bus station. She was expecting Mano.

Watching people get off the bus and not seeing Mano among

them left her feeling as if someone had kicked her in the stomach. Still she returned twice a week to the bus station to wait for him.

She was not alone in her waiting. A tall beautiful woman wearing long shiny blond braids coiled on top of her head like a crown was also always there. Lisa knew the woman was Dr. Petrescu's daughter, the haughty Olga to whom men used to tip their hats with respect and admiration; and who had accepted their homage with a slight nod of her head like a formidable princess, proud and remote. Lisa wondered why the distinguished Olga was sitting in a bus station all by herself, her eyes sizing up the descending passengers, her cheeks overly rouged.

Once Olga spoke to her: "Don't let it get you. Your sweetheart will show up. One of these days . . ."

"I know," she said blushing, "one of these days . . ."

The foolish little pride that had impregnated the air Lisa had breathed since her birth; the pride in holding back feelings to conform with what had been considered feminine; the constraining old-fashioned pride now prevented her from admitting her desperate yearning for Mano and the deep hurt his absence caused. She continued to wait for him at the bus station, return Olga's nod with a shy smile, and hope for a message through JOINT.

One evening three weeks after her return to Sighet, Lisa sat with Sandor the Handsome, Imre and Otto, in the restaurant at the Crown Hotel. They had just finished dinner when Drifter, Himy, Gyuri and Erno walked in.

Himy at once ordered a round of drinks.

"A man from Cluj came to JOINT today and brought this." Drifter gave Lisa an envelope. She saw her name on it and recognized the handwriting.

A couple of survivors had come in meanwhile. They all sat around the table.

The sliver of hope, the message, Lisa thought. She opened the envelope eagerly.

"Dear Lisa and Rozika," the letter began. "A thousand welcomes, a thousand greetings. I wish I could have welcomed you in person but alas! fate has decreed that I be in Cluj at this time though I plan to come to Sighet soon.

180

"I enrolled at the Cluj university. The formal term begins in September. I am now taking a preparatory summer course the university offers to Jewish undergraduates. My sister Mady believes it's absolutely essential that I take this course to make up for the lost year . . . It's because of this that I cannot presently come to Sighet.

"Ah, Sighet . . . We shall talk about many things when I'll be there. . . .

"My brother-in-law the judge is district chief justice. He is going out of his way to help Jews. I live with Mady and the judge, that's all the family I have now. . . .

"And so . . . I think often of Sighet and of you, my friends. I will try to come to Sighet before the fall term begins.

"Till then, be well and think of your friend Mano."

"P.S. Lisa dear, how should I put this to you . . . if you have time to spare, won't you come visit me in Cluj? If you have no money, I'll gladly send you a bus ticket. Please let me have your answer."

Lisa had finished reading the letter long before she became aware of a heavy silence. She took her eyes off the letter and saw everyone look at her, except Drifter. He was staring into an empty glass he held in his hands.

She folded the letter with meticulous care. Slowly, she tore it into many bits.

"He wants to come to Sighet," she said, scattering the bits of letter on the floor as though she was sprinkling confetti at midnight during a New Year Eve's party. "He wants to come at once. As soon as I call him."

"Will you call him?" someone asked.

She looked at the expectant faces around the table and knew they all wished her well, they all rooted for her. For an instant she was tempted to give them cause to cheer.

"No," she said with a hint of regret. But she had to deny Mano's rejection not so much for their sake as for her own. Her tone abruptly changed.

"Never!" she said forcefully.

Her mind now clearly ordered her what to do and she obeyed automatically: she reached for a glass of vodka calmly and in control, then downed the liquor. The stinging pain in her gut was melting, melting. It would soon vanish. As soon as the vodka coated her senses into a torpid mass of cold memories.

She took another drink.

The letter . . . "Dear Lisa and Rozika . . . I cannot come . . ." Absurd. That was not what he had said. She knew by heart what he had said from the moving train, that day in May. She knew every word, every syllable. It was: "I'll come back, I promise . . . I love you."

Mano would not put her off any longer. She was his Red, a little like Mady perhaps, and he would keep his promise now. Not shelve it for another time.

He had promised!

That afternoon in Budapest too. Has he forgotten in Cluj what had happened in Budapest?

. . . playing with three bullets, real bullets. Though she did not know at first they were real. She did not know then how bullets looked.

It was after she had written to him from school in Budapest that their relationship must be ended, finished. That she wouldn't see him anymore, not even in secret, because she had promised Mamma to stop seeing him. Then Mano came to Budapest. She skipped classes that morning to explain to him how things were . . . they said good-bye to each other solemnly. Good-bye forever, period. They parted heartbroken. In the afternoon he was again waiting in front of the school. No, he said, he wouldn't give her up, ever, ever . . . and kept tossing those metal objects from one hand to another. He asked her if she knew what they were. Bullets, he said, they were bullets from a pistol he had stolen from their lodger, an officer. He would kill himself, Mano said dramatically, blow his brains out rather than give her up. He made her touch the cold metal bullets and she began to cry.

"I love you," he said, kissing her eyes, "and you love me. We belong to each other . . . and I'll never give you up, I promise. . . ."

He had promised. . . .

His taste, his smell, suddenly came back to her. Her mind had turned sluggish, it failed to tell her what to do. Her heart now took over completely and she started to ache in a way she had never ached before. She knew she ached for him. But she also

182

knew that the letter would prevent them from ever again holding each other and her pain became excruciating.

She began to cry.

"Hush," someone said. "Hush . . . take another drink."

The dining room was full of them. In fact, there were no other diners in the restaurant, only Jews drinking, some crying, others lost in counting spots on the ceiling or the walls.

". . . right. Finish your drink, little sister."

"It will extinguish——"

"Fire!" someone yelled.

"There is no fire!" Drifter shouted. "Cool down . . ."

". . . smoke, I smell smoke——"

"They bake bread!" Lisa suddenly screamed. "That's it! Can't you smell? Bread, it's the smell of bread, bread . . ."

Himy poured her another drink:

"Sure, it smells . . . sure. But the fire; there is no fire."

She finished the drink and began to feel warm, relaxed, just a bit giddy. The pain was subsiding, till nothing hurt anymore, nothing burned.

"Tell me about shooting the dozen Nazis in the sewers of Warsaw, Drifter," she said.

"I only shot two, my girl. The rest got away."

"So what. You killed them, didn't you?"

"I'll tell you how I mowed down a Nazi Panzer battalion," someone volunteered. "Like this." He ran around the dining room squirting soda from a bottle. "And then the Nazis and their tanks evaporated. Puff!" He laughed and took another drink.

"We sure scared the shit out of them when we bombed Auschwitz, didn't we?" Otto asked giggling. He was drunk.

"You weren't even there. How do you know——"

"So I wasn't even there! So I was somewhere else! What does it matter? We shot them, that's what matters. We beat the shit out of those Nazi horse pricks, plucked out their eyes, made them eat their own *Dreck,* that's what matters. Isn't that so," he screamed, "isn't it?"

"Yeah yeah . . ."

"I strangled a Nazi with my bare hands, one night," Ezra said. "The dog didn't even know what was happening to him at first. I squeezed the life out of him bit by bit. As my fingers tightened

183

around his neck I kept saying, 'for my mother,' and gave another squeeze; 'for my father,' another one; 'for my sister Esterl,' another squeeze; and another for my brother, Sam; for my little brother Shloimele a special squeeze . . . I watched the Nazi dog die by my own hands . . . I heard his last gasp." Ezra began to cry very softly.

"Don't you worry, Ezra." Huna drank straight from the bottle. "I made them pay plenty . . . I did. Himmler the killer shat in his pants and piss dripped into his fancy boots when I jumped him that night. If it wasn't for the guard, I would have torn Himmler apart, peeled the skin off his rotten body inch by inch. But the guard pulled me off Himmler. So I grabbed his gun and killed the Nazi guard instead——"

"The Nazis were on their knees that night, groveling on their knees on the bank of the Danube, begging me to spare their stinking lives," Himy said. "Three of them, three groveling shitty Nazis. Two were from the SS. The other was Strimbely, the bastard. They were all pleading with me. But I ripped out their hearts with my own two hands. Then I saw those weren't hearts: they were bags full of noxious gas, smelly ugly gas . . . then I shot those dogs, and I bashed all of them, and stepped on Strimbely, and clobbered him, and kicked him, like this," he said, thumping the floor and pummeling the air.

They stood in the middle of the dining room in the Crown Hotel, jabbing, slugging, striking at figures they alone could see, smashing empty glasses against the wall, then drinking more. Lisa was tired, she closed her eyes but someone began to sing an old lullaby. She took another drink, joined in the song and clapped hands with the rest to the rhythm of almost forgotten songs about nightingales and the *one and only girl*.

It was near dawn. Nobody could remember any more lullabies or love songs. Their fantasies were exhausted. The survivors were drenched in sweat, spent. Otto suddenly jumped up, put a breadbasket on his head, then stuck a fork in it. He thrust his right arm forward in a Hitler salute, pushed his chest out and began to shriek an old song to an old tune, but with new words. Everyone roared along:

> Bring the fuse, one, two, three;
> Not for the Jews, Szálasi;

It is your turn, one, two, three,
To go and burn, Szálasi.

Here is an ass, one, two, three;
It's a fine Jewish ass, you can see.
Kiss that ass, one, two, three,
Before you burn, Szálasi.

"Dear Mano," Lisa wrote him the following morning, "we·ap-preciate your sentiments and wish you well in your studies. Re-gards, Lisa and Rozika.

"P.S. Thank you for your offer to pay for my trip to Cluj. I must decline it, though. I too am very busy now."

7

Early in July JOINT confirmed that Naomi was at the refugee shelter in Budapest. It would be a matter of a week to ten days, at most, before she would arrive in Sighet. The prospect of Naomi's return and the cooling between Rozika and Lisa, prompted Lisa at last to accept Naftuli's plea to move to his house.

She was packing when Rozika came into the room. Without lifting her eyes, Lisa continued to pack.

"You heard me come in, I know," Rozika said. "I see you are packing. Where are you going?"

"I am going to Naftuli's house." Lisa smoothed out her things, refolded them, then slipped them into a knapsack.

"Why?"

Lisa closed the knapsack, straightened up.

"You know why . . . you hardly speak to me." She looked directly into Rozika's eyes. "Why do I irritate you?"

It didn't matter anymore how it used to be, Lisa thought. What if once upon a time there were three? Things have changed, everything was upside down, askew. They had been three all right, once upon a time, and now Mariko her friend was dead. Lisa did not kill her. Why does Rozika hate her; she, Lisa, did not kill Mariko——

"I didn't kill Mariko!" Rozika shouted. "You think it's all my

186

fault. That's what you think, that's what all of you think! That it's my fault that Mariko is dead. Don't shake your head, Lisa. I can hear you think these things. . . ."

Rozika began to pace the room back and forth, pound her hand against her head and pull at her short, curly black hair. "They didn't check on credentials," she shouted, "the Nazis just grabbed . . . It wasn't my fault, I tell you. The Nazis didn't ask for me, they wanted Mariko. Mariko!" she cried out frantically, "Mariko! But it wasn't my turn to go! I was sick, I tell you, and she took care of me. She always took care of me."

Rozika kicked the door, ran to the window and threw it open, then stood before it for a while.

"They came that morning, the two SS," she said with sudden chilling calm, "and chose ten girls for field work. One of the SS pointed at me. No, I said, it wasn't my turn, I was out the day before. The SS slapped me. Then Mariko jumped down from the bunk and said she would go instead of me."

She yanked Lisa by her arms and screamed into her face:

"I had no choice, you see; Mariko jumped down from the bunk, shoved me back into mine, then joined the *Kommando*. It all happened so fast, I couldn't do a thing . . . She called at me as she left with the other nine: 'I'll bring back some potatoes' . . . and she was gone.

"She went because she wanted to," Rozika raved on, "she wanted to, do you understand? And then she died; just like that, she died on me. And do you know how she died? Of course you don't, no one does. Only I know. Oh, how well I know! I see it every night, night after night. . . ."

Her mouth was twisted, the perspiration on her dead-white face glowed.

"Because once we were three and you were part of it," she said shrilly, "I'll tell it to you, Lisa Engler, as a special favor. So you too can see how Mariko died."

Rozika took a deep breath and in a flat, dull voice, as if she were reciting a poem she knew by heart, she said:

"This is how she died: the *Kommando* went out that morning to work in a big potato field, outside the camp. At noon there was a half-hour break. Mariko asked the SS for a few potatoes. 'Get them from the bunker,' he said. The bunker was underground, a cellar full of potatoes stored loose in rows and rows and rows.

One on top of the other, from floor to ceiling. Mariko picked potatoes from the bottom. The potatoes came crashing down on her. Tons of potatoes. Like a wall of bricks. She was buried under them.

"After the noon break was over," she continued mechanically, "the SS sent a girl to fetch Mariko. She was in the bunker all right, the girl told me later, Mariko was, but all you could see of Mariko was a hand sticking out from under the potatoes. And it moved, the girl said, the hand moved. She was still alive, my Mariko. Strong, hanging on, hanging on . . . Each night I feel her struggle as though it was me there . . . under the potatoes. My fingers keep moving, moving. Clawing my way out to life. Digging, digging . . . with my fingers. I must dig myself out of the grave; I want to live. I am only eighteen. I have never made love. I don't want to die. I want to live . . . no matter how. With a crushed spine, broken limbs; just as long as I live. I scratch the earth with my fingers, that's all I can move . . . and I dig, keep digging every night till one night I'll dig myself out. . . ."

Rozika stopped abruptly, as if she had forgotten the next line.

"And *you*," she snarled, remembering what she forgot, "*you* blame me for her death, don't you?"

"No, no," Lisa said, but Rozika did not hear her:

"Don't you . . . don't you . . . don't you . . ."

8

Near the ruins of the Orthodox Synagogue, on a narrow winding street, was the Kahn house. It was a large house, its backyard full of trees, overgrown grass and weeds. A wide porch connected the house to a small cottage, just one room and a bathroom. Naftuli lived in the big house; Lisa was to have the cottage.

The morning of Lisa's move, he had closed the store and was waiting for her at the house. The store was in the Jewish Section. It had belonged to old Zalmen Kahn, who had been a grain merchant. Naftuli had reopened the store in April and was again trading in grain. He also dealt in lumber and truckloads of salt. Word got around he even dabbled in rugs.

"We'll be a family when Naomi returns," he said to Lisa cheerfully. "As soon as Miklos comes back, we'll make a real home here, the Kahn-Engler homestead."

His cajoling tone, the obvious eagerness with which he tried to please, grated on her. She was uncomfortable and wondered whether she should not pick up her knapsack and go. Yet his hangdog appearance blunted her sharp dislike. His lips were flaky, like peeling thin glue, and he sniffled as he wiped his head or nervously adjusted his tie. The tie was spotted, his pants baggy.

She'll stay, she decided; he is forlorn and uneasy, she ought to understand, feel sorry for him. Yes, she'll stay.

He took her through the house, pointing to furniture he had found stashed away in the homes of Gentile neighbors:

"At first they refused to return it. They claimed it belonged to them because we had abandoned it. They convinced themselves we left voluntarily . . . It wasn't easy to collect from the *goyim* believe me. The wrangling, the arguments! What the *goyim* did to us! What didn't they do? Even dismantled my father's store. Ripped out shelves, crushed the shutters. I can't keep any merchandise to speak of in the store, it might get cleaned out at night. Besides," he shrugged, "there's hardly any business in the Jewish Section. Who would come these days to do business in the Jewish Section? . . ."

He wiped his head, touched his tie.

"I wonder . . . hm . . . Would you, I mean could you . . . hm. It's closed, you see, and it's no use to you right now. And the big sign up there would help me. . . ."

His hangdog appearance now irritated her. He wouldn't hesitate to sham helplessness for her benefit alone. And she had felt sorry for him! Almost liked him, she reproached herself, while all along he was scheming to get something from her.

"Wait till my father returns," she said irately, "you can talk to him about it——"

"But——" He suddenly stopped, stared at her, then continued smoothly:

"Yes. But till then . . . expenses. It would help defray expenses——"

"You mean," she cut in, "using my father's business place would be a kind of rent for my room and board?"

"God forbid! Lisa! How can you say such a thing? I am like a brother to you, don't you know? Rent for staying here . . . I am embarrassed. Would a brother charge a sister rent? A sister, is there anything closer than that? Take from a sister? Now? After all we've been through? God Almighty would strike me dead— and I'd deserve it too—should I take a penny from you, a sister. If anything, I want to protect you like a brother should. . . ."

He blew his nose, shook his head several times.

"I am shocked, Lisa. That you should think that I . . . that a brother would take advantage of a sister! How can you suspect

Naftuli Kahn, your only relative right now, of . . ." He gave an indignant last tug to his tie. "Well, let's forget it."

"All right," she said with relief, "let's forget it."

She got up, walked towards the door. He followed her.

"I only meant," he said weakly, "I only meant THE HOUSE OF ENGLER AND SONS still means quality, even though the store is closed. And the big neon sign in the middle of town, even though the lights don't work any longer, the big neon sign could have helped me pick up business. Frankly, I wouldn't have thought that you'd refuse to help me. It doesn't put you out, after all."

Lisa crinkled her nose, as if the disgust he evoked in her affected her sense of smell. Her knapsack was still where she left it when she came into the house, near the door. All she had to do was bend down, pick it up and walk away. Suddenly she felt fatigued, worn out. The exertion of picking up and carrying the knapsack seemed beyond her physical strength.

"All right," she sighed, "you may open the store."

With jaunty steps, Naftuli walked her to the cottage. There was a bed, a painted chest of drawers, a round table and two chairs in the room. The window was bare, without curtains or shade.

The sun flooded the room. She thought of flowerpots with begonias. Of velvet smooth begonia petals she had put on her lips when she was a child. They used to wrap themselves in lace tablecloths or fringed silk piano covers, Mariko, Rozika and she, pretend they were grown-up ladies; and instead of lipstick and rouge, they had put begonia petals on their lips and cheeks.

She will get flowerpots and plant begonias, arrange them on the windowsill, Lisa promised herself, dress up the bare window. The flowers will grow there, in the sun.

"And this is your room." His voice was full again, ingratiating. "You won't have to share it with anyone, or sleep on a cot. A room entirely yours," he emphasized. "Like your own room at home, no?"

"No!" she snapped, stung by Naftuli's comparison. "No room can ever be like my own room was, don't you know that, you . . . you . . ."

To equate anything with what one had had before was blasphemy. A callous negation of a past that by necessity was becoming idealized. Nothing could be compared to that past, and nothing ought to be. Didn't Naftuli know that? Wasn't he there that evening when Drifter told them about the Mozart episode?

"Like the Mozart episode," Drifter had said that evening, before they started on their now-customary nightly drinking bouts. He was speaking of a new set of values—or did he say tools for survival?—which recreated the past into a perfect and beautiful unity.

"Not one note too many," Mozart had replied to the Austrian emperor who had complained of too many notes on the score commissioned from Mozart for the imperial chamber orchestra. The emperor wanted to simplify the score, have a few notes removed. "Not one note too many," Mozart insisted again, and the score remained as he had originally created it: perfect.

"As was our past before the slaughter," Drifter had said. "Each note, each breath of memory of that past is flawless. At this time, we need the remembrance of a perfect past. It's a matter of survival."

"Our past," he said slowly, "it left a void which can never be filled, never recaptured. Never. Only we, the survivors, can keep that past from total obliteration. There is no past without us . . . and contemplating a future is beyond our scope, right now. Beyond our strength too. Yet the present is an agony. That's why we turn to our past: simply to survive. Anything compared to that past pales; in fact, comparisons become unbearable, abominable. Nothing can even remotely match the perfection of that past. Not one note too many. . . ."

There were other people at Rozika's that evening, but now Drifter seemed to speak to Lisa only:

"We've lost everything we've ever had. To go on living, we now must relearn everything from the beginning. We must learn to feel and ache and love and trust and judge and think in a new way. We must create anew an entire system of thought and feeling and discover new ways of expression. When we'll have learned all that, perhaps we'll also be ready to mourn."

Drifter was right, Lisa thought, he was always right. One must relearn everything from the beginning. Until then, everything hurts all the time, brutally, endlessly.

To hell with Naftuli and his nonsense about an Engler-Kahn homestead, she thought angrily, she'll go away from here and get a room at the Pension Amity where several survivors lodged. She grabbed the knapsack effortlessly; now it had the weight of a feather.

"Let me tell you about the jewelry," Naftuli said hastily. "Listen——"

"I don't want to listen to you! Let go of my knapsack!"

"Please, Lisa! Stop twisting everything I say. Just listen——"

"No!"

"It concerns you, believe me——"

"Let go of my knapsack!"

"Give me a chance, will you?" He let go of the knapsack and stood on the threshold, blocking her exit. "I've overheard your father tell Miklos the name of the man he left a batch of jewels with," he said quickly.

Lisa stared at him. She let the knapsack slip out of her hands. He picked it up, then continued. "It was the last day in the cattle-car——"

"I'm thirsty." She went to the kitchen. Naftuli went after her.

"As I said, we were in the same cattlecar that last day, my folks and yours. I tried to tell you about it the day you came back to Sighet. You wouldn't listen to me then either. But you must listen to me now: I overheard your father tell Miklos he gave a batch of jewels to Dr. Petrescu the morning before your father was arrested. And that he never had a chance to tell your mother about it." He cleared his throat, coughed. "Dr. Petrescu would return the jewels only to an Engler. I know. I went to him in April, but he refused to even see me——"

"You went to him?" she erupted, "how dare you——"

"I went to see him just to make sure he wouldn't deny it," he said defensively. He grabbed her hand: "For Heaven's sake, Lisa, I tried to help, make sure . . . don't you believe me?"

She wrenched her hand away from his and began to laugh in his face. "You had doubts about Senator Petrescu? *You?*"

9

Dr. Mihai Petrescu, the scion of patrician landowners around Sighet, had been elected senator for Judetul Maramures in 1932. Petrescu had run for political office on the Liberal Party ticket, an act his peers deemed outrageous and subversive as well as an unpardonable deviation indelibly besmirching his character. Dr. Petrescu stood his ground on the parliament floor, amidst booing and hissing, to speak of political morality and the dictates of conscience till his solitary voice was drowned out by virulent orations extolling new racial theories.

"There goes Petrescu the philosopher," his colleagues ridiculed him. "He studies the sky, counts the stars, and stumbles into the ditch."

He stopped speaking up in parliament till one day, in late August 1940, a few days before the Vienna award of Romanian territory to Hungary became known, Dr. Petrescu, spoke up again, briefly. His last words were later often quoted:

"I call your attention to the fact that a strong chill pervades these chambers. I request, therefore, that the attendant be directed to close the windows forthwith."

When the voters heard of Dr. Petrescu's last words in parliament, they laughed. He had stumbled into the ditch again, they said, the old fool. He is cold in August. Whoever heard of such nonsense . . . ?

Only the Jews in Sighet did not laugh at Dr. Petrescu. Though they considered it odd to complain of cold in the midst of a heat wave, they assumed there was a deeper meaning in what the senator had said. A meaning so deep they themselves could not grasp it. Not yet. Meanwhile, they bowed when he passed them by on the street and looked on him as their champion.

During the Hungarian regime, Dr. Petrescu retired with his family to one of his country estates. He moved back to Sighet early in 1945 and took up residence again in his town house, behind the wall of hedges and the curved wrought-iron gate. His wife had died the year before and now he lived alone with his daughter, the beautiful and haughty Olga. In 1939 she had married Grigore Mosan, a Romanian officer, and went to live with him in Bucharest. Now she was back in Sighet by herself, shrouding her husband's absence in mystery by neither denying nor confirming strange rumors circulating in town. The Nazis had shot him as a spy, some whispered; but others maintained the Romanians had executed him as a traitor.

Then one day, early in June, news swept through town that Olga's husband was not dead after all. To the contrary: he was very much alive in Moscow, where the Russians were grooming him to become an important political commissar. His return was imminent—and that was why Olga was waiting at the bus station twice a week.

10

"Did I say 'doubts?'" Naftuli asked. "Of course not! I said 'just to make sure.' There is a difference, you know. Listen, Lisa, let's not argue, huh? You get yourself all worked up. Look at you: you've even broken out in blotches all over."

There were red spots on her arms, the size of peas. She became alarmed and let him take her by the hand, walk her to the cottage. He stopped at the door.

"You need some rest. I am concerned about you. You should stop fretting and lie down. Mull over what I've told you about the jewelry. We'll talk about it again tomorrow. You'll see things differently. Tomorrow——"

"No, Naftuli," she replied firmly. "We'll wait till my father returns. He'll take care of it."

But the idea of familiar objects within her reach gnawed at her mercilessly all day long as she lay on the bed anxiously watching the red spots change to a crop of hives that stayed for several hours on her arms, then disappeared only to reappear soon on her neck, chest or thighs. During the night she woke up several times shivering, chilled to the bone, the hives as large as saucers.

It was midmorning, next day, when she walked through the wrought-iron gate of the Petrescu mansion. Her hives were gone, her skin clear and her hand steady as she pulled the bell handle.

An old woman in a long black dress, a black scarf tied under her chin, opened the door.

"I wish to see the senator," Lisa said.

The old woman put her hand to her ear.

"My name is Lisa Engler."

Her hand still at her ear, the woman did not budge.

"Engler," Lisa said louder. "Please tell Dr. Petrescu an Engler wishes to see him."

"I am Dr. Petrescu. What can I do for you, my dear?"

The voice was gentle. A gallant-looking man, tall and imposing, with long white hair brushed back in the fashion of Greek Orthodox priests, stood behind the woman. His large forehead was lined, deep furrows extended from the corners of his mouth to his chin, and in the burst of wrinkles around his eyes there was a hint of sadness.

He beckoned her inside, then listened attentively to what she told him.

"Yes, there was a man," he said after she finished. "He came to see me a couple of months ago. A Mr. Kahn, I believe. Claimed to be a close Engler relative. I refused to see him, though. You understand, of course. I had promised Mr. Engler to hand over only to an Engler what he had given me for safekeeping. It's a great responsibility. I must make certain to keep my promise. Let's go, my dear, and get acquainted."

They went to a study lined with bookshelves from floor to ceiling. He sat down behind a large desk, picked a meerschaum pipe from a pipe stand and slowly stuffed the elaborately carved white bowl with tobacco.

"Take a seat, my dear. I wish to make it as painless for you as possible," he said as he lit the pipe. "I wish to help too, if I can, though it's not yet clear to me how I can be of help." He gazed dreamily at the bluish smoke rising from the pipe, watched it waft through the open window, dissolve in the balmy summer morning.

"Wars," he sighed. "How dreadfully uncivilized. They go on and on; never stop. Only take on different names, different ideologies. But basic motivations are always the same. Results too."

There was a sonorous lilt to his voice, she thought. A fugue performed on a double bass. She had better listen.

". . . were it but that mankind would at long last learn the fundamental principles of the good life," he was saying. "Knowledge and wisdom. They are different things, you know." He knocked the pipe against the desk, then struck a match to re-light it, sucking in his cheeks while he inhaled.

"Plato teaches that doing wrong is worse than suffering the wrong."

The statement bewildered her even as she remembered the senator said he wanted to help. She believed in his sincerity. But it was difficult to grasp the meaning of his words, discover the underlying theme of the fugue.

"I don't understand," she said apologetically. "Perhaps——"

"To avoid doing wrong is more important than being wronged. Do you understand now, my dear?"

She stared at him blankly.

"It means that the reality rather than the appearance of good-ness should be the supreme object of a person's effort. In other words, my dear, if you are really a good person, devoted to the practice of virtue, your soul is pure and, consequently, no one can harm you."

"Ah . . ." she said in a daze, "no one can harm me. . . ."

He looked at her with wide-open eyes, then touched his fore-head.

"I am sorry, my dear," he said regretfully. "Of course, this is not a propitious moment to discuss the Platonic Idea . . . how insensitive of me. Though in times of confusion it may point the way." He sighed again: "But first we have a certain matter to at-tend to, don't we?"

He selected a key from a bunch on a ring in his pocket, un-locked the lower drawer of the desk and took out a small card-board box.

He placed the box on top of the desk.

"This I received from an Engler and promised to return it to an Engler. You are an Engler. I hereby discharge my obligation. It is yours, Lisa Engler. Take it."

The box was sealed with tape. She peeled it off slowly. Her hands were steady, quite unrelated to her, as though someone else's fingers pulled the tape and lifted the lid. A beige handker-chief, its four corners tied in a knot, was inside the box.

A small bundle nestling in a pouch.

The handkerchief had brown borders, an AE monogram in one

corner. She recognized it instantly. It was her father's handkerchief.

Her fingers gripped the bundle, her knuckles turned white.

At last familiar contours were touching her palm. Their edges would worm themselves into her flesh, tear open her skin. She expected to see blood, to have its wetness soak her palm and feel its damp warmth. But her palm merely tingled and her fingers relaxed. She cupped her hand over the handkerchief.

Echoes of Dr. Petrescu's earlier monologue mingled with a light whirring in her head. She tried to remember what he said, sort out what he meant. The theme still eluded her. Maybe there was no theme.

"Untie the handkerchief," he prompted her, "make certain it's all there."

"Sure. Thank you." But her hand was paralyzed. She became confused, uncomfortable, and the desire to untie the handkerchief, lift the bundle out of the box changed to a burning need to do so. Her abdomen began to ache, as if the bundle was inside her, getting heavier and heavier, weighing her down. She must remove the bundle from the box at once, she told herself, it surely would relieve her abdominal cramps. She won't squander the jewels if she opens the bundle, she assured herself, she would merely touch them. Just touch them. A spasm in her stomach made her double over. She tried to move her hand again, but her cupped hand had stiffened into a protective cover over the open box holding the bundle of jewels.

She moaned. The cramps increased in intensity and frequency. She must ask the senator where the bathroom was.

"Sir, I feel awful——"

"Justifiedly, my dear. I understand."

"I mean——"

"I know what you mean. We'll try to help, believe me——"

"I mean, I am in pain and I would like to——"

"Certainly. One would like to find refuge from man's inhumanity to man. . . ."

She moaned again. The cramps were sharp now, unbearable, and she still could not move her hand. The senator had put the pipe to his mouth, drawn at it and found it was choked. He meticulously emptied the ashes from the pipe bowl into an ashtray.

"I find refuge in Plato," he said, keeping his eyes on the bowl as he cleaned it and Lisa stopped moaning. Warm urine was trickling down her legs. Her cramps ceased and her hand loosened. Then she gingerly lifted the handkerchief from the box.

He finished cleaning the bowl, then looked at her reflectively, compassion softening the wrinkles around his eyes.

"It may sound foolish," he said, "but you mustn't mind an old man's advice: reading Plato may give you new insights. Recharge you. Every bit helps. . . ."

He pulled a book from the bookshelf behind his desk and turned to Lisa, who clutched the bundle of jewels with both hands.

"A little refuge." He tugged lightly at her hands and tried to wedge the book between the bundle and her fingers.

Her grip tightened around the jewels.

"After you read the *Dialogues,* my dear, come up again to visit an old man." He now got hold of her fingers and tried to pry them loose from the bundle. "We could talk some more. . . ."

Lisa jerked her fingers free of him and again secured a firm grip on the bundle.

He sighed, then pushed the book under her arm:

"Meanwhile, I wish you good luck, my dear. Do let me know if I can be of any help. *Au revoir.*"

She locked the door of her room, placed the handkerchief in the center of the table, then sat down on a chair. She stared at the bundle, the knotted corners reminding her of a handle; the bowed handle of a dainty evening bag.

A bag or a pouch. A pouch-bag that contained familiar objects.

The nightmare would be over as soon as she touched the contours of familiar objects. Didn't she say this to herself *then* and *there?*

She opened the bundle with deliberate slowness. The sparkle of jewels, spilling on the table, leaped away from her. She quickly put both her hands over the jewels as if trying to save them from dissipating into thin air, then cautiously spread her fingers over them. Her glance brushed over a double strand of pearls, diamond rings and earrings, over gold brooches and bracelets, over many gold coins, napoleons and sovereigns. Then she saw the big gold pocket watch.

It was still looped to the gold chain.

When she touched the watch, it felt as if someone had abruptly siphoned off the oxygen from the room. She gasped, for she had the distinct feeling that the watch she was holding in her hand was ticking inside her.

How old had she been when Papa played the game with her? she wondered. He bounced her on his knees, she must have been a very small child, she thought, sitting on his lap, facing him. He supported her back with one hand, in the other he held the gold pocket watch looped to one end of the gold chain. The other end was fastened to his vest pocket. She could not imagine Papa without the chain across his chest. It was so much part of him, even as it dangled from the vest pocket while he rocked her back and forth on his knees holding the other end of the chain and the watch in his hand. He rocked along with her, his face touched hers and she stroked his long side-whiskers, enjoying the fragrance of the shaving lotion she smelled on him. She stroked his whiskers and the two of them rocked back and forth till suddenly he snapped the watch open, close to her face. The lid popped against her nose, she gave a little cry of pretended surprise then gleefully asked for more. More snap, pop, bounce; snap, pop, rock . . .

Afternoon shadows crept in through the window when she heard Naftuli puttering around outside.

She must have fallen asleep over the jewels, she reproached herself, seeing them scattered on the table. There was a gold coin on the floor, under the chair, and from the foot of the bed a diamond ring blinked at her. Between her sweaty palms, she was still clasping the watch.

In a panic, she gathered up the jewels, put them in the beige handkerchief and tied it in tight knots. How irresponsible of her to have let the jewels scatter. She must never again scatter them. She must preserve them intact until Papa and Miklos returned. The bundle must be protected.

Hurriedly, she left her room. Naftuli was on the porch.

"Here." She handed him the monogrammed handkerchief with the jewels. "You said you want to be like a brother to me. That I should trust you. All right, I trust you. You keep the jewels for me in a safe place till I ask for them. Whoever comes back first, Papa or Miklos——"

"I'll guard the jewels as if they were my own," he said, quickly taking the bundle from her. "You won't regret trusting me. Now I am like a brother to you; it makes me feel real good too. Trust. It's important. If we can't trust each other. . . ." He seemed moved, his eyes were misty. "Listen, you know the big safe in the living room. That's where we'll put the jewels, right now. Come on."

"Trust for trust," Naftuli said standing before the safe. "You'll be the only person, besides me, to know the combination to this safe. It's six, nine, seven. Watch." He turned the safe knob slowly: "Six to the right; left past nine and back to nine; then right to seven."

The steel door creaked as he opened it. A black cavern stared at her, obscuring an inner compartment with a small door. There was a musty smell coming from the inside of the safe. She pictured the bundle of jewels lying in that smell and she felt faint, nauseated. She turned her back to the safe, closed her eyes.

"All right," she said raising her hands, "just close the safe and be done with it."

"Sure, sure," he said, surprised. His hand went for the safe door but after a moment's hesitation he took a key from his wallet and, keeping his eyes on her back, unlocked the small door inside the safe. He shoved the bundle of jewels into the inner compartment, lightly pushed the small door shut, turned the key in the lock and put it back in his wallet. Then he slammed the door of the safe closed with a single turn of the knob.

"Remember," he said to her back, "the combination is six, nine, seven. Whenever you want the jewels, you know where they are."

11

"... whip in his hand, angelic smile on his face——"

"*Malach-hamoves, Malach-hamoves,*" they muttered shuddering, spitting. "Yeah, *Malach-hamoves* Mengele——"

"Conducting a selection, he was——"

"With a whip. A conductor with a baton-whip. Left, right, left——"

"Smile, left, smile, smile. . . ."

The breath of liquor and the rancid breath of fantasies of revenge hung in thick fumes in the room till they diluted them, as they did night after night, with self-lacerating purgings, high-pitched or pathetic, but still far from adequate to thoroughly clear the air.

Tonight they were in Imre's house. The cathartic drinking bouts always grew noisy and lasted till dawn. The *goyim* were spreading rumors that the Jews were having fun every night, drinking and singing; wasn't it peculiar that after all they claimed had happened to them these young Jews could still have a jolly good time; and what with so much booze and bawdy songs, the Jews may have made up those horror stories. . . .

"... then I grabbed the whip from him and whipped the

smirk off his face for good! Off!" Flicking his wrist, Abe slashed wildly through the air. "Off! Off with that smirk!"

"The smirk is still there," Huna screamed. "Don't stop!"

Lisa watched Abe's wrist dance in the air for a while. Then, tossing back her head, she gulped down a drink from the glass she held in her hand and jumped up.

"Enough!" She grabbed the invisible whip from Abe's hand. "Stop whipping him. The angel of death may become virtuous."

"You're crazy——"

"Listen," Lisa said, "the senator——"

"The senator? And who the hell is he?"

". . . explained. Even gave me the *Dialogues* of Plato——"

"You are not crazy, only drunk," Abe concluded.

"No, I am not drunk! Merely virtuous, according to the senator. A virtuous victim. That's me." She wiped her forehead, pirouetted around the room pointing to each one: "So are you; and you; and you. You too," she said to Drifter, and patted his back. All of a sudden she felt hot, took another drink, then smashed the empty glass against the wall.

"So much virtue. I can't bear it. It burns me." She reached for the bottle but Drifter had his hand on it. Their eyes met briefly, in a fleeting, sharp challenge, then she wrested the bottle from him and took a few swigs from it.

"That's better." She quivered, took one more swig.

"See that painting?" she asked, wobbling to the wall. "A Holbein. I ripped it up. There in the castle. I'll show you how." She clawed the wall with both her hands frantically. "Like that! In shreds. Kaput, kaput!"

Drifter moved towards her.

"Don't try to stop me," she yelled at him. "I have a virtuous soul and a burning heart."

"It burns me too." Ezra joined Lisa at the wall.

"Me too," Abe cried out.

Abruptly, she turned away from the wall.

"You killed Nazis, Drifter. Tell me how it felt." She closed her eyes to hold back tears. "It felt good to kill Nazis, ja, Drifter?"

He did not answer.

"Tell me the truth." Her voice was harsh, commanding. "It felt good to kill Nazis."

204

He stared at her tears escaping from under the tightly closed eyelids and touched his scar.

"All right," he said. "You want the truth. More and more pain. All right then: NO, goddammit, it did not feel good to kill—even Nazis. It only felt right. Goddamn right."

12

A retinue of hangers-on accompanied Himy everywhere. His secretary Ilona, the woman with long blond hair, was usually among them. Once in a while, the survivors heckled him for employing a *shiksa*.

"When Himy the Mogul employs *goyish* help," he would respond, winking, "remember: it's titled help. The best!"

Count Árpád von Tokay de Györ Hayduczy was Ilona's father. A descendant of the noble von Tokays and de Györs, Count Árpád had been singularly proud of the Hayduczy strain in his lineage. A footnote in the official Magyar national archives recorded that the national hero, General János dé Vitéz Hayduczy, had succumbed to the infidel at Mohács in 1526 only after he had valiantly fought the invading Turkish hordes in the defense of King and Motherland. Although this was true, it was only a partial truth. An unbiased, full disclosure of the fateful events at Mohács, Hungary's greatest national disaster on the field of battle, would have revealed that the noble general's army of hussars ran helter-skelter at the sight of Suleiman's hundred thousand Turkish warriors and that the general himself fled atop his horse shouting, "Transylvanian treachery wrought the Magyar debacle." Furthermore, were it not for his vain attempt to shake off a Magyar nobleman pulling at the mane of his horse, the general would have escaped with his life. But by the time János dé Vitéz Hayduczy recognized his own sovereign, King Lajos II, as the nobleman trying to steal his horse, it was too late for all of them: horse, king, and general were drowning in the waves of the Danube.

In 1913, at the age of twenty-three, Count Árpád was promoted to the rank of major in charge of the Austro-Hungarian Imperial Double Eagle Third Hussar Regiment, sent on a routine tour of training to Sziget and there met and fell in love with the beautiful Romanian girl, Elena Corcescu. Appealing to his sense of patriotism, the von Tokay de Györ Hayduczys vehemently rang the chauvinist alarm bell and warned Count Árpád of dire consequences. He married Elena anyhow, declaring *amor vincit omnia,* a curious motto for a nobleman schooled in the martial arts.

The scandal almost toppled the Hungarian branch of the Austro-Hungarian government. It aroused the Magyar aristocracy sufficiently to consider whether reprisals in Transylvania were now called for, since Romanian treachery was undoubtedly at the heart of the count's amorous affairs. Plans for the Transylvanian bloodbath were shelved temporarily only because World War I had broken out and old Count Géza, Árpád's father, disinherited his son even as the Austro-Hungarian imperial army conferred on him, *in absentia,* a dishonorable discharge.

Count Árpád and his bride now settled in Sziget, where he accepted a minor post in the city archival department. Their daughter, Ilona, was born in 1921. Ten years later the count died of consumption. Local Magyar sources, however, claimed he had put a bullet through his head to wipe out the shame he caused his class. It was also alleged that before committing suicide the count left a note which, in the tradition of his noble ancestor, General János dé Vitéz Hayduczy, had stated, "Beware of Transylvanian treachery!"

Whether the count left such a note was highly debatable. What he did unquestionably leave was a destitute wife and daughter, since Elena's folks—conforming to *their* sense of patriotism—had disinherited her the day she married the count and vowed never to as much as acknowledge the couple's existence or that of any issue.

Still, Elena's spirit was not broken. The thrust of her own pride in independence made her seek self-sufficiency without delay. She converted her small house into a boarding house and, revealing the convictions of her heart and mind, she named it Pension Amity.

Ilona's convictions, whether of the heart or mind, did not approximate those of Elena. Count Árpád had seen to that in the first ten years of Ilona's life.

Having renounced rank, fame and wealth in the throes of romantic grandiosity, the count now abhorred the vulgar necessity of earning a living. It became a painful and constant reminder of what he had left behind. Out of the purgatory of memories of pomp and opulence he convinced himself and Ilona that his fall into the common world was plotted by his country's traditional enemies, the Romanians and the Jews.

As Transylvania was under a Romanian regime at the time of Count Árpád's revealing insights, he wisely refrained from speaking out against it. So, wallowing in the glories of the past, as he did every evening sitting in the threadbare sofa in the shoddy living room, the full measure of his hatred was heaped on the Jews.

"Bolsheviks, the whole race of shifty-eyed, hook-nosed Jews, the Kuns, Luxemburgs, Trotskys, the Marxes. A different breed, a different heart, a different mind. Despicable. Dangerous, this race of chosen people. Chosen for what? Chosen to betray us, the God-fearing Christians. Chosen to foist the red revolution on us, wrest Transylvania from the bosom of its Motherland. Traitors! Antichrists! Beware of them!" He coughed and wheezed, spat up phlegm, then paused to catch his breath and continued to fulminate.

"Rich or poor, they are a pack of swindlers and traitors. Theirs is the covenant of the Elders of Zion, a cabal of Jewish bankers and Jewish bolsheviks. Degenerates with earlocks and caftans running the world. Corrupting the Christian soul, drinking Christian blood at their ritual murders. Stealing away my inheritance. . . ."

To steady his trembling hands and to ease the throb in his chest, he invented the ceremony of vestments. It meant removing from his old military wardrobe the dress uniform he wore as a hussar major, then, holding Ilona's hand in his own, reverently

208

touching the stripes, tassels and passementeries, the hussar shako, and finally touching with his lips the only family heirloom in his possession, an ancient scimitar supposedly having belonged to General János dé Vitéz Hayduczy.

"Someday we'll come into our own again," he promised Ilona. "When that day comes, the Jews will pay for their treachery!"

Loudly denouncing the Jews always relieved the count's distress to some degree. It was in the stillness of the nights, helplessly lying next to Elena, when scapegoating the Jews failed to cure the source of his deepest humiliation: his impotence.

Amor vincit omnia, he had defiantly proclaimed, yet all he had won in the end was a gray, slow decline into oblivion. Nothing was as it had been when the mere presence of Elena compelled his heart to dance a wild *csárdás* and the rustling of her skirts made his loins come alive with desire. Making love to the daughter of Ilie Corcescu, the great Transylvanian landowner, was an intense, orgiastic pleasure he had never experienced before. He was performing a sacred act. As if he were possessing Transylvania, not just Elena. He penetrated Elena the way his hussar regiment had penetrated towns, taken villages or occupied entire regions, swiftly and purposefully. Flooding her womb with streams of his sperm was the act of fertilizing the Transylvanian plateau, its valleys and peaks and plains, with countless von Tokay de Györ Hayduczys.

But gradually it all began to change, till even fantasies of taking Transylvania through Elena failed to induce erections. His ejaculations were pitiful little temors, thin and devitalized. He blamed the Jews for his impotence, for the drying out of his soul and the sapping of his virility. The night he impregnated Elena with Ilona had been the night of his last orgasm.

After the count's death, Elena made friends with people named Schwartz and Stein and Gold, the very elements responsible for her father's unhappiness, Ilona often brooded. While surrounded by her mother's world of ordinary people, of roomers, boarders, tradesmen, and Jews, Ilona dreamed of her father's old world and of a golden redress whereby her rank would be reinstated and her sordid privations ended.

Ilona's dream seemed to come true one September morning in 1940 when regiment upon regiment of hussar cavalry rode into town and the red-white-green Magyar flags decorated its streets. Dressed in the Magyar national costume, seven colorful skirts and the embroidered tight vest called *pruslik* which pushed up her breasts like two blushing peaches, she was appointed to welcome the hussars officially, which she did with the poise of a queen welcoming her victorious knights.

Her father's "someday" had arrived at last.

It stayed on till another September morning brought to town other regiments and she was left with nothing but a sinking feeling of being again deprived, cheated; of having become an outcast. That was in 1944, when the Red Army had taken the town and a group of Jews, obviously fugitives from the labor force, came out of nowhere and stayed at Pension Amity during the fighting. Her mother hid some of the fugitives in the cellars, some in the attic, even though a neighbor came to warn Elena that a band of Magyar soldiers had taken time off in the heat of battle to go from house to house in search of Jewish deserters. Ilona had been outraged by her mother's concern for the grubby Jews till that morning when Magyar soldiers were retreating while the Russians penetrated the town and Sandor the Handsome made love to Ilona in a dark corner in the cellar, next to her father's old military wardrobe.

The irony of Ilona von Tokay de Györ Hayduczy being the mistress of Sandor Cohn did not trouble her: being an outcast did. It terrified her. A new spirit due to the war and to politics was reshaping the world and she feared her own destruction in this world where a strange breed of Jews was boldly emerging once more. To avoid becoming a pariah she had to hold on to something. Or someone. The only *someone* she could hold on to was her lover. Ilona's survival now appeared to be bound up with Sandor and his people. Being accepted as "one of them" by the people she had been taught to despise was a necessity which slowly turned into an obsession, then into a crusade she waged under the banner of *amor vincit omnia*.

She must explain herself, Ilona thought, make them understand she had been manipulated by people and events; how anti-Semitism was as much part of her upbringing as the Ten Commandments was part of theirs.

210

She thought of Lisa Engler as the most likely to respond to her need. The Jews were treating Lisa in a special way, she had noticed, as if she was the Jewish counterpart of an Ilona von Tokay de Györ Hayduczy. Yes, Lisa could be the key to their world. Through her, Ilona might be accepted.

13

"Let's talk," Ilona told Lisa one day, "get to know each oth-er——"

"Why?"

"Because it might help——"

"Who might it help?" Lisa asked with deadly slowness.

"It might help, that's all," Ilona said, blushing.

"It won't help you with Sandor, if that's what you are after."

"Yes . . . I mean no." Ilona was confused, suddenly thrown by Lisa's direct questions. "Even so . . . I'd like to make friends with you. Just for yourself."

"I don't know . . ."

But the motion of the outstretched hand had created a small radiation which Lisa could not dismiss. Their talks were experimental at first, cautious probings of how deep and how far to go. Ilona was undaunted by setbacks. Her resolution to become "one of them" was recharged nightly in Sandor's arms, making it easier to overlook Lisa's aloofness and occasional hostility the next day.

She began to notice, though, Lisa's tight lips relax, her fists unclench when Ilona spoke of her childhood as an outcast. Once in a while, she even caught a spark of interest in Lisa's eyes, and the hope that Lisa would accept her as a friend, perhaps absolve her of any blame, made Ilona continue to hold out her hand.

Yet Ilona could never be quite sure if Lisa was listening to what she was saying or was slipping into another world. There would be hardly any change in Lisa, only a blank look in her eyes. Then Ilona knew Lisa had sealed herself off from the present and from stories of feuding families and a sickly father to step into a strange world, off limits to anyone except to *their* own. To the survivors. The Jews.

At times Ilona envied Lisa; but envy passed and she began to love her.

"I remember watching Jewish children from my window," Ilona told Lisa one evening, "and uniformed governesses, *fräuleins,* hovering over them. The children seemed different, not merely because they wore hand-embroidered starched little pinafores over fancy dresses. Rich or poor, all Jewish children looked different . . ." She lowered her head, closed her eyes and coughed. Dare she tell Lisa of her father's diatribes? Of Antichrist?

"It was inculcated in me to distrust you. To fear you," Ilona said. "Can't you see it was unavoidable——"

"No!"

"No, of course you wouldn't." Ilona opened her eyes. How much longer must she hold out her hand? She was frustrated. "It's such a clear-cut issue with you," she said reproachfully. "But then the Jews were lucky, weren't they. They always managed to be on the side of justice and——"

"And would you have liked to change places with me, Miss von Tokay de Györ Hayduczy, to be on the side of justice?" Lisa shot out, glaring at Ilona. She pressed her hands to her temples, waited a few seconds. "Did I perhaps forget a title, is that why you don't answer me?"

"Please——"

"You envied everything Jewish, didn't you?" Lisa screamed in her face, "as if only Jewish children had fancy dresses and starched pinafores! You even envy Jewish death, you *goy. Goy* . . ."

Each time she said *goy* she felt light, almost weightless. No more pounding in her head.

Lisa got drunk that night and next morning she hardly remembered anything.

"Listen," Drifter said to her the following day, "go easy on Ilona. I've seen documents, I've spoken to people. Did you know her mother was smuggling food into the ghettos daily? She also kept a Jewish family hidden in the pension cellar long after the Magyars deported the Jews from Sziget. It took guts."

He ran his fingers over his scar.

"It took more than guts. It took real humanity. So few had it, though. Elena Corcescu had it. A woman of valor among thousands. We must never forget that."

Lisa was silent.

"Himy gave Ilona a job," he continued, "because of Elena, not because of Sandor."

"Why should I concern myself with Ilona?" she said. "While I was rotting *then* and *there* she was having a good time and didn't give a damn about——"

"But her mother did!" Drifter cut in. "Ilona was nothing but a bystander——"

"A bystander?" she shouted. "Don't tell *me* about bystanders! Go tell it to the tree stump in my garden. Or to the hole in the wall in my room. Go, tell them about bystanders—peering from windows. Just don't talk to me about bystanders!"

"Give her a chance, girl——"

"You want me to give a chance to the daughter of the Jew-hater, Count Árpád von Tokay de Györ Hayduczy?" she asked shrilly.

"No. I want you to give a chance to the daughter of Elena Corcescu. She deserves it."

A few days later, Ilona said to Lisa: "I am sorry for the other night. It came off differently than the way it was meant. I am indeed a *goy* who has much to learn——"

"Sandor," Lisa said, "surely he'd teach you."

"He can't. Or he won't. It's too much to expect of him. I mean, our affair . . . I think he convinced himself it's separate, peripheral to everything else. Insulated by the night. I don't have the heart to dig into his soul. It would split him further, cause more torment. All I want is to hold on to him——"

"What about my torment, Ilona?"

214

"I thought of it. It must be awful for you to speak of these things with a *goy*. It really unnerves me. But Lisa," she said timidly, "these things ought to be talked about among . . . friends. To clear the air. . . ."

Lisa watched Ilona's cheeks turn to a soft, warm pink. Her own cheeks were burning.

"Can't you simply let things be, for a while," Lisa said. "Everything is still so terribly fresh, raw. It's cruel to dig. You understood it with Sandor——"

"I feel driven to understand why and how it happened. I am afraid that if I don't connect *now*, I never will. Like it's my last chance."

"Let me tell you something." Lisa paused. What Drifter had said to her the other day had struck root in her thoughts but still she had to be cautious even though she was getting less and less worked up in Ilona's presence, just like now. Daily contact made her see Ilona as an individual, apart from the mass of *goyim*. The daughter of Elena Corcescu.

"Let me tell you something," Lisa repeated amiably, "don't try to become the *other*. It won't work anyhow. Stay out of it and you'll live to become an old lady. A countess."

"I don't want to become a countess," Ilona said, "I want to become——"

"I know. You want to become the *other*." She really wants to become Ilona von Tokay de Györ Hayduczy *Cohn*. The thought piqued Lisa. Was she jealous of Ilona's love affair, of having someone to love? "It takes more than wanting it up here," she said touching her head. "It takes feeling the Jewish past inside here." She pointed to her heart.

"I do feel——"

"The taste of thousands of years of persecution? The Inquisition, the pogroms? Dreyfus? The entire insane system of blame, hate, of false and vile accusations, you feel all that? Myths about the conspiracy of the Elders of Zion——"

"What about it?" Ilona was abrupt. "What about the Elders of Zion?"

Lisa stared hard at Ilona. "That's exactly what I mean," she said wearily. "You are hooked to your past——"

"Unhook me, then. What about the conspiracy of the Elders of Zion?" Ilona asked tensely.

"Absurd." Lisa waved her hand impatiently. "Absurd, I tell you, this whole thing—you wanting to feel what a Jew feels without the experience of being one. A shortcut to history through my guts. I resent it——"

"Lisa," Ilona pleaded, "help me understand. What about the Elders of Zion?"

"It's preposterous!" she exclaimed, "you——"

Then she stopped in midsentence:

"All right," she said, "you want to know the truth about the conspiracy of the Elders of Zion. Which one should I tell, I wonder. Your entire history is full of Jewish conspiracies, isn't it? . . ." She screwed up her eyes as though she was concentrating: "I have it! Did you know the Mongols were in the pay of the Elders and that the Mongol invasion of Europe was nothing but a Jewish conspiracy? And what about the black plague? Another Jewish conspiracy to rule the world. . . ." (*eins, zwei, drei, vier . . . deutschland, deutschland über alles*)

Ilona was listening patiently to Lisa's mordant narrative till she noticed that certain look on her face. It only lasted a second.

"Why are you staring at me?" Lisa asked edgily, "what is it?"

"I am sorry." Ilona would have liked to put her arms around Lisa's shoulders. She suddenly looked like a frightened little girl. "We'll talk another day——"

"All right," she agreed, "after you tell me about the *Judenrein* paradise in Sziget."

"It wasn't the way you think it was," Ilona said. "Or maybe it was exactly as you expected it to be. After the Jews were deported everything went haywire; a terrible disruption. Nothing functioned the way it used to. You feared your own neighbor. The Germans. Then the looting began. Then there was dark. Lice . . ."

She looked thoughtfully at Lisa, sighed.

"All along I had a strange feeling of loss. Till one Sunday morning, on the Grand Corso, I knew exactly what was missing. It was a girl on a bicycle I used to see ride in the middle of the Corso, ringing the bell to wake up the dead. I missed not seeing that girl riding her bike. Crazy. I kept hoping she'd appear one day on the Corso."

Ilona reached for Lisa's hand.

"Did the *verboten* signs stay up," Lisa asked, leaving her hand in Ilona's, "the signs reading ENTRY FORBIDDEN TO DOGS AND JEWS?"

"Yes, they left the signs up for a while." She shuddered, clutching Lisa's hand. "How horrid it must have been for you, seeing those signs. At last, I am beginning to grasp what Drifter meant the other evening, that anti-Semitism was like a precious heirloom, handed down intact, with great care, from generation to generation. But now we'll dispose of that deadly heirloom, people like you and me. We'll make up for it, you'll see Lisa, it will be all right, you and I——"

"Stop patronizing me, damn it!" Lisa snapped, and angrily pulled away her hand. "And stop treating me as if I were a *goy*'s show Jew!"

"Please, I only mean to——"

"I don't give a hoot what you mean *now* when it is prudent to mean well. Where the hell were you when it counted?"

"You misinterpret my words, Lisa," she protested weakly, and began to weep. "I can't expiate the world's sins against you. But I am trying to expiate my own sins. *Mea culpa, mea culpa* . . . Can't you see how hard I am trying? Not only because of Sandor . . . What the *goyim* did to you, what *we* did to you, hurts *me. I* am ashamed. I don't envy your pinafores any longer . . . Spit in my face, slap me, kick me—and get it over with. Then we could begin to heal. Both of us. What must I do to make you believe I am sincere? Fall on my knees and beg your forgiveness? Here . . ."

She dropped to her knees.

"Will this help, Lisa?" she asked between sobs, "will it?"

Lisa looked at Ilona's hunched-over body for a long time, then lightly touched her long golden hair.

"It won't help me anymore, that's for sure," Lisa said slowly. "But crying helps, that I know. It may help you, Ilona."

14

By late July the rhythm of life was almost back to normal. And why not?

The Prislop and Solovan mountains were turning green in the background, the rivers Iza and Tisza hugged the town like moats around a castle, and the summer was beautiful once again in Sighet.

Main Street was waking up. Store shutters were raised, Jewish merchants, tailors, carpenters, began practicing their trades once again. Only the whores, Jewish beggars, Jewish children and Jewish old people were nowhere to be found. Farmers came to town twice a week to sell their produce in the Market Place, and a Red Cross truck brought back to Sighet Naomi, Eva, Dolly and Mitzi, Sandor the Handsome's sister.

Naomi went through the rooms in the Kahn house, swept her hands over the furniture, opened closets and shifted cans of Spam on the cupboard shelves in the big kitchen.

"Have you been to my house, Lisa? Is it still there?" Naomi's short hair was brushed back, her drawn face flushed. Tears brimmed in her gray eyes. "What now; when is Miklos coming home. What have you learned of him? Talk to me, Lisa. Just say something. . . ."

No, she hadn't been to her house, Lisa told her. It was all empty, Naftuli had said, everything was gone except the walls. No use going there. When Miklos returned, they would start fixing things up. Their house, Lisa's house.

"It's over, I keep telling myself," Naomi murmured. "Over, done with. No more Somerda, Glatz . . . or Klodzko. I am home. And as soon as Miklos returns . . .

"They grabbed him from me, there on the square," Naomi said, and her mouth hardened. "They announced that children would be given special treatment. I held on to Sonny. He hung onto my neck, his tiny arms clutched my neck right here, see?" She placed Lisa's hand on the nape of her neck. "It's all numb there. I don't feel a thing."

She kept Lisa's hand on the back of her neck.

" 'Mommy,' Sonny cried, 'no go. I stay, Mommy. Mommy.' He was so little. Not even two years old. . . ." She moved away from Lisa: "Oh God, how will I tell Miklos. . . ."

That evening they came to Naftuli's house. Himy the Mogul arrived early, holding Ilona on one arm and food and drink on the other.

"Just watch for this latest deal of mine with the Ruskies," he boasted between drinks. He was jolly, his eyes danced. "Quantity, quantity; that's where the profits are. Big, bigger, biggest. Like the American way of making bigger and better elephants, if you know what I mean. Though who needs elephants? I ask you. But Himy the Mogul's way to make bigger and better salt convoys, ah, that's something!" He smacked his lips, rubbed his hands. "The Ruskies appreciate me, that's sure. I mean, who gets them nylons, now that their *ciassi* craze is over? Nylons for trucks, that is? Himy the Mogul, that's who!"

His tone turned solemn, his eyes teary.

"Should I get through with the convoy smoothly, I'll have a park made where the Orthodox Synagogue was. I'll erect a monument there in memory of the Sighet Jews murdered by the Nazis. A monument inscribed with all the thousands of names. And whatever it costs, let it cost," he said, and opened another bottle of liquor.

"I'll also sponsor the first Jewish wedding. It's time to be fruitful and multiply again. Multiplying time has come. Enough tears." He looked suggestively at the women in the room and his glance lingered briefly on Naomi. He adjusted the knot of his flashy tie, smoothed the lapels of a new barbareeba suit he wore in her honor, swung his right arm forward in a wide arc to check the time on an enormous wristwatch.

Accurately reflecting Himy's major activities, the epithet Mogul had been lately expanded to include Don Juan as well. Himy the Don Juan Mogul. What a name! A title, almost. His chest heaved with pride whenever he thought of it. He was a celebrity in every sense. An *oisher* and a ladies' man. If only the Prince could see him now, Himy would brood sadly, and then buy Lisa another blouse or trinket. Both he and the Prince could have reaped the benefits Himy's remarkable reputation brought. There was plenty to go around, and still plenty left over, as they say.

Himy propositioned every woman he met as a matter of principle. With the exception of Lisa, there was hardly a woman in town he did not approach. Once in a while his propositions were as graceful as belches, but more often than not he encountered resounding success. He persevered with genuine conviction and never took *no* for an answer. Perseverance and pursuit was the formula for his success with women, he claimed. And his fanatical belief that of her six children his mother had loved him best.

He blazed forth and smiled, slept with every available woman an showered money around with a benevolence and generosity one instinctively knew was authentic. The survivors rooted for the success of his business schemes and cheered each time he bragged of a new amorous conquest, as if his masculine prowess was a reflection of their own virility.

In the midst of Himy's banter a woman walked in, shrunken and haggard and old-looking.

"*Shalom*, Jews," she said. "I was told I'd find most of you here."

They watched her standing in the doorway and wondered who she was.

"I am Leah Stein," she said faintly, "Gitl's mother."

Gitl, a classmate of Naomi, had been one of Sighet's beauties. A match with Chief Rabbi Rosenbaum's second son had been arranged for her by Reb Stein, her father. Two weeks before the wedding was to take place, a handsome Romanian officer, in full-dress uniform aglow with gold epaulettes and shiny brass buttons, came to see Reb Stein.

"Gitl and I have been in love with each other for over a year," the officer said. "I now have the honor to ask for your daughter's hand in marriage."

Reb Stein pointed to the door.

"I'd rather see her dead than marry a *goy*," the old man replied.

And so he did: next morning Gitl was found in a field of wheat on the outskirts of Sighet, in the arms of the officer. A double suicide.

At the mention of her name they recognized her. Himy took Leah by the hand and gently led her to a chair. Drifter brought her a glass of wine. Although Leah was not yet fifty years old, everyone stared with awe at her lean, dried-out and wasted face. To them the face of a middle-aged Jew was beautiful.

"Why *I* was spared, I don't know," she said, turning to Naomi. "Why not some of the younger ones? Why was *I* spared, what does God Almighty want of me? Could anyone tell me, why *me?*"

She sipped absentmindedly from the glass.

"I don't even know why I came back to Sighet. There on the square," she said closing her eyes, "it was as if an invisible hand guided me back to the right side after *Malach-Hamoves* Mengele had sent me to the left."

She spat three times at the mention of Mengele's name. So did the others.

"I did go to the left," she continued, "but everything was blurred there. I had lost my glasses, you see. I stepped out of the left column. No, an invisible hand drew me out of there. I told an SS I had lost my glasses. 'Where did you lose them, madam?' he asked me politely. I pointed to the mob on the right, though for all I knew I could have dropped the glasses in the cattle car. It was the hand, I tell you, pointing with my hand. '*Lauf*,' the SS said, 'run and get your glasses, we don't want you to miss seeing anything, *ja?*' I looked for my glasses. They were nowhere. The right column began to move. I was swept along. Now here I am."

She took another sip of her drink, looked at the young faces around her.

"Maybe I came back because of Gitl," she said defensively. "I must talk to her; there is so much to tell. That's all I have left now, my Gitl's grave."

Leah's words slowly made them turn inward, Himy and Gyuri, Imre, Huna, Lisa and Bozsi, Naomi, Naftuli, Eva and Otto, Dolly, and all the rest who were there that evening. They could not bear to look at each other. Each was walled off from the other, and all of them were walled off from the outside. Even Drifter was drinking and stared blankly at the ceiling.

Then Sandor the Handsome and his sister Mitzi arrived. Himy raised his hands in a limp salute. Otto pushed drinks to them, a few bobbed their heads.

Mitzi Cohn had always been a stunning woman. She didn't walk or stroll—she swaggered through town dressed in extravagant costumes, trailed by an entourage of young men who flitted around the pretty and rich Mitzi like moths around a flame. She was still stunning, though her beauty was now different. She was tall, had full breasts and held herself straight, all hundred twenty-five pounds of her. Her short black hair was curly and her eyes shone with the intensity of the Eternal Light before the Ark. Mitzi's movements were accompanied by a jingling sound. It came from a magnificent belt she wore that Sandor had discovered stuffed in the upholstery of a chair when he had moved back to their house. The belt, made of ancient gold coins looped together with silver hooks and eyes, was quite long. Mitzi had tied it in front, midwaist, its ends reaching to her knees, and the coins gave off cheerful little sounds each time she moved.

Ilona now got up slowly, walked over to Mitzi.

"How do you do," Ilona said warmly. "I am so happy to meet you at last. I've heard so much of you from Sandor, as I am sure you too heard of me."

Mitzi tilted her head to one side, contemplating her.

"And why should I have heard of you, Miss . . . Miss?"

"Hayduczy. Ilona von Tokay de Györ Hayduczy," she volunteered helpfully, then asked with astonishment: "Why should you have heard of me? Indeed. Don't you know who hid Sandor when he came back, who took care of——"

"It must have been you, apparently," Mitzi interrupted her.

Still contemplating Ilona, she tore off a coin from one of the loose ends of the belt.

"Here," Mitzi said, flinging the coin at Ilona. "For services rendered. Paid in full, by a Jew. Before witnesses. Now we are even."

Sandor got up but Lisa was next to Ilona ahead of him.

"Shhh . . ." she said, pulling Ilona away. "Shhh . . . You must learn to overlook things, you must. . . ." She filled up a glass with liquor. "You wanted to know what the *other* feels. Now you know. Drink up, Ilona. Maybe you'll get unhooked . . . someday. Let's drink."

". . . let's drink. Come on brothers and sisters," Huna was saying, "let's drink and let's sing. 'Bring the fuse, one two three'. . . ."

Bring the fuse, Lisa thought, yes. Why Leah Stein? Why not someone else? Mamma. Why not Mamma? Leah Stein has nothing but an overturned tombstone in the ransacked, desecrated Jewish cemetery. Lisa joined the crowd in the song, heard herself scream "Szálasy," spew out the name with rage. She had another drink, ran over to Leah, took her face between her hands and touched her eyes with her lips.

Leah put her arms around her.

"Go ahead and cry, *mein kind.* I understand. There are so many reasons to cry. It will relieve you. . . ."

But it did not relieve her.

She sat down, reached for another drink and quickly gulped it down, then tried to get up. She was shaky and sat down again.

"I'll help you," Ilona said.

Drifter saw them leave the room. He went after them.

"I'll take care of her," he said to Ilona outside the door. Ilona stepped back inside.

He put his arm around Lisa's waist and started to walk with her along the porch, towards the cottage. She stumbled on the way. He picked her up, then carried her in his arms, holding her tight.

There was fullness in the hot summer night, in the shadows and the sounds and the smell of jasmine coming from somewhere. The moon was shining. He could see her face clearly, every tiny freckle on it. He became aware of her breasts pressing against him, round and firm, and he stopped abruptly in the mid-

223

dle of the porch. She then slipped her hand through his unbuttoned shirt, touched the short hairs on his chest and snuggled up, inhaling the smell of his body, feeling the texture of his skin.

"It feels soft, warm," she murmured. "Smells good."

Carrying her towards the cottage, Drifter gently kissed her face. A light spasm made him quiver. He continued to kiss her cheeks, feeling a stirring in his groin, and he thought of how soft, how sweet she felt in his arms, like a cuddly little girl. But her breasts were pressing at his chest, increasing the heat inside him. He urgently kissed her mouth, then stopped again: he had a powerful erection. It was an extraordinary sensation, he had forgotten what it felt like.

"Lisa," he whispered, "I want you."

He thrust open the door of the cottage with his foot, then slammed it closed from the inside and sat down with her on the edge of the bed. Shafts of moonlight spilled into the room through the window. A bird trilled in the garden behind the cottage and the sound of a shot split the night. Instinctively, Lisa threw her arms around his neck.

"A drunken soldier," he soothed her. "Don't be afraid. I am with you."

He kissed her again, pushed his tongue into her mouth, moist and hot. She joined her tongue to his. A new liquid breath was permeating her body, making it throb.

He put her on the bed, then stood up.

"I love you, Lisa." His voice was mellow, a sigh. "I must have loved you for some time. Now I want to make love to you."

Yes, yes, Lisa wished to say, but her own excitement was choking her. The alcoholic haze had spent itself and she was now fully conscious of an aching desire to be held by someone, be fondled.

She reached for him.

He quickly took off his clothes, undressed her. He knelt on the floor, at the edge of the bed, caressed her breasts, circled her nipples with his tongue. Then he lay down next to her and guided her hands over his body.

Lisa knew there was going to be some pain in losing her virginity. But she was ready, all ready. Her entire body was pulsating. She willed herself to pretend, for a brief moment, that the hands cupping her breasts, gliding down her abdomen, playing with her pubes and vulva, belonged to Mano. But she saw Drifter's face, breathed in his breath and felt his body weigh down on her.

"Yes, Drifter," she panted, "make love to me. Now."

Drifter spread her legs apart with his knee. He felt her wetness, the musky smell.

Suddenly he rolled off her.

"Oh God," he groaned. "It's gone. I can't do it, Lisa."

He lay motionless on the bed, next to her, flat on his back. He was hurting. His nerves, like overtaut violin strings, were strung to the point of snapping and he wanted them to snap and relieve the strain at last. Get it over with. A restless craving remained in his loins, he had her smell in his nostrils, his mouth still retained the taste of her exploring tongue, and his receded penis was clammy. The accumulated tension reached an almost unbearable pitch.

With an effort, he got up and put on his clothes slowly, then turned towards the bed. He ought to say something to her, he thought, but did not know what. He saw her shape in the moonbeam, she was lying on her side with her back to him and had pulled the sheet up to her shoulders, her knees close to the wall, her head resting on her arm. He had a vague urge to stroke the curve of her hip, touch again the sinuous lines of her body. But he knew the urge was only in his head.

He sighed, then left the room, closing the door carefully.

15

He stayed away from her for four days. The fifth morning she walked into JOINT.

"I must speak to you," she said to him. "Now."

They went to the park, sat on a bench near the pavilion, facing each other. Her eyes scanned his face, searching for an answer, a clue.

He was silent.

"Why do you avoid me, Drifter?" she asked. "What have I done?"

"Done? You've done nothing." His heart hurt, in a new way. He was not used to that kind of hurt.

"But that night," she said haltingly, though her eyes looked straight into his eyes, "something did happen. To both of us. Tell me what happened that night, Drifter."

"There is nothing to tell. You know what happened——"

"Yes. But I know and I don't know. Let me tell you something." She always said this sentence in a certain way, with her chin thrust forward, a resoluteness in her eyes, Drifter mused. But the puckish expression, the childlike defiance, only exposed her vulnerability. He wanted to protect her, reassure her. He took her hand.

"Let me tell you something," she repeated. "What I do know is that I wanted you to make love to me. And so did you."

The pent-up tension of that night returned, perhaps merely the memory of the tension. He needs breathing space, he now realized. Release. Was that what he sought since that night?

"But we didn't make love," he said. "We didn't."

"We did, in a way. Because we both wanted to, very much. Didn't we, Drifter?"

"Yes. But——"

"The wish for making love was there. It made us belong to each other."

". . . we didn't make love though. We can't pretend we did when we didn't. It's not the same——"

"Is that why you avoid me, then?"

"No. No . . . I was embarrassed. I still am. Can't you see how it——"

"Embarrassed? Before me? . . ."

It was so obvious to him why he had to stay away from her. Why could she not see it his way? He had assumed his impotence was caused by the overwhelming need for a woman, long-delayed and now suddenly aroused by her, which he simply could not handle. He hadn't had a woman for more than a year. Or was it two, three years? He had lost count. That night with her, he was bursting with excitement, he wanted her so badly he could barely hold himself together. Like a starving man at the sight and smell of food. A ravenous beast wishing to glut, gorge himself with the stuff—and then unable to swallow even a crumb. He was out of order, a machine nonfunctional due to idleness. That was the reason he could not perform that night: the body-machine had forgotten how.

Her delving back to that night was beginning to confuse him, making him feel uncomfortable. His head started to ache.

". . . whose mess you cleaned up in the Emke Restaurant without a trace of embarrassment," she was saying, "and held my head while I vomited my way from Budapest back to Sighet and protected me like a father protects a child; you embarrassed before me?"

"It's different now. Can't you see? . . ."

"It's different now," she said, "yes. Because now you know

you love me. That's what's different now. And that's what embarrasses you. Or frightens you."

He took a long time to answer.

"No. I was embarrassed because I was impotent; it never happened to me before. That night had nothing to do with love. . . ."

The instant he said those words, he felt he was lying although he was telling the truth. The thought almost split his head. Impossible. He was telling her a lie and yet it was true: that night, he believed, had nothing to do with love, with Drifter and Lisa; it had to do with overstimulation.

It didn't quite balance, though, he now knew. The proportions weren't just right. Could it be that Lisa had stumbled on insights before he did?

He was groping for answers himself.

How can one make love, he wondered, saturate in carnal pleasure, come apart, unglue in ecstasy, when the smell of singed flesh mingles with the scent of sex? Sex and death and love, all coming together that night, had been too much to cope with. His body had rebelled and refused to carry out his lustful desires. What kind of animal was Zoltan Feldman to be aroused by sex even before he mourned properly—or had even learned how to mourn.

Why did he tell her he loved her?

He reached into his pockets for aspirin tablets, the ones he picked up regularly at JOINT. Little white pills, chewable, sealed in small packets. They were shipped directly from America. Over there they understood that filling empty stomachs was not enough. They must have known that heads would ache, split into splinters sometimes. He dug into his pockets, his fingers nervously searching for the little packets with the pills.

He has never been in love, he thought while tearing open a small packet he found at last in his shirt pocket. How could he have said to Lisa, "I must have loved you for some time"?

He must have been thinking of *Piroshka*. She was the only one he has loved. His one and only little girl.

His headache was now subsiding. No, he never loved anyone in a passionate, romantic way. He cared for Elsa, of course he did. She was his wife. Elsa Mendelbaum was his wife.

When the time had come for him to settle down—he was

twenty-one then—his family first sent him on the traditional last fling, the Prague-Vienna-Budapest circuit. It was the path sons of wealthy fathers had treaded for generations prior to their taking on the bonds of matrimony.

His marriage to Elsa was appropriate. A good match. In those days similar backgrounds augured compatibility. Parents' sober choice of a mate took precedence over youthful emotions, which were more often than not temporary, like April showers. Compared to the few lasting marriages born out of spontaneous love his arranged marriage may have seemed prosaic, yet he had liked the solid base of unadulterated domesticity Elsa had brought to his life. The amalgamation of the two big lumber firms in the district after their marriage, the Feldmans with the Mendelbaums, had allowed him to continue, at his leisure, his graduate work in law and political science at the university.

There had been a healthy rhythm to their lives. The evenings of chamber music when Elsa listened to him and his group play Dvorak's Terzetto in C Major; or other evenings when she served Turkish coffee for him and his guests in the study, then discreetly closed the door behind her to let them discuss business or political matters in complete privacy. Still, he was not in love with Elsa. He appreciated her, was truly fond of her. Their sexual relationship was satisfying. Their coupling was enjoyable but without inner explosions. His life was good, he was pleased: it was predictable and controllable.

Then came *Piroshka* and it all changed. The child evoked in him the spontaneous spark of love his marriage did not. She was an extension of him, yet simultaneously a completely unique entity linked irrevocably with him. A breathtaking innocence he adored; a gossamer love, like her blond curls, wrapped around his soul, regulating his heartbeat.

He sighed, closed his eyes.

He used to puff his cheeks and her little fists punched them lightly. He then ejected the air, hissing, "Psssss." She giggled. "Again, Papush, again." He shook his head as he was supposed to. The game was on. "For a kiss?" Her bright blue eyes shone as he quickly nodded, puffed his cheeks again and she smacked a kiss on his face.

The day he was called into the Jewish labor force the five-year-old *Piroshka* had said, "I'll wait for you Papush; I'll wait for you forever." But he never returned, as he had promised her. It was not up to him, of course. Still. He could have perhaps saved her. He should have tried to save her. Or have been with her to the end.

The pain of *Piroshka*'s loss suddenly clawed at him with a fresh intensity. It was beyond the horrendous reality of a child's death by murder. It was the specific agony of *Piroshka* Feldman's death, his own. He was dying her death to be with her and knew he could never recapture her, not even in death, as if *Piroshka* Feldman had never existed.

He turned to Lisa. He does not love her; he is not embarrassed to tell her so. Perhaps just a little guilty.

"Listen," he said dully, "I told you, I wasn't with a woman for over a year; then all of a sudden I realized——"

He stopped abruptly, the pain in his head stabbed at him violently. He must never tell her he loves her. He does not love her. He only loved *Piroshka*; and thinking of her, he said:

". . . how much I love you. But I should sort out my own feelings first."

He saw her lips quiver and thought she would cry. How can he love her when he hasn't yet had time to mourn; what kind of a monster was he?

"We are all crippled," he said. The past was crippling him; the present too. Wasn't it his duty to have brought Lisa home from Budapest? He had to make sure at least one child survives so that all children would survive through her. Just like then. . . .

His headache was excruciating. He tore open another aspirin packet.

"Like during the Warsaw uprising. I had saved a few Jews from the ghetto, did you know?" he asked, chewing a pill. "There was a little girl, a lovely blond child. Yadwiga. Her parents had been shot to death by the Nazis. . . ."

the tatra air, mr. weinfeld said . . .
yadwiga . . . said it smelled like home . . .
we are going home, the child said . . . not to *kenyérmező*
gewalt, yidn, we are lost, it's over . . . over . . .

"Are you listening, Lisa?" Her eyes were on his face, unblinking, staring at him, but he was sure she did not hear him. He continued anyhow: "I placed her with a couple of Jews I smuggled into Hungary. Provided them with false papers. From Hungary they were to cross into Romania, then make their way to Constanta, where there were boats to take them to Eretz Ysroel. One of these days I should look up Yadwiga."

Lisa was now softly humming a melody. It reminded him of an old Gypsy song.

"I must go to Eretz." He was slightly distracted by the song and wished he could remember the words. ". . . or roam through Europe, see what's to be done there. Learn a new way to mourn. Perhaps act it out. . . ."

But the child needs him, she has no one.

Then he suddenly remembered the song Lisa was still humming: It was *The one and only girl to love.* He sighed, his heart was hurting him once more in that strange way, but the sigh turned into a gasp because he felt a hard-on again.

Not again, he thought, not now. No. Not yet. Someday perhaps, someday he'll hold her anew, someday when he'll be free of . . . but not now. It was what had to be.

"That night," he said with excessive calm, "that night showed me . . ." He wanted her. Now? Now! The whirlpool inside him returned. But she speaks of belonging. Belonging, love. Commitments he cannot yet consider. Not before he belongs to himself, to the present. Not before he has mourned.

". . . how fettered we are. How restricted. The trick is to juggle the present without bruising the past, or the other way around. I haven't yet learned how to do that."

His headache was gone, he was in control of himself. There are things for him to do; the world is waiting. He took a deep breath.

Lisa had stopped humming and was listening intently to him.

"Yes," she said. "Let me tell you something, Drifter." Her face was luminous, a blush of red underneath the freckles, her eyes sparkled and her hair retained the sun. Why can't he let himself love her? he thought, the world can wait. Just love her, blot out all else. Love her and heal.

"Love should not be pieced together with a song," she said, "or be a substitute for . . ." She could not complete her thought and shrugged her shoulders. "It should be a joyous belonging, without equivocation. A *coup de foudre.* The one and only choice, regardless of reason. . . ."

231

He looked at her with surprise. There was a new dimension in her. She was awakening, gathering tools for independence, gaining fresh strength; asserting herself stubbornly, defiantly even, and facing her feelings without embarrassment. She was going to come through all right, he thought, and felt respect for her, above all gratefulness, for he knew she could still hold him. Yet he instinctively trusted her to release him.

"I want to go away, Lisa," he said. "Alone. I made some money with Himy. I'd like you to have it. I must get away from here to learn at last to mourn, to live and love without guilt. It's the only way to survive, don't you think so?"

It scared her, the thought of his leaving, and she bent down quickly, brushed her hands over the short grass growing in front of the bench. The soft blades touched her palms, lightly and familiarly.

Then she looked up at him smiling:

"Yes, Drifter. It's the only way."

BOOK V

"Set me as a seal upon thine heart."
—Song of Songs, 8:6

1

Life went on.

Storekeepers were busy with customers, the Market Place teemed with vendors and buyers. Only the clubhouse in Malom Kert was boarded up and the surface of the Samson tennis courts was cracked all over, though the mountains surrounding the town looked more and more like the sentinels of old.

Sighet was beautiful again.

Deathcamp survivors arrived daily. They ached and cried and got angry, then took a deep breath and with the help of JOINT, of Himy, or by themselves began to restructure their lives. For what else was there to do? And does not the Bible teach that a living dog is better than a dead lion?

At night gangs of thieves roamed the town. People walking on the streets after dark were ambushed, robbed of their clothes and left stark naked in alleys or doorways. Those who resisted the attackers were found in the morning with slashed throats or a bullet in their heads. Those who wisely yielded lived to tell of their ordeal although they could not identify who exactly their attackers were.

Even so, the *goyim* claimed that the night raiders were none other than *Ivan*. The Russian soldier, the Russian occupation force, the Red Army, the *goyim* disparagingly called *Ivan*. He was blamed for everything.

"Who but Ivan would do such vile things," the *goyim* said. "First our watches, then our women. Now our clothes. How bestial! Ivan the brute. Ivan the barbarian."

The Jews were skeptical.

"Watches yes; women yes. Soldiers stealing civilian clothes? No! Homegrown thugs, former heroes of the Crossed Arrows Party, crawling out from the woodwork during the night disguised as Russian soldiers, yes!"

Some *goyim* with a lyrical bent, inspired by the first version of Russian bestiality, created new ballads to the tune of *Mack the Knife*. Ballads about carnage, eerie nights, and slant-eyed Asiatic savages with red stars on their sleeves and horns on their foreheads. The Jews refused to sing along even though the melody of *Mack the Knife* was haunting. Instead, they hummed the French hit *J'attendrai*.

That was when whispers of Commie-loving Jews who brought the Red Menace into this world gradually began to spread around town.

August 6 and August 9 came and went by like other ordinary days. On August 10 Gyuri sent word to Himy and Imre to meet him for lunch at the Crown Hotel.

"There was a horrible explosion in the Pacific." Gyuri was chain-smoking. Each time he lit a cigarette his hands trembled. "It was yesterday. The worst ever. I've just learned from a certain source that before yesterday's detonation there was a similar one a few days earlier. I wanted you to know at once of such news."

He stopped talking as a Russian soldier walked in the restaurant. His cap pushed back on his head, the soldier seemed carefree, loose like his unbuttoned, unbelted tunic. He looked around, then took a seat at an unoccupied table next to where Gyuri, Himy and Imre sat.

The three friends pulled their chairs closer to the table and Gyuri lowered his voice: "There is bedlam at the *kommandatura*. What happened in the Pacific, I want to know. And who did what to whom?"

The soldier was paying no attention to them. He ran his fingers over the white tablecloth with a pleased expression, flapped open the white table napkin, then tied it neatly around his neck.

"It had to do with the sun, a terrible explosion of the sun," Gyuri continued in a hush.

Himy and Imre agreed. They too had heard strange rumors this morning of an awesome phenomenon, a supernatural one to be sure: part of the sun had fallen on Japan. Hell from Heaven. It had burned the entire complex of islands in the Pacific, and Hirohito and Tojo had surrendered instantly. Not much was left of Japan. The heat generated by that terrible explosion was now permeating other continents, scorching the earth in its wake. People insisted that the mildly warm summer days had abruptly become sweltering and that these hot days were precursors of the scorching to come to Sighet. Some of the town's people could even detect a change in the shape of the sun: it wasn't round anymore, they said, it looked like the moon, because a portion of the sun, the part which fell over Japan, was missing. That was why the sun looked like the moon.

While they talked, the Russian soldier had taken an apple out of his pocket. He breathed vigorously on it, gave it a quick sheen with the napkin and put it on the table, in front of him. He looked around for a few seconds, then, reaching over Gyuri's shoulders, grabbed a knife from their table and began peeling the apple.

The conversation halted for a moment, then Gyuri continued as if nothing had happened: "Everyone is jumpy at the *kommandatura*. I wonder what's going on. A new war?"

The Russian had meticulously peeled the apple and had cut it into quarters. He reached over Gyuri's shoulders again, this time retrieving a fork from their table, and stuck it into a quarter. Impaling each quarter with a florid movement of his little finger, he ate the apple slowly. When he finished, he wiped his mouth with the edge of the tablecloth and got up.

Imre had been watching the soldier from the corner of his eyes since he came in. His presence had not been acknowledged by anyone. The waiters had passed him by without stopping to pour water in the glass on his table or to show him a menu. Everyone pretended the Rusky was not there, Imre mused, as if denying his presence would make him vanish like a bad dream. It won't help, he bristled; such an approach is doomed to fail. And maybe underneath, the Russian soldier was a plain human being, a bit frightened and confused, just like them.

"You know," he said to Gyuri and Himy, "we ought to have a heart. We ought to know better too: a little show of friendship could be more effective than a lot of snubbing."

By now the soldier was near the door. He stopped and turned around, then took off the napkin, still tied around his neck like a bib. He carefully refolded the napkin to its original folds and put it back on the table. His eyes fell on a stain on the tablecloth. He blushed, then rubbed it with the sleeve of his tunic but the stain on the tablecloth remained. He shrugged his shoulders, smoothed again the tablecloth with his palm and picked up the knife and fork.

"Spasiba, tovarish." He pressed the knife and fork in Gyuri's hand. *"Harasho,"* he said with a shy smile, *"kulturna, harasho."*

2

But early next morning *kulturna* was not quite *harasho* nor were the hearts of the Jews particularly keen on friendship with the Russians. In fact, the Jews were shocked, alarmed, and angry, precisely in that order when Yosl and Abe brought the news that Erno the engineer had been dragged out of his bed during the night and taken to Villa Grodl.

"With my own eyes I saw Erno handcuffed between two Ruskies," Yosl said.

"And I shadowed them to the Grodl," Abe added. "I heard screams. I swear."

The Jewish shopkeepers pulled down their store shutters and marched to the park.

"The Grodl again," they grumbled. "The former headquarters of the Hungarian secret police. Of the Gestapo. Splotches of Jewish blood still on its walls——"

"Now the NKVD. It carries on with the tradition. Our liberators, the Russians, taking a leaf from the Nazis," they seethed.

By noon the park was jammed with people. Every Jew in Sighet was there. Even the peasants in the market had closed up their stalls or tied up their bundles and came to the park.

It was hot. Some looked at the sky and thought another piece of the sun was going to get unhinged and fall on them, as had

239

happened in Japan. They became frightened and considered disbanding. Then the additional news reached them that Erno was not alone at the Grodl: six to ten more Jews had been picked up by the Russians and taken there.

The Jews forgot all about the sky and the sun, shook their fists and began to shout.

"Action!" someone yelled.

It was Huna the Butcher.

"Yes, action!" the crowd shouted back, "let's show them!"

Huna jumped on a bench in the center of the park. He was tall, his bony face bathed in sweat, his eyes bulged.

"Chaverim!" he yelled. "Brothers, listen! Jews are again in the Grodl!"

An ominous dirge rose from the crowd:

"The Grodl, the Grodl!"

"Are we going to let them do it to us anew and just stand by?" he screamed.

"No! Never!"

"Action! Action! Now!"

"To the Grodl!" Huna thundered.

Suddenly Imre jumped on the bench, next to Huna.

"Hold it!" he shouted, "hold it!" Imre's blond hair seemed to melt under the sun and the crowd, mirrored in his eyeglasses, was dwarfed and distorted by the convexity of the lenses. "Hear me out first," he yelled and grabbed Huna's arm. "Facts, let's have facts first. Consider——"

Huna wrenched his arm free. "Facts, consider," he mimicked Imre. "Scream and yell and kick up a fuss if they try as much as touch us, isn't that what you said not long ago, Mr. Imre? Well then, they touched us," Huna bellowed. "Think with your head not with your ass! As for me, I am through chewing the cud with my pants full of shit. I am not afraid of them! Facts, facts . . . up their asses! Let's go!"

"No, no! Wait!"

". . . for another pogrom?"

"Slaughter——"

"Jews in the Grodl!"

"But listen," Imre yelled and Huna yelled back:

"No! Shut up and you listen!" Saliva dribbled from the corners of his mouth, a vein in his thick neck throbbed furiously.

"And let the world listen too: a tooth for a tooth! The same justice for all! No more is Jewish blood cheaper than *goyish* blood!"

His shrieks slashed through the air and a hysterical shiver rippled through the crowd:

"Yes—no more cheap Jewish blood."

"No more! Never! Never!"

"Turd and manure they made of us!" Huna continued to yell. "That was all they considered Jews good for! All right, we'll show them right now what Jews are good for!" He pulled out a long butcher's knife tucked in his belt, held it up and pushed Imre aside. "We have nothing to lose! We've lost all in the crematoria in Auschwitz!"

"Dachau!"

"Treblinka!"

"To the Grodl!" Huna screamed and the crowd saw the butcher's knife glint in the sun.

"Burn the fucking place!" they yelled.

"Burn the Grodl, burn the Grodl! Yes! Burn the Grodl!" The frenzied crowd stomped and rasped under the hot sun: "Burn the Grodl! Burn the Grodl!"

Gyuri suddenly pushed forward. No one had seen him before. He hopped onto the bench next to Huna and Imre and caught Huna's raised arm holding the knife.

"Wait!" Gyuri shouted, "wait and hear me out!"

"Let's hear him!" Imre yelled.

"No! To the Grodl!"

". . . and burn it!"

"Listen!" Gyuri was shouting, "I've just come from the *kommandatura*. Erno had been arrested, it's true; but only him, no one else. He is in the Grodl——"

"Why?" someone screamed, "what's the charge?"

"Been denounced as subversive by one of the town's patriots." Gyuri's lips were thinly drawn. "Erno has nothing to fear if he is innocent——"

"If, if!" Huna angrily pushed aside Gyuri and Imre. "If! Bullshit! While we haggle, they are torturing a Jew. Maybe killed him already, or shipped him to Siberia. Gestapo, NKVD, It's the same, don't you see! Let's go!" He jumped off the bench.

"Wait! Wait!" Gyuri was flailing his arms, yelling, but the crowd closed behind Huna and began to follow him.

Gyuri's cry now pierced the crowd: "Vad, remember Vad!" A few turned around. "You want another Vad? Vad! Vad!"

Huna now stopped near the end of the park and heard Gyuri scream:

"They are ready for you as they were ready in Vad for the peasant demonstrators! With machine guns in front of the Grodl!"

"Then let's arm!" Huna yelled from the head of the crowd. "I have knives, a few guns——"

"Give me a chance," Gyuri began but someone shouted:

"Who gave my mother a chance?"

". . . my little son . . ."

". . . my father . . ."

"Wait till sundown, that's all I ask!" Gyuri said. "If I can't get Erno out by sundown, then you lead us, Huna."

It was now late in the afternoon. The sun had stayed in the sky intact and its inflamed red had mellowed to rust. The peasants hitched the horses up to their wagons and carts and drove back to their villages. A few *goyim,* who had joined the crowd during the afternoon, stayed for a while, then they went home to their families and their suppers.

The Jews remained in the park, waiting for Gyuri.

"We have time," they said, "lots of time. Nobody is waiting for us."

"After Erno had restored electric power to the town," someone recalled, "he discovered all his family's belongings in the home of Karmany."

"A bastard," someone else said, "a former Hungarian gendarme with cocky feathers in his shako. A son of a bitch."

"Karmany refused to return anything to Erno. He claimed it was an award from the Hungarian police department."

"Erno had to get an injunction from city court to get back what was his."

"And Karmany now cooks up a little revenge . . ."

"Bastards," Himy cursed, "sons of bitches, the whole stinking lot. The Ruskies, they should have checked with us before dragging a Jew out of his bed. A little friendship goes a long way, what Imre? A little talk about salt and trucks and profits between the *tovarishes* and me will go a longer way. Leave it to Himy the Mogul, I say."

He noticed Olga Petrescu enter the park and walked up to her.

"Miss Petrescu." He bowed. "You come to the park. For what?"

Olga looked through him.

"It's strictly a Jewish matter this business today," he continued. "Did you know that, Miss Petrescu?"

She was still looking past him.

"Permit me to introduce myself: I am Himy the Mogul, at your service. Some call me Himy the Don Juan Mogul. But you just call me Himy. And as long as you are waiting," he said obligingly, "why not wait together with me and my friends?"

She shrugged her shoulders and followed him.

"Meet the friends of Himy the Mogul," he proudly said to her, "Miss Lisa, Imre . . ."

Himy fawned over Olga like a peacock in heat trying to arouse an indifferent hen. Lisa noticed Olga's eyes aimlessly wandering over the people in the park and wished Olga would at least acknowledge Himy's presence with a glance. Even such slight recognition could have probably put him at ease, soften the rigid lines of his terse smile.

Then she thought again of Drifter, as she had done several times during the day; what would he have said; done? Would he have been with Huna or Gyuri?

3

It was way past sundown when Gyuri returned to the park with Erno. They got up on a bench and Gyuri placed his hand on Erno's shoulder.

"Here he is, free and in one piece," he told a cheering crowd. "A stiff drink and he'll be as good as new. We could all use a drink, I bet. It's open house at Naftuli Kahn's. Let's all go there."

Naftuli received them with food and drinks and an unctuous smile. He had lately become a generous host. There were always plenty of bottles of liquor and cans of Russian caviar on his table. He even paid Anna to deliver fresh eggs and milk regularly to the house. A few Jews thought of Naftuli's burst of hospitality as concrete expressions of thanks for Naomi's survival. But those who remembered his previous penuriousness were slower to make sense of his present prodigality. A number of Jews wondered just where indeed Naftuli had found money for such fancy spreads. Some Jews also noted how well stocked he kept the premises of THE HOUSE OF ENGLER AND SONS, always piled with fresh merchandise. Naftuli himself was eager to dispel speculation about his prosperity: "A little luck on the black market, that's all. It can happen to anyone, no?"

* * *

Huna slapped Erno on the back, shook hands with Gyuri.

"You were right this time. Still, we must be ready——"

"Yeah. Keep alert," Abe said. "Organize night patrols——"

"First we must learn self-defense," someone said.

"Sure, Huna could teach us."

"Huna, yeah. He was the only one who had guts."

"But guts alone's not enough," Huna said bashfully, as if ill at ease with his newly won prestige. "Would Erno be here tonight if it wasn't for Gyuri?"

"It wasn't my doing," Gyuri said, without further elaborating on this point. "But this I can tell: it was Karmany who denounced Erno. He is a dangerous man, this Karmany. He should be watched."

"He will be," Himy said. "I promise, I promise. Leave it to Himy the Mogul." He poured himself a drink. "Enough talk. It's time to celebrate. Celebration time is here. Let's drink and dance." He raised his glass, winked at Olga. *"Lechaim!"* he said, and downed the drink.

The fingers of Tzofi the musician deftly ran over the accordion keys. His eyes were closed, a beautiful smile on his face and an unlit cigarette between his lips. He was playing the *hora*.

Just like in the olden days at the Habonim Zionist meetings, Lisa reflected, watching the crowd dance *Hava Nagila*. There was nothing to celebrate then, she reminded herself. And now? Now, mourning properly becomes a celebration of sorts. Hadn't Drifter been trying to tell her that? She saw the drink in front of her and pushed it aside. She had no taste for liquor tonight: the taste of loneliness was in her mouth. She got up to go to her cottage to cry away that taste.

Someone grabbed her hand and she found herself in a circle of dancers. All, except Olga and Erno, were dancing, whirling and stomping and clapping. Lisa danced along with them for a while, then broke away, pulled Huna into the center of the circle and linked opposite arms with him. The rest of the dancers stopped, widened the circle while continuing to sing, clap and step up the pace each time Lisa and Huna changed arms. They were dancing faster and faster, the room began to spin and the people in it fuse into an amorphous ring orbiting with the spinning room.

"Harasho. How nice."

A tall Russian captain, with black hair, a proud aquiline nose, high cheekbones under deep-set dark eyes, stood at the door smiling at the now motionless crowd. A man in a Russian officer's uniform, addressing them in fluent Romanian, in a warm friendly manner, was such an unusual sight that it stunned the crowd and, for a moment, he seemed to them to be the earthly incarnation of a good *malach,* an angel who had come to watch over them.

"Go on dancing. It is good to dance," the captain urged, but no one moved. The crowd still stared at him in wonder.

He stepped into the room, walked up to Huna and Lisa.

"Please," he said and put his hands on her waist, twisting her gently to the right, then to the left, "dance with me."

She did not wish to dance anymore, thank you, she wanted to say. She really wanted to go to her room all along to wash away that lonely taste with—what? Tears? No, that doesn't help. Perhaps touching contours of familiar objects might. Yes, after the party will be over she'll go to the safe (six, nine, seven, wasn't that the combination?), take out Papa's watch, hold it in her hand. But she must be careful not to scatter the rest of the jewels. No, no, she doesn't want to dance with the captain and breathless, flushed, she waved her hand and said:

"I'll gladly dance with you, captain," then danced with him as if all her life she had been dancing only with him.

When they stopped Gyuri announced:

"This is Captain Leonid Nicolaievich Yashenko. A friend. It is he who cleared Erno of the charges. Without the captain's help Erno wouldn't be here tonight." He poured vodka into two glasses, offered one to Captain Yashenko and raised the other.

"To your health, captain," Gyuri said solemnly. *"Nazdorovie!"*

"Lechaim!" the captain responded and the Hebrew word coming from his lips galvanized the crowd. Pushing Lisa aside, they surged towards him, vying to shake his hands, at least touch him. A miracle at last: the captain was one of them: *amchu.* A Jew!

It was late in the night when Olga Petrescu tapped Erno on the shoulder:

"You've suffered enough today. Come, Jew, let's fuck. You'll forget all the bad things, for a while."

4

After they had stopped dancing, and the people crowded around the captain, Lisa left the room. The breeze on the porch restored evenness to her breathing. She listened for a few minutes to the laughter and music filtering out, then went into her own room, closed the door, and opened the window wide.

Her skin was tender, hot, as though sunburned. The captain's hands on her waist, she mused, had been like a band holding her together. She felt feverish, got undressed and stretched out on the bed. She began to shiver, still feeling hot. It was going to be one of those wide-awake nights, she thought, the same as the first night she had come back to Sighet.

Or the first night of liberation.

That first night without armed SS guards, without dogs, without Nazis. That first night of freedom.

The Russian army was ten kilometers from Weisswasser, the camp she had been brought to from Auschwitz in December. During the day the Nazis in charge of Weisswasser had taken to their heels dressed in civilian clothes, their heads pulled down between their shoulders, headless freaks running to surrender to the Americans. They were very specific on that, the Nazis: they were not going to surrender to the Russians or even to the English or the French. Only to the Americans. The factory SS supervisor too went over to the Americans but *he* wanted to bring them proof of his sterling record: a live Jewess with number A-7665 tattooed on her arm: Lisa Engler.

She had run back to her bunk, run away from the SS supervisor, and lay on her back with eyes closed to disconnect herself from the inmates' frenzied commotion. Frenchmen from a nearby prisoners of war camp had come over to the women's camp in the afternoon and had assured them the war was indeed over. But the women were too frightened to leave camp. They were still darting about, their pent-up tensions giving way to hysterical laughter, weepy lamentations and gloomy silences.

She just lay on her bunk, the rush of emotions almost paralyzing her. All her nerves were greedily absorbing the meaning of that first night of freedom, but her body was helpless even to stir. She did not mind that numbness, it was only a physical insensibility. She knew it was over, the nightmare had come to an end, and she wanted to feel its impact fully, till it blotted out all other sensation. She wanted to be sure to always remember that night, be sensitized forever by its horrible greatness, always to recall the density of her feelings, the enormous leaden heaviness of an imminent but uncertain rite of passage.

She was still fully awake when the Red Army rolled into the village at sunrise.

It was the morning of May 8.

She had run outside the camp and she saw them, sleepy-eyed on their huge tanks, the first Russian soldiers she had ever seen. She remembered one soldier rubbing his eyes, looking at her with disbelief, rubbing his eyes again, then throwing her a package of cigarettes wrapped in a daisy-patterned kerchief.

The songs and laughter from the room had now died down. She heard Naftuli say, "Any time friends, just any time," then lock the kitchen door.

The leaden heaviness of that other night returned, total recall as she had wished it. She started to cry, first softly, like a whimpering child. She did not know then that that first night ending one nightmare was the beginning of another.

Papa.

Mano.

Drifter.

5

Next morning she went to the Market Place to see Anna. In front of her stall, Anna was goading shoppers to buy her produce. When she saw Lisa, she took a basket from the cart.

"I picked them this morning." She removed grape leaves from the top of the basket. "It's for you, miss. You can still see the dew on them." The basket was filled with purple-red raspberries and firm, luscious cherries the color of burgundy wine. Anna refused to take money.

"God forbid!" she exclaimed, crossing herself. "Never. Not from you, miss. I want to share a little from what I have. Isn't that what the good Lord wants us to do?"

"Look what Anna gave me," she said, bursting into Tibor's drugstore in the center of Main Street. Tibor had returned from Dachau a month earlier and had opened up the store with help from JOINT and Himy. The store had become one of the survivors' social centers. There wasn't a day someone didn't come by to hear the latest news and Tibor's crackling comments.

"Here, Tibor." Lisa scooped out a handful of cherries and raspberries from the basket. "Help yourself."

"Could I have some too?" a voice called from the back of the store, and Captain Yashenko came forward. "I was wondering what happened to my dancing partner last night? Disappeared, like Cinderella . . . I have her glass slipper, though," he said laughing. "It will fit you, I'm sure."

"Do you think so?" She blushed, for she was hoping, suddenly and unaccountably, that he was right. "Till we find out," she said shyly, and held out to him her cupped hands holding the fruit, "please have some. They were picked this morning."

"What's your name, *devushka,*" he asked, "won't you tell me your name first?"

"Lisa Engler," she answered, still holding out her hands. He took a few berries, ate them slowly, keeping his eyes on her face.

"Lisa," he then said softly, pronouncing the name with the mellow Russian sound of *Ljisa.* "What a lovely name. Come on a picnic with me, Lisa, this afternoon," he urged. "You too Tibor. Close up the store, bring some friends along, if you wish." He glanced at his wristwatch. "We could meet here at three o'clock. Will you come, Lisa?"

"Yes, Captain Yashenko. I will come."

A Jeep was parked in front of the drugstore when Lisa returned with Ilona and Himy. Tibor had closed the store and was talking with Imre and Bozsi. A Russian driver sat at the wheel holding on his lap a tray covered with a white napkin.

Captain Yashenko took Lisa's hand and got in the front seat of the Jeep with her. The rest sat in the back.

"Where to?" the captain asked.

"To the Malom Kert," Himy suggested.

On their way a Russian lieutenant waved them to a stop. The captain asked him to join them.

"I didn't invite Grisha Keroff," he told Lisa later, "and I apologize for an unexpected guest. But once he saw us . . ."

They sat on the grass under a willow. Lieutenant Keroff, also speaking Romanian fluently, his eyes darting from one person to another, swamped them with questions. Who were they? What did they do? And what did they think of the war?

"Comrade Grisha," the captain said after a while, "relax, will you? You can get into historical dialectics later. There is a proper time for everything. Now it's time to eat and drink to friendship among all peoples." He motioned to the driver, then took off his military jacket and unbuttoned his tunic. "Come," he said to Lisa, "come and sit near me."

He held her hands and touched each one of her fingers separately, stroked them one by one, then caressed them lightly, as if pleased that all ten were there.

"The peoples of the Soviet Union won the war," Keroff was saying. "The Americanski, did they stop Hitler?

"Did the English? The French?" he asked triumphantly, as no one had answered. *"Nyet!* It took us, the strong, peace-loving peoples of the Soviet Union, to bring the war to an end. Stalingrad, that's where victory began. Once we started rolling in our tanks nobody could stop us. The Americanski, the English, hah! All soft, all mush."

"With respect, lieutenant," Himy said, "with great respect, lieutenant, sir, comrade, weren't the tanks you rolled in American Sherman tanks?"

"So what if they were?" he replied with heat. "There was a fascist-imperialist war the capitalists brought upon themselves which they couldn't have won without our help. Look at what happened even now: for years the Americanski tried to defeat Japan and couldn't. But as soon as the Soviet Union declared war on Japan, boom! the war was over!"

"I see, lieutenant, comrade, sir," Himy said seriously. He noticed Imre biting his lips, grimacing to attract his attention. Himy winked at him, noisily blew his nose in a polka-dotted handkerchief, tapped a cigarette on the lid of a large cigarette case, then lit the cigarette with a lighter. "I see what you mean," he said at last. "The Soviet Union declares war on Japan just before that big explosion, the boom! as you've just said. How clever. And that big boom, you must have done it, a Russian boom, no?"

"Konyeshna, of course!" Lieutenant Keroff snapped.

The *zsids,* Keroff thought, always provoking, always resorting to their old tricks. Like this capitalist here, tapping a gold cigarette case, using a gold lighter. The big boom indeed! What did he mean, that sarcastic jackass of a *zsid,* the Soviets do not have their own scientists? He looked at them testily, noticed Yashenko holding hands with the red-haired girl.

These *zsids,* he thought again, they cling to each other like magnets. With all the upheaval going on they still manage to find each other. Uncanny. Then he remembered these Jews with whom he sat under the willow were Nazi victims, after all. A little more patience . . .

He motioned them closer with his index finger.

"Stalin, a great man of the people, leave it to him. He knows what to do. About bombs too. He will bring peace and justice to the world. See this?" He slapped his left leg. It gave a hollow, wooden sound. "I lost it in Stalingrad. And see this?" He slapped his other leg. "Healthy flesh. But if Stalin wants it, I'll give him this one too."

He took a long drink.

"You people will be educated," he said. "You will learn in proper time, as the comrade captain just said, about communism, about our new way of life."

"Tell us *now* about that new way of life, please lieutenant," Lisa asked.

He looked at her with interest. Her cheeks were aglow, as if a bulb was lit inside her. His eyes skimmed over her blouse molding her breasts.

"Your new way of life," Lisa reminded him.

"Ah yes, the new order. The Soviet state is the bastion of the people," he said fervently. "The beacon for world revolution." He leaned against the trunk of the willow, reached for a leaf, took it between his lips and looked into the far distance.

"Think of a country where everyone is free and everyone is equal," he said, chewing the leaf. "Such a country is the Union of Soviet Socialist Republics, where the root of all evil, class differences, has been extirpated and there is now but one class: the proletariat. Each gives according to his ability and receives according to his needs."

Lieutenant Keroff looked at their serious faces, threw away the leaf and closed his eyes to enjoy the image of his land. The vastness of Mother Russia humbled him; his love for her was endless. Then he pulled himself together, opened his eyes and continued to instruct:

"Who takes care of the just distribution of economic and social responsibilities and benefits in a classless society? The answer is: The Communist Party. The party provides all the people with jobs, houses, education, health care. The competitive and exploitative drives, the tools of capitalists, have been eliminated in the Soviet Union. There is no profiteering, no unemployment. Religion, the opium of the suppressed peoples, has no place in an emancipated state like the Soviet Union. The religious mumbo jumbo . . ."

Captain Yashenko stood up.

"Come, Lisa," he said quietly, "let's take a walk. He is a truly dedicated man. He can go on like this for another hour."

They walked along the Iza, the captain holding Lisa's hands. They walked in step, without speaking. The river flowed slowly, almost silently. It washed gently against its banks, depositing little wet pebbles, brownish-green leaves, nibbling bits of earth from the shore.

Lisa's fingers were interlocked with the captain's. Everything else ceased to affect her except the sensation of his fingers touching hers. It was all that mattered, all she wanted to feel at that moment, and she knew that that moment was elemental, pure, and nothing else intruded into that moment, nothing. As if all were starting from the beginning.

They stopped and he held both her hands in his.

"Golubka," he said, "little dove. I could hardly wait for this morning to find you. I wanted you to know that last night, when I saw you, something happened to me."

He again saw her as he saw her from the doorway, dancing with perfect grace, bend and turn and arch with supple, gentle strength, radiating an innocence in motion that touched his heart against his will but that he would not, perhaps could not, stifle. As if a connection that had always been on the verge of occurring had at last clicked into place. It was an unexpected feeling, overwhelming and strange, that inner wave that went through him, and he thought of a warm soft dove and knew he had to hold her.

He pulled her close to him, took her face between his hands.

"Within the hour I shall have to leave. Orders. I must speak to you frankly, straightforwardly, for there isn't much time. I wish to find you here when I come back, in a few days, perhaps in a week. I know I'll be back, that's certain, if you tell me you'll still be here."

She rested her head on his chest, looked up at him:

"Yes, Leonid, I'll wait for you to come back." She was happy. She smiled. "No matter how long it takes, I'll wait."

6

Next day the town was agog: Bozsi and Imre were planning to get married the following Friday afternoon. The news stirred up Jews and *goyim* alike. The former were confused, the latter scandalized. A Jewish wedding, the *goyim* muttered, how can the Jews think of propagating, of loving, when only a year ago . . .

"That's precisely the point," Imre said a few days before the wedding. "The *goyim* think we are through, finished. That the Jews are kaput. Well, they'll see how kaput I am." He playfully smacked Bozsi's back. "I am getting married, that's how kaput I am. We'll make babies again. Jewish babies."

His friends nodded slowly, thoughtfully, and just wondered.

"Getting drunk every night," Imre continued, "is no solution. One still wakes up in the morning with the same pain in the gut. We cannot drink away our misery——"

"So what else is new?" Otto said bitterly, then opened his guitar case, took out the instrument.

"We are alive, that's what's new! We are not caving in, that's what's new! We'll go on living like men——"

"Who first need facts," Abe quipped, thinking back to Imre's stand during the Erno protest.

"You still don't understand, do you?" Imre asked patiently, and adjusted his glasses on the bridge of his nose. "There is a long road between caving in and rushing headlong into a hail of bullets. That road is called 'the middle road.' Look," he said taking off his glasses, "I want to live with my eyes open because I've had it with the old song about God, America and England; I am through with that type of ostrich strategy. But I don't want to gallivant around the world either, searching for new opportunities. I am home here, this is my land——"

"Don't make me laugh, buddy, with this new song of yours, 'I am home here'!" Otto plucked a guitar string after each word. "Some song," he said. "It stinks."

"Have you heard the latest story?" Tibor cut in, "about the Devil on a motorcycle who had been tailgating the limousine in which Truman, Churchill and Stalin were riding on the *autobahn?*" Without waiting for an answer, he proceeded: "Irritated by the Devil's pursuit, Truman takes out of his wallet a batch of hundred-dollar bills, opens the car window and throws $25,000 to the Devil, who doesn't even bother to pick up the money but continues to pursue them. Now Churchill reaches in his wallet for a batch of English pounds, opens the window and throws £10,000 to the Devil, who still continues to pursue them, again without even bothering to pick up the money. Eventually Stalin takes a slip of paper from his pocket, writes a few words on it and throws the note to the Devil. Now the Devil picks up the note, reads it, then quickly turns his motorcycle around and speeds away in the opposite direction. Miffed that the Devil rejected their bribes but not Stalin's, Truman and Churchill ask: 'What did you promise in your note, Marshal Stalin, to have persuaded the Devil to leave us?' 'My friends,' Stalin replies with a sly smile, 'I promised him nothing. I simply wrote, 'This road leads directly to Russia.'"

The men laughed. Tibor took a deep drag on his cigarette.

"What's the matter with you, Imre," he said, "can't you see where this road leads?"

"What about you? I don't see you making an about-face——"

"Just wait till my little sister writes to me from the convalescent camp in Sweden that she is well again. Will I make an about-face then! By the time the Ruskies slap their paws on this country I'll be somewhere else, you can bet your eyeteeth on that! I'll be somewhere else, read about the takeover while puffing on a Havana cigar, shake my head, roll my eyes and exclaim, 'Tsk, tsk, what a shame!' Then go on about my business——"

"With such a cynical attitude, why the hell did you bother to open a drugstore," Imre retorted, "what for?"

"For work. It keeps me from getting depressed while I'm waiting for news from my sister. But if I smell foul play even before I hear from her, I lock the door, turn the key over to whoever cares to have it and leave. Free, easy and without regrets."

"My valise is packed. All ready, under the bed," Yosl said.

"Mine too," said Ezra.

"Everyone is in transit," Otto remarked wryly, "only our friend Imre digs in."

Imre put his glasses back on, looked at them as though they were naughty kids bent on mischief, too far gone to be straightened out. He shook his head in disappointment and gravely said:

"I refuse to apologize or to be embarrassed for loving this land. Maybe this land *is* like a whore—so I am going to help rehabilitate the whore. Restructure her. There's a good chance, my friends, to do something important right here where a new society is being constructed. I am tired of always running somewhere else. I am here, not somewhere else, therefore I want to be part of *this* society. I am convinced we have an opportunity here, at last, for a decent life. That's why I am settling down, getting married. Dig in, as you said, and have children. Perpetuate something else than loneliness. Children; continuity. It's the only way to win——"

"And Jews will be peers of *goyim* from now on," Otto cracked.

"Yes!" Imre shouted. "Defeatist attitudes like yours notwithstanding. Yes, a thousand times yes! We are all part of humanity, aren't we? What was this war all about? About individual freedom, wasn't it? If I can't believe in that, after all we've gone through, I might as well lie down and die."

7

Imre did not lie down and die. To the contrary. In the end all Jews had their hands or fingers in the wedding for it was, they realized, a singularly meaningful event in Sighet, this first marriage of deathcamp survivors. Prior to the wedding each Jew brought the couple a present—a special goblet, a *kiddush* cup, an old silver condiment holder shaped like a fish, a *mezuzzah*, priceless "little somethings"—considering there wasn't much to give from.

Himy was paying all the wedding expenses, of course. Wasn't it he who called attention to the fact that the time was ripe to multiply?

"What an event!" he exclaimed, mopping his forehead each time he met a Jew. "We'll have the best at this wedding, the Mogul says so. Money is no object. Food, drinks, the best! It's going to be a feast. A jubilee. The first wedding after the slaughter. It will be remembered, I promise. It must be remembered!"

Even Mayor Barka got into the act and announced he personally would officiate at the marriage ceremony.

"Then let Senator Petrescu be there too," Imre told Lisa. "Won't you please ask him to come?"

* * *

Two days before the wedding Lisa went to the Petrescu mansion. The senator was sitting in the garden, shielded from the sun under an umbrella, reading. He listened with interest to her.

"It's an honor to be invited," he said. "Yes, I shall attend the wedding."

On the ground near him was a pile of books, some with markers between the pages, others lying open, face down. He pointed to the book he was holding in his hand:

"Plato. *The Republic.* Extraordinary. Each time I read it I find new meaning in Plato's vision." He remembered something, his face became animated: "Oh yes, what did you think of Plato's *Dialogues?*"

"Nothing. I haven't read it yet." The senator's remoteness irked her. He could relate to her only through books. She now regretted coming here.

". . . the prisoner in the cave recognizes as reality nothing but the shadows of those objects," the senator was saying. She tittered, then wondered whether he heard her. He was eagerly leafing through a book. No, he did not even hear her. The book again, the only relevancy in his life.

"Ah! I found the place," he said genially. "After the prisoner is freed from the cave he believes the objects he now sees are not as real as the shadows of those objects he formerly saw. The proposition is then to make him gradually grow accustomed to light after he has left behind the cave and its shadows," he droned on, a faint hum in his voice, "so that he may clearly perceive things in the upper world. . . ."

She watched his finger on the page move along each line and wondered whether he knew.

"Here it is!" he called out enthusiastically. "Let me read it to you: 'In the world of knowledge, the last thing to be perceived and only with great difficulty is the essential Form of Goodness.'"

Lisa's eyes were now on the senator's lips though the meaning of the words eluded her. She wondered again whether he knew what was said about his daughter Olga.

There were rumors of orgies and debauchery, of nightly depravities beyond imagining that the town's talebearers carried around like choice tidbits to tickle prurient palates.

"The harlot, the slut," they dished out the dirt while dishing out their soup, "the whore. She gives *our kind* a bad name."

"Ah!" The senator was keyed up: "Now comes the *crux* of Plato's philosophy: 'Once it is perceived, the conclusion must follow that, for all things, this is the cause of whatever is right and good. . . . Without having had a vision of this Form no one can act with wisdom, either in his own life or in matters of state. . . .'"

Lisa abhored the cant, the smugness with which the *goyim* condemned Olga. Still, the question hung in the air: what had happened to the haughty Olga of former days? The mystery kept the townspeople in a dither of speculation as they wagged their heads, clacked their tongues and whispered of remedies such as stoning.

Was it connected with her husband's absence? Everyone wondered.

". . . and now," the senator continued, "we arrive at last at the central thesis. Listen: '. . . the summit of the intelligible world is reached in philosophic discussion . . . through the discourse of reason . . . until he has grasped by pure intelligence the very nature of Goodness itself. This journey is what we call Dialectic.'"

Olga Petrescu picked a different man every night. It did not seem to matter to her who he was, Lisa reflected, as long as he was Jewish. And as long as the mark of suffering was on his body. She went for the maimed, the ashen-faced men. Lisa had watched Olga come to their nightly drinking bouts, sit by herself for a while and eye the men with detachment, tap an emaciated, pathetic-looking man on the shoulder and beckon to him with a nod of her head. Then leave with him.

On the Petrescu grounds behind the mansion there was a carriage house which was connected to Olga's quarters. The men with whom she slept in the carriage house never spoke of those nights. If her name came up in conversation, they merely raised their eyebrows or pretended not to hear. They were as much at a loss to understand the motives behind her apparent promiscuity as anyone else. Yet they felt a kinship with her. To them Olga Petrescu too was a victim like themselves, and instead of being flippant or brash about having slept with her, they became her silent accomplices.

Only Himy pursued her in earnest, flamboyantly and persistently, in his own fashion. He sent her flowers and bonbons and courted her like an adolescent in the grip of first love, gawking and blushing and fidgeting whenever he was near her. She never picked him. She passed him up like a teacher skipping over the obviously best prepared pupil. His zest for indiscriminate love affairs waned with each night she passed him up for someone else till he had no desire for any other amorous pursuit except that of Olga. He even began to look like the ashen-faced men Olga was picking night after night.

The senator was now gently tugging Lisa's hand.

"Are you day dreaming, my dear?" He closed the book. "Pure intelligence," he said, looking out into the horizon, "the very nature of Goodness itself."

"I am so lonely. Sick with loneliness."

She put her head in his lap, wishing he would pat it, assure her that all would be well. That the nightmare was over and that Leonid would come soon.

Surprised, the senator gazed at the head in his lap. He cleared his throat, stroked her head lightly, barely touching.

"Don't cry, my dear. Have a cup of tea. It will calm you, I am sure."

8

". . . and by virtue of the power vested in me by the citizens of this great city," Mayor Barka said sonorously, "I now pronounce you man and wife." He shook hands with Imre and before giving Bozsi their marriage license he gallantly kissed her hand.

Now Senator Petrescu stepped closer to the bride and groom, brushed back his long white hair with his hand, then hooked his thumbs into the wide leather cincture girding him. The Romanian national costume he wore for the occasion, hand-embroidered white linen shirt over baggy white linen pants, made him look like a folk prophet who had come to bless or exhort, depending on the congregation.

"I am deeply moved to have witnessed this marriage," he orated, raising his hands and eyebrows. "This is no ordinary marriage: it is, against all odds, an irrevocable reaffirmation of life, a postulate of Jewish faith. Furthermore, and to paraphrase the great English philosopher Alfred North Whitehead, I submit that once the visible world is apprehended in all its aspects, the conclusion must be drawn, which conclusion I do draw, that the only remaining advantage this miserable world continues to have is represented by the Jewish people; as long as they exist our ultimate freedom is a viable proposition. . . ."

261

Ilona had been watching the crowd listen to the senator—polite but bored. Then his last words seemed to have piqued their interest. A few smirked. Some laughed, others whistled.

". . . and if the Jews were no more, this planet would cease to be human," he intoned, bowing as someone whistled, "Phew!"

". . . it sure was a close call," someone else called out behind Ilona.

Yes, it had been a close call, and it almost ceased to be human that afternoon, Ilona thought. Her mother had been alerted in the nick of time, the Jewish family had just fled from the cellar when two men from the Magyar secret police barged in. They picked up Ilona anyhow. For questioning, they said, smirking. Why did she hide those Jews, the men wanted to know. For money or Jewish prick? Tell us, they said, is it true a Jewish prick is small? A piece is missing, eh? It must have been money then, where is it? Come on, let's share it, Miss Ilona von Tokay de Györ Hayduczy. You are a fine example of Magyar patriotism, fucking Jews . . . One of them grabbed her breasts as screams were filtering through the walls. They were in the Grodl.

It had been a close call indeed.

What would have happened, she had often wondered, if Count Aristide de Taszilo had not have stormed in at that moment, ordered them to release her at once, then rage and curse at their stupidity for arresting a genuine Hayduczy while slimy *agents-provocateurs* infiltrated the city, hid Jews and . . . it almost ceased to be human.

Aristide. Poor Aristide. Without his plumed shako, the intricate passementeries criss-crossing his padded officer's uniform, without his monocle, the black shiny boots and gleaming spurs—divested of military and sartorial paraphernalia he was a slight, little man with a hairless effeminate body, his small genitals lost in his pubic hair. "We'll comb it out," Ilona had told him, laughing, "don't worry Aristide. We'll make it grow a bit. Look how it's grown already . . . No, you don't have to mount me. I'll do it for you. There . . . there . . ."

The first time she had an orgasm was with Sandor. Right there in the cellar, near her father's military wardrobe.

Ilona looked at the wedding crowd, one big circle of friends and strangers belonging to the same family. Only she, Ilona, was the outcast. Not the outcast, she instantly corrected herself, merely the outsider. She saw Lisa walk over to Rozika and watched them embrace. Himy beamed and smiled, nervously touched his pocket holding the two wedding rings, boisterously predicting that nine months hence there would be a *bris.*

"What a celebration *that* will be. The first Jewish baby! Just think!" he bubbled, dashing to the end of the garden to help set up the *huppah.*

Although Imre and Bozsi were legally married now, Ilona knew they would not be considered truly married until after the religious ceremony had taken place. Ilona was learning, bit by bit, about ritual laws and their meanings. Those she could study, find out their origins. What she still could not find out was what else, besides knowledge and a fervent wish, was needed to be "one of them." She had been trying so hard! She had even taken Lisa's advice and had spoken to Sandor of her wish to learn how to be Jewish. She could envision Sandor's humiliation in the Jewish labor force, compelled to wear the yellow Star of David. Sandor then told her it was no humiliation to wear the Star of David; the humiliation was that the *goyim* used the star to defile, to slur . . . and besides, Sandor said, the persecution started much earlier, way back, one thousand, nine hundred and forty-five years ago, to be exact; it has become a way of life to hate the Jews, come now Ilonka, you surely know, you've heard your Count Aristide de Taszilo's vile rantings (yes, yes, he hated Jewish men, he called them perverts, Jewish perverts), bring the fuse, string up the Jews; you cannot will it with a snap of your finger or an impulse of your heart or a decision of your mind to be Jewish. Unless you have *goyish* spittle on your cheek, cossack boots on your back and Nazi . . . no, you'll never be one of us, Sandor said, never.

She was not *amchu*, not one of them. Not yet.

The men were fastening a white wool *tallis* to four poles. They were improvising a *huppah*, the marriage canopy under which the rabbi recites the traditional blessings and the couple exchange the Hebrew marriage vows. Ilona had read up on Jewish wedding customs and knew that after the vows are said under the *huppah*, the groom crushes a glass beneath his foot. The *goyim* believed this gesture to be a symbolic piercing of the

263

bride's virginity, but Ilona now knew better: the crushing of the glass under the *huppah* was to recall Nebuchadnezzar's destruction of King Solomon's temple in Jerusalem.

How odd, she mused, that even in moments of pure joy such as weddings the Jews should wish to be reminded of ancestral tragedies. That memory, she had learned, was supposed to keep alive their determination to rebuild the temple, someday. A rather unconventional method for her taste. If she were *amchu* she could probably feel that memory, or its effect, just like the rest of them, she thought, looking around.

She saw Mitzi holding on to Sandor's arm, Himy sniffling, his eyes teary. Naftuli had his arm around Naomi's shoulders, and Mrs. Stein sobbed loudly, pronouncing Gitl's name again and again. All of them—Abe, Ezra, Huna and Gyuri, Dolly and Eva— all seemed different. An indefinable difference they all shared. Why, Mother of God, why can't she become one of them? As the Moabite Ruth had?

The *huppah* was up, the afternoon was serene. The cloudless blue sky stretched over the town, like a cosmic canopy of love and peace. All was quiet. Ilona sensed the importance of the moment, the incredible happening of a Jewish resurrection—the wedding. A strange emotion fleetingly touched her heart, like a scalpel's tip, and for an instant Ilona tasted Jewish pain. But only for an instant.

Bride and groom stood under the *huppah*. A young man, the former assistant *dayyan*, was reciting the blessings.

"*Harai at mekudeshes li*," Imre repeated after him, placing on Bozsi's finger the thin gold band Himy handed him, ". . . *Moshe v'Yisroel*."

What did those words mean? What magic did they contain? Ilona wondered again as she noticed a sudden transformation in the Jews as though a mysterious power had taken hold of them, given them an exclusive inner vision.

Then Imre broke the glass with his foot. The sound of shattering glass flashed the memory of the sacked temple, yet seeing the Jews' profound reaction Ilona sensed that that sound triggered other, more recent and infinitely more painful memories. Tears streaking their cheeks, the Jews skipped and danced, and screamed and shouted and cried out desperately, obsessively: "*Mazel tov, mazel tov! Lechaim*—to life! Life! Life! Life!"

Lisa too wept. Her lips moved feverishly, as if under a spell, repeating the same words over and over: Moshe and Israel, Moshe and Israel, till at last the words soaked her soul as summer rains soak parched earth, till at last her mind absorbed the meaning of those words. She was somebody, an individual rooted in history, an organism whose past was undeniable and whose continuity, each time the foot of a groom shattered a glass, was undeniable too, despite the world's attempt to do away with her. She was a descendant of Moses, a shoot of Israel. Like the sky above her in which she was one of the innumerable stars. An element and a part of the whole.

"I belong," she realized, "I am," and the revelation gave her immense peace, a sad happiness.

From the back, someone embraced her.

"Leonid," she whispered, without moving.

He turned her around, tightened his hold, then kissed her.

"*Maya dusha*. My soul, my very own soul. I am so happy to have found you."

"I love you," she said.

That night they made love and that night the moon swelled to twice its size. A cow in Anna's village calved twins, and the village deaf-mute suddenly began to speak.

9

During the next several days there were many other strange signs: spinsters found husbands, barren women became pregnant. Fruit trees hung heavy with juicy plums, peaches, apples and pears, till one night the branches could no longer hold the weight of such abundance: all the fruit, swarming with thousands of tiny worms, fell to the ground. Hardly anyone noticed the rotten fruit. Even Anna failed to see the rot, for she said to Lisa:

"All those strange signs, miss. The village sage interprets them. He says something is in the air. Something which never before was there. Bears sleep in the summer, dogs don't bark, and owls hoot during the day. But the nightingales also sing. See what I mean?

"This is the summer of new life," Anna whispered conspiratorially to Lisa, "you listen to me. The village sage says it's love, that's what's in the air. Good tidings, all those strange signs. It means love will bring luck and plenty throughout the year, till next summer at least." She gently patted her bulging stomach: "Twins, that's what I am going to have. You'll see, miss . . ."

These magical signs recharged the weary country people with the promise of rebirth and infused the survivors with strange desires. After Imre's wedding a change of mood came over them. A frantic search for pairing, for bonding, replaced the nightly drinking bouts. Imre had been right. The alcohol did not seem to have worked. Human touch was now to be the answer.

"Yes, time to multiply," Himy went on saying with a gentle, bemused look of reverie. His voice, though, lacked resonance, his flashy suits hung loosely on him and the old bounce was gone from his gait. Olga still refused to notice him.

Tzofi the musician married Esther and Motke married Beila. Her younger sister Mirele, who returned to Sighet on the eve of their wedding, was going to marry Yosl.

"Don't," Beila advised. "You are only fifteen; he is twice your age."

"So what. Yosl promised to be as good to me as Papa was. I'll marry Yosl."

Huna fell in love with Dolly, the pampered daughter of a wealthy merchant.

"You'll be like a princess to me," he said to her, "marry me."

"But——"

"Times have changed. Marry me."

"But—"

"Marry me, marry me."

Rozika wanted to marry Antal, a gangster.

"Not him," her brother, Moritz, begged. "Please, not Antal the Gangster. An extortionist. He's been in jail . . . Please."

"He shed the old skin in Auschwitz," Rozika said, and paid no heed to Moritz. Antal smiled, smoothed his pomaded blond hair, hung around Rozika constantly and whenever others were present kissed her hands with his thick lips.

One morning Moritz walked into Rozika's room and found Antal in bed with her.

"All right," he said to the grinning Antal. "I'll make you a partner in my haberdashery. The wedding will take place within a week. But I am warning you, Antal, watch out! All I have left is this one sister. Watch out!"

Only Otto delayed marrying Eva, his childhood sweetheart.

"Let's wait a little while longer," he said to her, running his fingers over the curves of his guitar. "I am not yet unthawed. When I'll remember the names of flowers, or create songs again, then . . ."

Ezra reread a small ad in the newspaper, something about men

267

with experience in traffic and transportation being wanted by a Jewish firm in Bucharest, a veiled reference to Jews being smuggled into Eretz Ysroel. One day he bought a one-way bus ticket to Bucharest, pulled out his valise from under the bed and left town the same afternoon.

Next morning the bus brought from Bucharest, *via* Cluj, Paul Berger, a doctor of internal medicine and an enthusiast of external Nature. He came to pick edelweiss on mountaintops and stayed long enough to be charmed by the little town nestled in the Carpathian lap. He decided to practice in Sighet and in no time opened an office on Main Street. The doctor was handsome, Jewish and single. Mitzi fell in love with him at once, but Paul remained aloof to her advances.

"He is shy," Mitzi concluded. To overcome his shyness she launched a series of parties in his honor—at which he never showed up.

Undaunted, Mitzi continued throwing parties. Because of Paul's absence the parties turned into poker games that visibly shortened her belt of gold coins.

One evening Tibor brought along Eva to such a poker party. Her eyes became glued to a purple silk blouse Mitzi wore.

"It has been such a long time," Eva said to Mitzi. "Let me feel it for a second." She smoothed out a crease in the blouse no one had noticed before. "How lovely," she said.

While awaiting Paul's imminent surrender Mitzi had acquired a knack for poker. She went at it zestfully, with a full heart and full purse as she did this evening, although now her gambling was more reckless than usual. She was playing with Tibor, Himy and Gyuri, raising their bets, piling money on the table, intermittently glancing at the door, and losing.

"I raise you again!" she said to Himy during a particularly tense round in which only the two of them were left to play. Mitzi threw her last banknote into the pot. "Let me see your hand," she challenged Himy.

He showed his cards: royal flush.

"And now," Himy said, noticing Mitzi tear a coin off her belt, "we'll stop the game——"

"Not when I lose. The Prince would consider it bad form," she twitted. "Loser calls the shots. I lost, I call the shots. Even though *he* stood me up again . . ." She began dealing another hand.

268

"I'll get him for you," Himy said, and called Abe over: "Go look for him; and don't come back without him."

The cards were dealt, Tibor and Gyuri had placed their bets. So had Mitzi. Her coin was in the pot, and all eyes were on Himy.

"No money," he said to Mitzi, shaking his head, "no poker. And no gold coin. Period. Himy the Mogul says so." He sighed, put his hand over his heart: "The Prince would agree. I know. Would never take advantage of a dame with gold coins and a yen for——"

"Play!" Mitzi commanded. "Prince or no Prince, you play!"

"I said no gold coin." He pushed his cards to the center of the table, reached for his jacket and tie.

"Hold on," Tibor laughed nervously. "This is a friendly game, isn't it? How about Mitzi using something else instead of a gold coin?"

Her eyes fell on Eva. Mitzi slowly unbuttoned her purple blouse, pausing after each button to relish the baffled looks on her friends' faces. She slithered out of the sleeves and threw the blouse on the table among the banknotes. She stood up, stretched out one arm and pointed to the blouse:

"That's my bet!" She was bare from the waist up, her jutting breasts defiantly directed to Himy: "Now can we play?"

She lost the purple blouse, and Paul arrived escorted by Abe.

"The game is over," Mitzi told the party, "now be so kind as to go." She locked the door after them, took the key out of its lock.

"So nice of you to have come." She advanced towards Paul. "I've been waiting."

10

And life went on.

Then Imre had an idea. "Those knitting machines are idle in the basement," he told JOINT officials, "they should be made operable again." He spoke to them of young men and women returning from camps. "They need rehabilitation in many areas. Learn a Trade to earn a living."

JOINT agreed to subsidize a training program. The machines were brought up from the basement and Itzik Berg, a knitter who had worked in the original factory, was made instructor, foreman and Technical head of the project. Imre volunteered to be its overall chairman and Lisa volunteered to help out with administrative details. She went to the factory daily, for a couple of hours, to work in the office.

"They need me now," she told Naomi, who could now think only of tomorrow.

Tomorrow which would bring Miklos home.

"A man who had been with him in the Buna factory in Auschwitz came back the other day," she told Lisa. "The man told me that two days before the Russians had liberated Auschwitz Miklos had been shipped out. God, help me! Bring him back already! Don't you hear me? Hey, God, listen to me!" she cried out, then turned to Lisa in desolation: "He is deaf again, this God of ours. He is so old, maybe he died, who knows . . ."

Yes, maybe he died, Lisa thought, maybe he never existed; then again, maybe he existed but really never gave a damn one way or another. Or maybe he is just human, this great God of ours. Who knows?

"Certainly God will help, Naomi," she said reassuringly. "He always almost does. Miklos will be back soon, you'll see."

"Yes, tomorrow. Tomorrow." She perked up: "And what will Miklos say, I wonder, about you and Leonid?"

"What should he say?" Lisa was surprised. "What *is* there to say?"

"Oh Lisa, don't you see? Life goes on, as it always does. Things rarely change. Leonid is a communist, a Russian, a soldier. He will have to leave you."

"Yes, I know," she answered evenly, and it occurred to her how pleasant Naomi was with Leonid, a bit flirtatious at times. How Naftuli kowtowed to him and how her friends called Leonid *kapitan* and how everyone in her crowd smiled and bowed to him. "What's the objection, Naomi: breaking the rules because I love a man who is not *our kind* or breaking the rules because I love a man who will leave me?"

"The whole town talks about your romance with the Rusky and you talk of . . . what?" Naomi seemed genuinely puzzled. "I can't even make sense of your questions. Don't you think of your future? After all, you are somebody. An Engler. What will Miklos say when he learns you are involved with a Russian communist soldier——"

"He'll say *coup de foudre* and be glad for me," she answered impetuously. "And Miklos won't give a damn what others say." She wanted to cry and laugh, or just scream. Instead, she lashed out: "On the dunghill did you think that you'd ever care again what others say? Did you care what they said when you ate putrid potatoes or moldy bread? Or stole a rag? Or smelled the stink and saw the flames. . . ." The world was falling apart before it had a chance to be put firmly back together, Lisa thought, and she became angry at her own grief over it.

"Let me tell you something, sister-in-law. I love Leonid Yashenko, the Russian communist soldier who can't marry me. So what? So what, Naomi, if he can't marry me? The world is up-side down, they've almost destroyed us and we are still half dead but you are concerned with form . . . This is insane!"

Naomi was crying and Lisa watched her cry. In a little while she said: "I love Leonid, don't you understand? I am surviving because I am still able to love."

Naomi wiped her tears. "But that's not all there is—love," she said stubbornly. "Once we've come out of there alive, we must think ahead. About tomorrow. Don't you want a family, chil-dren?"

"How can I know yet what I want? All I know is I love Leonid. It keeps me going; it makes me want to face another day. Chil-dren, you say . . . I don't know." She became visibly upset, bit-ing her lips. "I don't really give a damn what others say," she finally said. "It doesn't matter to me."

Being with Leonid was all that mattered to her now, she thought. When he brought her home at night they walked hand in hand on the street and she was not afraid any longer. She was not afraid of memories and she was not afraid to speak of them. Russian night patrols stopped them: *Kto idyot?* who goes there? they asked. Leonid put his arms around her shoulders, an-swered, *Svoii, svoii*, our own. She was not going to let anyone take this security away from her.

"He and I are one," she said and remembered, without bitter-ness, her return to Sighet. "I came back here to belong again. But there was no one. Mano——"

"He wanted to come back," Naomi said, "didn't he?"

"No, he didn't." There, it was out at last and she felt relieved. "Mano asked me casually, very casually, to go visit him in Cluj. I was too confused, thought it would be humiliating to tell the truth. I still don't understand Mano's reasons for staying away, but I don't feel humiliated any longer."

"Then what about Drifter? He cared, didn't he?"

"Yes. The time wasn't right though. Too soon, perhaps. We brought each other substitutions . . . Oh, I don't know!"

She was tired, the old feeling of being squeezed dry by outside events returned and she wanted instant deliverance. To crawl back into the shell she had created for herself but which she had been slowly shedding since she had met Leonid. Even if she could reassemble the cracked bits of the discarded shell, she thought, it would fit her no more. She was herself now, without swaddling clothes, still raw, still tender, her own skin exposed and hurting sometimes. But it was pure Lisa Engler.

"I have a lover." She lingered deliberately on each word to give birth to her feelings unambiguously, enduringly, in a verbal bundle. "It doesn't matter if he marries me or not. What matters is to recognize what's important to me, then the pluck to stand by that recognition. I love Leonid. He *is* important to my life. I *won't* give him up."

11

And Leonid made love to her as if nothing else mattered to him either.

That first evening, when he had gone to the Kahn house as Captain Yashenko, political intelligence officer attached to the Fifth Army of the Byelorussian front, it was on an off-duty mercy mission. Those Jewish survivors had to be guided into a course of action that would preclude flare-ups similar to that morning's; either commit yourselves to us, or leave at once, he intended to advise them, we do not tolerate fence straddlers. He was taking a chance of being accused of favoritism. Still, he had to do it. Angry and hurt, those young people were emotionally too worked up to manage another confrontation coolly, another bout. Yes, he wanted to help stir them towards survival—and *that* was worth taking a chance for.

But as he stepped into the room, he saw her dance and forgot why he had come. For days thereafter, while he was away, he couldn't get her out of his mind. After they became lovers, he felt a unique exhilaration, an intense state of well-being never before experienced and he made love with her as if indeed nothing else mattered to him—as if the impending arrival of Colonel Alexandr Michailovich Marcovski was of little concern to him. Yet it mattered very much to him, he told himself, of course it mattered. . . .

Leonid Nicolaievich Yashenko, born Leib Yashenberg, grew up in Iasi, the capital of the Romanian province of Moldavia. His father, Nachum Yashenberg, was a modest man although his vast knowledge of Hebrew sacred texts had earned him the name of Reb Nachum, an unmistakable sign of high esteem in the Iasi Jewish community. He was modest, although his reputation as the best grain merchant in the area had spread over both banks of the Prut, the river between the provinces Moldavia and Bessarabia. Reb Nachum's prosperity and his peers' respect entitled him to one of the five honor seats at the eastern wall of the main Iasi synagogue, yet Reb Nachum chose to pray with his old friends in the old *stibl* in the cramped Jewish quarters where he had once lived. But when it came to his only son Leibele, whose unusual memory was the wonder and talk of the Jewish community, Reb Nachum's pride was boundless.

". . . another honor scholarship," he told his friends at the *stibl*, where he went every evening to recite the *maariv*. "Leibele was accepted at the gymnasium."

". . . *nu? nu?* How is Leibele with Torah?"

Reb Nachum's proudest day came when he told them of Leibele's acceptance at Alexandru Cuza University, an achievement rarely attained by a Jewish youth.

"Let it be for the good," Reb Nachum's friends said, "the boy will be in a *goyish* world. Let it be for the good only, so much *goyish* knowledge."

At the time Leonid enrolled at the university, he was a confirmed Marxist, the head of an underground communist cell.

But it began with Dora. Her golden hair was neatly braided, her intelligent gray eyes often settled on him and her fleeting smile would leave a dimple on her chin. They were both fifteen when they met in the home of Dr. Iancu Marciuc, the professor of history at the Iasi Gymnasium, where a few handpicked students met weekly for extracurricular history lessons the professor had volunteered to give.

That was how it began. He fell in love with Dora while Marciuc taught him political history and science for the next five

275

years. Marciuc became Leonid's mentor, a secular father-substitute. Though at times repelled by Marciuc's insistent hold, Leonid was flattered at having been anointed as the great professor's favorite disciple. The young man let it happen, allowed Marciuc to swallow him up, possess his mind. The nature of exchange, the theory of surplus value, the exploitation of labor, the manipulation of production and distribution in the capitalist system, and the ineluctable necessity of liberating the world proletariat through a social revolution—these eluded Reb Nachum, no matter how often Leonid had tried to enlighten him if for no other reason than to maintain an affectionate father-son relationship.

"Don't burden him with modern socialist theories," Marciuc would counsel. "Your old man is the expert of the old world. Let him be. But you—you shall become the expert at making a new world. I'll teach you how."

Marciuc's thin short fingers drummed the table as he expounded Marxist-Leninist theories and proposed methods to eradicate class differences. Revolutionary consciousness must be brought to the workers by their intellectual leaders, Marciuc emphasized, drumming the table; the Communist Party must consist of full-time, disciplined men capable of acting as one man. Discipline, *discipline* was essential to the life of the Party. The Party which must come first, second, third, etc., for the Party was one's mother, one's father; it was one's lover. Marciuc drummed and pounded the table: the Party gives its members identity; the Party alone matters.

When the light fell at a certain angle, the thick lenses of Marciuc's pince-nez glared. There seemed to be nothing behind the lenses but two cavities. A blind man pounding the table. A vertical frown in the middle of his forehead separated Marciuc's thin blond eyebrows. His hair, washed-out yellow, was straight and coarse and never stayed parted. Wisps of hair fell on his forehead, right on top of the frown. His face was elongated, his body short and chunky. He smoked constantly and rolled his own cigarettes, spat bits of tobacco around the room as he talked and rubbed a brown stain on his right middle finger with his thumb, all at the same time.

None of Marciuc's habits mattered. He was their new seer, the apostle rightfully threatening the old world with thunder and lightning and proclaiming, with infectious conviction, the Party as the only possible savior. When he finally confronted Leonid it seemed an obvious and just solution.

"There is no other way," Marciuc said, and Leonid could see nothing behind the lenses. "You must defect." Dora nodded. "To intellectualize is a bourgeois vice; our ideas need to be put into practice. I've taught you well. Couldn't have done more for my own son. The logical conclusion is to work now directly under and for the Communist Party. Dora will go with you."

He and Dora defected to Russia in 1938.

The night before defection, he sat in his father's study for a long time. He kissed the old man, whom he found asleep over an ancient scroll.

"Pray for me," he whispered to the sleeping Reb Nachum. "Pray—*daven* as only you can *daven*. *Daven* for your Leibele. And love Mamma for me."

When they got to Russia he and Dora became lovers, as she had promised. Then one day, without warning, he was sent to a special training school in Moscow. He graduated with the rank of lieutenant. It was 1941. The Germans had just broken their non-aggression pact with Russia. He never saw Dora again.

By 1943 the *Wehrmacht* was pushed back from Stalingrad and the Red Army began its thrust to the West through the Ukraine. Leonid's unit was among the first to enter Moldavia in August 1944. He went to Iasi to look for his family. He found no one. The entire Jewish community, he was told, had been transported to Transnistria.

Until its surrender to Russia in August 23, 1944, Romania had been an Axis ally, though an unwilling one at times. The SS had been pressing the Romanian government to turn over to them its Jewish population, close to six hundred thousand souls. The government refused at first, preferring to dispose of the Jews in Romanian style. Thousands of Jews were murdered during the Iasi pogrom in June 1941. But by late 1942 over two hundred thousand Jews were shipped to Transnistria, the Ukrainian section between the rivers Bug and Dniester under German jurisdiction. There the Jews were placed in ghettos, along with native Russian Jews, and left to the mercy of *Einsatzgruppe* D, who were aided in their Jew-killing missions by zealous Romanian army units and Ukrainian defectors.

From Iasi Leonid went back to Transnistria, combed through every ghetto, pored over whatever documents he could find, questioned whoever was coherent enough to answer him. He found not a trace of the Yashenbergs.

On his way to Berlin with the Red Army, he went through every extermination and concentration camp the Russians liberated. He also went through camps liberated by the Allies. He went through

Treblinka	Auschwitz	Maidanek	Buchenwald	
Mathausen	Babi Yar	Belzec	Bershad	Sobibor
Chelmno	Ponary	Janov	Pustkov	
Theresienstad	Bergen-Belsen	Weisswasser	Dachau	

and never found the Yashenbergs. Not even a memory of them.

He saw those places and he still could smell the stink of those cesspools and see the mountains of corpses, the mountains of human hair and the mountains of shoes. All one could do in the face of such colossal horror was to bow one's head in shame for being a member of the human race. He also knew that what had been perpetrated upon the Jews precluded forgiveness and he wondered, sometimes, if there was anything in the world that could ever heal the survivors' wounds. But he wished he could, perhaps, heal Lisa's loneliness.

And that, he hoped, Colonel Marcovski would understand.

12

And though he made love with her as if nothing mattered, his
heart was rent by yesterday's shadows, while his mind was keen-
ly aware of five-cornered star-shaped shadows looming ahead of
him which adumbrated tomorrow and which, with the absolute
faith of a Party member, he welcomed unconditionally. First and
foremost, he was a communist whose actions would never be determined by bourgeois sentimentality. His love affair with Lisa
was a very special one, but regardless of its special status, the
affair would never veer him away from the communist path he
had chosen to travel. Neither would it prevent him from carrying
out tasks assigned to Captain Leonid Nicolaievich Yashenko, recently appointed first adjutant to Colonel Marcovski.

"The year I was born, Moldavia was still called Regat," he said
to her the evening of the day he learned of his appointment. He
was in an expansive mood, wished for light diversion and light
love, so that his judgmental perceptions could stay finely honed,
unblunted by emotionality. Grisha Keroff, appointed the colonel's second adjutant, had hinted in the morning that Marcovski
had been one of the original communists who had taken part in
the October uprising, had stormed the Winter Palace in Petrograd, and in the early years of the Bolshevik Revolution had been
on the Council of People's Commissars headed by Lenin. Keroff

had done his homework, it was obvious to Yashenko, particularly when Keroff called Marcovski the Stenka Razin of the Communist Party for having put Party loyalty above all else. "He proved his mettle," Keroff said, and Yashenko had refrained from further questioning Keroff but nodded knowingly, as if to indicate that he too had done his homework and then some.

As matters stood, the importance of Colonel Alexandr Michailovich Marcovski was amply clear to Yashenko.

He reached for Lisa's hands, pressed her fingers lightly. He could barely wait for the encounter with the colonel, his entire system was keyed up, set to go. The precision tuning perfect. Marcovski would not regret choosing him first adjutant.

"The year I was born was an important year. I'll give you ten reasons, one for each finger." A somewhat unorthodox method to refresh one's memory on obscure or esoteric points, he thought, and laughed nervously, but a pleasantly stimulating one.

He tugged gently at her fingers, one by one, as he began:

"It was the year the Bolsheviks dissolved the Russian Constituent Assembly in Petrograd; the year they transferred the Soviet government to Moscow; the year of the Brest-Litovsk Treaty between Russia and the Central Powers; the year the Kaiser abdicated; the year of the Armistice signed by the Allies and Germany——"

"It was 1918!" she interrupted, full of spirit, "the best year in the world's history. Because you were born." The ease with which he spanned a variety of topics reminded her of a magician pulling out rabbits from someone else's hat, and she chuckled with delight. His mere presence was magic, she thought, a magic shield against the outside world. He was her talisman, hers alone, someone who could bring about miracles, find rabbits and free Erno. Leonid could make wishes come true. Lying close to him, she felt his breath, his touch, and a warm flow ran through her, as if a magic transfusion has just taken place, and she thought that through him even she possessed a speck of that magic.

She could probably perform a trick or two of her own, she boldly thought, and all of a sudden remembered the secret game she had played long ago. A grandfather clock, chimes, she now faintly recalled, and a game called *a wish fulfilled for a contract fulfilled*. How about contracting with herself that Leonid would enumerate all the ten reasons and then . . . Then what? Yes, then Miklos will be home in ten days! That was her wish. It will come true.

"Five more reasons," she said smiling, and stretched out her other hand eagerly. "You said ten, Leonyushka." That was the contract. He will fulfill it, she was certain, and all will be well. Miklos will be home at last, in ten days.

"Georgi Plekhanov, the Marxist theoretician died," he continued with an indulgent smile, "Czar Nicholas and his family were executed; Igor Stravinsky composed *The Soldier's Story* . . ."

He was slowing down. The game will be lost, she thought anxiously. He must give two more reasons so that Miklos would be home ten days from now. She blushed with embarrassment at how childish this game was, after all, and thought of letting it go at that. But just in case, she quickly told herself, she ought to make sure Miklos will be back. Just in case . . .

"Two more reasons, Leonyushka. Please."

"Alexandr Blok wrote *The Twelve*, one of the greatest revolutionary poems." He now pulled her closer: "I want you. Let's . . ."

But it was important. He had promised ten reasons and the contract was for ten. She became frantic. The contract she had made with herself must be fulfilled. Bend the rules, just a bit. The game must be won. Hurry.

"And Count Istvan Tisza was assassinated," she whispered. She could think of nothing else; but as long as the contract had been fulfilled her wish too would be fulfilled.

She sighed with relief and turned to him, love in her eyes.

Next day he brought her a Matrushka doll. It was an oversized flat-bottomed wooden egg, split horizontally midway, on which a face was painted.

"It reminds me of you," he said, twisting open the doll. Nine successively smaller dolls nested inside, the smallest the size of a thimble. "There is more to a doll than meets the eye. Just like you."

281

13

The tenth day was up and it did not bring Miklos. It brought, instead, Colonel Alexandr Michailovich Marcovski, Military Governor of the Eastern Region, Occupied Territories.

The colonel had been expected to arrive the following week and the staff had been planning an elaborate reception. His premature arrival at the *kommandatura* flustered everyone.

Colonel Marcovski, ignoring the general mix-up, strode through the *kommandatura* and headed straight for his office.

"Summon First Adjutant Captain Yashenko!" he barked at his secretary after half an hour. *"Davai, davai!"*

Within minutes, Yashenko was in the office. His back to the door, Marcovski faced a window overlooking Main Street. Yashenko looked at the short bulky figure, the blond hair mixed with gray covering the back of his head, waited a few seconds, then cleared his throat:

"At your service, Comrade Colonel Marcovski."

Marcovski turned around slowly, his head bent, sprinkling cigarette ash on the floor. The cigarette was in a long white holder. He ejected the stub into an ashtray on the desk, then lifted his head.

Leonid stared at the plain green field uniform, the wide leather belt around the portly waist and the wisps of hair on the fore-

282

head. The vertical frown in its center had hardened into a permanent crease, and the pince-nez was gone. Otherwise, the man looked the same.

"Dr. Iancu Marciuc!" Leonid exclaimed.

"Not any more,' Marcovski grinned, and shook Leonid's hand. *"Kak djela?"* he asked, "how are you, my boy?"

"At your service," he answered unhesitatingly, though he was still aghast, awed.

Marcovski sat down at his desk, opened a folder, glanced at it while drumming his fingers on the desk top. His fingers seemed thinner, more spidery, Yashenko thought. The old ambiguous feeling, that peculiar mixture of revulsion and attraction, returned for a moment and Yashenko understood in a flash the Marciuc-Marcovski role in his own life—at least he thought he understood.

"Good record." Marcovski inserted another cigarette in the holder. "I've been following your development all along." His instinct to pick neophytes had not misled him. This one here, Yashenko, had all the ingredients, as Marcovski had sensed the instant he had heard the boy's questions in class, saw his eager eyes. "Not bad at all," Marcovski added, remembering that Yashenko reacted positively to flattery.

"Yes, comrade," Yashenko said briskly, though he was wound up, flipping pages and pages in his memory. The name Marcovski or Marciuc did not show up. How far back should be search? The man was around fifty, it must have been during the Revolution. The rumors were probably accurate. But the name did not show up. What was Marciuc-Marcovski's real name?

"Well my boy, *now* we'll put the theoretical approach into practical use. The real thing . . . and you'll be the one to help me. *You* were my choice. Though Keroff is also a good man." He smiled briefly, emphasized the words: "I chose you over him. For old times' sake as well as for your potential. Our goals are in sight." Marcovski reached for his attaché case, took a small key from his breast pocket and opened the case. He handed Yashenko a thick file.

"It's all there," Marcovski said. "Stay here, read it through. Work begins as of now." He got up, walked to the window again. The people on Main Street looked like rag dolls, aimlessly walking in different directions.

"The reins will be tightened. The Romanian Communist Party shall begin the tightening." He pointed across Main Street, to the Crown Hotel where the headquarters of the Democratic Party Bloc was. "But we'll hold the reins. One year, that's the deadline."

Yes, Yashenko thought, he knew how it was done. Manipulating power was the ultimate power and how it was done depended on one's style. Had Marcovski retained Marciuc's style?

"What about the girl?" Marcovski asked lightly.

"Which one?" Yashenko sounded casual, the question did not seem to throw him off balance.

"You tell me."

"There is one in Budapest. I saw her not long ago, on my last assignment there." He had said good-bye to her after telling her he had been transferred to another region.

"Good." He shrugged, tapped his fingers on the desk. "It's war and a soldier is a soldier. Women *are* necessary. There are plenty of cunts in the market these days."

"Yashenko did not reply."

"What about Lisa Engler?" Marcovski asked.

"Just a girl. She doesn't interfere much." Marcovski did not waste any time in getting all the facts. Yashenko bristled, and wondered if Keroff was the one who supplied them. Even so, a soldier is a soldier and it's war. Still, Marcovski's lewd remark, his attempt to reduce the affair to a sordid little distraction bothered him.

"As long as it stays that way." Marcovski's voice was thin, cutting. Yashenko looked into his eyes, the pince-nez was not shielding them any more. A watery-blue slit peered back at him from under half-closed lids. There was a fleeting chill in the room.

"No slipups," Marcovski continued. He knew the girl was an Auschwitz survivor, the dossier on Lisa Engler was very detailed. Keroff has done a thorough job. Will he have to break up this one too? Marcovski pondered.

"Though this is a slightly different affair," he remarked. "The girl is an Auschwitz survivor."

Yashenko nodded. How much longer must he hold back from asking him about the Yashenbergs, he wondered. Even Party discipline does not preclude a normal interest in one's parents. Particularly since Marcovski was Marciuc . . .

"Comrade colonel," Yashenko asked bluntly, "What happened to my parents?"

"I was beginning to wonder when you'd ask," Marcovski said lighting a cigarette. He looked squarely into Yashenko's face: "I followed through with our agreement. A week after your departure I personally handed your father the first of the four notes you wrote ahead of time to comfort him, notes, you should remember, you wrote on my advice. And then I mailed the remaining three notes to him during the following year. Just as we agreed."

"We also agreed you'd protect my parents once I had gone, comrade colonel," Yashenko said quietly. "Did you, comrade?" Questioning Marcovski was audacious, but it was not really Marcovski he questioned. It was Marciuc. "On my word as a comrade," Marciuc had said, "if you defect I'll protect your parents."

"As long as I could, my boy." Marcovski got up, came around his desk. "And I did, as long as I was in Iasi. I kept the Iron Guard goons off them till early in 1940, when I was recalled to Moscow, where, by the way, I had something to do with your progress . . ." He placed his hand on Yashenko's shoulder. "The first major wartime pogrom in Romania occurred in June 1941. It was in Iasi. I am sorry."

Yashenko said nothing. Anger prevented him from speaking. Anger and pain. For even though his search in Iasi, Transnistria, and the camps had failed to produce the slightest clue to his parents' fate, encountering Marciuc after so many years brought about the crazy, irrational hope that he had taken them along when he returned to Russia and had saved them. That the Yashenbergs were alive, after all.

The weight of Marcovski's hand on his shoulder reminded Yashenko that Marciuc's first and last loyalty belonged to the Party and that nothing, nobody could have prevailed upon him to jeopardize its safety. Yashenko was furious with Marciuc for shattering his momentary illusion of hope; and the clearer it became to Yashenko that expecting Marciuc to rescue the Yashenbergs against all odds was sheer lunacy, the more he blamed Marciuc for his parents' deaths. The specter of the 1941 Iasi pogrom made Yashenko shiver, for it had been one of the most hideous displays of Romanian savagery: bloodthirsty soldiers, having satisfied their lust for plunder, murdered thousands of Jews, then crammed the remainder in cattle cars, without food or water, and shipped them into the unknown, a phantom train traveling with no specific destination till that human cargo died of suffocation or Romanian bullets.

He suppressed a sob and held on to the desk to steady himself.

"It was a blow, my boy," Marcovski acknowledged, grim-faced. "I understand how you must feel. But you must get ahold of yourself and overcome it. Reproach, that is self-reproach, is ultimately counterproductive. Now that I've made you first adjutant . . ."

Was his new position a payoff, Yashenko reflected, so that the matter of the Yashenbergs would be squared away? He became furious all over again with Marcovski for so crassly underestimating him, if indeed that was the reason for his promotion. He recognized, though, that he could never substantiate his suspicion nor could he rationally blame Marciuc for his parents' deaths. It was his own howl of pain coming from the notion that Marciuc should have done the impossible, stretched the limits to save the Yashenbergs, a notion born out of wishful thinking that would chafe at him for the rest of life, destroy his peace of mind, grind away the sharp edges of clarity and dedication his work required. This he could not allow to happen to him. For his own sake then, and for the sake of fair play, he must admit that the odds against the Yashenbergs had been overwhelming and that Marciuc had done what could be done under such harrowing circumstances.

No, the position of first adjutant to Colonel Marcovski would never be the bribe Comrade Marciuc might have intended it to be. Instead, it would become the most appropriate platform for Captain Yashenko to carry out his duties as political intelligence officer and member of the Communist Party. For, in fact, he had been trained to be that and was going to be just that. The Party's goals were his own; and he was totally committed to give of himself fully to achieve those goals.

". . . remember," he heard the colonel say, "the Party——"

". . . is first." Yashenko's voice was choked but then he recalled Marciuc deplored any show of emotions. Bleeding hearts made him squeamish, he used to say. "The Party is first, second, third," Yashenko said calmly, "I know, comrade colonel. I always knew. I've been taught well. The Party does come first."

"All right then. You've had your time off for a bit of play too. I don't begrudge it. But no slipups now, as I've said. This is war, all-out war. And it's just beginning."

14

The day Colonel Marcovski came to Sighet, Yankel Schwartz also arrived in town. He walked along Main Street, shook hands with the survivors, smiled at passers-by.

"I am back. Bergen-Belsen . . ."

"At last," the Jews said. "A great scholar in Jewish law has returned."

"Reb Schwartz, Yankel's father, may his soul rest in peace, always hoped Yankel would become a *doctor rabbiner.*"

"With so few left, who knows, Yankel could become the chief rabbi of Romania . . ."

Yankel kept smiling; his Adam's apple bobbed up and down like a piston in a pump.

He seemed to be the same Yankel as he was before the deportations, lanky and thin, with wavy blond hair and rosy cheeks, a truly learned young man with degrees from the Szatmerer *yeshiva* and the Liceul Dragos Voda: the wonder Talmudist who could recite by heart sections from the *Gemara* and *Mishna*; the secular student who hung out with Otto and Imre, with Gyuri, Mano and Tibor, yearning to be accepted in that clique as one of them and declaiming passages from *Hamlet* to impress them; the young man who failed, despite his shining erudition and valiant

288

attempts to worm himself into their midst, to be part of that clique.

Reb Schwartz had periodically turned to Yankel:

"Stick to the Talmud, son. The *goyish* scribblers will only kick your soul around like a pebble on the beach. You'll change, become an *apikoros,* a renegade, may I never live to see the day."

Reb Schwartz's fears were thought exaggerated, for it seemed, at the time, that what would happen to Yankel would be the fulfillment of his father's wish: he was going to become a *doctor rabbiner.*

"But you always wanted to be something else," Lisa said sipping coffee with Yankel in her small office. He had come to pick up his rations at JOINT and stopped by her office. "Did you know then what it was you really wanted?"

He finished the coffee and thought, yes, even then he knew what he wanted, for he always knew what he did not want: gluey thick Judaism, its disciplines, its harsh morality extolling anonymity and modesty, while all along he wished to be accepted by the clique, to dazzle them with his wit and sophistication. And he wanted someone like Lisa Engler to be his girl.

It was too late then as it was too late now. Damn it. Then it was Mano, now it's the Rusky bastard.

The razor-sharp cutting event of an evening long ago when he had wanted to kiss her came back to him. That summer evening, and the girl with teasing green eyes exuding the sweet smell of girlhood. Laughing, bantering, she was a little coquette, a bitch. She dubbed him "Yankel the Laureate, Poet or Rabbi, as you like it." He had pulled her towards him, towering over her. With a lofty gesture, she raised her hand, lightly tapped at his chest with the tip of her forefinger, as though his mere touch violated her dignity, and whispered, taking aim as if she were swinging a heavy ax:

"*You* can't kiss me. Haven't you heard? I am Mano's sweetheart. And don't you ever forget that, Yankel."

He did not forget that nor did he forget what he wanted. He was going to get it too, now. He wanted it so badly, the thought of it alone made him dizzy and accelerated his salivary secretion. He wanted deference, respect, acceptance, the intangible ingredients of power. Yes, power. It was what he always wanted, along with a chance to get out of his constricting Jewish skin. Out. He would seek the power to do it now.

"Yes, I always knew what I *really* wanted," he said smoothly to Lisa. "What about you, though? Is it true that you . . ."

She let him hang on for a while to the unfinished sentence, then asked:

"Is it true what, Yankel?" She knew what he meant and was repelled by his obliqueness. It rankled her that now, after all that had happened to them, the Yankel Schwartzes had learned nothing.

"Well, you know," he gurgled, his Adam's apple going up and down, up and down, "hm, I mean——"

"Oh Yankel," she interrupted him impatiently, disdainfully, "can't you come out straight and say what you mean? Here, I'll say it for you: you want to know whether the Russian and I sleep together."

Yankel's Adam's apple came to a standstill midway in his throat and she repressed a smile.

"Yes, we do." She tightened the cover of the Nescafé jar, put it in a drawer and got up. "I have work to do now. Good day, Yankel."

Yankel Schwartz moved in with a new friend, one of the members of the Democratic Party Bloc, the DPB for short. Soon thereafter Yankel joined the Romanian Communist Party and was made secretary to the assistant executive chairman of the local People's Literary Association. The association was the formal government arm in charge of all publications in Judetul Maramures and the informal watchdog over what was written in them. Yankel also started to write a play which, he hoped, would at last earn him the reputation he deserved.

And Reb Schwartz did not live to see the day Yankel changed his name to Ion Negrescu. It was August 30, 1945.

15

One morning, the first week in September, Lisa found a message on her desk: *The Tiplea brothers robbed your bunker.* Who had placed the note on her desk? Who were the Tiplea brothers, she wondered; and why now; why not sooner, or why at all?

She looked again at the note in her hand, then noticed her arms were full of red little spots. Prickly heat, she thought when her fingers began to itch. She quickly dropped the note on the desk, as if by getting rid of it she would also get rid of the rash. She could get rid of the note, she realized, but not the rash. She instantly knew that to get rid of the rash she would have to act on the information contained in the note, as she had acted when Naftuli spoke to her of the jewels held by Senator Petrescu.

The itching in her fingers ceased as suddenly as it had started and the rash was gone. That was it, then! The note was a long-delayed sliver of hope. A mysterious sign only she could interpret. Of course! The note meant that Miklos would be home soon, as soon as she would touch the contours of familiar objects. Like the ones that had been buried in the bunker. She should not have bent the rules of the game with Leonid, that time. Tricks do not work, she should have known that. Touching familiar contours, *that* will bring Miklos back. It was a good contract.

She went to Gyuri's office before noon. Although he was now chief of police, he was informal and friendly with Lisa.

"Snitches. Stoolies settling scores," he said after he read the note, then turned to a file cabinet, pulled out a file.

"Yes, that's them!" He read out loud: "Petru and Chirie Tiplea, presently residing in the village of Vad. 1936 to 1940, members of the Iron Guard. 1940 to 1944, members of the Crossed Arrows Party. During Hungarian occupation Chirie employed as delivery boy . . ." He stopped reading a loud, his eyes raced through the rest of the file.

"So that's it!" he said. "Did you know Chirie Tiplea had worked in 1942 as a delivery boy at THE HOUSE OF ENGLER AND SONS?"

She was as surprised as he was.

"These are dangerous fellows. Hooligans," he concluded. "You should stay away from them. Let me deal with them," he said obligingly.

There was a contract she had to fulfill. She alone must first touch the contours of familiar objects, otherwise it wouldn't work again. This time there must be no tricks, no substitutions.

"I want to do it myself, Gyuri," she said. "Please."

Gyuri filled out a search warrant, signed it, then held the warrant in his hand.

"Let me provide you with escort at least. Those guys are ruffians."

She shook her head.

"Then you must ask Captain Yashenko to drive you there," he said, "or else I can't let you have the warrant."

The crystalline rocks of the immense Pietros Peak glistened under the morning's sun rays as Yashenko drove Lisa over the small bridge across the Iza, towards Vad. The sky was clear, spotless, an uncorrupted Transylvanian blue. Marigolds and cornflowers blanketed the countryside. Peasant women came out of small thatched houses, leaned against carved, painted wood gates and stared at the car making its way along the narrow dusty road.

When they arrived at Vad it was near noon. The Tiplea house was at the end of the village. Yashenko stopped the car several houses away, helped Lisa out, then opened his jacket and lit a cigarette.

He should not be here at all, he thought, watching her walk to the Tiplea house. Yet once she told him that to receive the search warrant she had promised Gyuri to ask him to accompany her to Vad, he could not refuse her request. He was relieved, though, when she insisted on facing the Tiplea brothers alone. A confrontation with these fellows at this time would have run counter to Party policy. "Woo the peasantry," was Marcovski's directive, "get them on our side."

He took off his jacket, rolled down the windows, then stepped out of the car and watched Lisa stop before two men standing in front of the last house on the road.

"Good day," she said as she stopped before them. "Are you the Tiplea brothers?" One of the men, the one with bushy eyebrows, blinked, while the hefty man showed no reaction. "Then it is you," she continued calmly, for she had rehearsed this scene in her mind all morning. "I understand one of you gentlemen had worked——"

"Cut the crap," the hefty man said. "What do you want?" He wiped his hands on the face of a shirt that bore a monogram on the left side. She stepped up closer and recognized the familiar initials.

"Right," she said. "You and your brother opened a bunker in my parents' house and removed its contents. I want them back."

"Chirie, did you hear the lady?" the hefty man asked the other.

Chirie spat a few times, then said under his breath, "Are you going to answer the slut?"

"Why not," Petru grinned. "She ain't that bad to look at."

"Shit. Get it over with."

"What's the hurry, Chirie? Let's give this fine lady her due. To think she came all the way from the city to visit peasants." He bowed to her: "What can I do for you, madame?"

"I've told you already!" She raised her voice: "I want the contents of my parents' bunker back!"

"Really? You kidding . . ." Petru spun around, then farted. "Did you hear that, Chirie? She wants the contents of her parents' bunker, that's all the fine city lady wants." His voice changed to a squeak: "The contents of my parents' bunker," he mimicked. "What should we do, Chirie?"

"Shit. Kick her in the ass, Petru."

"Stop this . . . this comedy!" she shouted. "I have a search warrant . . . but . . . I'd rather not cause a commotion." It took all her willpower to utter these words. Her head ached, something made her gag. She loathed the jeering brothers. Hated them. She was terrified by the violence of her hatred pounding at her throat.

"A search warrant?" Petru screamed, and Chirie yelled at him: "I told you to ax that turd, Nicolai Caliniu——"

"This bitch, who does she think she is——"

". . . but you thought you'd buy the snake off with a few shirts——"

". . . the filthy *zsid* city lady!"

"Yeah!" Chirie yelled, "right you are, Petru! She still thinks she's the fucking rich lady of the fucking rich Engler *zsids* and can get whatever her pissed-off little heart desires. But no more, you hear, no more!" He hollered at the top of his voice, shaking his fists at her: "The filthy rich bastards have had it! It's our turn now to wear their silk shirts and sleep under their silk down comforters!"

She covered her ears with her hands. The down comforters again, just like *then* and *there*, when oldtimers viciously taunted, blamed; denounced; reproached; indicted; hated every new inmate for having slept covered by what the oldtimers were convinced were silk comforters, while they had slept covered with lice, shrouded in the smoke billowing from the chimneys. Except that *then* and *there* silk comforters symbolized freedom while here——

"It's finished, over!" Chirie continued to rage. "No more fancy comforters for the *zsids!* Chirie, do this, do that; sweep the floor, bow and scrape before the wealthy Englers! The rotten scum! Our time has come now, you'll kiss my ass and suck my cock, you whore——"

Yashenko was suddenly near her, a revolver in his hand.

"I give you three seconds to open that door!" he shouted. "Three!" He grabbed Lisa's hand, himself kicked the door open.

There was a familiar tablecloth on the table, familiar curtains over the windows. She knew that in the drawers and closets, under the bed and in trunks, she would find the contents of the bunker, all familiar things with familiar contours.

She walked to a dresser, picked up a pair of four-branched silver candelabra.

"That's all, Leonid," she said crying. "Let's go now, quickly. Please."

16

The cemetery and the charred frame of the Orthodox Synagogue were the only Jewish landmarks left in Sighet. The synagogue was chosen for the service and Himy took charge.

The rubble from the fire was carted away, rows of folding chairs replaced the wooden pews and a lectern was placed where the Ark had stood. The singed, jagged walls of the building were topped by a star-studded dark sky, for the roof of the synagogue had been destroyed by the fire, too. Oil lamps shed light on the lectern and hundreds of thick, short candles flickered in the courtyard.

It was the eve of Yom Kippur.

"The five-thousand-seven-hundred-and-fifth Eve of Yom Kippur," Himy said from the lectern, facing the jam-packed congregation. All wore striped inmates' garments, even those who had not been in camps. "September, nineteenhundredfortyfive. What a date. The first Eve of Yom Kippur after the *horban*. The slaughter." His voice was strained, his eyes glistened with tears. "The Sacred Texts have been destroyed by our enemies. We have no more Sacred Texts and now, on the Eve of this Yom Kippur I don't know what to say. Or how to say it. It's just as well: the old texts wouldn't do anymore. Perhaps the time has come to write a new text. Perhaps tonight we'll do it. We need a new text."

He stepped down from the lectern.

There was silence in the roofless synagogue, a primal, awful silence.

Then Eva walked up to the lectern.

"Kol Nidre," she sang the traditional chant, *"ve' esarai, ush-vooai, vikonamai* . . . all vows and promises made unwittingly . . . shall be considered null and void . . ." She stopped in the middle of the chant, just before she came to the customary plea for forgiveness directed to God to pardon the iniquities of His People . . . as He has forgiven them from Egypt until now.

"I will not sing any more of it," she said, then slowly walked away from the lectern.

It was an impulse that made Lisa take her place. Or was it a hand drawing her up there? Yes, an invisible hand had summoned her to the lectern and an inner voice commanded her to remember how a year ago in Auschwitz word had spread that the onset of Yom Kippur, the holy Eve of Yom Kippur, would be at sundown that very day. Who started the rumor, who checked on its accuracy, or who kept count of the coming and passing of days and nights, Lisa did not know. No one knew. It was not important. What was important was to know and to feel that the Eve of Yom Kippur would come at sundown that very day.

At the lectern, Lisa was silent.

Have you forgotten, the voice asked, that Yom Kippur begins on its eve with chanting of the *Kol Nidre* and is followed by fasting till sundown next day so that one can fully concentrate on spiritual cleansing through atonement and through begging forgiveness from our God?

Have you forgotten, the voice further asked, have you forgotten that Yom Kippur, the Day of Atonement, is the holiest day in the year observed by Jews everywhere in the world?

Tell them, the voice urged, how that day was observed in another world as well. Tell them how it was observed in Hell. In Auschwitz.

Tell them, the voice insisted, of fasting in Auschwitz, from sundown to sundown, so that the Jews *there* could fully concentrate on atoning for their sins. Come on, Lisa Engler, tell them of sin. Of Yom Kippur in Auschwitz.

But such musings were not part of her thinking *then* and *there*, she wanted to answer the voice, they were not part of her

297

thoughts *then* and *there*, so many years ago, so many worlds ago. So many lives ago.

Then tell them of what was in your thoughts, the voice ordered. You must; you are a witness and a witness must speak.

Lisa was silent at the lectern. She stared at the Jews in front of her and shivered.

This is a new ritual, the voice informed her, you don't have to speak: they can hear your thoughts, see the pumping of your heart. You are them.

Then and *there* i only knew, or wanted to know, how to win another day, wrestle with the night, and endure starvation.

THE JEWS NODDED: THEY HEARD WHAT SHE THOUGHT.

Hunger was a driving force that made me fight death, perhaps against my will, a death i could or could not really fathom; still, a death that clung to me every instant, a ubiquitous presence that had become a familiar part of me, my own contour: me. Death and hunger owned me. Whatever i did or whoever i was, *then* and *there*, was the consequence of my obsequiousness to my two demanding, harsh, exquisitely cruel masters. With a puppet's mentality, a robot's reactions, i was enslaved to them. Death, tell me to run: i gallop. Hunger, order me to dig in filth till my nails break: i greedily grab withered potato peels, the decayed core of a cabbage, and chew with ecstasy, for i am extricating the sweetness of a ripe mango and the cool bouquet of smooth wine made of juicy tokay grapes. i worship you, Hunger, for you are my Lord; the wonders you perform are ceaseless. With a flick of your fingers you can make me eat partridge laced with truffles and suck the delicate flavor of steamed artichoke leaves dripping with lemon-flavored butter. My allegiance is yours, my Lord Hunger, yours and Death's alone. You crack the whip and i submit to your caress, as a lover submits to the beloved, for in the darkness of my horizon you alone shine and can flood my dry mouth with delectable tastes, such supreme culinary delights that i wish for death to retain the rapture forever.

i was absolved of everything, *then* and *there*, of all custom, all ties, all loyalties, all love, all bonds, all humanity. i owed my loyalty, my love, to my new gods, the Lord of Hunger and the Lord of Death. Though the Lord of Hunger was more demanding than the Lord of Death, it was Hunger i fell desperately in love with.

298

YES, THE EYES OF THE CONGREGANTS SAID, WE UNDERSTAND. WE KNOW.

Yom Kippur, which begins with fasting at sundown, in no way should interfere with the worship of *my* new gods.

NO, IN NO WAY, NEVER. WE KNOW. WE KNOW.

The day before Yom Kippur: supper had been distributed capriciously in the middle of the afternoon. There, in that world, hours or blocks of time were meaningless. Sweet was bitter, good was bad, ugly was beautiful, noon was midnight, dawn was dusk. But nothing really mattered, for the penumbra of my two Lords determined all things—all things dead though sometimes they seemed living. The slice of bread was not stale: yes my Lord, the slice was a loaf, crunchy and still warm from the oven (oven oven oven which oven which oven which bread bread bread oven oven) steaming goodness as i bite into it. Oh no, my Lord, the chip was not my tooth nor is it a worm in the bread. It is a tiny raisin you graciously stuck in the bread to titillate my senses. The concavity of my stomach is merely an optical illusion. Yes, my stomach is full, i am bursting from overeating, Hosanna, Hosanna to you my Lord and i thank you for the daily bread you so generously bestowed upon me. Amen.

AMEN, THE CONGREGANTS ANSWERED SILENTLY.

And then came the night when my other Lord laid claim on me. But i do not want to tell you about my cavorting with Lord Death—or perhaps i do, for in that place nothing was what it seemed to be, and although i was in love with Lord Hunger it was Lord Death who made love to me. It was a passion-filled night with Death, my only lover *then* and *there*. i wish i could tell you more about that night of abandon i had with him but i cannot, for right now my heart beats too fast and the veins in my temples throb and i think my head will split—and a muscle in the pit of my stomach tightens, tightens and it hurts just now, oh how it hurts! Tears well in my eyes and i am pulsating, my toes are numb—where are my feet? my hands tremble, please Death, do not hug me with such fervor, please, no more of this, please . . . but I give in, i cannot resist him.

i am cavorting with him, my lover the Lord of Death, and someone—something?—intrudes, breaks up my intimacy with Death, my lover Death. He lets go of me just as he was ready to take full possession of me, and he listens to that someone, something. We both listen. It is a chant. It comes from far away. From another world. i want to remain in the strangulating embrace of my lover that would climax in total peace, inertness, and i would never again ache, never again be hungry. Don't leave me Lord Death, don't let the chant chase you away. The chant makes me think, or feel, and it hurts. It hurts.

The chant. It insinuates itself. The moon filters in in pitiful rays through slits in the plank walls and falls on a woman standing in the middle of the barrack. The woman chants. i listen, *then* and *there*, for Lord Death, my lover, left me unfulfilled and exhausted from our love play. He is angry with me, i think as i listen to the chant. Lord Death has promised me the supreme climax, nothingness, and i yearn for it, but the chant rips into me and i almost forget about nothingness till, in the last moment, i am saved by my other lord, Lord Hunger, who stirs right next to me. My saliva runs profusely, the chant becomes just sound, i can even block it out, for i am going to feast on chunks of tender squab and nightingale tongues moistened with nectar, and the taste of pomegranates shall sweeten my sour breath.

It is morning. Barrels full of filthy dark liquid they call coffee are brought into the barrack. No matter. The nauseating liquid wets shriveled guts and everybody usually guzzles it down in seconds, but this morning nobody drinks. Something lingers in the air, i do not know what. There are no quarrels, no shrieks this morning, there is a peculiar quietude. What is it? i look to the center of the barrack for an answer, search for a shadowy figure i faintly remember from the night before. i think i detect a shadow, and i almost remember its purpose when the whip or the whistle propels me outdoors, and i stand at attention to be counted. i watch breathlessly at the pointing hand while we are counted and sigh with relief when it points in another direction, not mine . . .

YES, THE SURVIVORS NODDED, WE KNOW HOW IT WAS. WE KNOW. WE SAW THAT FINGER.

And then i march. Rags covering my feet are lost in the mud and i march barefoot. i hear the clank of my tin spoon against my tin bowl, both spoon and bowl dangling from a rope tied around my waist. The noise is reassuring, it blots out faint echoes of a chant, and the dance of the tin spoon banging against the tin bowl synchronizes with the cadence of marching.

300

EINS ZWEI DREI VIER, ZERO; ZERO, ZERO, LINKS. LINKS LINKS, THE SURVIVORS REMEMBERED.

The noise of the spoon and bowl, the noise of the marching, screens out the chant. i am hungry and spittle drools from my mouth as i look at the well-fed dogs prancing along the column. i hear shouts and i am marching, marching, and i am consumed with hunger.

i carry a huge rock in my arms, and i know that tomorrow i will take it back to where i took it from today. What am i saying my Lord? the rock is a pie, i'll bite into it, my Lord, and i won't think the pie is a brick from a legend i once knew. It was a legend about people carrying bricks like the pie i carry in my arms. Why did they carry those bricks? To build what? My head aches, oh how it aches. i cannot place the legend because i know it is not a legend. i am going mad. i ache and i parch.

i look up and see the sun is almost at its zenith. Soon the main meal will be distributed, the good soup. Some days they dump a few rotten potatoes in the soup and i pray that today will be that day.

The whistle blows and we are lashed into columns again. We march back to camp for the soup. i do not want to waste any seconds. Quivering with expectation, i disentangle the spoon and the bowl from the rope around my waist, then clutch my survival utensils in my hands. i am ready.

We have arrived at the distribution place. While we are whipped into rows of five, i converse with one of my Lords. He promises a regal banquet today and reprimands me for not drinking the morning liquid. "There was a shadow the night before," i say to him, "and i looked for it again this morning." He shakes his head reproachfully. "Beware," he admonishes me, "do not wander" (or did he say "do not wonder"?)

A giant in a silver-steel uniform struts towards the barrels. With a pompous gesture, he points the whip to the top of the barrel. A smaller uniformed giant jumps to remove the lid of the barrel. Steam rises from the barrel. i think i am inhaling it, though i merely gasp and swallow foul air. i smell potatoes and keep inhaling and gasping, and blissful visions of what is to come envelop me. i begin to sway back and forth to a rhythm i hear inside my head, a strange chant; and the clouds of steam carry me into happiness.

"Hey you!" A bark. i keep swaying.

"Come forward, bitch!" The same bark. Someone gives me a push from the back. i realize i am first in line for the soup. i want to run, leap to the barrel, but each step becomes an obstacle i struggle to overcome. What, who is holding me back . . . let go of me, there is the barrel, the soup, steam clouds of happiness. i am plodding ahead, towards the uniformed giant, whip in his hand.

The chant again. It is firmly embedded in my head and i clutch the bowl and spoon in my hand for dear life. i am near the barrel and note that the giant's badge on the military hat shows a skull and cross bones

and all at once i know where i am.

He dips into the barrel with a big ladle.

"Your bowl, stupid!" he yells. i glance at him and recognize the image of my lover on the badge. The recognition calms me, i feel at ease.

"Move, scum of the earth!" he yells again. i come close to him and the aroma rising from the barrel intoxicates me. i let go of the bowl and spoon and straighten out my arms. With a clink, the bowl and spoon meet my thigh.

"Look!" he shouts, lifting the ladle and lets the soup splash back in the barrel. i see bits of meat and potatoes drip back in the barrel and each splash evokes the beat of the chant in my head. In my heart too. The chant is familiar—yes, it is an affirmation of something, i do not know of what, but it does not matter because i remember what the chant is. It is the *Kol Nidre* and all at once i know who i am.

THE SURVIVORS NODDED AGAIN: WE DID NOT FORGET, WE NEVER FORGOT, THOUGH WE DID NOT WANT TO REMEMBER.

i put my arms behind my back and lock my hands:

"*Nein*," i say.

NEIN! LISA SAID DISTINCTLY IN THE EERIE SILENCE AND THE CONGREGATION ANSWERED IN ONE VOICE: NEIN!

"What?" the uniformed giant screams at me. "You don't want to eat, you Jew shit?" Furiously, he dips the ladle again into the barrel, lifts it out heavy with soup and throws it in my face, then one by one he kicks at the barrels. They topple. Steaming soup pours on the ground and i watch it seep into the earth.

The soup is on my face, it is warm. It dribbles over my mouth. i restrain my tongue's urge to lick the tepid liquid oozing down my face. The soup keeps dripping from my lips onto my chest and i begin to sway like a *davening* Jew because

all at once i know *i am* a Jew and i know it is Yom Kippur in Auschwitz.

The Day of Atonement in Hell.

Lisa gazed at the striped-clad Jews, then raised her eyes to the sky. It was the same starry sky that had looked down on her in Auschwitz, day after day, night after night. She lifted her hands, pointed to the sky and said:

"It is God who must atone, not I."

Someone walked up to the lectern and gently put his arms around her shoulders. Yashenko faced the survivors together with Lisa. When they stepped down, after a while, the Jews touched him lightly as they passed by.

At home that night Yashenko's fingers stroked the tattooed number on Lisa's left arm, several times.

"I wish I could make all those numbers my own if they could lessen the pain of the memory," he said and began to weep.

17

Next day Dr. Max Rausk returned to Sighet. The following morning he came to Naftuli's house.

"I was with Miklos Engler in Auschwitz, in the Buna," he said, "till January when the Nazis began liquidating the camp. The Russians were close by. The inmates were put in transports, some shipped out in freight trains, others put in marching column. Miklos and I were in one of the marching columns."

He coughed, held a handkerchief to his mouth.

"We were more dead than alive. *Muselmans*. Walking skeletons. There was no food. We dug for roots in the frozen ground, drank melted snow. Rags wrapped around our feet were lost in the snow. Still we were forced to march. We marched barefoot. We didn't even know where we were marching to.

"We marched and marched. Then the air raids came, the bombs. We still marched, driven by the SS. By that time there were only a few of us left . . ."

He stopped, looked around.

"Please help me," he said to Naftuli, "this is agony."

"He can't help you," Naomi whispered. "You are the witness. You must tell."

Dr. Rausk turned to Lisa.

"You are the witness," she echoed, "you must tell."

"We hadn't eaten for several days. It was freezing, it never stopped snowing. We were in a forest. Miklos couldn't walk any longer. His legs were frozen, so were his hands. I supported him for a while, others did too. Then one morning he just lay down in the snow . . ."

Lisa ran out into the street. In the afternoon Yashenko found her in Anna's cart in the market place, lying in the hay, knees drawn up to her chin and her left thumb in her mouth.

BOOK VI

"Therefore shall a man leave his father and his mother, and shall cleave unto his wife: and they shall be one flesh."

—Genesis 2:24

1

The summer was over.

On unpaved streets, fall rains had soaked the summer's dust and left dark puddles and caked mud. Horses drawing carriages and oxen pulling carts splattered mud on houses and passers-by. The trees, the parks and the mountains were stripped of vivid colors. The magic of the first post-war summer that had lulled the people into believing in the promise of approaching bliss was forgotten.

Life went on as if nothing had changed except the season.

Yet a change other than seasonal had been coming all along, at an irrepressible tempo, forecasting fateful consequences. Although people later claimed that the change took them by surprise and that it came swiftly, overnight, while the town slept, so to speak, the fact was that the people were too exhausted by war and politics, too overcome by malaise, to have bothered to notice the obvious.

It was on the morning a Democratic Party Bloc antisabotage squad swooped down on Imre's store that the people had to acknowledge, at last, a change, which had not only been coming all along, but had arrived, unyielding, and which would affect them for a long time to come.

By October 1945, the DPB had become the dominant political umbrella under which parties of all shades, ranging from moderate to progressive and including the Romanian Communist Party, were gathered. After the Red Army had ousted the Nazis in the fall of 1944, the prewar National Peasants and Liberal parties had reconstituted themselves under the leadership of Iuliu Maniu and Gheorghe Tatarescu, respectively. The Romanian provisional government all along had been promising free national elections within the year, and the DPB even paid lip service to Maniu, an underground war hero and symbol of resistance during the Nazi occupation. Eventually, the provisional government passed an economic antisabotage act to stem black-market activities. People shrugged their shoulders and said it was high time for such a step. But the creation of antisabotage squads to enforce the law caused concern to some, particularly since the squads consisted solely of members of the DPB who also belonged to the Romanian Communist Party. They arbitrarily barged into stores, demanded invoices and inspected books, wreaked havoc with the merchandise and arrested anyone on the slightest suspicion of having violated the law. Special courts, set up to deal with the so-called lawbreakers, rendered summary judgments within three days of arrest, while the accused were kept in jail.

The same morning the DPB antisabotage squad descended on Imre's store, the city employees were applying finishing touches to next day's parade to celebrate the anniversary of the Red Revolution. Portraits of Stalin, Lenin and Marx were plastered over buildings, the Crown Hotel was bedecked with red flags and carpenters were busy erecting a reviewing stand in the middle of the Grand Corso, on the side of the park. Though these preparations had been in progress all week long, the town's people behaved as if they were unaware of what was going on. But when a black automobile, a red star painted on one of its side doors and a Romanian flag on the other, parked in front of Imre's store the car was instantly identified as belonging to an antisabotage squad and *then* the people began to wonder, anxiously, if there was a connection between the forthcoming celebration and the activities of the DPB squad.

310

"No price tag on the merchandise displayed in the window," the antisabotage goons told Imre. "Outright sabotage!"

"You are joking," Imre said. "The price tag is still there, see for yourselves. It simply fell off the merchandise when your car screeched to a halt before my store and rattled the window." He pointed to the price tag in the fold of the merchandise: "It was tagged on before you arrived——"

"Bullshit. You are a saboteur, an enemy of the people. A capitalist. We charge you with hiking prices, black marketeering, crimes against the people, subversive activities . . ."

2

Next day at noon, as soon as the parade was over, the Red
Army brass and its staff trooped over to the banquet hall at the
kommandatura. Long tables groaned under the weight of bowls
of caviar and platters of sturgeon, of bottles of vodka arranged in
rows like endless centerpieces. By midafternoon toasting Marx
and Lenin was still going strong, though a few men began to
slobber over names of war heroes such as Rokossovski and Voro-
shilov. Still, the celebrants drank heartily, now and then spilling
vodka as they raised goblets filled to the brim, simultaneously
pointing their thumbs upwards, calling out ott harasho, then
guzzling the vodka in one gulp.

The tempo increased, the empty vodka bottles multiplied.
Glasses were continually refilled, a perfect drinking rhythm had
been reached. There was no slackening now.

Grisha Keroff was moved, his stump throbbed. It always
throbbed when his feelings were aroused. He turned to Marcovski:

"With your permission, comrade colonel." Marcovski nodded
and Keroff pulled his revolver out of its holster, aimed at the ceiling, pulled the trigger. The shot brought everyone to his feet.
Keroff refilled his glass, waited till each man did likewise.

"To our savior, Joseph Stalin!" he shouted, and as one the men snapped to attention, their chests expanded, their eyes flashed.

"To Joseph Stalin, Russia's savior!" they shouted in unison, quickly drained their drinks and smashed the empty glasses against the wall.

The throb in Keroff's stump was diminishing and he thought, with anticipation, that the drinking would at last begin in earnest. The toast to Stalin had now been properly made, terse and to the point, signaling that everyone was at liberty to drink himself into happiness, or painlessness. They could revel in the glories of war, the fire in the Russian heart. The Russian spirit, for centuries abused and exploited by bloodsucking aristocrats and bourgeois brigands, could freely soar as it revealed its stupendous wounds and bathed in the balm of cascades of vodka.

The drunken Keroff hopped, dragging his artificial leg behind him. "Stalin," he cried, "*Batyushka* Stalin, ask something of me. Anything. You are Russia, *Batyushka*, and I love Russia." His eyes filled with tears. He ran his fingers over a row of medals pinned on his uniform, then slapped his good leg.

"Ask for this one too, *Batyushka*; you can have it. It's yours. I love Russia. The war was my wedding."

He noticed Yashenko.

"And the *zsid* has a woman," Keroff mumbled before he passed out.

Marcovski inserted a cigarette in his holder and looked over the debris in the banquet hall. It was late in the evening and the celebration was over. Most of the men had been able to make it on their own and had departed. A few, too drunk even to stir, were sprawled on chairs, under tables. Only Keroff, flat on his back, was on top of a table, his good leg dangling from the knee down over the edge, while his artificial leg extended rigidly into space.

Postwar depression, battle fatigue, Marcovski mused, flicking ashes on the floor, physical depletion. It was the same in his days too though he and his peers took it differently. Even drinking was different. They had the stamina to go through old-fashioned drinking bouts without passing out and without giving in to self-pity or sentimentalism.

313

For a fraction of a second Marcovski permitted himself to delve into the past. A pretty girl with long black braids and eyes as clear as the blue summer sky. Yet it was different in his days. It had to be. A lay, that's all a woman was, a good fuck or maybe not so good a fuck, so what. Black hair or blond, blue eyes or some other color, it didn't really matter. Fornication was legitimate and there was plenty of it, but when it came to the Party, love was tangential to their lives. It never interfered with their destiny. The sole involvement which had captivated him and his comrades was the Revolution. That was their real passion. That separated the boys from the men and that aroused their manhood. No hard-on comparable to that. Worth the jail in Odessa, even worth having been tortured by the Okrana.

He carefully killed the cigarette in a saucer, then motioned to Yashenko.

"How is the girl?" Marcovski asked nonchalantly. "She is getting inside you, eh?" The question was a mere prurient peek into an affair, small talk about an ordinary war romance, insignificant and passing. A man-to-man exchange of intimacies . . .

"Comrade colonel," Yashenko said, "the girl belongs to a different world, another system. How could she get inside me?" He had promised Lisa the night before he would try to get Imre out of jail and had been wondering all evening, during the partying, how to accomplish that. Freeing Imre was not the same as freeing Erno. Erno had been picked up by Red security, whereas Imre was in the hands of the civil authorities. The Imre incident was strictly a local, internal matter the occupation forces were supposed to stay away from. But . . .

"Precisely," Marcovski agreed. "She is the offshoot of a system you chose to leave. Never forget that." Reproach and enticement suffused his voice, and Yashenko reexperienced the old peculiar mixture of revulsion and flattery.

"How can I forget?" he said and remembered the feel of her round shoulders, the sweet softness of her body synergizing with his. "How can I forget the red star?" he repeated, forcing himself back into the immediate present. His head began to ache. Imre, he shouldn't forget Imre either.

He must clear it with Marcovski, though, if he was to undertake anything on Imre's behalf. Be cautious, he warned himself. In the last few minutes, he noticed, Marcovski's face had changed: the eye slits had narrowed, the teasing smile of camaraderie had turned into a predatory expression.

"Ah! That's what I expect to hear from my finest neophyte, my protégé. That's what you are, you know. Like a son almost. I am responsible for you." Marcovski laughed. It was a short, curt laugh. He cleared his throat: "All right. Now back to business. This Maniu trend. It's got to stop. To allow resuscitation of national pride runs counter to our interests—at this point. Maniu is from the old guard, nothing can change *that*. He will have to be, hm . . . silenced. We must project and thus avoid embarrassments. The ethnic personality cult is out. Out! Besides, the Romanians still have their little King Mihai; it should keep them at bay for the moment."

"Yes, of course you are right," Yashenko said. "The Maniu conflict is inevitable."

Marcovski now gestured in the direction of the Crown Hotel.

"How are *they* doing?"

"Over-doing, in my opinion." Yashenko walked to the window, looked across the street. On the roof of the hotel the large painted sign reading DEMOCRATIC PARTY BLOC HEADQUARTERS—JUDETUL MARAMURES was topped by a red star and a still larger sign reading ROMANIAN COMMUNIST PARTY.

"How's that?" Marcovski asked.

"In their zeal to prove their worth, the local chieftains take foolish and precipitant actions. It may boomerang——"

"What did they do?"

"For instance, they arrest a man they claim has violated the antisabotage act. Except that the man hasn't. He is innocent."

"So?"

"So they shouldn't have arrested him, particularly since the whole town knows the man to be innocent. Furthermore, the man is an earnest believer in reconstructing the old system——"

"Hm. It's foolish indeed, in that case. But still, it's a local matter, It doesn't concern us."

"It should, comrade colonel. We are in charge——"

"Yashenko, such petty squabbles, minor injustices, mean little to me. We can't be bogged down with trifles. The scope of our work must not be deflected by caring how justice, on local levels, works. Besides, we have agreed to a *hands-off* attitude in domestic matters——"

"Only in terms of public consumption, comrade colonel. That's why I am clearing it with you before I——"

"No! Absolutely no interference——"

"Comrade colonel, the man is innocent! He also happens to be a Jewish survivor of fascist persecutions. We can't——"

"Yes we can—and we will!" Marcovski exploded. "So that's why you are so worked up: the man is a Jew, your woman's buddy probably, isn't that so?" He ejected the cigarette from the holder, then inserted another one that he lit with the still burning stub. He dropped the stub on the floor, crushed it with the tip of his boot and now calmly said, "You are pushing, Yashenko, pushing much too hard. Watch out. I shall not stand for that!"

"It seemed to me a routine matter, comrade colonel." The intensity of Marcovski's outburst surprised Yashenko. He had never had cause to suspect Marcovski of anti-Semitic feelings, and in all the years he had known him as Marciuc, Yashenko couldn't recall one instant when he lost his temper. The colonel's present volatility worried him. "I retract my suggestion, comrade colonel," he added.

"You had better!" Marcovski snapped. "And while you're retracting, you might as well do a full job of it!" He unbuckled his belt, leaned back in the chair, pounded the table with his fist. "Tell me about the religious happening in the burned-out synagogue. Start your retraction *there* . . ."

Yashenko was alarmed for an instant. What should he tell Marcovski? What could he tell? He didn't even remember how it all happened. All he remembered was seeing Lisa dressed in striped garments, tears flowing down her cheeks, stand before the congregation and staring into their faces, forging with them an eerie bond, a silent communion. He had wished to be part of that ritual, be one of them. Perhaps he was one of them. Yes, he was one of them . . . The stars, or the flames from the oil lamps, shone on her moist cheeks, her large green eyes had become immense, bottomless, like the sea; and the congregation fed off her, leaving her empty and enervated. He had watched her for a while till suddenly he could not bear seeing her at once inside and outside her own experience, and aching, aching. The agony was too much; the silence devastating. He had to relieve some of her pain, and some of his own. What, who, compelled him to walk up to the lectern, touch her, try to share her suffering? The purgation was for himself too. And he broke down that night, weighed down afresh by his own losses, by the memory of the camps. The bittersweet taste of Zyklon B was in his mouth, he was gasping for air and choking. She had comforted him, rocked his head in her arms till the pain spilled out of his heart and made room for memories he had forgotten to remember.

"That religious happening was an unconventional *Kol Nidre* service," Yashenko said slowly. "Yom Kippur being the Jews' most——"

"I know all about that!" Marcovski thundered, and the force of his statement startled Yashenko. "But did the comrade captain have to go to the *stibl* and *daven?* Or did First Adjutant Captain Yashenko think he was *amchu?*"

Stibl. Daven. Amchu. These words stunned Yashenko. How could Marciuc Marcovski know of such expressions only Jews use unless . . . No, it can't be . . .

"Exposing yourself like a bleeding heart sentimentalist! Retract that if you can! How long do you think I'll protect you?"

Yashenko thought, he must not jump to conclusions, his memory was overburdened, playing tricks with him. It was useless, though. The blurry images refused to dissolve. Stubbornly, like a mechanism turned on by remote control, the images now resolved themselves into clear pictures.

"Even if I am partial to you," Markovski threatened, "I have the strength to cut out my own heart for the sake of the Party!"

Of course! The words of the famed Sasha Markenberg, the Stenka Razin of the Communist Party, as Keroff had called Marcovski. But Markenberg was the young Jewish intellectual from Odessa whereas Marcovski was—is Markenberg the young Jewish intellectual who had sacrificed his sweetheart for the sake of the Party? Was it in 1918 or 1919 when the youngest member of the Cheka, the twenty-two-year-old Sasha Markenberg, had arrested a group of counterrevolutionaries? His own sweetheart was among them, but Markenberg treated her as he had to treat the enemies of the Soviet State. As Marcovski or Marciuc would: ordered the execution of the entire group.

". . . then your scuffle with the villagers," Marcovski was saying, "the brothers . . ."

"Tiplea." Yashenko wanted Marcovski to go on talking, or shouting, so that he could collect himself, pull his thoughts

317

together. His headache had slipped into his chest and was causing him pain. He had to overcome the notion that the pain in his
chest would cease if he would bodily attack Marcovski. Or just
shake him by the shoulders, shout in his face "Shalom, brother!
You are *amchu*, one of us, after all! What if I *davened*, brother
Marcovski? It was Erev Yom Kippur, even brother Markenberg
knew that. But brother Marciuc never let on; he manipulated the
whole Iasi cell, but most of all he manipulated me, me, his own
kind, me . . ."

"Yes, the Tiplea brothers," Marcovski said curtly. His fingers
now drummed the table, the vertical crease in his forehead deep-
ened. "Your acts smelled of petit-bourgeois sentimentality," he
shouted. "Retract *that* if you can! They were also counterproductive to the Party's interests at a time when the country folk, the
peasantry, should be allied with us. Instead, you antagonize
them! I am warning you: don't ever act in collision with my policies, Yashenko! Understand?"

Yashenko nodded though he knew he was expected to say
something, admit his errors. Yet too much was converging on
him to be able to deal with all his emotions at once. He therefore
played for time and kept nodding while his mind sorted out
what was what.

From the way Marcovski was still going at it, pounding and
drumming the table and shouting, Yashenko concluded the colonel had inadvertently dropped a few telling clues as to his origins, slips of the tongue the colonel was not even aware of. Yashenko resolved not to let on that he had picked up the clues—
not until . . .

". . . you are not just anybody! You are the man *I* picked, understand? *I, I,* Alexandr Michailovich Marcovski, *I've* picked
you! Your actions reflect on my judgment, damn it, can't you see
that? You cannot jeopardize our influence because . . . because
of your prick, damn it! And you are an idiot to boot: don't you
see you jeopardize her too? Did you think Keroff would just
stand by idly while you fraternize with capitalists? He's been after me to settle your affair with a brief order, a signature . . ."

. . . then why indeed didn't Marcovski settle the matter with
a brief order, a snap of his finger and a flick of his cigarette, Yashenko wondered. Was he holding Lisa as a pawn? Or was it

Marcovski's own feud with Keroff? How about another perspective, Yashenko thought all of a sudden: ordinary humanity, for instance. Would that be so out of character? Perhaps compensating for a rash act in one's youth. Dedication to a cause had not made a cynic out of him; why then should he assume it had made a brute out of Marcovski? Perhaps Marcovski had been moved, after all was said and done, by the one thing the three of them undeniably had in common, the one thing they were born with, regardless of geography and politics: their Jewish roots.

". . . yet I refuse," Marcovski said, then slowly inserted a cigarette in the holder, peered at Yashenko and waited a few seconds.

"Don't bother with the light." Marcovski lit his cigarette. "Has the girl bewitched you?" he asked snippily.

"The girl hasn't bewitched me." Yashenko managed to sound calm in spite of a spasm in his chest. "She hasn't bewitched me, comrade colonel, but I ache for her, at times. She has suffered, comrade colonel, I can't retract that. Her ordeal was beyond imagining. The camps . . . I've seen them. She is a victim of fascist-imperialist forces——"

"Hold it." Marcovski's voice was now even, the crease in his forehead smoothed out. "Sit down, Yashenko. Let's get a few concepts into proper focus." He waited till Yashenko sat down, opposite him, offered a cigarette which Yashenko took, then continued: "Your woman, Engler, she is a victim, yes. At the same time she is proof of the bourgeoisie's inherent weakness and bent for self-destruction. The Marxist doctrine that——"

"The fate of the Jews is indissolubly linked with the emancipating struggle of the international proletariat," Yashenko finished the sentence for him reflexively, in a flat voice. "I know."

"Good. You know what's worth knowing. It's also worth knowing that fun is fun, nothing more. It passes . . . as your fling with the girl will pass. Men in your position will always have the pick of the crop as long as they take their women to bed, not to their hearts. Nothing must interfere with your destiny, Yashenko, nothing. The Party——"

"Comes first, second, third . . . I know, comrade colonel," Yashenko said mechanically. But why doesn't it work out, he

319

brooded, why? Something was running amok in his guts, destiny, struggle, emancipation, Marx; it was cutting into him. Come on, Markenberg, be a *mensch*, don't you see the girl bleeds?

"Good. Only the Party is a permanent reality. Sentimentalism is a cheap commodity and, besides, it's a petit-bourgeois vice. Cheating on the Party." He paused, then asked softly: "Are you guilty of that?"

"Never." His reply was firm; the pain in his chest increased. Never, he thought again; but the girl bleeds. He bleeds. They all bleed.

". . . you've overcome your own petit-bourgeois background," Marcovski purred, "shed tribal ties before they could drag you down as they dragged Jews down for centuries. . . ."

How can he speak of Jews, Yashenko wondered, without blinking an eye?

". . . because Professor Marciuc had opened your eyes and you acquired historical consciousness which made you into an ardent socialist imbued with idealism. *That* was appropriate for *then.* You've come thus far, as a result of my manipulation, because I am convinced *now* you are ready for the next step, the one following youthful idealism: sober, practical materialism. I speak as your mentor, Yashenko, not as your superior: you must adhere to the Party line without a scintilla of deviation. I know you can—I groomed you. What looms ahead of you is the summit, and you must keep up with the march of progress to insure your place there. The summit is power, the apex: world communism. Those who don't have the stamina to get there must fall by the wayside. One's mettle is tested. Those who stumble or get weighed down by sentiment must be left behind; those who don't have the vision must be rendered ineffective. Every great cause requires sacrifices, selflessness. Can you do it, my boy? Do you have what it takes?"

"Yes!" Yashenko replied with the fervor of the young student in Marciuc's class, "yes, comrade, I can do anything for the Party. I have the stamina——"

"I know you do. Now listen: there is just one path for men like you and me and time is of the essence. We cannot waste it to pick up cripples on the path to the summit——"

"But the girl." The pain in Yashenko's chest had become unbearable, it erased the zeal in his voice. "The girl . . . she . . ."

320

Marcovski looked at him in surprise.

"Oh, the girl again. She is innocent, is that what you're trying to tell me? Well, in a way she is innocent, and in a way she isn't, because she has become a force of history which may cause an infection, destroy your entire fabric of thought. I don't particularly call that innocence, do you?"

They were silent for a while, then Marcovski reached for Yashenko's hands.

"All right. Listen: I too have seen the camps. The Jews' annihilation by Hitler was the terrible price they paid for having opted to stay as an individual group, by themselves, as Jews, instead of joining us in our socialist struggle for world revolution. Their massacre could have been avoided if . . . if they had worked for international socialism and the emancipation of the world proletariat. But even those Jews who were genuine socialists looked for Zionist justification in Marxism—and there is no such thing, of course. Thus, the Jews' socialism had major elements of petit-bourgeois ethnic patriotism and was ineffective to stem the tide to the camps. . . ."

He lit a cigarette, watched the smoke.

"Don't worry though. Remember Marx again: the Jews have survived not in spite of history, but because of it."

The drunken Keroff now stirred. He glided off the table, his crude artificial leg banged the floor. Marcovski and Yashenko turned their eyes in his direction.

"Now then," Marcovski snapped. "I've had enough of this. Bleeding hearts make me squeamish. Start winding down with her. She means trouble for you."

3

Next day in jail Imre was adamant. He refused to admit there had been no price tag on display in the window.

"No, goddammit! No!" he yelled at Gyuri, who tried to persuade him to cooperate with the authorities. "I violated no law! I wouldn't pervert the truth to keep the books balanced. . . ."

"Grow up, man," Yankel Schwartz advised him the following day. "Just admit a little infraction. You'll come out smelling almost clean. There are all kinds of truths . . . You can satisfy everyone."

"Go to hell. I know of only one kind of truth."

The third morning in jail, Imre woke up to thuds and screams coming from the adjacent cell. The screams came from Bozsi, he recognized her voice. Someone was beating her up, pummeling and kicking her.

The screams stopped in the afternoon, after Imre made a simple deal with his jailers: in return for dropping charges of economic sabotage made against him, he would apply at once for membership in the DPB.

"But I wasn't jailed," Bozsi assured him later, "how could you have heard me scream. . . ."

"It sounded like you, it must have been you," Imre said. "The moans I heard were yours. I couldn't bear them. That's why I gave in."

After Imre's arrest and release many shopkeepers joined the DPB. At the Crown Hotel they attended biweekly educational meetings where regular roll calls and rigorous drills in how to interpret history and economics kept them on their toes and in line. Members were instructed to learn by heart certain sections assigned to them from a recently-published book entitled *History of the Romanian Communist Party*. The book was unofficially referred to as the *Caca Book* because it was made of a cheap, greenish paper and because its contents, it was whispered, were as smelly as shit.

4

The window shades were framed by light coming from a streetlamp and thinned out the darkness in the room. She was lying on her stomach, close to him. The pillow was pushed down, to the foot of the bed, her face in the bend of one arm, her other arm resting on his chest.

Yashenko listened to her breathing. It was even and soft, barely audible. He could not tell if she was awake or sleeping and he wondered if she ever had dreams. She had never spoken to him of dreams. Tenderly, he touched her hand on his chest. Her fingers were warm, and quivered slightly at his touch.

He wished he knew what she was thinking, lying next to him, for her physical and emotional state had become important to him, much more so than a wartime romance, albeit a special one, would justify. The realization startled him, and he pondered whether indeed the romance was getting out of hand, beyond the finite perimeters he had originally envisioned. He had found, lately, that making love to her was not just an erotic act: it was a joyous merging, the knowledge of flesh with love, an undiluted pleasure that let him soar to dizzying heights and made him feel indomitable. He had never before made love so happily.

Still, he brooded, if he lost control over the affair it was unintentional; the order of priorities must be reexamined, placed in proper perspective, and his affair with Lisa toned down. A sinking feeling in his gut warned him of his own ambivalence and he shifted his thoughts, on purpose, to Marcovski who obviously had sensed his dilemma before he, Yashenko himself, knew there was one. That was why the old Bolshevik had put on a masterful performance the other night! Wooing Yashenko, manipulating him and finally dangling before him the supreme award, power, in return for uncontested allegiance to the Party, to which, in point of fact, he was pledged under any circumstances. Yes, it had been an admirable performance, Yashenko thought, and acknowledged his own vacillation between respect for Marcovski's astuteness and resentment at having his own loyalty doubted.

The thought of power, though, quickened Yashenko's heartbeat. He had not actively sought it, nor had he privately schemed to get it. But he was a pragmatist: when offered to him he would accept it without hesitation. Some men chose to become a doctor, an architect, a pilot, a teacher. He had chosen to become a social revolutionary. A communist. That was his profession. He would give of himself to that profession unstintingly because it was a good one and, like any other man, he would not refuse power when it came his way. Cripples could never stop him from marching. He would merely try to heal, in passing.

He reached in the dark for a cigarette on the night table. Her hand slipped off his chest, stayed inert on the bed for a few seconds, then groped for him. When she found him, her palms pressed lightly on his shoulders.

"You were brooding, Leonyushka," she whispered.

"No, *golubka*, I was merely wondering——"

"Oh." She sat up and kissed him. "What about?"

"I wondered if you have dreams."

"Oh?"

"Do you?"

She was silent.

"Please tell me: do you?"

"Yes," she said slowly, then took the pillow from the foot of the bed, lay down on her stomach again and covered her head with the pillow.

"Tell me your dream."

He waited a little, then turned her around. "Please, Lisa. Tell me your dream. I so want to know. Share it with me."

"All right." She breathed hard for a while. "All right. I dreamed of a house. I always dream of the same house. I dream of an enormous house made of bread. Everything in the house is made of bread: the walls, the ceilings, the floors. The furniture and the windows. Everything is bread. Walls in some of the rooms are made of white bread, others of *challah*. The bread is warm, soft, just baked. I smell the sweet smell of good bread. The lamps are made of little buns, the beds of rolls. Some chairs are made of *croissants*, a few of pastry dough. Nobody lives in the house but I go there every day. Every day. I walk through the rooms and eat the house of bread. I eat the chairs, or I nibble at the walls. I eat. I eat. That's my dream."

She paused.

"I'm sorry," she said. "That's the only dream I have. The only one. The house of bread. I have no other dreams."

She shivered and he embraced her.

"Let me tell you something, Leonyushka," she said in his arms. "Hunger had kept me alive, *then* and *there*. It's insane to say that hunger can keep someone alive. Crazy. But *then* and *there* was a crazy world. Everything was upside down. Hunger saved me from dying. Now you know."

"Now I know," he said in a hush.

"You would have expected mass suicides or at least a great number of suicides. But there were hardly any suicides at all. Do you know why? Because you felt nothing but hunger. We knew no other reality—except the reality of death, of course. Nothing else was real. But the first reality was hunger, even when the chimneys belched fire. I had thought at first they were bakery chimneys, though I must have known all along what they really were."

She sat up abruptly, covered her mouth with her hand. What made her say that? she wondered, she had wanted to say something else. Was it his closeness, the magic of his love, which made her feel safe and strong, permitting her to formulate ugly, terrible truths which she had been denying? She took a deep breath.

"I had believed *then* and *there*," she said, the words coming in a steady irrepressible flow, "that the world was ignorant of what was being done to us; that as soon as it learned about the horror it would move heaven and earth to rescue us."

She laughed in a queer way.

"I was a simpleton, of course, to have had such ideas . . . The chimneys belched fire and we were doomed. It's all very clear to me now. Should the war have ended later, a week or a month later, I would have been dead. All of us would have been dead. Our doom was only a matter of time; but we didn't know that. But the world knew. It knew and it didn't give a damn. Right, Leonyushka?"

He said nothing.

"The world didn't care about the Jews, right, Leonyushka?"

He still said nothing.

"Right, Leonyushka?"

"Yes," he murmured. "The world didn't care about us."

She nodded and said, "We didn't know the world didn't care because all we knew was hunger. If the Nazis had given us an extra crumb, another bite of bread, maybe we would have had the energy to figure out things, understand that it was hopeless, see the doom in store for us. . . ."

The Party, he thought. The Russo-German pact. Bershad, Transnistria. Then Babi Yar, just outside Kiev. 33,000 Jews. One day he must take time out to count that far. Farther, much farther. It would take him months, perhaps years. A lifetime. The Yashenbergs: Iasi, Transnistria, Babi Yar? Would the locale make a difference?

". . . and in our stupor we took it for granted Roosevelt and Churchill and Stalin had no inkling the Nazis were exterminating us. We had harnessed every ounce of energy to scrounge for food instead of to think. It was one or the other: think out matters, conclude we were doomed, and make a dash to the electrified fences; or blindly follow our instinct of self-preservation. Thinking was suspended and hunger took over. It made us fight for food. Nothing else mattered. . . ."

But the summit, he thought again, and his heart was heavy, the summit mattered too. Time marched on; it did not wait while do-gooders bent down to pick up cripples. Nothing could bring

327

back the Yashenbergs anyhow. And Lisa? She was young, she would heal. . . .

"The world is now judging us, I hear. The world which had been outside the electrified fences sits in judgment over the world which had been inside those fences. Did you know a civilian tribunal in Cluj is trying one Magda Terecky for having slept with the *Lagerführer* of Camp C in Birkenau?"

"Yes," he said. "I know."

Dawn was breaking through the rim around the window shades. The room was unfolding into a soft milky whiteness.

"Terecky saved her mother and two cousins from the chimneys. That's all she did. In return she had to sleep with the *Lagerführer*. The judges judging Terecky," she asked angrily, "how many people did they save from the chimneys? . . . Terecky had bread, lots of bread. The entire camp must have been jealous of her. There wasn't a woman who wouldn't have eagerly changed places with her. Bread meant life."

She looked at him. His eyes seemed moist and had changed into mirrors in which she saw herself, as she was *then* and *there*, her head shaven in a grotesque pattern of little clumps of bristles the *Aufseherin's* scissors failed to snip off, an eyesore in rags, prowling in the back of the infirmary near a room said to be the inmates' brothel. Grunts and groans draw her nearer, she perches on a ledge, looks through the window and sees bodies copulating, chunks of bread on the floor, a woman eats during copulation. She stands close to the entrance of the brothel, waiting. Perhaps a man from the *Scheisskommando,* the shit brigade that comes once a week to the women's camp to clean shit houses, perhaps such a man would choose her. Once the men from the *Scheisskommando* finish cleaning the rows and rows of ditches over which women crouch, baring their abscessed buttocks to piss and shit while the men scoop it out from under them with pails attached to long sticks, they go to the brothel. Perhaps one of them would offer her a slice of bread in return for going in there with him. But nobody does.

She threw her arms around Leonid.

"Hold me," she sobbed. "Don't let go of me, just hold me. Magda Terecky could have been me."

* * *

328

Another night.

"Brooding again, Leonyushka?"

"No . . . No." An unaccountable yearning to know more of her, of her life prior to what she called *then* and *there*, had kept him awake. Or was it his need to validate himself, relive his own past through her memories?

"No, no," she echoed. "But it's yes, yes. Please, Leonyushka, don't shut me out. . . ."

"All right," he said quickly. "I want to know how it was with you before you . . . before the——"

"*Then* and *there*," she helped him. "I don't remember. Don't ask me to."

"You should remember and speak of it, Lisa. It will do you good. It will do us good."

"I can't do it," she murmured. "I can't. Please . . ." She turned away from him, to the wall, pulled the cover over her head.

He pulled back the cover, slipped his arm under her and held her tight to his chest.

"I've caused you anguish. Forgive me. Forgive me . . . It's against my will to hurt you, ever. . . ."

Her body stiffened suddenly. He held on to her even tighter, tighter, almost crushing her in his embrace, and waited, patiently, for her to say something.

"That's what Papa said," she whispered, "once a year."

Her words were thorns, perhaps barbed wire tearing into her own flesh, he thought, feeling her heart beat in his palm. The fluttering of an injured bird, dying, dying. Warmth, caring, should make her renascent; he must not let go.

"When," he asked, "when did your Papa say that?"

"On the eve of Yom Kippur. After Mamma lit the candles . . ."

Did her mother wear a white lace shawl, he wondered, as Rifka Yashenberg did?

". . . and my brothers and I stood near her," she went on, "waiting for Papa. 'If I caused you anguish,' he said to us, 'forgive me. It was against my will.' Then . . ."

"Then what?"

. . . then Leonid clearly saw Nachum Yashenberg pick up the

blue velvet bag with the Star of David embroidered on it in which his son Leibele had respectfully placed the prayer book, the immaculate white *kitl* and the soft-soled slippers.

". . . we went to the synagogue," she said faintly, "and prayed that God should inscribe us in the Book of Life."

He remembered an old song, *es brent yidn, in der stetl brent*, but he hummed the lullaby Nachum Yashenberg had sung to a small boy, *under your cradle, little one*, till he and she fell asleep in each other's arms.

5

Then the letter from Drifter arrived. The stamps were French, the date on the envelope was August 28, 1945.

"There is another world besides Sighet and Auschwitz," the letter began, "the two major poles of your existence which, at this time, exclude the reality of the ordinary world. It is from this ordinary world, ulcerated, ravaged and hideous, that I write you.

"My whereabouts are not important. By the time these lines reach you I'll be far from the place I am now. I don't know where that place will be—I only know it will be somewhere else.

"There is a chance, out here, to redeem one's humanity. Or one's self-respect.

"We start from scratch, invent new rites for old passages, re-feel feelings and rename things. We make up new words and create a new language to express the ugly realities unveiled by auschwitzmaidanek or buchenwaldbergenbelsen or treblinkada-chau or theresienstadtlodzvilna or chelmnoponaryheilhitler.

"The extermination camps are open. Anyone can safely stroll through them, particularly since the camps have undergone subtle changes. The Americans, the French, the English, the average good guys, have begun to cosmeticize the abominable: they call extermination camps 'concentration' camps and drown the smell of evil in clouds of antiseptic deodorants. They have toned down reality, made it more tolerable. After all, one must consider that the impact of deathcamps *post facto* on the observer, visitor, tourist, or curiosity seeker, might not be merely one of guilt and shame. The visible results of naked power, mountains of human hair, for instance, might produce an involuntary hard-on, make the ordinary man vicariously experience the ultimate high of a global orgasm. Surely such a horrible thrill must be denied for the sake of *kultur*, no?

"And who can tell, maybe some day the deathcamps will be parks, fields, playgrounds or parts of *autobahns*.

"And the extermination camps now smell like mere concentration camps. . . .

"Still, when my view of the sky is blocked by mountains of corpses I wonder if the world had been born necrophiliac, if the *goyim* have some perverse atavistic addiction to Jewish corpses. How else can one account for it?

"My hatred of evil overwhelms me. And my shame on behalf of humanity. And my pain.

"Numbers begin to emerge. It is staggering, even to me. Tell me, Lisa, have you ever counted up to a million? A hundred thousand? Of course not. How then can one comprehend the murder of millions? Impossible, dear girl, simply impossible. One man's death touches us deeply; even the death of ten men. A hundred. Beyond that? How can one weep for the incomprehensible? The sheer magnitude of the numbers makes those numbers meaningless. I can't comprehend millions. Yet they killed us in millions.

"Six millions, they say.

"We were even screwed by the numbers.

"The world is now bent to find an answer as to who should bear the guilt for the slaughter.

"An army of experts, who call themselves psychiatrists, sociologists, psychologists, social workers, or other such impressive titles, has invaded the displaced persons camps. They interview the survivors in depth, they analyze, use intimidating tape recorders while they dig and twist with their questions, ifs and buts and how comes, then set up charts and graphs and theorize about sheep being led to slaughter, about the victims being their own executioners, about lack of cohesion in Jewish communities. A grand requiem to exculpate the democratic world's failure to save the Jews from Nazi butchery. Not to mention the silence of Christendom.

"The experts don't know what the hell they are talking about! Have they ever been forsaken by everyone, hunted down like rats? Have they ever been starved, weaponless, killed by their neighbors? Have they ever seen their own mothers and fathers murdered? Have they ever faced, with their hands tied behind their backs, the awesome bestiality of the swastika-mad? Clothed and well fed, armed to the teeth, they speak of courage and wonder why the Jews permitted their own extermination. It could have been them, but for the grace of being an American, an Englishman. . . .

"The world is in ashes and the good guys screw us with their own guilt.

"Out of the ashes, as impossible as it seems, the world will be reborn again. It always has. The question is: reborn to what?

"It is because of this question that I am in the *Bricha.*

"You've never heard of the *Bricha?* Why should you have? But if you did, you might be here, next to me, and not in Sighet, the phony island with illusory promises. I know, I know: the world is full of Sighets.

"The *Bricha* is a business like any other except this: it buys and collects used merchandise, rubbish and rags as it were, then transports the cargo to an ancient land. There the air, sky, sun, the earth and all living matter, charged with the molecules of two thousand years of our ancestors' yearning to return home, rejuvenate the rubbish into vital matter again.

"I mean, the *Bricha* is in the business of rescuing Jewish lives from the hellholes of Europe and rehabilitating them by bringing them back home to the soil of the primal source: Eretz Ysroel.

"The *Bricha* claims every Jew. It needs every Jew.

"The experts will learn that despite their charts and brilliant theories only a Jewish sovereign state would have prevented the Nazi slaughter.

"Such a state will be built, mark my words. In the process we shall redeem our humanity and wrest our long-denied right to be equal to the *other.*

333

"That is why I work in the *Bricha*.

"What about you?"

In the evening she translated the letter to Leonid.
"Let me hear it again," he said. "Slowly . . ."

6

Yankel Schwartz glanced at Lisa sitting behind a small desk in her tiny JOINT office and thought of his own office at DPB headquarters, a spacious room befitting Ion Negrescu, now assistant chairman of the People's Literary Association, an important man in town. He had no reason to feel ill at ease in the presence of a mere JOINT employee, as Lisa was, and he cleared his throat, vigorously:

"As I've told you, the statement has to be read tonight at the general membership meeting at headquarters. It's a short statement, it won't be any skin off your back but it would show the Party you are cooperative——"

"I repeat: I won't read anything publicly unless I see it beforehand."

He shouldn't allow himself to be provoked, he thought, realizing how deeply her rejection was stinging him, for more than his reputation as a skillful negotiator was at stake, as far as the DPB was concerned. For a second he contemplated letting her read the statement that was neatly folded in his breast pocket only to dismiss the idea at once. The statement written by him was a strongly worded indictment of the prewar bourgeois class, among other things. The very reason he had suggested to the executive committee that Lisa Engler read it was that denunciation

335

coming from one's own ranks gives the illusion of genuine repentance.

"I'd gladly let you read the statement," he said, trying to sound sincere and persuasive in the same breath, "if I had a copy. But I don't. Nobody does. Party rules. It's in the vault, at headquarters, till formally read tonight. It will be you, I hope." He cajoled: "You won't regret helping out a friend, I promise you——"

"Not sight unseen——"

"Why are you so stubborn? Besides, you like Reds, don't you? I mean, surely . . ." He stopped midsentence, his Adam's apple bobbing up and down a few times. He looked at her, helpless, and she watched him impassively for a while.

"I know exactly what you mean," she said. "The answer is still *no*."

"You are making a mistake," he now said gravely. "I mean, a friend like me won't hold a refusal against you. But the DPB . . ." He shrugged his shoulders. "Can't you see the direction of the compass needle? It's evident that it points to Moscow. Wise up, Lisa, before it's too late."

She had closed the ledger on which she was working when Yankel walked in, pushed it to the center of the desk and relaxed. He was the former bathetic Yankel all over again, she realized, striving hard to impress, as he must have thought he did one prewar afternoon when, arms flailing, chin thrust out, one foot forward, he wildly declaimed before a gathering of her friends:

> Oh, what a rogue and peasant slave am I!
> Is it not monstrous that this player here,
> But in a fiction, in a dream of passion,
> Could force his soul . . .
> For Hecuba?
> What's Hecuba to him, or he to Hecuba
> That he should weep for her?

"Are you suggesting I become a member of the Romanian Communist Party?" she asked, holding back a giggle that memory evoked.

"And why not? Indeed, why not become a Party member?"

336

She looked at him skeptically.

"Why not?" he insisted. "What do you have against the Party?"

"Nothing. I just don't want to——"

"Listen!" he exclaimed without hearing her and jumped up as if shocked by an electric current. "I'll sponsor you myself! What a *coup* that would be! Am I glad I thought of it! Of course, of course! You should join the *élite* early in the game, while we still want you. The *plebs* will be coerced to follow, believe me."

Lisa snickered and Yankel, uncertain as to how to interpret it, wagged his forefinger before her eyes.

"Get smart, Lisa. Don't miss the boat. Just think: Ion Negrescu and Lisa Engler. What a team *that* could be! I see it all: I write and you speak. Who is better qualified than us, victims of fascist-imperialist oppression, to spread the teachings of Lenin and Stalin? With our education and intelligence you and I could become the Romanian Communist Party's dialecticians and theoreticians like Engels, Marx, and Plekhanov. And with drive and ambition, we could go far; we would be *somebodies* in Party hierarchy!"

She had barely contained herself from laughing out loud at Yankel's pompous effusions, yet, as he now sat down, small beads of perspiration dotting his upper lip, his body slightly twitching, she felt a chill run down her spine.

"Have you tasted power?" he asked, his eyes closed, his voice thick. "Have you? I have. It's everything a man dreams of, everything a man ever wants. Power makes the ugly beautiful, the weak strong. Power cures when nothing else can cure. The essence of potency, the crest of pleasure, is power. I want it. How I want it . . . and I'll get it!"

He sighed, then opened his eyes.

"The Party is power and I am part of the Party. As such, I have power. I am power. I don't quake in my boots any longer, afraid of being called *zsidan* again. Nobody would ever dare call Ion Negrescu 'kike.'"

"You stupid sycophant!" She gave an angry shove to the ledger, which fell to the floor with a thud. "You are a coward and a bootlicker, not just a buffoon! They're mopping up their own filth with you, can't you see? You're being duped. Duped!"

A few youngsters from the factory, hearing loud voices, had stopped before her open door.

"You think you have power!" She got up, glared at Yankel. "Wake up, man, and smell the dunghill. But you can't, because they've smeared your eyes and plugged your ears with . . . antiseptic deodorant, Comrade Negrescu!"

"You have a Commie for a lover, a real live Red," he retorted, "but you play hard to get when it comes to the Romanian Communist Party. I wonder why——." The statement, he suddenly thought, he must keep his head!

"Look," he said in a different tone of voice, "I ask you, for old times' sake, to read the statement tonight. Will you?"

"No," she said flatly, looking through him. "What's Ion Negrescu to me or I to Ion Negrescu that I should weep for him?"

7

Next day Gyuri told Himy about Lisa's confrontation with Yankel.

"His cheeks burned in shame before the brass," Gyuri recalled, "when he reported Lisa's snub."

The executive committee had a short session prior to the general meeting that evening. Where was the girl? they had asked, was she coming tonight? Yankel fretted, rubbed his nose and ran his fingers through his damp hair. The committee listened to him in cold silence for a while. It was not such a great idea to ask her in the first place, Yankel said. There are other, better qualified prospects, more forceful voices, deserving of a break. (Yankel looked to Gyuri for backing, some sign of support; we are old buddies, yes? I am in trouble, not much, but at least nod your head. Gyuri looked away, why should he be lumped with Yankel? We all must look out for ourselves, yes?)

Yankel sputtered: "I don't think she'd add any prestige to us, comrades," he said, "none at all." He suggested he himself read the statement calling for a spontaneous mass demonstration in support of the Romanian Communist Party, questioning Iuliu Maniu's motives for having gone underground during the war and branding Sighet's prewar merchants leeches and enemies of the people. "Won't it be more effective if Ion Negrescu reads the call for Party allegiance and not Lisa Engler; who was she, after all, comrades? A nobody, a nothing. Listen to me, please, comrades——"

"Comrades my ass!" the Party secretary finally thundered, "bunglers are no comrades! And you bungled it, didn't you? It was your brainchild, this idea of having her read the statement tonight, the entire scheme was yours. You were itching to show us you were up to replacing the chairman of the People's Literary Association . . . You'd better confess to your own ineptitude, mister! We don't equivocate here, remember!" The secretary banged his fist on the table. "We are here to deliver, carry out orders, not to think! The girl is absolutely unimportant," the secretary shouted. "It is her name we want, not her voice, idiot! That sign, THE HOUSE OF ENGLER AND SONS, is still up there, reminding the town. It has to go! Go, go! Who the hell cares about the girl? But she is making us look like fools. Her connections . . . with certain people. We cannot touch her. And you, Schwartz, undertook to con her into cooperating! She'll come voluntarily, you said. Well, you are an asshole, Mister Schwartz!"

"Perhaps she should have read that statement, after all," Gyuri told Himy. "She's made Yankel look ridiculous, a bumbling schoolboy; and she's placed herself squarely on the other side, ideologically speaking. How long do you think she can count on special consideration?"

"I will speak to the captain," Himy said.

8

Himy Lieber filled out his fancy suits again. He was putting on weight and was beginning to look like his old self. He was a satisfied man, even a happy man: the relentless pursuit of Olga Petrescu, which had kept him in a perpetual emotional turmoil and had made him lose weight, had finally come to an end. He was Olga's lover.

Himy still rented a room at Elena Corcescu's Pension Amity to provide needy survivors with a place to stay, and he still slipped a few banknotes into their pockets when no one looked. Salt, more than ever, was going strong as a black-market commodity and his deals with the Russians were still highly profitable, the stringent enforcement of the antisabotage act notwithstanding. Gossip had it that he had highly placed protectors; what other reason could have kept the DPB squads from scrupulously avoiding his office and never questioning him on any aspects of his business?

Although his deals with the Russians continued smoothly, there was now an added dimension to their relationship: a social one. After the business transactions were over, the Russians offered Himy a drink or, on rare occasions, a Russian would go to Himy's office, tarry a while in his chair, shifting one leg over the other, then offer Himy a cigarette.

"We don't discuss business and we don't discuss women," Himy had told Imre. "Do you think suddenly the Ruskies appreciate Himy the Mogul?" He laughed, tapped his forehead, then arched his left arm over his head and touched the tip of his right ear.

"As if I wouldn't know. They use me as an unofficial conduit, dropping hints of this or that to come, trying to worm out information from me . . . I simply nod, *da, da*. Let them think what they will, Himy the Mogul knows the score. I've been apprenticed to others as cunning as they are. Swastikas, crossed arrows or hammer and sickle, it's all politics in the end. The point is to keep your head, understand the game. While it's good for us, I play along. This way at least we know what's what. . . ."

And so, Himy went about his business purposefully but in a less boisterous manner. He sighed often and beamed once in a while at the wall or the window or at a stray cat on the street.

"Himy the Mogul doesn't brag," he answered to questions about Olga. "What can I say . . . it's hard to resist me. So it happened, as it was bound to happen, that's all. Just forget the *Don Juan* in my name."

Olga had slept with every available Jew in town. No one was left, except Himy. She picked him one evening at Mitzi's. Olga had come in waving her hand, in a brief greeting, looked around for a while then her eyes fell on Himy who, like an emaciated sick puppy, sat by himself in a corner.

"Jew," she said to him. "Your time has come. Let's go."

That first night he made love to her in a state of reverent ecstasy as if, overcome by religious fervor, he was worshiping at the shrine of a goddess. He was possessed, that first night, by an incredible rapture and passionate awe. He sucked the pink nipples of her breasts as though he were drinking the nectar of the gods and played between her legs as though the folds of her vulva were the exquisite petals of a flower. His hands, his lips, his tongue, touched and licked her flesh till he had her moisture on his fingers and the smell of come in his nostrils. The head of his penis rubbed the folds and creases between her legs and gently teased the hardened tip of her clitoris. In the warmth of her ooze, he slid his penis into the mouth of her vagina, almost thrusting it into the tempting, demanding hot cavity, then withdrew it to go back into the folds of her flesh, back and forth, back and forth, till her closed fists opened and her tight lips slackened. He then went into her deeply, lustfully, pumped and thrashed for both of them, for she was passively lying under him, spread-eagled. He went on pumping and thrashing till he felt himself stretched to the utmost, till the intensity of his craving reached its apex and then dissolved into liquid pleasure, primordial and thick. Till, in the sublime explosion of orgasm, man and goddess merged.

The third night, unable to hold back any longer, Olga's rigid body slowly began to move under him.

After she came, she turned on him.

"Don't get me in heat, and don't make love to me," she instructed him. "Just fuck."

He nodded and murmured, "Olga, my Olga."

Each time she charged him to perform sex mechanically, he took her with more passion, more caring.

"I told you not to arouse me!" she berated him another night. "You are ruining my plan, Jew man."

Jumping out of bed, she stood before him, hands on hips, the shadow of her magnificent hips and great breasts on the wall, looming enormous, overflowing the ceiling.

"I hate you! The others were feeble little men, coming in little gasps like self-conscious little farts. But you! You're an aroused bull getting into me, kneading me into a mass of . . . feelings. You have no right to do this! I forbid it. I service you, that's all! That's all!"

He took her hand, put it on his erect penis and pressed and released her fingers till she squeezed and massaged without help from him.

"Don't love me," she murmured weakly, massaging his penis. "Don't make me feel. Please . . ."

He grabbed her hips, pulled her close and made her straddle him. Her hands on his shoulders, her knees bent, she sheathed him with her vagina and rode him up and down, back and forth, in a frenzied, uninhibited joyride she no longer wanted to disavow; nor could she stop it. Till drenched in the sweat of fulfillment and of sensual fever, her mouth hungrily, rapaciously drew in his lips and her hot tongue licked his cheeks, his eyes, the hard folds of his ears, and throbbing, panting, she said yes . . . yes.

Since that night Olga had quit showing up at parties, roaming the streets looking for men, or waiting at the bus station.

Himy too stopped seeing his friends in the evenings.

She told him her story one night while he held her hands.

Grigore Mosan, the handsome Romanian air force lieutenant, ace pilot and decorated hero, had been the idol of the people before he had married Olga. He had deserved their love, for it was his deed alone which had soothed inflamed Romanian national pride on the mournful and crucial day of August 30, 1940, when part of Transylvania was transferred to the Magyars. Whenever that loss was mentioned, the Romanian people laughed instead of lopping off Magyar heads, as was the custom. laughed and laughed, remembering Mosan's deed, till tears came to their eyes.

The area of the award included Rasadel, a small town in the southern section of Transylvania which henceforth would be on the new border. Rasadel had been an important Romanian military air base, with a supply depot and a dozen fighter planes.

On August 29 six Hungarian officers arrived at the base to make preparations for a smooth takeover scheduled for the next day. Mosan, a native of Transylvania who spoke fluent Romanian and Hungarian, was in command. He greeted the Hungarians courteously, and after mutual assurances of goodwill, in which neither party believed, supplied them with sharpened pencils and large writing pads, walked with them through the air base and watched them take copious notes on every item, piece of equipment, and plane.

The transfer was to go into effect next day at twenty-two hundred hours. Before that came to pass, Mosan suggested it would be fitting to seal the new spirit of cooperation between two neighbor nations whose common ally was the great leader himself, Adolf Hitler, with a celebration worthy of the event and of such an exalted protector. Mosan's proposal of an evening of diversion at the Athené Palace, the famed bordello in Cluj, was heartily accepted.

The eager celebrants arrived at the Athené that evening after an hour's drive from the Rasadel base. They feasted on *vinete, ciorba*, crisply roasted suckling pig, and on the beaks of ducks soaked in champagne-flavored oyster sauce, a powerful

344

aphrodisiac personally prepared by the lady of the house, Madame Adelaide. Their gastronomic appetites amply satisfied, the guests' sexual appetites were next catered to by an exotic *corps* of whores, who led the men to bed amidst whispers of promised orgies that would make the Arabian Nights and *Walpurgisnacht* look like church picnics.

Mosan's disappearance after the first toast was noticed only by Madame Adelaïde.

Once back on the base, Mosan loaded an old cargo plane with oil drums, communication components, spare parts, weapons, ammunition, whatever was transportable and valuable, and flew to a farm where Romanian partisans were in hiding. He unloaded the cargo and returned with two partisan pilots. Mosan reloaded the cargo plane, the two pilots got into fighters and all went off to the farm. They repeated the process five times.

In the morning, after the Hungarian officers had sobered up, they drove back to Rasadel. They found empty hangars, a ransacked supply depot, no planes and no Grigore Mosan. Crestfallen, they stared at their detailed inventory schedules and looked around again. At last they found something: a Romanian flag fluttering on top of the deserted control tower. One of the Hungarian officers furiously ripped up the flag—after he read a note pinned on it:

"Come and get it or take it up with Hitler."

Several days later, on September 3, King Carol II personally decorated Grigore Mosan and promoted him to lieutenant colonel, a three-rank jump no one begrudged.

The king's gesture in rewarding Mosan for his defiance struck the truncated country as either cynical, sincerely contrite or fruitlessly propitiatory. In any case, three days later, on September 6, the king was deposed and sent into exile. It was not merely the loss of Transylvania the nation would not forgive Carol for: it was also his alliance with the Axis, which had brought about such great territorial losses.

Olga had met Mosan in 1942 at a reception in the royal palace in Bucharest. They were soon married with the blessing of King Mihai, Carol's son, and became the sweethearts of the newspaper-reading and radio-listening public. They were the symbolic golden couple of the ancient Romanian folk tale: he Knight Fru-

mos, who slew the seven-headed dragon, and she Princess Teodora, who would live together with her knight happily ever after.

"Yes, it was like a fairy tale, in the beginning," Olga admitted.
"Then around the middle of 1943 it all changed. He'd get mysterious phone calls at night and would rush out of the house. If I
picked up the phone, there would be a click on the other end of
the line. I questioned him about the calls. 'Military business,'
was his standard answer. Then he stayed away overnight. When
he was home, he was exhausted. Women were still sending him
perfumed little *billets-doux*, threw kisses at him. It must have
been one of those women keeping Grigore away from me, I decided. But he denied everything. Military business, he insisted.
All night? All night, he shouted at me, all night, understand? Get
used to the idea, he said. What about the phone calls? . . . The
fights between us turned bitter, ugly . . . Desperate."

Himy's grip tightened around her hands.

"Yes," he said, "I understand."

But she was not sure if he really understood, if anyone could
understand that night . . . that particular night she had stood
naked before Grigore. "Grigore," she had said, "look at me,
please look at me." He had turned around. "Am I not pretty?"
she had asked. "You are beautiful." He caressed her breasts, the
flatness of her stomach, the triangular softness of dense silky hair
below. He had seemed so tired, moving his hand slowly on her
body and trying to steady his trembling hand. "Then why," she
had asked him, "why don't you make love to me anymore? Don't
you love me?" He had whispered: "I do, oh I do . . . just trust
me . . . a little longer . . ." He fell asleep in the middle of the
sentence. She did not even hear what he had said, she desired
him so fiercely; she felt the heat between her legs, a heart tucked
into the vulva and pulsing to a strange rhythm: "I am the other,
the other, the other woman; I am the other, the other, the other
woman." She became that other woman, she was that other
woman to whom Grigore was making love and could feel him inside her as that other woman must have felt him; and standing
naked in front of the sleeping Grigore, she masturbated until she
had the release that that other woman had experienced.

She could not bring herself to tell Himy of that night. No man
would understand.

"I was sick with jealousy," she said. "I became convinced he had another woman. When Grigore didn't come home for two nights in a row, I couldn't bear the thought of him sleeping with that other woman. I called headquarters. His adjutant was surprised. Weren't we supposed to go away on a vacation, a short holiday? he asked. That was what the lieutenant colonel had said to him when he took three days' leave. I waited one more night, and in the morning I called again. 'What kind of an air force are you running?' I screamed at a general. 'For months Grigore Mosan had been gallivanting around at night, and you know nothing. He may be sleeping with your wife right now, or with Queen Mother Elena, and you know of nothing!' Next night the Gestapo grabbed Grigore in front of our house. Two days later they let me visit him. He was lying on a stretcher. Every bone in his body was broken. The general was there too. 'He's yours,' the SS told him, 'he's your officer. You finish him. It's an order.'

"He pulled the trigger," she said, "but it is as though I gave him the gun."

The Gestapo had tortured Grigore Mosan without interruption for twenty-four hours before he broke down. He then confessed to his underground activities, his connection with the Romanian resistance movement led by Maniu, and admitted having piloted rescue flights of political and Jewish refugees from Bucharest to Constanta and Istanbul. He told them everything about himself. When the Gestapo pressed for the whereabouts of Maniu, Mosan passed out and never regained consciousness. At that point he would have been useless to the Gestapo anyhow: his fingers were broken, his jaw fractured, his larynx crushed. So the Gestapo ordered the general to shoot.

The Gestapo kept Grigore Mosan's role in the Romanian resistance movement top secret. The Nazis did not need national martyrs. The Romanians were ordered, though, to give him a state funeral, with all the pomp, solemnity and propaganda due a great soldier fallen while fighting the enemies of his country, the underground antifascist elements led by Iuliu Maniu.

"Hush, hush . . . enough crying. Enough tears," Himy said. "You didn't kill him. Grigore Mosan knew the odds and he chose them because he knew in his heart he had to. Olga, my Olga . . . You paid for everything. You paid and you paid. Now let us live. We still can. I promise you."

He kissed her hands, held them to his heart:

"I love you."

9

As soon as Gyuri left, Himy went to see Yashenko.

"I remember the first time I had the good fortune of meeting you, captain," he said. "It's not quite a year ago. 'Go while you can,' you had advised us. It sure was good advice."

Yashenko poured drinks, and the memory cut into him sharply: the look of pain in the eyes of those who had just come back to Sighet, prompting him to suggest that they set down stakes somewhere else, where the regime would be less demanding, less invasive; find a quiet spot on earth where they could first catch their breath and lick their wounds. Their Jewishness had seemed secondary then; he had been reacting to human beings, battered and blighted and deserving a break. Now, in retrospect, he wondered whether their Jewishness was indeed of small consequence to him.

"I have great respect for you, captain," Himy said. "So do the Jews in town. We think of you as our unofficial friend. A *chaver*, if you don't mind my saying. Permit me to be blunt. You see, captain, I don't have a honeyed tongue and I'm not familiar with fancy words. All I have is a heart and this thing inside." He touched his head. "Suddenly something is set off, it begins to click and then it starts manufacturing thoughts. It's my heart and mind that made me come to see you, captain."

349

"Say what's in your heart first, *chaver* Himy. Then the mind should not object."

"Thank you. It's about Lisa I want to speak."

"Yes, let's speak of Lisa." It was a breath of fresh air to speak of her with someone other than Marcovski. The use of her first name spanned a bridge of intimacy between him and Himy that he welcomed. Friends, ordinary guys unburdening their hearts to each other.

". . . you see, captain, her brother Laszlo was my best friend. My only friend," Himy said staring at his hands, at the nervous movements of his fingers.

"They laughed at how I talked, they poked fun at my clothes. Laszlo showed me proper posture; how to shake hands; how to eat with a knife and fork. He taught me how to make a Windsor knot in my tie."

He spread his palms on the top of the table, looked directly into Yashenko's eyes.

"My friend Laszlo is dead," he said. "So is Lisa's other brother. She has no family, no close relatives to look after her. She is a young woman, all alone. She has survived the slaughter, yet she may wither away. I owe it to my friend Laszlo to be concerned about his sister. I care, like a brother, what happens to Lisa."

"I care too. As a man."

"Yes, captain, I know. I'm here because of that."

Himy finished his drink. "The Torah teaches to weigh one's words before speaking. I have weighed my words. Now I'll speak: I am here to ask you to stop seeing Lisa, captain."

"What? What did you say?" But he knew at once what Himy had said, what the surrogate brother of Lisa Engler was trying to tell Captain Leonid Nicolaievich Yashenko: free her, Himy was pleading with the fine captain, free the *golubka* so that she may start to build her own permanent nest somewhere, have a family with children, children with curly red hair and lots of freckles.

"What happened?" Yashenko asked, and for an instant he felt frozen or empty inside, he wasn't sure which, and he had a sensation of weightlessness, of dread, of being out of control and of falling into an abyss. "Tell me what happened. Don't hold back."

Himy told him of Lisa's encounter with Yankel and of the episode with the Party.

"But it's not just that," Himy said. "The time has come for her

350

to get married, have her own family to care for. She must belong, before it's too late. She'll get poisoned otherwise. Gangrene of the soul."

"I can't marry her, you know that," Yashenko said. "She is not a Russian citizen and . . ." The words died in his mouth. The abyss was dark, airless. He was suffocating. What about the summit, he thought and quickly opened his jacket, the summit to which he, Captain Yashenko, brilliant officer, the heir of political genes, was expected to ascend. Love comes and goes, the motions will always be the same. Only partners change. The Party alone endures becuse the partners are permanent though the motions change. No, it is the other way around. Or was it? How could he be sure, at the bottom of the abyss, how could he be sure of anything? Of course, he now remembered: the Party comes first, second . . . Progress feeds on sacrifice. The *golubka* is an albatross.

". . . and I wish I could marry her," he said.

"I know, captain. But you can't. That's why I ask you, with respect, to stop seeing Lisa. I'm talking out of place. I apologize. Still, I must do what I know in my heart to be right. It's a man's obligation to listen to his heart. My heart tells me that if the sister of Laszlo Engler is in trouble, then Himy Lieber must help. As long as you are here she is not in trouble, of course. But when you're gone, captain, that's when she'll be in trouble. Lots of trouble. You wouldn't want that."

"No. I wouldn't want that." He had not wanted the Yashenbergs to get in trouble either. He had refused to leave Iasi till Marciuc had vouched for their safety. Then he left.

"Nothing can happen to her while you are still here. That's why I ask you, as her brother would have asked you, please stop seeing her now, when your influence can still protect her. She'll think it's another woman. . . ."

(oh my god, what am i doing? olga, olga. but it has to be done, it has to be said, may god forgive me. i know the score. i could never sleep at night if lisa becomes a victim again)

"She would want to leave Sighet, I'm sure," Himy said. "Wasn't it your own advice, 'Go while you can, you've suffered enough'? I'll help her leave town, take care of every detail. I give you my word, she'll get to the West in safety."

Yashenko thought of the Matrushka doll Lisa kept on top of

her dresser. Once a week she twisted open the dolls nesting in each other and lined them up, side by side, all ten of them to see the limits, she said, and at the same time the possibilities of their endlessness, all contained within one system.

Himy got up. "Another thing, captain. Have you thought of your own safety? How safe is it for you now? You've called me a *chaver*. All right then, I'll say this too: I've heard rumors . . . In my position, you know, they tell me what they think I ought to know. But I also know what they might not want me to know. I have my own sources, if you know what I mean. *Chaver* Yashenko, watch out. They talk about you. A certain lieutenant . . . he's no friend of yours. You can still straighten everything out, if you hurry. Let her go. Now."

The Matrushka doll, Yashenko thought, the little mother doll.

"You spoke to me man to man," he told Himy. "It is my turn now to speak to you in the same way. Listen, friend: I am a Marxist, an active communist. I'll always be one even as I shall always remember an old man teaching a young boy, before his *bar mitzvah*, how to bind *tefillin* on his arm and head. . . ."

Yashenko stopped to steady his voice. "So you see, there are vital issues I must consider and I shall. But I need a little time to read my own mind and heart clearly." The abyss, the suffocating sensation was returning to him. "Often, I gnash my teeth in sheer rage: I have seen the camps. I don't know what, or how long, it would take to make the survivors whole again. I even doubt that they can ever be whole again . . . Yet this I know: a main consideration which shall determine my future actions shall be Lisa's safety. She means a lot to me, *chaver* Himy."

10

During the night the first winter snow had covered the town and Solovan was all white. The *crivatz*, a vicious wind blowing in from the Ukraine, howled all night long and in the morning lashed at chestnut vendors who were setting up drum-shaped sheet-steel stoves on Main Street. Through holes cut into the drums' walls, the vendors dumped burning coal, inhaled deeply and puckered their lips, then blew air into the holes, repeating the inhaling and exhaling until the coals glowed. On top of the red-hot stoves they roasted chestnuts, rolling them with fingers wrapped in singed rags, so that by noon the aroma of roasted chestnuts was all over the Grand Corso. People walking by stopped at the stoves, warmed their hands and thumped their feet, then bought a few chestnuts.

The early winter also brought Popov, the famous Russian clown, to town to entertain the troops at an exclusively Russian show, a gala evening to which only one civilian, the Romanian Communist Party secretary, had been formally invited. Another civilian in the auditorium was Lisa.

She was there without a formal invitation, sitting with Leonid in the center of the second row, directly behind Marcovski who was between two generals. Yashenko knew—as he must have known when he had impulsively asked Lisa to accompany him—that he defied more than just protocol. Yet this thought, far from upsetting him, gave him a small taste of autonomy which he enjoyed beyond expectation.

"Why did you take me along?" she asked him later that night. "I was the only civilian, besides the Party secretary. There were hundreds of eyes on my back, as if I were some sort of a freak."

"Well," he said lightly, "now they know you are not. Now they know you are real. The colonel——"

"He didn't even notice me."

"That's what he wanted everyone to believe; but he noticed you." Yashenko was familiar with Marcovski's ploys: changing the subject of a conversation in midsentence, pouncing forward with an apparently irrelevant question to throw one off balance; the leisurely but meticulous way he dropped ashes in ashtrays, rather than on the floor as was his habit, as if neatness was uppermost on his mind while, in fact, he was cunningly probing and searching for the adversary's weak spot or spots. The colonel's mental acuity was sharpest when he pretended least interest.

"He knew you were there." Yashenko wished to end this topic. "Let's talk of something else. Wasn't Popov——"

"But there was tension, Leonid. Perhaps it wasn't right for you to have taken me there."

"It's done," he said, slightly nettled that she still pursued the matter. "Don't upset yourself." But it was he who was getting upset. "Can't a man take his girl to a show, want her to have a good time, without causing a revolution?"

"Not when she is from the other side," she blurted, "like I am. *Verboten.* Or haven't you heard? It's all over town——"

"Then damn the town!" Startled, he acknowledged her vexation which made his own resentment flare up. Of course she had cause to be bitter, he told himself, and wondered if his anger was directed at her petulance or if it was his own independent anger now joining ranks with her bitterness. Was this their first quarrel? The idea that they were behaving like ordinary lovers made him feel good. Still, he should ferret out what it was that truly angered him. She had simply exposed again the status quo in her own terms; and by doing that, she had made him instantly aware that the status quo had become intolerable to both of them.

It was hot in the room. He removed his tunic, then his shirt too. Bare-chested, he stood before the open window and let a gust of wind cool him.

He needed time to know precisely what it was that disturbed him. Yes, he needed time to look into himself, as he had told Himy. All he knew for certain was his own irritation, caused by misty, vague feelings he could not or dared not name. Yet these feelings lacerated him like a tight saddle strap rubbing the flesh raw. He often had to tell himself that the reasons he turned to communism were still valid, could still stand up under sharp scrutiny. Even so, the once glorious drumbeat now had a hollow sound which dismayed him.

Recently, faint memories from his early youth were coming to life in his heart and mind, doggedly competing with visions of Marcovski's summit. Reb Yashenberg saying the *kiddush* Friday night over the sacramental wine, a special hug Rifka Yashenberg had given to a little boy, the shape of a certain *mezzuzah* on the doorpost, images evoking his submerged identity, fought with passages from Lenin's *What Is to Be Done*? The Party's absolute claim on him and its jealousy of Lisa filled him with frustration and only reinforced his link with her. Himy's request that he stop seeing her was cutting savagely into him, adding to his caldron of conflicts.

Should he wait till the vague, misty feelings inside him took shape at their own pace, or should he force their birthing now, looking into her eyes to make it easier for him to speak of what he felt?

The molten blackness of the sky was dusted with countless flickering stars. He saw himself up there, marching alongside Marcovski towards the summit while mechanically living, acting, breeding as determined by a new science, or a new technology, called political genetics.

He closed the window, turned to her.

"Four years ago," he said quietly, "I remember watching the dawning of a spring day from the porch of a secluded house in a forest, near a river. It was, for me, a very special awakening: the night before I had finished my training in intelligence and I had become a card-carrying member of the Communist Party of the Soviet Union. I watched the dawn and listened to the forest. All was still, not a sound. An incredibly peaceful and beautiful mo-

355

ment, drowsy and tender. The river rolled by and it caught the rays of the sun in its flow. I watched the sun play with the river and I thought it was the absolute, perfect dawn befitting the dawn of my new life. Then suddenly the stillness was shattered from across the river. A peasant woman on the bank was washing linen, pounding it against a washboard. Thud. Thud. The dawn was gone and it left in its wake a crisp morning, exhilarating and beautiful. But its loveliness began to hurt me. The woman seemed to pound at my heart. Thud. Thud. I remembered the river Bahlui flowing by Iasi and I wept. There, in the sun and in the forest, homesickness wrung my heart the way the woman was wringing her linen. So I wept. After a while I stopped weeping and went ahead on my course laid out before me, as a disciplined comrade would do, and I tried to put that moment of weakness out of my mind."

He locked his arms around her, fitted her to him. At last, he thought, he was uncovering the root of his anger. The revelation uplifted him as it filled him with a strange excitement: he perceived what it was he truly wanted and sensed that a synchrony of events and feelings had led him inexorably to this night and to this moment. Now, he knew, he would act.

"That dawn has haunted me ever since, just as I have been homesick ever since. I am not denying it any longer. I am homesick, I have been homesick since I've left my people. And yet, when I am with you, my homesickness is healing. So, you see, I need you at my side all the time."

She held her breath to suspend all movement, force time to a standstill, spellbind and bewitch the night, the place, into an enchanted garden to last a hundred years, to endow this Moment with all that Magic.

"I love you, Lisa," he said and thought of her little gestures, traits he cherished. The way she swung open the door for him even before he had a chance to knock. How she drank vodka in one gulp, first saying *ott harasho*, closing her eyes, then the slight shudder. The steely, stubborn strength lodged in her chin. The way she crinkled her nose or brushed her hair. The light blush on her face when she told him "I love you" in Russian: *Ya tyebia lyublu*, and her shyness when she asked him *Te minya lyubish?* do you love me?

Oh yes, he loves her very much.

"I want you to be my wife," he said, "and to have children with me, to walk together on the street, arm in arm, to say to a friend, 'Meet my wife, Lisa Yashenko' . . ."

She thought: I am dreaming; the dream will fragment and vanish as soon as I wake up. Yet, even as she thought this thought her mind was already hungrily absorbing the dream and holding onto it, to remember it after she wakes up: Leonid and she, husband and wife. Lisa Yashenko, happy to meet you . . .

"I've become a free man," he continued. "I don't know the exact instant my heart and mind crossed the forbidden frontier. But I know, without a doubt, they have crossed it."

It must have started a long time ago, he thought, the emancipation of Leonid Nicolaievich Yashenko. Was it when Stalin had signed the pact with Hitler? Or when Yashenko went back to Iasi, to Transistria? When he first saw the Treblinka deathcamp and explained to his sergeant the meaning of a *Vernichtungslager*?

It must have been a continuous process without his knowing it.

But she was the catalyst, he thought, and he gratefully held her closer.

"You were right just now," he said. "As far as the Party is concerned, you are *verboten*. But that's wrong. Love should never be *verboten* and a man should never be ordered whom to love or not to love. It degrades him, reduces him to a cipher. It kills his spirit and he becomes a commodity. I am a human being, not a commodity. A free man," he concluded, "and I love you. I now exercise the right of a free man: I ask you to be my wife. Lisa, will you marry me?"

Her hands trembled as she touched his eyes, his cheeks, his mouth. She was waking up from the dream, and it did not vanish. The warmth of his body soothed and invigorated her and she was slowly overcome by a new feeling, stirring and beautiful, which she knew was hope.

"Yes, Leonyushka," she whispered. "Yes, yes. I will marry you whenever and wherever you want me to. I will."

11

"Are you suicidal, Yashenko?" Marcovski accosted him next morning, "or merely insane?"

"I think neither, comrade colonel," he answered.

"Taking her to the Popov performance was not the act of a sane man."

The colonel's gruffness induced in Yashenko a peculiar stimulation, an oddly pleasant feeling like a slight touch on inflamed tissue around an aching tooth. It reduced, temporarily, pain.

"Since when is plain decency madness or lethal?" Yashenko asked calmly.

"Rubbish. Explain yourself, Yashenko."

"At your service, comrade colonel." Last night's renaissance and happiness should not make him reckless, Yashenko cautioned himself. To the contrary, he should prudently explore all possibilities. Prove himself a worthy disciple of the master himself.

"My relationship with the girl will have to be terminated soon," Yashenko said smoothly, "you've said so yourself. Before that happened I wanted to do a kind act, without an ulterior motive. Out of ordinary human decency. For instance, make her laugh again. She hasn't laughed for over a year; perhaps she's forgotten what laughter or plain fun is all about. I took her to Popov hoping he could make her laugh again."

"A touching sentiment. But you went against the rules again, damn it! In your position, you can't indulge yourself in dispensing kind acts without prior clearance! You are losing your head over a skirt——"

"I didn't mean to," Yashenko said. "But you see, comrade colonel, the girl has suffered——"

"And so have millions of others!" Marcovski retorted. "She's suffered, she's suffered, that's all I hear, damn it! Has she an exclusive license on suffering? It was war, damn it, war! It *is* war. What do you expect? Roses wrapped around bombs?"

"But her suffering was not due to the war. She suffered solely because she is Jewish," he replied.

"I know," Marcovski said. "So what?"

"I too am Jewish."

"I know that too. As I just said: so what?"

"I thought it would make a difference, that's all. Considering that you too are Jewish . . ."

They sized each other up in silence. Yashenko watched the colonel fastidiously drop ashes in the ashtray. Marcovski's eyes narrowed slightly without changing his facial expression.

"That's where you miscalculate," Marcovski said evenly, "that my being Jewish would make a difference. I often wondered how long it would take you to find out. How did you find out? Never mind that, it's not important. What is important is that while I don't deny I was born to Jewish parents I don't boast about it either. The fact is, it doesn't really matter."

"A *Vernichtungslager* matters."

"To whom? I am a communist, and now you know of what vintage. That matters. That I am a communist."

"I am a communist too, of a much later vintage, of course. But I am also Jewish."

"Being Jewish is a pure accident of birth, an inconsequential trademark, from my point of view."

"But the *Vernichtungslager* were created for Jews. To exterminate those who were born Jewish by pure accident of birth, as you say. To carry out your proposition to its logical conclusion, since being Jewish is an inconsequential trademark, anti-Semitism then also becomes inconsequential."

"Not at all. Rather, from a certain vantage point, unavoidable. In fact, I would like to see anti-Semitism eradicated, considering that it obscures the class struggle. We went through all that before!"

Marcovski stubbed the cigarette in the ashtray.

"Yashenko," he said soothingly. "You are losing your grip. Your perspectives are out of kilter. This entire dialogue is superfluous. You know the questions and know all the answers. You know them as well as I do. You are infused with my ideological teaching. Your provocations don't fool me. I am simply being lenient towards you, for the moment. I consider you a kind of a son of mine, you know. A son of my mind."

"Yes. But so is Keroff."

"A father sires different children. They all have their use——"

"Comrade groomed to replace comrade——"

"Why not, if need be. The Party must prevail. Always. But Keroff's anti-Semitism is not programmed; that is, not by the Party. It came to him with his mother's milk. Even so, Keroff will tone down, I'll see to it. He is nothing but an errand boy. You, on the other hand, are on a different plane. You have your eyes open, understand the nature of political dictates, the mechanism of power. You are a realist. You'll go places, I've told you. But you mustn't waver."

"Then let's level with each other, Comrade Marciuc." The reference to their past was purposeful. Yashenko knew Marcovski would understand.

The colonel nodded and Yashenko now embarked on a new track. "I've been indoctrinated by you. You've made me a communist for life. I agree that progress without sacrifice is impossible. I am prepared, as I've told you, to make the sacrifice. The girl, for instance. I'll give her up right now, if you so order me, without batting an eye. But first prove to me it's for the good of the Party."

"I don't have to give you any justification. I could settle the issue this instant. With a snap of my fingers."

"Precisely." Yashenko thought again of the touch bringing relief to inflamed tissue. "Of course you could, comrade colonel. But Comrade Marciuc would first engage in a dialogue with his neophyte, elucidate the nature of the problem, then together

360

with him reach a theoretical conclusion. The pragmatic solution would follow thereafter."

Marcovski cracked a smile, lit a cigarette. "The old give-and-take. Fine. Let me hear your proposition."

"The Party could capitalize on Lisa Engler," Yashenko said, expecting a hail of laughter or a stern reprimand from Marcovski as "Party" and "capitalize" were antithetic. The colonel merely stared at him. "Having experienced the unjust oppression by fascist-imperialist forces," he then continued seriously, "she is a ripe subject for conversion to communism since the most likely bulwark against future persecutions is obviously the USSR. She could be a showcase," Yashenko went on, "should she become a convert. It could also bring us a whole batch of converts. The way I see it, she is a bourgeois symbol that could be dramatically used to our advantage. Should Lisa Engler be given Russian citizenship the gesture would emphatically cast us in the role of liberators, not occupiers——"

"Russian citizenship! Come now Yashenko . . . don't let yourself be carried away. Stick to probabilities, not possibilities. All right then: You propose that she be used as a lure. And what about her Jewishness?"

"Being Jewish should not be a liability with us. Didn't you say it was inconsequential?"

"Ah yes, as far as I am concerned. I shed my traditional tribal cloak before you were born, Yashenko. Many, many years before you were born. When I was eleven years old, to be exact, and saw a Cossack kick a Jew . . . but this is irrelevant. What is relevant to our dialogue is that your subject, Lisa Engler, is Jewish. In fact I suspect Auschwitz reinforced her Jewish identity to the hilt——"

"Ideology can be enhanced by identity."

"I wonder if you've become indeed infected, as I predicted you might. . . . But let's proceed. Now then: how can a specific identity, Jewish identity in this case, buttress communism?"

"Have you seen a Jewish wedding? Seen them dance the *hora*?"

Marcovski raised his eyebrows.

"I've seen a wedding in town, a while ago," Yashenko said. "All participants were deathcamp survivors. Weakened, emo-

tionally shattered. Then comes the ancient wedding ceremony
and at the mere mention of certain words the cripples become
giants, beautiful. . . ."

(and Lisa radiated. he saw her from behind the tree where he
had stood for a while watching the wedding scene. her lips
moved, forming the same words over and over. he read her lips:
moses and israel, moses and israel. how beautiful, he thought,
this girl standing under the sky, alone, yet part of an endless
chain linking the sky and the earth, affirming continuity, life.
then he walked over to her)

"The Jews have a flair for emotional outbursts," Marcovski
said dryly.

"The exuberance with which they dance the *hora* and sing
shalom, alenu shalom is a sort of spiritual ecstasy. The frailest
Jew leaps, flies as if he had wings. They transport themselves
somewhere with unmatched fervor——"

"All right, they dance like demons when it comes to the *hora*.
What does it have to do with identity?"

"Their ethnic dances, religious ceremonies and cultural tradi-
tions give them immense strength and pride, particularly *now*
when they have been stripped of everything else. It generates
emotions that could fuel them to walk barefoot from here to Jerusalem, or carry the red flag seven times around the world, depending in whose cause they enlist."

"You miss the point, Yashenko. They would never carry the
red flag around the world, as you suggest. Not as plain comrades,
that is. They would carry it as Jewish comrades. That's why your
proposition is not sound."

"An inconsequential trademark, 'Jewish.' You said so yourself.
Harnessing the energy released by Jewish identity——"

"Individual identity allowed to flourish would create class
distinctions," Marcovski said didactically, "and Jewish identity
would inevitably bring religion."

Yashenko listened in silence.

"The political emancipation of the Jew, the Christian, the religious man in general," Marcovski went on, "is the emancipation
of the state from religion in general. Brush up on Marx, my boy.
It will sharpen your thinking."

Another great performance, Yashenko mused. The master magician was at his tricks again. No wonder Marciuc had been able

362

to mold his students' thoughts like putty. They had held their breath to make sure they caught the professor's every word, every nuance.

"To be specific," the colonel said, "communism is not anti-Jewish. It's anticosmopolitan. The Jew, on the other hand, was historically the eternal cosmopolitan even as basically he was true all along only to teachings of his religion."

"The emancipation of the Jew from usury," Marcovski continued, "from trading, what Marx called 'huckstering,' the Jew's secular religion as it were, would be the self-emancipation of our time. In the final analysis, you see, the emancipation of the Jew is the emancipation of mankind from Judaism. Human emancipation, in short, requires the eradication of capitalism. And that's our job, yours and mine."

Marcovski stopped, looked gravely at Yashenko. "The time is ripe for world communism, Yashenko. Hard-core communism, without little pockets of individual identities. Our personal feelings do not matter. Only the Party matters. That's our identity. Don't you agree?"

No! Yashenko wanted to shout, but remembering the Marciuc of olden days he knew it was futile to argue with him once the professor was engaged in reshuffling theories and ideas into what seemed sequentially logical postulates, as he was doing just now. A fanatical Bolshevik of the Old Guard who was also a brilliant dialectician was not a likely candidate for deviation, Yashenko knew. Why then continue the argument? "The Jews are free in the Soviet Union," Marcovski would say, and theoretically he would be right. "In the Soviet Union there exists no discrimination. To wit: the Jews have their own autonomous *oblast*, Birobidzhan." True. "And have not a great number of Jews been prominent as leaders in the war?" Yes. "Reaped great honors and hailed as heroes?" Yes. "Then what's your point, my boy?"

That was exactly the point, Yashenko thought: I know the Jews are now free in the Soviet Union, but I know there is a fatal flaw somewhere. I cannot prove it yet. But I know, in my gut, the Jews will have a rough time living as Jews.

"Don't you agree?" Marcovski asked again, louder this time.

"Certainly," Yashenko replied quickly, though he was not sure any longer what the question had been. "Yes, of course," he added, thinking again of Marciuc the consummate prophet firing his disciples with pure ideals of absolute brotherhood and of absolute justice.

Marciuc the prophet had become Marcovski the apostle, Yashenko concluded, relentlessly proselyting the new creed to the world, with orthodox fervor, authoritatively proclaiming it to be the one and only true creed. Marcovski would violently deny that this creed, world communism, was religion, although he would agree that the creed required absolute faith, unswerving commitment and the abjuring of all previous ties.

The new orthodoxy Marcovski preached would ultimately result in a Communist Grand Inquisition, Yashenko suddenly realized, and envisioned Marcovski a Torquemada of political religion at the summit of his power, convoking a Communist Eucharistic Congress in the Kremlin for spiritual union with Joseph Stalin.

He was hallucinating, Yashenko assured himself, and a half smile crossed his face.

"Ah," Marcovski said, "you recognize your own folly. Good. The question whether the girl could become a liability or an asset to the Party should be answered: in view of her Jewish identity she would become a liability, and it is recommended, therefore, that any and all relations with her be severed."

Marcovski ejected the cigarette from his holder, got up and stretched. He walked over to the window. Puffs of smoke, rising from chestnut vendors' steel stoves, hovered over the Grand Corso.

"In a curious way I am fond of you, Yashenko. As I've said, you are like a son to me."

He turned to Yashenko. "You spoke of decency. So; I am not prohibiting your seeing her. Not yet. Do let her know there is still a measure of human kindness to be found among comrades, even in the heart of an old Bolshevik . . . Teach her how to laugh again. The time limit is the end of the year. Thereafter, the romance is over. Finished. That's an order!"

12

It was his turn, that night, to lay bare his past before Lisa. He did it deliberately, gladly, for confiding in her gave him first relief, then freedom to transcend the encapsulation born of his rigorous training, even as this freedom, he felt, was binding him closer to her. But he held nothing back. He spoke of Rifka and Nachum Yashenberg, of his years in Iasi, of his becoming a communist through Marciuc, of his defection to Russia with Dora, of their abrupt separation. Then, he told her, came the war years, his long march with the Red Army from Moscow to Berlin, all leading to a prized and special post with Marcovski, one of the top commissars of the MGB, the ministry of state security, whose responsibility was internal security including espionage and counterespionage, political supervision of the armed forces and enforcement of security measures in the occupied zone.

He finally told her he believed Marcovski was playing a macabre game with him, that of simultaneously giving and taking back, to induce a conditioned reflex which Marcovski would solely manipulate.

"And yet," Yashenko continued wistfully, "I also think, at times, that in an odd way he is trying to help us . . . Like today, when he spoke to me. There was something about him, something intangible yet real. It's a hope that maybe . . . maybe. It was folly on my part but for an instant I believed with all my heart that he, a Jew who has seen what the Nazis did to Jews, could be persuaded to let us marry——"

Sasha Markenberg, he thought, what did Sasha Markenberg feel when he had ordered the execution of his own sweetheart?

"Marcovski brought me back to reality quickly," he said. "That coldhearted bastard uses even hope to try to inveigle me into carelessness. He leaves me with no alternative: it's clear, we must defect to the West."

Marcovski was enigmatic, yes; dangerous, and unpredictable. But he was Marcovski's trainee, Yashenko reflected with confidence, and the idea of standing up to his old teacher suddenly excited him.

"First, I'll contrive to get you to Budapest with the colonel's permission. We'll invent some reason for it . . . How about your uncle, or was it a cousin, who recently arrived at Budapest from . . . ?"

"A convalescent camp in Sweden," she said. Why indeed couldn't it be true, she thought. Uncle Haskell, dear Uncle David. Why couldn't it be true? And who was mourning them? Who? "It's one of my uncles, though I don't know which one. It's hard to decide."

"I see," he said. "You don't know which one came back though you received word that your uncle would not return to Sighet and that he's asking you to go see him. Isn't that so?"

"Yes," she whispered, "I wish I could see . . . my uncle."

"And once we are there," he said quickly, "I'll contact certain parties."

He was familiar with dossiers on every underground group, whether they called themselves rescue operations, runners, smugglers. Or patriots, as the Hungarian Renaissance Party called itself. It was part of his work to keep tabs on every saboteur, spy, *agent-provocateur* and counterintelligence agent within a radius of five hundred kilometers. There was hardly a defection the MGB did not know about. Security was familiar with Jewish rescue teams as well. The *Bricha*, for example. As yet, the MGB did not hinder these operations, not unless it had information that political people, disguised as Jewish refugees, had infiltrated a team. But such cases were rare.

". . . the *Bricha*," he said, his hand on her stomach, "I'll try to contact them."

He closed his eyes and imagined her carrying his child, the flat stomach rounding out, his seed growing inside her, growing, having a child. Children, lots of children, with freckles and without freckles, red-haired and black curly-haired, named Rifka and Rachel and Nachum and Andras and Miklos and Hannah and Haskell and David and Laszlo and . . . and there were so many names, so many. Too many.

"We'll create anew out there. A family, a people. We'll go on forever—because we'll never forget," he said.

13

During the past two weeks fiery shooting stars raced nightly across the winter sky, and bleating black sheep roamed the mountains. These strange signs passed unnoticed. The art of interpreting celestial and terrestrial phenomena, as it was practiced in the days when Shlomo's son Haskell was born, had been long forgotten, or the significance of those signs may have simply escaped the Jews whose minds were now agitated by certain rumors: England, it was said, was preventing survivors of Nazi butchery from landing on the shores of the Promised Land.

"Impossible," they said at first. "Rusky propaganda to besmear the British." Then someone asked: "Remember God, America and England?"

"The Balfour Declaration——"

"Ask Attlee about it. . . ."

"The *mashumeds* are back."

Himy, who seemed to know more about what was going on because he said nothing, merely mopped his forehead and often blew his nose.

"Yes," he finally said one day. "Survivors of Nazi deathcamps landing on the shores of Eretz Ysroel are hunted down by the British, put in camps, behind barbed wires, in Cyprus. . . ."

Once the reality of detention camps in Cyprus had been

confirmed by other sources as well—JOINT, secret radio broadcasts, a few damning and chiding articles in the government-controlled papers *Scanteia* and *Romania Libera*—an exodus fever broke out among the survivors. Many flocked to Constanta and embarked on rotting boats to sail to Haifa, to Tel Aviv.

"The British will deny you permission to land," they were warned.

"We'll try anyhow——"

". . . and put you behind barbed wires, in Cyprus——"

"It doesn't matter! We'll break out!"

"The world is not with you. The United Nations——"

"The world never was. We just didn't know it then. Now we know. We trust only ourselves. We cannot be dissuaded."

Motke and Esther, Mirele and Yosl, packed their valises.

"Next year in Jerusalem," they said.

Moritz wanted to go, but Antal refused.

"You and your sister go," he grinned. "I am a member of the Romanian Communist Party! I'll mind the store. . . ." Rozika begged her brother to wait a while longer, to give her a chance to persuade Antal to go along with them.

When Sandor the Handsome said good-bye to Ilona she did not weep.

"I must go away," he said, and Ilona nodded.

"My place is somewhere else," he said.

"Take me with you," she asked, "I'll help——"

"No," he said. "It's not your fight."

"It could be, if you'd let me."

"No. From now on, I'll fight my own battles."

"Then may God be with you. I'll pray that your fight is successful. And remember: I love you, I'll always love you, no matter what. Remember."

14

The first week in December, on a Monday morning, the opportunity for which Yashenko waited presented itself.

"Coordinate reports at once," Marcovski told him and Keroff. "Prepare security projections. A meeting with the chief of staff has been called for next Monday morning at Budapest headquarters. We'll leave at dawn, this Thursday."

Keroff left the room to carry out orders without delay and Yashenko stepped closer to Marcovski's desk.

"Comrade colonel," he asked formally, "may I be permitted to speak to you off the record?"

"Go ahead, Yashenko." He unbuckled his belt, stretched out in the chair. "Come on, what's on your mind? I'm in a fine mood today." He pointed to his epaulettes. "There may be another star after next Monday's meeting. Then the road to the summit is open."

Marcovski smiled. He had never yet failed in his assignments and he wouldn't fail this time either. Particularly this time. He ought to put out of his mind a remark, a teasing sweet irritant, the chief has passed before assigning him to his present post. The remark had haunted Marcovski ever since. At odd moments he even heard himself say it, involuntarily, without moving his lips. A queer ventriloquism he could not contain. The chief had said, "You are superior to Abakumov; everyone knows that. Now you'll prove it once more, and then . . ." The remark was left hanging in the air, whimsically dangling a variety of possibilities before him.

Of course he would prove it to the chief. The opportunity, the final test, had arrived.

He looked at Yashenko through the thin line of half-closed eyelids.

"And you, my boy, shall rise with me. We understand each other, eh? A little reeducation, though, would really clinch it."

Yashenko nodded, cleared his throat.

"How is the girl?" Marcovski's smile was benign. "Has she learned to laugh again?"

"That's what I want to speak to you about." The uncle in Budapest, Yashenko thought, who does not want to come back to Sighet but who is the sole surviving family member. Marcovski wouldn't refuse——

"What is it?" He poked Yashenko with his elbow. "Is she pregnant?" The question was gratuitous, a spicy little dig to establish the old camaraderie. Yashenko, hearing his own fantasies voiced, read into Marcovski's bantering a subtle signal and, unable to resist it, said impulsively:

"Yes, she is." He paused for an instant, just long enough to savor the taste of the words in his mouth, then his mind began to race. He knew he had to think fast, improvise a new strategy and bluff his way out with great care. *Is she pregnant* was unexpected, yet he had perceived at once the break he sought: Marcovski would recoil from nothing in order to hush up a scandal that would reflect on his ability to maintain discipline among his handpicked men.

"She is six weeks' pregnant," Yashenko added.

Marcovski glared at him, unblinking, and pushed some loose strands of hair on his damp forehead into place.

"What do you intend to do about it?" Marcovski opened a drawer, then slammed it closed. Keroff had suggested settling the romance weeks ago by having the girl deported. Marcovski had always suspected Keroff was from the NKGB, and by allowing him to attend to that matter he could have found out in one stroke whether Keroff was planted by the chief or by Abakumov, the rising star in the NKGB. He cursed under his breath.

"She tried to get help." Yashenko spoke slowly, avoiding the word *abortion*. "The doctors refused."

"Yob tvoyu maty!" The colonel cursed loudly. Why didn't he let Keroff attend to this matter in time? Marcovski had had no qualms in ordering Dora separated from Yashenko soon after they had defected to the USSR. What had possessed him now to lapse into a moment of indulgence? he wondered angrily. Teach her how to laugh! What an absurd touch of sentimentality.

"The unanticipated mishap," Yashenko said, "may be remedied without repercussions——"

"Why don't the doctors want to help her? Is it a matter of money?"

"No. Life, death, the Nazis, with the Jewish doctors. As to the Christian doctors, they've suddenly become law-abiding although . . ."

"Although what?" Marcovski became attentive.

"Although they are known to have performed such operations. The law is not all that stringent. I suspect they simply don't want to cooperate with Jews and hide behind the law——"

"And what about you? Aren't you moved by the girl's suffering?" Marcovski asked abruptly. "She has suffered, you've said yourself how much she has suffered and cried out about human indecency—and called for a touch of decency to restore some of her trust in people."

Maybe he was pushing too far, Yashenko thought; but then he had a visceral feeling he was on the right track.

"She is Jewish," Marcovski prodded, "and now it means nothing to you?"

"It does," Yashenko said. "That is why I ask your permission to take her along to Budapest. I know of a cooperative doctor there."

"And after the operation?"

"After . . ." Yashenko shrugged his shoulders. "It's over, that's all. I've gotten myself a bit too deeply involved. Time has come for me to get uninvolved. I wish to take care of the doctor and be done with it." He looked calmly at Marcovski as if he really meant every word he had said and knew that Lisa would understand why he must speak this way: it was for their future, for a new beginning somewhere else, for they must get away from

372

here where day is night, sweet is bitter, love is hate, friendship is cunning.

The crease on Marcovski's forehead smoothed out, his eyes opened wide. "Don't you feel anything special in that heart of yours, Yashenko? Having listened to your views on Jewishness I came to the conclusion that Jewish hearts bleed for each other."

"Comrade colonel, I've given a lot of thought to our last conversation on this subject. I am Jewish by an accident of birth but I am a communist by deliberate choice. I choose to march with you." Yashenko straightened out, thinking he must be careful, tread gingerly and not overdo it. Let Marcovski call the tune. If this plan doesn't work, there is always the uncle scheme.

"You direct me what to do," Yashenko added gravely.

"You'll bring her to Budapest, that's what you'll do!" Marcovski snapped, and Yashenko could barely restrain himself from shouting with joy. The master manipulator had taken the bait: to secure Yashenko's unswerving loyalty, Marcovski was going to become his benefactor! And who knows, Yashenko mused, perhaps the colonel believed that one decent deed could, at last, wipe his slate clean of the Markenberg and Marciuc past; appease, if not erase, nasty shadows that troubled his sleep.

"After she has seen the doctor in Budapest," Marcovski continued, "maybe I'll find a job for her. I also need an official *tolmacher* during this trip. She'll do. And meanwhile, you treat this girl nicely, my boy, like a . . . *mensch*. That's an order!"

15

"The impetus carried me away," Yashenko told Lisa in the evening, "and being flexible about the rules of the game. We've won the first round."

But his nerves and wits were ground down, almost used up. He stretched, pulled her to him. Her closeness melted away the tension.

"Once across," he said, "I'll contact the *Bricha*; and till we'll be on our way we'll have to live in DP camps. I know how hard it will be for you . . . Another camp, even though a DP camp. It won't be for long, you'll see. Without money——"

"We have lots of money, Leonyushka," she exclaimed. "Don't you worry about money."

"What?"

"A bundle, we have a bundle. Mamma's diamond earrings alone should be worth a fortune. We have lots of gold sovereigns and napoleons and——"

"What are you talking about, Lisa?"

"About the bundle. The bundle I gave Naftuli for safekeeping. I'll take it back now. The bundle is in the safe, in the living room. Six, nine, seven. That's the combination."

"Why . . . why didn't you mention it before?"

"I . . . I don't know." She was stammering. "I just don't know why I couldn't speak to you about the bundle . . . It was connected with Miklos . . . a beige monogrammed handkerchief . . . I just couldn't face it . . . that I would have to take charge . . . don't be angry——"

"I am not," he said, "I understand."

"But now it's different, isn't it, Leonyushka. Now *you'll* take charge. I'll ask Naftuli to return it to me——"

"Let me think it over."

Later he said: "Yes, it would mean a lot taking the bundle along. It would also mean taking a risk asking for the bundle *now*."

"But it's mine . . ."

"Of course; and you want it back just before you are going away on a holiday with me. What for? To wear the jewels? Or do you think you could trust Naftuli with the truth?"

The look of guile on Naftuli's face and his hands reaching out every month for her share of household expenses came to her mind. She shook her head. "No, I wouldn't trust Naftuli."

"Is there anyone else you could trust?"

"Yes! Yes, there is. Himy, I could trust Himy with my life. He is like a brother to me."

"I know. Yes, Himy."

"I could also trust Ilona," she said. "I am sure."

"Himy," Yashenko said. "Although you may be right about Ilona too——"

"And Olga," She had friends, real friends. Three friends—and Leonyushka. She was rich.

"Empower Himy in writing to request, on your behalf, the return of the bundle from Naftuli. Then ask Himy to deliver it on his next trip to Budapest to an address I'll give you tomorrow," he said. "Make sure Himy speaks to Naftuli one week after you and I have left Sighet. I know Himy will understand. . . ."

Naomi helped her pack.

"Going on a honeymoon," Naomi smiled. "You'll tell me about Budapest when you return." She looked in the valise. "What's that?"

"My Matrushka doll."

"What's a Matrushka doll?"

"Dolls within dolls. Each doll a part of the other yet separate. Just like people."

"I see." She took her eyes off the doll, looked in the distance: "Will you stroll on Vaci Utca, windowshop . . . ?"

16

At daybreak Thursday morning the dark green military limousine was rolling along the highway. The colonel sat in front, next to the driver. In the back, between Yashenko and Keroff, Lisa looked out the window apprehensively, watching the white landscape roll by and the gray clouds hanging in the distance. She thought of jasmine and acacia fragrance, of familiar textures and colors, of people she knew.

Perhaps she should have gone to the house one last time, she brooded, to touch the wall with frame marks on it.

She would think of the past later, she went on brooding, sort it out later, in freedom, with Leonid's help. What mattered now was what was ahead.

The sight of the frontier coming towards them frightened her. She was traveling in a limousine, not a cattle car, she reminded herself; there were documents to prove the legitimacy of her being there. Documents, there were many documents, with seals and signatures and stamps. She must relax. Someday, oh someday, she would travel with her own passport, perhaps a blue one with a white star of David on its cover. Then she would not tense up at a border. She wished she could hold on to Leonid's arm, but Keroff's stern presence was forbidding. He sat at her left, stiffly, and had not yet uttered a word.

The limousine reached the crossing point between Romania and Hungary at Mátészalka. The border, a strip of land between two gates, was patrolled by a pair of Russian soldiers. Along the side of the gates were two wooden huts, a puny flag fluttering on top of each. One was the Romanian, the other the Hungarian flag.

"The tricolors of my youth," Lisa said.

Grisha Keroff stirred: "You don't like them?"

"I've honored both of them. But the flags only mocked me."

One of the flags in particular, she thought, mocked her Papa. It had cruelly mocked Papa. It was the Hungarian flag.

The sun shone so brightly that morning. It was the first week of September, in 1940. Fall was the most beautiful season in Sighet, she now remembered, or was it spring? Everything was beautiful to her till that September morning. She remembered having looked at the mountains on that morning, how assertive they were, how safe; and the blue mist over the mountain peaks was like an ethereal union of sky and earth.

The parade was on. A parade on a September morning that would stay with her for as long as she lived. For even now, as she sat in the limousine, she could feel the breeze of that morning on her skin and distinctly hear the clap of hooves on the pavement on the Grand Corso, see hussars sitting erect on horses, colorful passementeries webbing the front of their uniforms, see their gold epaulettes, brass buttons, tassels, shakos with bright plumes. They held the reins in gloved hands, the spurs on their shiny black boots dug into the horses that pranced and trotted while the hussars looked down on the people jamming the streets. The people shouted LONG LIVE OUR SAVIORS, HAIL THE MAGYARS. Columns of hussars were joined by columns of foot soldiers pouring in from the western end of Sighet. And Sighet changed to Sziget.

It was a big day indeed: the Magyars were taking over Transylvania, two-thirds of it.

The people were ecstatic, they shouted and waved flags.

There were flags everywhere. Large silk flags on top of the city hall, on all public buildings: on schools, courts, churches, the post office. The flags billowed and fluttered in the breeze. Each house on the Grand Corso was bedecked with flags, somewhat smaller than those on top of the official buildings.

All these flags had been donated to the town by Andras Engler, the man who loved the Magyars, loved their lullabies and love songs, who was loyal to the country where he and his parents were born, who every year, on March 15, made Lisa listen to him solemnly recite Sandor Petröfi's patriotic poem *Talpra Magyar, Rise up, Magyar,* the poem that had been the anthem of the 1848 Hungarian revolution.

At last they had returned, his Magyars as of old, Papa said when he underwrote bedecking the town with welcoming flags.

She and Papa stood on the curb, watched the hussars and foot soldiers. The sun shone brightly. Papa held her hands. He was tall and elegant, a red-white-green cockade in his lapel. Silver-gray hair framed his handsome face, the sideburns brushed to a sheen. The beating of his heart seemed to induce a gentle stir in the gold chain across his chest.

His green eyes were full of tears.

He stood at attention, saluting a large flag a foot soldier carried. The flag had the Magyar emblem embroidered in vibrant, sharp colors, and Papa could not restrain himself any longer: he sobbed for joy.

Traffic on the highway was light. There were no civilian cars on the road, only military vehicles and trucks in convoys. The afternoon had turned dark early and snow was falling heavily, charging the windshield in a continuous gusty, whirling dance, like feathers and puffs of eiderdown jerkily shaken loose from an enormous comforter. She watched the dancing snowflakes disappear under the blades of the windshield wipers—the inexorable squashing of snowflakes into dribbling liquid.

But first the snowflakes danced.

(the hermetically sealed shower room was called *Brausebad.* it had no windows. there were little recessed openings in the ceiling, little innocuous-looking spouts . . . then the Jews, like the snowflakes, danced. a dance of terror and agony and death.)

She began to shiver and Grisha Keroff turned to her.

He had not liked the idea of her coming along; and the colonel's reluctance to permit him to deal with her in the usual manner had left him wondering if there were any secret links between those three. Hasn't there always been, he brooded, a conspiracy among *zsids?* Yet the instant someone tries to break up that conspiracy they yell *pogrom!*

As a little boy he had had a mutt to whom he was inordinately attached. It was his only companion, his only toy. He had nothing else. One summer the dog got infested with ticks. By the time Keroff pulled all the ticks out, it was too late. They had practically drained the mutt of its blood. Keroff was heartsick, angry that whole summer, cried out in his sleep; if he could have at least found a nest of ticks in the woods, destroy and squash the parasites under his foot, burn them. Revenge the death of his mutt . . .

Whenever he thought of *zsids* he remembered his mutt, and the old anger and pain returned. They are in the thick of everything, the *zsids*, and are everywhere. Even tried to run away with the Revolution—Trotsky and his ilk—by spewing out international brotherhood to becloud their real goal: that of sucking Russia dry of its blood. But Stalin, who clearly recognized their conniving and huckstering, was well on the way to solving the *zsid* problem when the war came. Now that the war is over, Stalin will continue tackling the purging of traitors and the Russian people will, at last, have a *zsid*-free country.

Still, what was it, he wondered, that made every *zsid* stay on top and always get ahead. Cosmopolitans, the lot of them, so different from humanity; a maze of invisible threads linking the *zsid* from Bialystok or Odessa or anywhere in Russia to the *zsid* in Rome, Paris, New York. How can one fight such a widespread and subtle net of international subversion? The *zsids* in Russia proclaim themselves comrades. The question is: what kind of comrades? Soviet comrades or *zsid* comrades? Meanwhile, one has to watch them, day and night, so as to prevent the infestation of one's own country.

"Aren't you feeling well?" Keroff now asked Lisa rather loudly, to show the colonel he bore no grudge for having her along although, at the time, Keroff had inquired why they needed a *tolmacher* when the three men spoke Romanian fluently. "But none of us speaks Hungarian, lieutenant!" Marcovski had bellowed, "and she does! We are going to Budapest, not Bucharest, remember?"

"Or are you cold?" Keroff wanted to know.

"Yes, I am," she said, still shivering. "Winter came early this year."

"Ah, you should experience winter in Russia: then you'd know what real cold is! Russia," he sighed, "I miss her. The birch trees——"

"You love your country, lieutenant," she said. "Isn't it wonderful to love . . . one's country. An added dimension."

"Well said indeed, Lisa," he replied pleasantly. "May I call you by your first name?" He saw her nod. "And you call me Grisha."

"If you wish."

"You are right, Lisa, I love Russia." He was feeling uncomfortable; being cramped in annoyed him. He could not stretch out in the car and his stump throbbed.

"I have good reason to love Russia." He tried not to think of the pain in his stump. "My grandfather was a *muzhik* who kissed the hem the lord's cloak on whose land he toiled, from dawn till dusk, and then went to bed hungry. Now look at the *muzhik's* grandson: a lieutenant in the Red Army! Without our glorious revolution, I too would be toiling on land, kissing the lord's cloak, going to bed on an empty stomach." He forgot about his discomfort. "My grandfather, his father and grandfather, were illiterate folk; thought the division of classes God-given. The same God who handed down the Ten Commandments to your Moses also handed down a design for a class-structured society——"

"*Slushi,*" the colonel said turning to them. "Listen, how about some singing?"

Keroff started on a marching song.

"Lisa," he said after a few bars, "don't you want to sing too?"

"Yes, of course," she said. "Leonid, teach me the song."

They were still singing *Moskva Maya* when they arrived at Budapest. It was past midnight, the snow had stopped falling. The limousine pulled up in front of a big apartment house, on Andrassy Ut where the Russian high command and its staff were billeted.

Lisa and Leonid had a room to themselves. It was Marcovski's *prix de douleur*, Yashenko told her smiling.

Six plaster cherubs, their wings and some of their toes

chipped, were clustered around a hole in the center of the high ceiling. Had the cherubs held a sparkling Bohemian crystal chandelier or a handpainted Herend fixture? she wondered. Then she saw the big four-poster bed with a floral canopy and the frown on her face smoothed out. She touched the carved posters, fluffed up the pillows. Tomorrow morning she will wake up with him beside her, she thought; she won't have to look for hollows on the pillow to convince herself he had been there indeed. How she dreaded the loneliness of that brief moment in the morning, the searching for someone who was no longer there, whose earlier presence was attested to merely by impressions left on the pillow!

They stood beside the bed, she slowly gliding her hand on one of the posters, and the thought of waking up with him in the morning exhilarated her. She moaned with pleasure. Thousands of little ants had suddenly invaded her vulva and were making her tingle inside. The prurient sensation rose to her fingertips, and she took hold of him with such feral passion that they both staggered for a moment. As she covered his face with tiny kisses, the tingling inside her became exquisite, urgent, and her mouth and tongue continued to kiss him while her hands tore buttons open and unbuckled belts, pulled off his jacket, opened his pants. The urgency in her was greater than when he aroused her, for now the arousal was induced by the thought of waking up with him beside her in the morning, a thought that accelerated and heightened her own desires and made her the sexual initiator she had never been before.

17

Next morning Lisa went to the Korvin Department Store, bought a pair of gray corduroy trousers, a wool sweater and a navy beret. She would put these items at the bottom of her valise, under her own clothing, as Leonid had told her to do. She also bought him a short sheepskin coat that was too bulky to fit in the valise and even though it was a few sizes big on her, she decided to wear it.

The city was damp and bleak. People trudged sluggishly along streets full of rubble, courtesy of one year of Nazi occupation, thank you, she thought vindictively. The Russians' siege of Budapest followed by the final rout of the Nazis in February 1945, had left the city in ruins.

Old squares had new names: Engels Square, November 7 Square. The embankments on the Danube were now called Groza Peter and Belgrade. Everything was negotiable, she concluded: the Magyars' slavish homage to their former Nazi masters could be restyled and easily converted into a treaty with their former enemies, the Soviet Union. A full reversal in national sentiment could be accomplished overnight; the Magyars would hardly know the difference—since the one fixed element, creating a sense of unity and purpose, would always be there. That element was the "patriotic" song. Sometimes the Magyars marched to the tune of "The Carpathian snowy peaks we claim, we claim, we claim," at other times they rallied to shrieks of "bring the fuse . . . string up the Jews."

On the Pest bank of the Danube the stolid gray parliament building stood scarred and lusterless like an impotent man who has, at last, given up even the pretense of manhood. Lisa sat on a bench for a while, staring at the colliding blocks of ice floating on the Danube. The six bridges that had linked Buda to Pest had been blown up by the Nazis during the siege and were not yet reconstructed. She looked across the river, to the terraced hills of Buda, some of which bore lovely names like "Rose Hill." She looked in the direction of the royal palace where the regent, Admiral Horthy Miklós had lived, then to the steep Gellert Hill that had prompted the Magyars to boast that the city's landmarks had attracted even the great Prince of Wales. Yes, the hill and its landmarks were famous: the Citadel; the statue of the martyred St. Gellert, the city's patron saint; and the swanky Gellert Hotel that had an indoor swimming pool called Champagne Baths where the water fizzled and frothed just like champagne, while outside the Magyars sang "bring the fuse."

To rid herself of a creeping depression, she walked at a brisk pace along the deserted bank, till she found herself at the foot of Margit Bridge, before a path leading to a small island in the Danube, Margit Sziget. It had been a charming little island with a lovely beach, a fine restaurant and heartwarming Gypsy music, where her father had taken her when he had visited her in Budapest during the year she was in school there.

She turned her back to Margit Sziget, abruptly, loathing not merely Budapest as it was now or as she remembered it to have been when the Jews failed to see the rot behind the charming facade, but loathing the Magyars as well who had delivered the Jews of Hungary to Hitler with an eagerness and speed unparalleled by the other Nazi allies.

She returned to her room on Andrassy Ut, stretched out on the canopied bed. Nothing has changed, she concluded again, even though old slogans and principles had been swiftly painted over in fashionable red. Only the prevailing sentiments about Jews, she sensed, retained the perennial venomous color of anti-Semitism. What else could one expect from the upright citizens of Magyarország who claimed to have known nothing of Kenyérmezö and the sealed cattle cars?

18

Marcovski turned to Yashenko during a recess.

"Well?"

"I've reached him by telephone. Saturday the doctor goes to the country. He'll come back late that night. It's all set for Sunday morning."

"This time there mustn't be any accidents!" Marcovski warned.

19

At first the driver could not find the restaurant. He drove them through sloshy streets dim from missing or broken bulbs in sad-looking lamp posts. Keroff switched on a small light in the roof of the limousine, then noticed the fur hat she wore.

"The *kushma,* it suits you nicely. You could almost pass for a Russian woman. But the coat . . ." He shook his head: "You are too thin——"

"The coat is a present from Leonid. He had me buy it today," she said, as they had agreed she would. "Maybe I should exchange it tomorrow for a smaller size."

"Not tomorrow," Yashenko interjected. "You can do that on Monday. Let's spend tomorrow and Sunday together. On Monday I'll be busy. Work."

Marcovski coughed.

"What are you doing tomorrow, the two of you?" Keroff's question was friendly.

"There is a French film, with Harry Baur and Annabella," Lisa said.

"She wants to see this movie, *Taras Bulba,*" Yashenko explained. "I'll take her."

"Good, Yashenko. You do that," Marcovski said, and coughed again. He turned to Lisa: "The movie, that's fine . . . relieves the mind for a few hours." His hand made a gesture as if to pat her cheek, or knee, then it changed direction. Marcovski reached into his pocket for the cigarette holder.

"The famous Taras Bulba," Keroff said, "the old Cossack chieftain. He was a colonel, did you know?"

They arrived at the restaurant. While the driver held open the door for them, Keroff continued: "Yes, he was a colonel, the fearless Taras Bulba. Known for an implacable heart when it came to duty and country. Like Stenka Razin . . . Taras Bulba had two sons, Andrei and Ostap. Shot Andrei with his own hands for having betrayed his comrades for the sake of a Polish woman; then the Poles tortured Ostap to death. . . ."

Before the entrance of the restaurant she stopped for an instant. It was the Emke. Then, between the colonel and Yashenko, she walked in slowly.

The damask table cloths were smudged, the stemmed goblets coated with fingerprints and lip marks. The zither, covered with oilcloth, was pushed in a corner. Tired, weary-looking waiters were galavanized into action when the party of Russians appeared at the door.

Bowing, the headwaiter led them to a center table, pulled out a chair, arched his arm elegantly: "Won't you sit down, honored lady?" He bowed again. "Please."

The menu was soiled. Waiters rearranged the dull silverware and plates, poured water in glasses. She picked up a glass, examined it, then, sneering, put it back on the table. A waiter promptly removed the glass, brought another one and wiped it with a napkin inside and out several times.

How they grovel and crawl when they smell power, she thought; they fawn around her, address her with deference as if she were a titled lady, all because they think she has power. Smugly, she reclined in her chair, enjoying their toadying. Why not, the previous dinner she had here . . . Or was she enjoying the piquant taste of power, as transient and banal as it was, nonetheless power?

She turned her attention to the waiter pouring wine. His face seemed familiar, yet she was certain she had never seen the man before. She kept thinking of the last dinner here, with Drifter and Rozika and Bozsi.

She sampled the wine.

"Vinegar," she said half in jest, "not vintage tokay."

Marcovski snapped his fingers:

"Vintage tokay!" he barked at the bowing waiter.

After dinner she impatiently watched the waiter clear the table. His face still puzzled her, she was not sure if he was the same waiter who had poured the wine just now, or if he was the waiter who had once held before her a covered dish with shimmering sauce in it. Each waiter could have been the earlier one.

Her head ached. A peculiar smell, reminding her of scorched food, perhaps seared meat, infiltrated the dining room.

The waiter dropped a crumb in her lap, inadvertently.

"Where are your manners?" she snarled at him. The waiter mumbled a few unintelligible words, bent down to pick up a fork from the floor. As he straightened up, she caught a sharp glint in his eyes, full of hate. Triggered, she jumped up and grabbed a plate to hurl it at him, but Yashenko, as if by accident, knocked the plate out of her hand.

"Better clean up the mess," he sternly told the waiter, pointing to the broken china on the floor, "and make a good job of it."

Yes, she thought, and gasped for air. Leonid was right: retaliating at this level was not the way to even scores and besides, her scores can never be evened. But still . . .

"Careful," she warned the waiter, "and next time, better watch out!"

20

Saturday Lisa went to the movies to see *Taras Bulba* and Yashenko went to make arrangements for their defection.

"It's settled," he told her in the evening. "We'll take the train, tomorrow morning, to Sopron. At night we'll cross into Austria as Katinka and Lajos Halász."

The false identification papers were in his pocket but he was reluctant to show them to Lisa, for he would then have to speak of the characters he had been forced to deal with. The pressure of time had made him turn to the Hungarian Renaissance Party after he had learned that the next border crossing, under the aegis of the *Bricha,* was not scheduled until the following Wednesday night. Yashenko and Lisa had to cross on the next night, Sunday. The only organization prepared to smuggle them across the border in time was the Hungarian Renaissance Party. Its members, proclaiming themselves the new patriots, were in fact nothing but leftovers from Szálasi's Crossed Arrows gang, greedy merchants handling political flesh, smugglers trafficking in blood and money. Yashenko had dealt with them from the seeming vantage point of a superior instructing their leader to put across the border the Hálasz couple his department wanted to expel, unofficially. But the fact that Yashenko had to scheme with these brigands still offended him.

He was determined not to allow his anger to dampen his concentration, and to maintain his alertness unimpaired for the next twenty-four hours. There are ways and means to deal with gangsters, at the right time. Always at the right time, he reminded himself, and there was a trace of a smile in his eyes as he suddenly recalled a forgotten verse from Ecclesiastes: "To every thing there is a season . . ."

"Once we've crossed into Austria, we'll stay in the Allied section of Vienna till my contact gives word to travel to Salzburg," he said calmly. "There the *Bricha* will get in touch with us, take us to Munich, in the American zone of Germany."

He wondered how long she had been shivering. Her teeth chattered slightly, sounding like glass beads children shake playfully in a paper bag. He nestled her securely in his arms: "Don't be afraid, my love. We'll make it."

They were at the train station at daybreak. Yashenko changed in the men's room and emerged looking like one of the many civilians milling about on the platform. He joined Lisa in the unventilated waiting room, opened a newspaper, the *Nepszava*, and pretended to read it. She leaned her head on his shoulder and feigned sleep.

Make believe she was Lisa Yashenko; she and her husband Leonid were ordinary people, doing ordinary things on an ordinary Sunday morning: an excursion to the country, some sightseeing, perhaps visiting some friends. A smile crossed her face. Lisa Yashenko, happy to meet you. Yes, oh yes. Someday soon.

The train arrived. The passengers rushed to the compartments, sweeping her and Yashenko along.

"Going to visit his parents in Sopron," she told the conductor when he stepped into the compartment, together with a Russian soldier, to check identification papers. She pointed to the sleeping Leonid. "Like clockwork, my husband visits them every month. . . ."

It was early afternoon when they arrived at Sopron, a western border town in Hungary. The town, dating back to Roman settlements in Panonia, was at the foothills of the Austrian Alps, near Lake Fertö.

"Sopron is associated with the Széchenyi, the Esterházy and the de Györ families," she said. "There is a museum here——"

"We'll forgo sightseeing today. Let's find the school instead."
He smiled but there was a slight edge in his voice. "We have a
rendezvous in the school."

She stopped a passerby, then turned to Yashenko: "You want
to know where the school is?" she asked him casually in Hungarian.

"*Igen,*" he answered jovially, "yes."

After she got directions, she turned to him again: "You've
heard the gentleman. It's a long walk, two kilometers at least.
What do you say?"

"*Menyünk,*" Yashenko said, "let's go."

She thanked the man for the detailed directions, then started
walking with Yashenko towards the outskirts of the town. When
they reached the school, it was the middle of the afternoon.

All was quiet, soundless and colorless. A courtyard in the foreground of the building was covered with several inches of snow,
and the building itself blended into the faraway mountains and
the sky. This ashen eeriness was punctuated by a large hand
pump in the center of the yard. A child's knitted red wool cap
was wrapped around the mouth of the pump spout, and the water, which had filtered through the wool cap, had turned into
jagged, scalloped ice, like a fringe of lace. The pump handle,
frozen midway, pointed east.

One classroom, close to the entrance, had been left open. A
part of the Cyrillic alphabet was on the blackboard.

"It's incomplete." He chalked in the rest of the alphabet,
rubbed the chalk dust off his hands.

Shadows, taupe and slate, enveloped the room.

"Don't be afraid, *golubka,*" he said in the semidarkness, holding her hands, "we are so near. Almost there, on the other side of
the mountain. A few more hours."

"Yes," she said. "I love you."

"And I love you." He thought he again heard the sound of
glass beads playfully shaken by children in a paper bag and took
her in his arms. "Don't worry," he said.

"Don't worry," she echoed, and opened his coat, nestled to
him, but still she was scared and cold and shivering. Her hands
trembled as she slipped them under his sweater, seeking reassurance from the warmth of his body, and she thought he must be

392

scared too, maybe cold, for he reached into her bosom, touched her breasts, and then her fright melted into a rising need for him, draining off tension as they lay down on the floor.

It was pitch-black in the room. Through the window they saw the bleached night, a few stars in the sky.

"After this is over, you'll never be afraid again."

"I am not afraid anymore," she said.

"It will be clear crossing tonight. They should be here in another hour."

He started to hum a tune. It was a Russian war ballad called *Tomnaya Notch,* a bittersweet song of love and loneliness—and of hope.

"Join me," he asked her.

He peered at his luminous wristwatch dial. "It's past nine o'clock. They'll be here soon."

They continued to hum together. All was still, save for their soft humming and the hoarse cawing of a crow.

After a while, she asked him, "Do you remember a fairy tale called *The Seven-Headed Dragon?*"

An old Romanian folktale, it told how the dragon, a monster whose seven heads were greed, fear, envy, hate, war, pestilence and death, was holding Princess Teodora a prisoner in his mountain cave. Undetected by the dragon, the handsome knight Frumos found his way into the cave. Laying his head in the princess' lap, he waited for midnight, the only time when the dragon could be slain. But midnight found Frumos fast asleep in the lap of the princess, who began to weep. Her hot tears, falling on his cheeks, woke him. He drew his sword instantly, killed the seven-headed dragon, and lived with Princess Teodora happily ever after.

Yashenko pressed Lisa closer to him.

"Yes," he said, "I remember the fairy tale."

She put her head in his lap, kissed both his hands and whispered: "Papa predicted that some day my Knight would come. He was right: you *are* my Knight."

Then the sound of an approaching car broke into their fragile dream.

21

She ran to the window. The car stopped at the gate, in front of the courtyard.

"They came for us in style." She groped in the dark for her valise, then linked fingers with Yashenko, waiting.

There were steps in the corridor followed by a kick on the door, flinging it open. Two figures stood in the doorway, one of them scanning the room with a flashlight.

"There they are!" Keroff's voice was exultant as he beamed the flashlight on them.

"Yob tvoyu maty!" Marcovski shouted, switching on the electric light. "So that's how you carry out orders, you miserable son of a bitch!"

"I'll explain——"

"Shove your explanation up your ass, Yashenko! I ought to shoot you with my own hands as I would shoot a mad dog. Like Taras Bulba shot his son Andrei." He angrily kicked over a small chair. "But you're not even worth a bullet, you stinking traitor!"

The coat had given them away, she thought in a panic; Marcovski and Keroff realized the coat was not for her; they were caught because of her!

Struck by dumb, animal terror, she was paralyzed for an instant till the image of a girl and a man on the floor, loving each other tenderly, cut across her inner eye, sweeping away the terrible fear. In that instant, she knew she must fight back, do something quickly before it was too late.

The gun was under Leonid's sweater, in the holster over his right hip. Lisa let go of Yashenko's hand and pressed her right shoulder against his left arm, hugging his back with her right arm. She deftly slipped her hand inside his coat, towards his right hip, her fingers feeling for the holster.

Fast, Lisa. Pull out the gun and shoot them. Quickly. You are not afraid. Do it for Leonid and Lisa Yashenko.

Her fingers touched the butt of the gun.

We must escape, Leonid and I. Our only chance of survival was in loving each other.

She jerked at the gun.

Having sensed Lisa's intention as she moved her arm behind his back, Yashenko had unerringly placed his hand on his hip, over the coat and was now exerting tremendous pressure on her hand, inside his coat. At the same time he swung his other arm over her shoulder, clutching it tightly.

She felt his fingers pressing her shoulder and the weight of his grip on her hand.

But I must shoot them; the girl and the man must escape. I must help them. Please, Leonyushka, your hand is a steely clasp immobilizing my hand. Please!

Again she tried to jerk the gun free.

Then she saw a gun barrel stare her in the face.

It was Keroff's weapon. Marcovski was pointing his gun at Yashenko.

"Your gun!" Marcovski snarled. *"Davai!"*

Yashenko unbuttoned his coat slowly, removed the gun from the holster, after prying loose her fingers.

The girl and the man, they must escape! They have suffered enough!

"Don't hurt us anymore!" Lisa cried out to Marcovski. "Have mercy!"

"Keroff, tell him what a fool he is!" the colonel shouted without looking at her. There was a book on the floor and Marcovski sent it flying with a kick. His face was contorted, damp strands of hair hung over his forehead and the lids were so nearly closed that his eyes seemed to have disappeared in their sockets.

A blind man kicking books!

She knew then she had failed to protect the girl and the man, and the terrible, paralyzing white fright returned.

"Tell him!" Marcovski ordered Keroff.

"I wanted to see *Taras Bulba* myself," Keroff said, looking now at Lisa, now at Yashenko. "But the two of you were already gone when I went to fetch you——"

He is lying, she wanted to scream, he did not really want to see the movie; he hates us. He hates Leonid. Keroff is a Jew-hater, a modern Chmielnicki, please, could someone help, please . . .

She slipped her right arm back around Yashenko's waist, over the coat, and held on to him.

"I drove to the movie house in time to see you kiss her," Keroff told Yashenko.

And you hate him for that too, she wanted to scream again, but now that the fear had come back, it held her dangling over a vast void, helpless and breathless.

She clutched Yashenko's waist tighter and her arm began to pulsate, gently.

". . . then she entered the movie house alone." Keroff touched his artificial leg. "I followed you in the car. The Hungarian Renaissance Party! Cutthroat hooligans!"

He turned to Lisa: "He is a deserter. I had to do it!"

"No!" she heard herself scream, "no!"

Their children, what will happen to their children, their silken black curls. What will happen to them?

She must do something now, now, she thought frantically. If only she knew what to do. Perhaps she ought to agree with Keroff. Maybe *then* their love would not be *verboten.*

"Yes," she screamed, "yes!"

Her arm around Leonid throbbed, a thousand little needles pricked at it, and she tightened, tightened her hold on him till she was not scared anymore, just hurting, so terribly hurting all over as if someone was carving her up, little by little, starting with the shoulder joints, cutting her off from Leonid.

Keroff now brusquely turned to Marcovski: "Your orders, comrade colonel!"

"They are under arrest! Haven't you noticed? Or did you think we came for a social visit, eh?" He gave a last kick to a chair. *"Davai!"* he yelled, "let's go!"

396

Marcovski stormed out of the room and Keroff prodded Lisa and Yashenko after him with the barrel of his gun. They marched through the courtyard towards the gate.

"I'll start the car, comrade colonel." Keroff dashed ahead, into the street.

From close by a voice cried out: *Death to the tyrant, long live Magyarország.*

Then a shot rang out.

Outside the entrance Keroff fell forward.

Marcovski quickly slammed the gate. They stayed inside the courtyard, listening. Echoes of the shot had died down while sounds of a song, a strange blend of the Magyar national anthem and *String up the Jews,* faded into the night.

Then it was quiet again, as if nothing had happened.

Marcovski wiped his forehead.

"*Yob tvoyu maty!*" he rasped under his breath. "What a fucked-up mess! I should have shot you like a snake, a traitor. You've betrayed me, you scum. *They* shot Keroff instead. He was a good man, Keroff, not a traitor like you!" And now he would never know if Keroff was the chief's man or Abakumov's. "What a fucked-up mess," he said again.

"Sir," Lisa said through chattering teeth, "I implore you: give us freedom. I love him. He is all I have. My life. Without him I'll never be whole." She was in the snow, on her knees, tugging his winter coat, sobbing. "Haven't you ever loved? Hasn't anyone ever loved you? Please," she grabbed his hands, "please have mercy——"

"Mercy?" Marcovski said leaving his hand in hers for an instant before pulling it away. "Mercy, eh? Did you know I was going to get you a job at the embassy because . . . you are a *medele*, after all? Did you know that? But you connived with him and lied to me. The girl is with child indeed!

"*Nyet!*" he added harshly. "Let's go. *Davai, davai!*"

"Comrade!" The words had been suffocating Yashenko. Everything had happened so fast. From the moment the flashlight had searched the classroom till the shooting of Keroff only several minutes had passed. Yet time and space had no more meaning for him. He had had the feeling that it all was happening to others at an agonizingly slow pace, while he was a spectator, from a different plane, in a different time sequence, gripped and mesmerized and fascinated into numbness by the victims' life-and-death struggle. He desperately tried to step into the pressing reality, fight the numbness. Split images bombarded his mental eye, images of winged children with freckled hair flying towards Jerusalem under an astonishingly blue sky, Jerusalem now a city washed over by black tidal waves; of a brilliant political gene killed off and sunk below the summit, at the bottom of the Caspian Sea; and in *der stetl brent.* . . .

Then he heard Lisa sob and knew that the rules of the game had been suspended, a new rule was being forged: anything goes. A freestyle match—unlike life till now.

"Comrade colonel." His voice was clear now and he picked Lisa up from the snow, put his arms around her shoulders. "Let us go."

"You are mad."

"No, I am not. You can do it. With a flick of your fingers. Manipulate, arrange——"

"Shut up!"

"But you went along with all this! You implied——"

"I implied nothing!"

"Yet you knew how I felt!"

"Yes, I knew you went berserk and got infected with alien notions. You are sick——"

"Then I am useless to you."

"Oh no, I've invested a lot in you. My reputation. You will be cured."

"There will be a scandal——"

"Scandal? What scandal? Who is there to tell——"

"Goddammit!" Yashenko exploded, the last vestiges of confusion overcome by outrage, "I'll tell!"

"Who is there to believe you?"

"Keroff," Yashenko blurted, "did you set him up?"

"Yes, you are sick. I'll take it upon myself to rehabilitate you. You'll be mended, be my boy again."

How does one appeal to an old Bolshevik or to a boa constrictor? Yashenko's frenzied mind was searching, searching for an opening, a way out, for the ultimate weapon.

"*Chaver* Markenberg," he said quickly, "how many of us have been left alive after the big slaughter? Tell me, *chaver,* tell me! You know statistics, figures; tell me how many? And tell me again to my face that being a *zsid* is inconsequential! You are a *zsid*, and that's not inconsequential, damn it, else you would have done away with me a long time ago!"

"Wrong, wrong again! You should know better, I trained you myself. Nothing matters except the Party. Not you, not her, nobody, nothing! I don't care how many *zsids* are alive," he hissed, "all I care about is the Party! You are alive because you are useful to the Party, not because you are a *zsid!* As long as the Party needs you, *I* need you——"

"Markenberg, be a *mensch!* For once in your life, be a real *mensch:* let us go! You'll sleep better——"

"Never! You'll stay——"

"Then let her go alone, without me." He was terribly tired suddenly, drained dry of energy and hope, for he knew in his heart that there would be no reprieve, no pity, and that Marcovski would consider nothing except the Party, in short- and long-range terms. "You've got me, and you've got me good. What do you need her for? She is unimportant to you; why be saddled with her? Let her go, I tell you. I'll be in debt to you for the rest of my life. Let her go, Markenberg, Marciuc, Marcovski. Whoever you are, comrade colonel, let her go!"

A shiver went through Marcovski, but then the cold and the wind may have made him shiver, and he abruptly swung open the gate.

"Nyet!" he shouted. *"Davai, davai!"*

They dragged Keroff's body through the snow, put him in the back of the car.

"To the Sopron *kommandatura!"* Marcovski ordered.

Yashenko was at the wheel. He fumbled with the ignition key, then pressed on the gas pedal several times till the motor started. Marcovski lit a cigarette, pulled out the ashtray underneath the dashboard.

"Yob tvoyu maty!" he cursed again. *"Mensch, mensch!* What does all that mean, anyhow?" He took a few drags at his cigarette, furiously, then killed it in the ashtray.

"All right already!" he barked at Yashenko. "Dig a bit into every man and you find a fucked-up bleeding Jewish heart. All right: the *medele* can go. Now. Turn back."

Yashenko swung the wheel westward.

"Please say *yes,* my love. Quickly." His voice was insistent, heavy. "There is so little time; always so little time; and the dragon has too many heads. I am sorry.

She put her hand over his, on the wheel, firmly pressing it. Everything had been so near, just over there, across the unknown mountain on the horizon.

"No." She was calm, almost serene. Her chin was set. He knew she was beyond persuasion. "I won't ever leave you of my own free will. I'll stay with you till they tear us apart."

Marcovski stalked into the Sopron *kommandatura*.

"What kind of security do you have around here?" he raged. "Deserters everywhere and you warm your asses in the room and drink tea to dilute whatever shitty little brains you have. *I* must come down from Budapest with my adjutants and a *tolmacher* to chase deserters! On your toes, miserable worms! Go after the rats who shot Lieutenant Keroff, the great war hero. Arrest every cocksucking, slimy Hungarian Renaissance Party member! I'll make them pay for this!"

On the way back to Budapest, Marcovski told Yashenko in Russian:

"It's over for good, the bleeding-heart bit. I want that goddamn star on my epaulettes and neither Keroff, the girl, nor you can make me lose it. I am fully squared up with you. From now on, I owe you nothing. But you, you shall always be in my debt. I am saving you on behalf of the Party. That's why, in good time, you'll come along with me to the summit, even if I have to drag you along. I'll give you cause to be grateful to me for the rest of your life."

They reached Budapest.

"You move in with me till the chiefs of staff meeting is over," Marcovski said as they drove on Andrassy Ut. "When we get back to Sighet, I'll start to process orders for your next assignment."

The car came to a stop in front of the building.

"Your new post will be in the Dombas," Marcovski said coolly. "And should you try another *coup,* the girl goes to Siberia, express."

400

BOOK VII

"Life begins where Death appears to be,
And where things mold and rot, your eyes may see
The poppies below most red."
                    —Zalman Shneour, *Manginot Hazugot*

1

Naomi watched Lisa unpack.

"Are you ill?" she asked. "You have a strange look. What happened, tell me."

"There is nothing to tell, Naomi." She cradled the Matrushka doll in her hands, then put it away in a drawer. "The holiday is over. That's all."

Something else was over too, she thought. The drive to get up in the morning, to face another day, and then still another day, and on and on. If she could only escape into a painless blur, never have to wake up again.

"But while it lasted," Naomi wanted to know, "did you have a good time?"

"Yes. I had a grand time."

What was Dombas? Where was it? When would he have to go?

"I am glad," Naomi said. "We celebrated Sylvester Eve at the Crown Hotel. Music, dancing, confetti at midnight. Everyone showed up, even Mrs. Stein. Life goes on, it has to, doesn't it Lisa?"

"Yes, Naomi. Life goes on."

Does life go on in Dombas? she wondered. If only she had prostrated herself before Marcovski, kissed his feet . . .

"... I went to the party with Gyuri. Himy and Olga were there. They are in love, one can tell by looking at them. ..."

... told the colonel how it was, how Leonid has made her want to live. Even taught her how to laugh again. It wasn't worth living without him. Marcovski might as well have shot her through the heart, a nice clean little hole like one of the spout holes in the *Brausebad,* and be done with her.

"Gyuri told me, confidentially, there will be elections soon. A new era is in the offing," Naomi said, running her fingers through her hair.

There was no future in it, so what? Lisa remembered having once challenged Naomi's warning that one day Leonid would be gone. Although then she had told Naomi what she had believed to be true, now Lisa knew how naive she had been. Of course she had wanted a future as she wanted one now, desperately, intensely. She must have wanted a future the instant she had walked with Leonid on the bank of the Iza, that first afternoon in the Malom Kert. Yes, after the unfathomable horror—perhaps because of it—she wanted to marry, have a family, children. Reaffirm life as Lisa Yashenko, happy to meet you. There was nothing she had ever wanted more vehemently, with greater passion, than to have a future with Leonid.

2

"Let's not speak of parting," she asked of him. "The night there will be no knock on my door, I'll know you've gone. If we don't say good-bye to each other, it's as if we never parted."

They pretended that each night was like the one before and that the one to come would be like the one that had just passed. They pretended to cheat time, knowing that time could not be cheated. They also knew that each night brought them inexorably closer to a night that would be different from the one that had just passed. Still, they did not speak of parting.

Then one night, a week after their return from Budapest, they both wept in each other's arms.

"Let's speak of it," he said. "It will hurt less."

"No."

"Then let's speak of our love for each other which——"

". . . which should last forever."

"Yes. It will last forever if we dream and keep on dreaming that some day . . ."

Yet Yashenko himself could barely cope with his own pain of separation and with his own fears. Marcovski was pushing him away only to lure him back again. A never-ending power game intended to reduce him to the state of a dog salivating at the sound of his master's bell. Yashenko had to keep his wits about him constantly, and the effort was depleting him. There were days when he wondered if the effort was worth it. He knew where the Dombas was and knew what it was.

But there were days he doubted Marcovski would make good his threat to send him there. The colonel might keep him close by for safety's sake, on a short leash, Yashenko thought, even as he was not sure of this course either. He was not privy any longer to the files Marcovski kept under lock and key in his bulging briefcase, though he was requested to sit in on certain conferences. He and the colonel had not spoken of the Sopron affair since that night in Budapest. Lisa's name was never mentioned. He had dreaded curtailment of his movements, an unofficial house arrest of which the staff would be unaware, disguised perhaps by Marcovski's invitation to move in with him. Instead, Marcovski chose to maintain the appearance of normalcy. At the end of each workday, Marcovski routinely glanced at his wristwatch and announced: "7:45; get ready to be dismissed, Yashenko."

It was a terrible thing for Lisa and him: loving under the shadow of imminent parting, wrestling with doubts, uncertainties—and the chancy hope of a change of mind by Marcovski. Yashenko fought hard to keep himself together. Still, he was not sure he could be strong for both of them or, even if he could be, whether he should. He wanted her to be strong on her own, independent of him. How else was she going to make it?

"Golubka," he said to her one night, "cry if you must, but you must never cave in. Never. There are many kinds of dying and many kinds of living. I want you to live wholesomely. Don't succumb to your despair. Think of the *Muselmans.* . . ."

Groups of two and of three women sit against the wall or bunch up together at night in a bunk. They sway back and forth and talk of meals, sighing and panting, and suck in their cheeks and lick their swollen lips in a trancelike ecstasy. They talk of feasts and banquets, of eating orgies they conjure up, and describe the preparation of every tasty meal they ate there. They exchange recipes, teach each other how to cook that meal, going over and over every ingredient, every condiment, in slow, husky voices till, chewing and swallowing as if they were actually eating those mouth-watering meals, they whip themselves into a sensuous rapture and flee reality for a fantasy world—from which eventually there is no return. Once they succumb to hallucinations of cooking and eating, they become irreversible addicts and soon can do nothing except mentally cook and eat, day and night, while they waste into skeletons, held together by paper-thin flesh, turning into human vegetables that the SS call *Muselmans* and sweep into carts and dump into the crematoria.

"Giving up hope can reduce anyone to an emotional *Muselman*," he said. "Whether we are together or apart, I'll always love you. You must never turn into an emotional *Muselman;* you must be strong to keep our dream alive. Then I too can be strong."

She stifled a sob and wished she could die for the love of him, die that moment in his arms and then it would be forever.

"Help me," he said. "Help me, my love. I too ache for both of us."

She pulled his head into her lap and began rocking him gently. Her tears fell on his cheeks.

"I'll try," she whispered, "I'll try to be strong for the love of you."

They stayed awake during the nights, begrudging sleep that would have robbed them of consciously being aware of each other, made love, consoled each other, and dreamed their dreams aloud.

Their dreams took them beyond mountains, to a place where the sky was blue, deep deep blue, a blue to be found nowhere in the world except there. People watched the arrival of a boat. *Shalom, shalom,* they shouted. The boat anchored, passengers disembarked. There he is, coming down the ramp; there she is, waiting for me; oh how I longed to hold you. . . .

Dombas was a penal colony in the Ukraine, she had learned from Himy, where the anthracite mines were. A ten-year prison sentence could be commuted to two years of voluntary work in the anthracite mines.

What was the penalty for dreaming, she wondered, how many years?

He said to her: "'If you cannot pass, you must return'; my father once quoted this folk proverb to me and added: 'What *we* say is that if you cannot pass, you must pass.'"

They embraced and in the nakedness of body and spirit they cleaved to each other and became one.

"Let's escape into another kind of freedom. That too could be forever," she said to him another night. "It won't hurt as much as waking up from dreams does."

"No. Dying is acceptable *only* when one's time comes. Not before; never, never before. It's a sin to die before one's time, remember that."

"I wish I had no wish."
"I love you."
"But the dragon—"
"There will always be a dragon somewhere."
"It's heartbreaking, the dream."
"I love you."

". . . these are the saddest hours of my life," he told her. "Yet I'll go on, limping at times, but go on I shall. Promise me that you too shall go on; that no matter what, you shall go on."

"I don't know how . . . Teach me how to limp."

He pulled her closer, held on to her for a while, then said:

"There will be moments, I know, when the temptation to give up will be almost irresistible; when resigning myself to defeat will seem easier by far than carrying on; when self-pity will sap my energies; when yelling 'foul' will fall on deaf ears and when the seven-headed dragon will seem to have taken over. When dying will seem the only way out. It will be then that I'll think back to how it was when I had you in my arms and I'll go on, limping. I'll tell myself that I have no reason to gripe because once in my life, if even briefly, I had no peer: I was the luckiest man on earth for having been able to love absolutely, for having dared, planned and schemed and dreamed as though I was the most powerful man alive. And I was, I'll remind myself when even limping will be hard, for I let myself feel with every fiber in my body, I didn't skimp or hold back my feelings, and I didn't lie down and die before my time . . . So you see, beloved, when I'll be bitter and lonely and sick of life, I'll think of us and I will remember that once I had a pure and perfect time because I was not afraid to love and dream. And I'll go on limping as I'll remember that once in my life I was a total human being, that, without reservation, I lived up to what was in my heart. And then I'll be glad for having been born."

3

Early in the evening, at the end of January, Himy and Olga came to visit Lisa. They sat in the living room speaking of many things, yet nothing in particular. Lisa threw a log on the fire and Himy wiped his forehead.

At eight o'clock Lisa got up.

"Now," Olga whispered to Himy. He reached Lisa at the door.

"I expect Leonid," she said.

"I know."

She walked towards the cottage slowly. Himy followed her in the room. They sat down facing each other.

By then Lisa knew. The back of her head felt monstrously big and all she could think of was how to make it easier for Himy.

The minutes ticked away in silence.

"I knew it would come," she said quietly. "You don't have to be afraid to tell me."

He took her hands. How much can a human being take? How much was not too much?

"The captain made me promise I would take care of you. Let me keep my promise."

She stared at him without blinking.

"He came to see me this morning, before his departure." Himy spoke haltingly, as if the balance of the universe depended on each word he uttered.

(and last night was the last night; we made love last night, the last time we made love was last night; love lasted last night to last)

"The captain told me what happened in Sopron." He scrutinized her anxiously, as he had scrutinized Yashenko's drawn face that morning and had listened to his quavering voice: *"Chaver* Himy, I've done what my heart and mind told me to do. I've lost . . . for the time being. Can her surrogate brother forgive me?" and Himy nodded and wanted to tell Yashenko that losing does not preclude another chance at winning but his own voice was choked. "Please take care of her, *chaver,* please," Leonid simply said, and walked away.

Himy wished Lisa would scream, pound, curse the sky, so he too could scream along with her, shake his fists and curse this rotten world, charge God with shamelessness for heaping so much sorrow on the survivors of Nazi hell. Quarrel and question Him about the way He was running the world. Himy's own heart would have been less heavy if both he and Lisa had yelled and cried and blamed someone for their pain.

But she just sat silently, her arms dangling at her sides . . . and she swayed her head from right to left and left to right . . . wilted and fragile like a little old woman . . . and he thought she was blinking . . . that something was stuck under her eyelids . . . and imagined he faintly heard sand scratching against a dry, stony surface . . . and his own eyes began to smart.

And she just sat silently, without blinking, staring at him or perhaps beyond him. Himy stifled a sob.

"We'll go on, won't we?" he asked softly. "I promised to look out for you, like an adopted brother, if you don't mind. Laszlo was my best friend and the captain a real *chaver,* a man of integrity and great strength. I owe it to him and to Laszlo. Let me take care of you. . . ."

(i love you, my darling, oh how I love you; do you know how much i love you? i am not what i was, for loving you has changed me into a loving being. what will happen now?)

". . . the captain thinks you should get back the jewels from

Naftuli and go away, beyond the mountains, he said. You two have a dream, right?"

(left, right, left . . . they all lost their minds to speak of burning . . . in his own sweet voice he dreamed a dream . . . it was a lullaby the last dream he sang . . . not a farewell goodbye)

". . . it can be done," he said soothingly, "we can make part of the dream come true soon."

With a short, moaning wail, she got up.

"I have contacts with the *Bricha*," Himy said.

Her eyes were fixed, as if in a permanent stare, eastwards.

". . . Lisa, speak to me. Say something. A word. Himy will help . . . anything you want . . . I am their *macher*, immune . . . just tell me what you want to do . . . please, Lisa."

But he knew she did not hear him. He stayed with her that night and each time she cried out he patted her lovingly and murmured "Hush, little sister, hush. We'll get through this too . . . we will."

4

Gyuri listened politely to Himy, though after hearing the first few sentences Gyuri had his mind made up.

". . . and since Naftuli refused to discuss the matter with me," Himy was saying, "I came to see you. Kahn says it's none of my business what had or hadn't transpired between him and Lisa and she is too distraught to know, or even care, what goes on. But somebody must care, damn it! Particularly now when she is so vulnerable without that 'special protection' we, her friends, must safeguard her the best way we can."

Gyuri thoughtfully lit a cigarette, offered one to Himy.

"She shouldn't have turned over a bundle of jewels to a . . . to a Naftuli Kahn," Himy said, aware that he had to watch his words. Gyuri and Naomi had become a twosome, the whole town buzzed with the news.

"But what the hell," Himy continued lightly, "we all know the jewels belong to Lisa. I have affidavits from Senator Petrescu. Speak to Kahn, won't you. The words of the chief of police carry weight."

Gyuri felt put upon. Yes, he thought, he could do something, but no, he did not want to get involved. Considerations other than Naomi were at stake: the office of state prosecutor was available. It was a more prestigious position than the one he held

413

presently. Being chief of police meant local stature; being state prosecutor meant a slice of the national pie. It could bring him Bucharest, the national government, all the way. Little squabbles concerning gold and diamonds, little frauds and cheats, should not compel him to distribute justice with a blindfold over his eyes. He may need every vote he can get, from the left and from the right, from the betrayed and from the betrayers.

"Can't Lisa settle it amicably with Naftuli?"

"He is slippery like quicksilver," Himy replied. "She has spoken to him about the jewels. She asked for them back. He minced words. He was busy, the combination to the safe was broken, he must bring in a specialist tomorrow, next week or next month. Kahn might stop shamming if you'd speak to him. You are the law, my friend. It should mean something, even to Kahn."

"I don't wish to take sides——"

"Sides? What sides?" To hell with the twosome, Himy thought, he had weighed his words long enough.

"Did I ask you to take sides?" Himy angrily asked. "There are no sides to the truth, even a child knows that. The truth is that Lisa gave jewels, which belonged to her family, to Kahn for safe-keeping; and that these jewels had been held, till her return to Sighet, by Senator Petrescu. But then you know all this, what the hell is the matter with you?"

Gyuri, annoyed with Himy, raised his eyebrows.

"Kahn is up to his old tricks," Himy continued. "He tries to wriggle out of returning the jewels to Lisa. Is there another side to this matter, Mr. Chief of Police, sir?"

Gyuri's annoyance turned to resentment. He did not need Himy the Mogul to lecture Gyuri the Lawyer on law. On the other hand, an unofficial Rusky *macher* can easily be made to stay within the law, even a child knows that. And ties of old friendships can be stretched only so far. But a lawyer worthy of his degree would bear in mind that there is justice and *justice* and never loses his cool.

"If it only were that simple," Gyuri said smoothly. "Who saw Lisa give the jewels to Kahn? Did you?" he asked. "I did not. She says, he says. What do you know about the rules of evidence?"

"Nothing, goddammit, nothing!" Himy yelled. "But I do know

she's telling the truth, and that's enough for me. I also know that slimy Kahn character is trying to swindle her."

He spat on the floor, got up, put his coat on.

"I'll get Lisa to make an official complaint, then you'll be forced to take action."

"And I," Gyuri replied calmly, "I shall dismiss the complaint for lack of evidence."

Before any process to recover the jewels was to be started, Himy had persuaded Lisa to move to the Pension Amity.

"Let me handle the rest," he asked. "Once I recover the jewels for you, we can start thinking of a journey beyond the mountains. I have promised to take care of you. I intend to keep my promise."

Himy then requested on her behalf a convocation of a *bet din*, a religious court under Jewish law which settles disputes among Jews without resorting to secular law.

At first, Naftuli refused to participate.

"A *bet din* is to be presided over by a rabbi or a *dayyan* versed in matters of Jewish law. It is written," Naftuli said. "And since there is no *dayyan*, nor a rabbi in Sighet, a *bet din* cannot be held."

"What is written is 'Thou shall not steal,'" Himy replied. "Your sudden concern for legality fools no one. I ask you to submit to voluntary arbitration. We'll find three scholars versed in rabbinic law, have no fear."

Himy then asked Moshe Fuchs, the Talmudist, to preside at the *bet din* and to get two more scholars who would qualify as the other judges.

"Isaiah teaches to seek justice, relieve the oppressed," Moshe Fuchs said. "It is a duty I shall not shirk." As soon as he found the additional judges, Oskar Baum and Menachem Tauber, he informed Naftuli that a *bet din* would be convened within three days to render a judgment in a dispute between Engler and Kahn. Himy Lieber was to represent Engler. Would Kahn designate his spokesman?

The Jews in town were upset at the turn of events. A *bet din* after Auschwitz? Who would have believed that such a thing would ever again be necessary. Through fire and brimstone, hasn't that been enough? And would Kahn dare defy the summons of the first post-Auschwitz *bet din?*

Naftuli sensed the importance of this *bet din.* Should he decline to appear before it, he would be stigmatized for the rest of his life. No Jew would ever do business with him. Should he appear and then refuse to comply with the verdict of the *bet din,* he would be excommunicated from the community.

Let them, Naftuli Kahn decided, let them excommunicate him from a nonexistent community; and if Jews won't do business with him, others will. Himy wants a show, let him have it. He, Naftuli Kahn, can't lose either way.

"I'll represent myself," he said, and appeared before the *bet din.*

"This is our case," Himy told the judges. They listened to him relate how it was Naftuli who first brought to Lisa's attention the existence of her parents' jewels the first day she had arrived in Sighet and how Senator Petrescu, after refusing to hand them over to Naftuli, had returned them to her. Then he submitted Senator Petrescu's affidavit, which gave the history of how he had received them from Andras Engler and had promised to hold them until an Engler returned to Sighet.

"I'll guard them as if they were my own," Himy quoted Naftuli as having said to Lisa, "and so he did. Once he slammed the jewels into his steel safe, Naftuli Kahn made good on his pledge and then some: he guarded them, then used them as if they were indeed his own."

"What a terrible *shande,* what a horrible shame," Himy said, "that now, after the world has almost cheated us out of our lives, I should stand before a *bet din* and claim that a Jew cheated another Jew! Tell the truth," he called out, "Jew, tell the truth! It's not too late."

All eyes turned to Naftuli. He sat crumpled up, like the suit he wore, an aggrieved expression on his face, and looked up sighing, then shook his head.

"Naftuli Kahn shakes his head," Himy said. "He humbly sits before this tribunal, a picture of . . . what? Of integrity or deceit? Of innocence or of greed? Of honesty or of cunning? I'll tell you. He appears to be a picture of integrity, of innocence, of honesty. But, in fact, he is a man of deceit, greed, and cunning. Before the Jewish Community, it is of lying, stealing, and fraud

416

that I accuse Naftuli Kahn, a Jew who used every trick and false-hood to cheat Lisa Engler, another Jew.

"That I should have to point a finger at a Jew and accuse him of robbing another Jew, now, after the *horban,* is a *shande,* I tell you! Yet I do so. For would it not be a greater *shande* to do nothing about it? Somewhere in the Scriptures it is written, and you learned *rabonim* surely know where, that to be complacent about injustice is as great a sin as being guilty of injustice. So I must point my finger at this man who schemed and cheated and exploited a girl's aloneness and used and connived and manipulated that aloneness till she gave in; till she said all right, you may open my father's store; till she said, here, hold the jewels for me; you speak of trust, she said, that I should trust someone: you. I have no one else, she said, so I trust you, Naftuli Kahn, I trust you. And Naftuli Kahn said, 'May God strike me dead if I would take anything from you.' Well, *Rebonoshelolom,* strike him, strike him now, but do not strike him dead; just strike his soul into admitting his sin, for he brazenly defrauded this girl; so strike him, that we may know there is a *Rebonoshelolom!*"

Perspiration dripped from Himy's face onto the wide lapels of his light brown jacket. He let it drip. Something ached in him. He let it ache.

"Indeed the Almighty's ways are strange," Himy said. "God shows mercy to cattle and birds. And now to hyenas too. What must I do to unmask the scoundrel? Should I perhaps tell of how Naftuli Kahn became an *oisher?* Of how he had the premises of THE HOUSE OF ENGLER AND SONS stocked full of merchandise for which he paid cold cash? Yes, cold cash. I should know, for I was the expediter who delivered to him, in my trucks, goods I had picked up for him in Budapest. He paid at once, I tell you, cash on delivery. Should I tell of all this, I would do it merely to point out that Naftuli Kahn became an *oisher* soon after Lisa Engler had moved into his house and gave him the jewels for safe-keeping.

". . . 'I am like a brother to you,' Naftuli Kahn told Lisa Engler. A brother? A brother who cheats a sister? . . . *Rebonoshelolom,* is there no limit to darkness?"

Himy's voice broke. Then he turned with great dignity to Naftuli:

"You called yourself a brother of Lisa Engler. I'll tell you what kind of brother you were. It is told how two men met. 'Who gouged out your eyes?' the first man asks the second. 'My enemy gouged out one of my eyes, my brother gouged out the other,' is the reply. 'Which eye did your brother gouge out?' the questioner wants to know, and the blind man replies: 'The one which has the deeper gash.' "

It was a conspiracy to besmear his name, Naftuli blatantly claimed. The whole thing was a lie, he said, the complaint based on no evidence whatsoever. Yes, he paid Lieber cash for goods. So what? He, Naftuli, had made a few clever deals. Was that a sin? Jewels. He never heard of jewels before, never saw a bundle of jewels. He did not know what they were talking about. Lisa Engler never gave him any jewels. If she had jewels she may have squandered them while she cavorted with a godless Rusky. Maybe she blew her baubles in Budapest, on her recent fling with him . . . who knows? Naftuli Kahn was no one's keeper, that's for sure. He never received any jewels and never saw any jewels. The whole thing was a trumped-up charge. Period.

But Moshe Fuchs and the two judges knew better. They did not see it Naftuli's way. The facts and circumstantial evidence were too strongly against him.

The *bet din* found in favor of Lisa Engler. Its verdict was that the jewels, in accordance with the itemized list signed by Senator Petrescu, be returned to her within twenty-four hours; and if such action was no longer possible, a sum of money equivalent to the current fair value of the jewels, to be determined by the members of the *bet din*, was awarded to her to be paid at the end of the prescribed period.

Nothing happened within the twenty-four hours, nor thereafter.

"Try and collect," Naftuli sneered at Himy, "or go and sue me."

418

5

The Jews' preoccupation with the *bet din* ceased the morning Otto was found in his room hanging from the lighting fixture, the cord from a curtain used for the noose. His guitar was smashed to pieces.

His friends buried and mourned him without words; only Moshe Fuchs recited the *kaddish* on the day of the funeral. None could bring themselves to speak of Otto's death, his own final solution to problems evidently insoluble. It was a dreadful demonstration, the destructive power in one's own hand.

Otto's death was absorbed during the following week's long binge of drunkenness. What sobered them up was the news that Antal had been expelled from the Romanian Communist Party and thrown in jail. He was found guilty of deviational behavior, a verdict understood by all to be the expression of the Party secretary's shame at having been cuckolded by Antal. Antal was sentenced to two years at hard labor. Giving in to Rozika's pleas, Moritz got Antal out of jail with a bribe and then the three of them left Sighet one evening without saying good-bye to anyone.

Lisa and Ilona spent much of their free time together. Their former emotionally charged discussions had turned into quiet conversations, and each was so completely at ease with the other as to permit protracted silences to bespeak their loneliness. They each lived in their dreams, and although they never spoke of them, each knew the other dreamed of *someday* as if the mass of gray winter clouds, which hovered in the background and obscured the mountains and the sky, was not there; as if instead of the bleak horizon there stood a sunny green mountain waiting to be climbed *someday*.

6

"Straight as a rod and handsome," Himy told Olga. "Wears an English uniform with the Star of David on his sleeve. A Jewish soldier from the Jewish Brigade! It warms my heart."

"I am glad when your heart is warmed," she said. "It has been chilled by so much sadness——"

"The empty victory of the *bet din's* judgment can be offset," he said. "The soldier has two British immigration permits to Eretz. All he has to do is insert the names of two relatives. One could be his brother or sister."

A faint smile creased the skin around his eyes. She wondered if it was a smile or a muscle contracted to hold back something in his eyes.

"One name could be the soldier's brother or sister," he repeated slowly, "the other could be his wife's. If he could find one."

Olga said nothing.

"The *bet din* left her more bitter than I imagined it would," Himy continued. "She's withdrawn, spends much time with Ilona. We must help her before it's too late."

"Would marrying be the answer?" Olga finally asked.

"Someday she'll get married." He patted Olga's hand gently. "I am not an insensitive soul . . . I don't think of marriage *now*. I only think she'd be better off somewhere else. In Eretz, for instance. She could marry the soldier *pro forma,* that's all I had in mind. Should they change their minds later and wish to stay married . . ." He shrugged his shoulders.

Lisa and Ariel met in Imre's house.

"Look who I found," Himy announced cheerfully one evening, walking in with Olga and Ariel. "An old friend of mine, Ariel Halevi. Let's celebrate," he said, giving Imre a bottle. *"Lechaim."*

Thereafter Ariel waited for Lisa at the factory each day, walked her home and spoke to her of his life in Eretz.

"I was just seventeen when I joined a *hakshara* training camp in Poland. I learned farming and self-defense. A year later I was ready for *kibbutz* life. In 1936 I got a certificate of immigration. As Orthodox Jews, my folks were against my going. But I went anyway."

He spoke of his early *kibbutz* life, of his bout with malaria and of building a settlement in the Judaean hills with a pioneer group of young men and women; of patrolling the *kibbutz* around the clock to guard against Arab marauders; of the harsh, dry *chamsin* wind that made him homesick for the old country's green mountains and pleasant breezes.

"The land was a vast desert before we settled it," he told her, "cracked and dried. We worked at it with care and patience. We soaked it with our sweat. And now, where the desert was, there is life. There are flowers and green grass, and trees with fruit and wells with water under a deep blue sky. . . ."

(. . . deep, deep blue . . . *shalom shalom* they shout as the boat anchors and passengers disembark . . . oh how I long to hold you)

She began to listen to him avidly, greedily, and dreamed of that remarkable land where she and Leonid might meet someday.

"I have seen the deathcamps firsthand," he said to her one evening. "I was in the Jewish Brigade, with the British forces, riding into Neugamme in a tank marked with a big blue-and-white Star of David. The prisoners kissed the tank—those who could walk; others crawled to take a look at the Star before they died. Those who were alive were too weak to even speak. Tears just rolled

422

down their faces. I remember thinking what a miracle it was they could still weep."

He gently held her hands.

"Tended with kindness and compassion you should be, you Jewish women who survived; nurtured back to life with love and care, then you too shall bloom as our land blooms. You are precious beyond worth, beyond value, you women who carry the seed of our future: a Jewish nation."

He kissed her hands gently, barely brushing them with his lips, as if her hands were too fragile for anything more than the light touch of a breath.

"Be my wife, Lisa," he said solemnly. "I offer you a fresh start in Zion, where wounds heal faster. Come with me there."

"Go," Himy said. "Go and mend, little sister. Life is perfect for no one. Only moments are perfect, for some. Thank God you've had some."

"Go," said Olga. "Leonid will always be with you; nothing will wipe out your love for him. But bitterness could make you forget."

"Go," Ilona said. "There is nothing anymore to keep you here."

But Mekkel, Ariel's brother, was quite upset.

"What about me?" he asked Himy, who went to see him. "My brother came here to fetch what was left of our family, that's me and Sarah, our sister. If Ariel takes Sarah and this Lisa girl on his immigration permits what happens to me? I want to go to the Holy Land too!"

"The Messiah hasn't come yet and you never believed in Zionism," Himy said to the Orthodox Mekkel. "What's this sudden conversion?"

Mekkel pondered for a while. "Well," he said, "a man can change, no?"

"Yes," Himy replied. "I promise to get you to Eretz Ysroel within the next six months if you let her go instead of you. I'll place the money in escrow if Lisa Engler's name is written in on one of the immigration permits."

"It's a deal!" Mekkel said.

* * *

Lisa listened in a daze to all of them planning her future and went along apologetically, as if she were intruding in someone else's dreams and invading the privacy of total strangers; for all along she clearly envisioned Leonid descending the ramp of a boat.

One morning, on her way to the factory, she met Anna the washerwoman.

"Were they twins?" she asked, pointing to Anna's belly.

"Yes, miss. Dead twins." Anna crossed herself. "But hope is not dead. I am pregnant again. The good Lord wants life to go on."

"I know," Lisa said, "as if nothing had happened . . ."

Then Mekkel wanted more money in escrow.

"She comes from an assimilated family," he rationalized. "Andras Engler was not a *Talmud-hacham*. Then there was the Rusky. The whole town knows about it. Why should my kid brother marry a someone who is not a virgin and whose father was an ignoramus?"

"How much more?" Himy asked.

"You see——"

"Just tell me: how much more?"

"All right, I'll tell you: twice as much. . . ."

The deal was on.

The evening before the civil wedding was to take place, there was a small party in Olga's cottage. Next morning they were in the mayor's office waiting for Ariel.

Mekkel alone showed up.

"Blood is thicker than water," he said. "I made Ariel see the light. My name is in on the second permit."

In the evening Lisa walked into Ilona's room. In the drawer of her night table she found a bottle of pills labeled VERONAL, took the bottle and went into her own room. Then she swallowed the pills and lay down on her bed.

424

7

The cherry pit was scrubbed clean and buried in the grove.

She was three years old that summer afternoon when she had tasted cherries for the first time. Her mother had playfully hung a pair of double twigs with unblemished cherries behind Lisa's ears. Each time she moved her head, the cherries gently pecked at her cheeks.

"Mamma, where do cherries live?"

"On trees. They grow on cherry trees."

"I want a cherry tree," she said.

"Maybe someday you'll have a tree," Rachel replied. "You must begin at the beginning though: plant and prune and nurture——"

"A cherry tree now," Lisa interrupted, "now, Mamma."

"Next year, maybe. We'll plant one in the grove, watch it grow——"

"Now, now!" She shook her head and the cherries, dangling like pendent earrings, tapped her face. She held up her palm to Rachel. There was a cherry pit in it. "Will this make a cherry tree?"

"Yes," Andras said quickly, "it will make a cherry tree."

They dug a small hole in the grove near the apple tree, buried the pit and raked earth over it. Andras hugged her, and she put her arms around his neck.

"Will the pit make a tree soon?" she asked, nuzzling up to him. "Soon, tomorrow? Please, please Papa, make it tomorrow. I know you can."

Early next morning Andras carried her in his arms to the grove. A young sapling, its bark light and smooth, was planted where the pit had been buried.

"See," Andras said, "your wish is fulfilled. The pit grew into a cherry tree, overnight. Just for you."

Where is my tree? she wants to ask, where is my tree now? but the words float and swirl around her like puffs of down she cannot see because her eyelids are weighed down by lead or sealed with wax, and the attempt to speak or to see fractures and shatters a weightless all-encompassing softness, snug and warm, that holds her together. She will stay in this softness then, she belongs there, where all is light and painless. It is a world full of people who love each other, who laugh and are happy. It is her world. She is small, people hug and pinch her cheeks and count her freckles, bounce her on their knees and give her presents, clap their hands approvingly at whatever she says and dance around her. Someone grabs her into the circle to dance and stomp along with them and holds her by the waist.

"No," she wants to say, "I am too small to dance with you; can't you see I am only a little girl?"

"Papa," she wants to wail, "make them stop."

Her words rise from the deep, travel through currents of air and leave her mouth as soundless speech.

They continue to swing her around and she begins to cry.

"Papa," she wants to moan, "please make them stop. I know you can."

She hears faint sounds, hushing. In a haze she sees long golden hair.

"You mustn't stop," someone says. "You must keep going."

A cup is held to her mouth. The liquid is bitter and hot, it burns her palate. She spits out the liquid and clenches her teeth.

Two people, one on each side, hold her under the arms and force her to run, almost dragging her. Can't they see it is too

426

much for her, she wants to scream, it hurts! Her feet refuse to move and her knees buckle under.

"Please, Papa," she moans, "please . . ."

They don't listen to her Papa, those who make her walk. Why don't people listen to Papa anymore? He could always do what she had asked him to do. Why not now?

She wants to reach out for the others who are there in the room with her, but her arms are not free. What, who is holding her back? But those others are all there, she can see them in the corners of the room flattened against the wall like cardboard figures. They stand against the wall and watch, silently, her agonized walk. She is limping.

Don't hide, she wants to tell those cardboard figures, don't hide from me. Don't pretend you don't see me. I am yours, you've created me, made me what I am; you are responsible for me. Can't you see I want to rest? Help me, she wants to tell them, please help me. I want to stop walking. Or limping. I am so tired! I want to rest.

The cardboard figures come closer to her now; only a shadow she cannot recognize remains in the corner.

"Let's play dominoes," Laszlo says. He wears the soccer team's uniform, the white jersey sweat shirt across which the name SAMSON is printed in blue. They play dominoes and she wins, she always wins, and Laszlo fades away.

Miklos now walks with her on a street lined with chestnut trees, redolent of scents of acacia and jasmine. He has his arm around her shoulders. Why is he supporting her? She can walk by herself! He holds her too tight. She pushes him away but then she stumbles. He holds her tight again and speaks to her of art and literature; but she is tired, she wants to go to sleep. It's late. "Not yet," he says gently, and keeps talking of poetry and love, of ethics and morality and law, of the dignity of man and of humanity, of reason and beauty and faith, hallmarks of civilization that uplifted mankind from its brutish origins. From a radio, music filters through a window and Miklos listens intently for a few seconds. "It's Schubert's *Die Forelle*," he says, and keeps walking with her without paying heed to her pleas to stop. He now points to the end of the street. "There is a surprise for you," he says, "you'll find your cherry tree. Come on," he encourages her,

427

"don't you want to see your cherry tree? Try, try. You can make it if you try." With an immense effort, she makes it to the end of the street. The cherry tree is scraggly and brittle, its bark crawls with lice and cockroaches, its stunted branches are full of ticks and the cherries are rotten. The tree begins to dwarf before her eyes till it shrinks to the size of a cherry pit. She is a little girl again and begins to cry. "I don't want the pit," she screams, "what happened to my cherry tree? I want my lovely cherry tree. It grew just for me."

Suddenly Uncle Haskell appears, holding in his hands a box wrapped in tissue paper. He gives her the box and she eagerly rips off the paper, opens the box. It's a present from Uncle Haskell, the cardboard figures say, and shake their heads in wonder. Uncle Haskell has never given a present to anyone, never in his life. See, you are special, they say, Lisa Engler is a special little girl. And lucky, oh how lucky. Uncle Haskell has given her a present!

The present is a miniature white enameled cooking range. It has two small burners on top. She runs her fingers over it in amazement. What a lovely present! Someone points to the front of the range; to a knob. She pulls at it and out comes a grill. An oven! someone says, laughing, how clever!

She begins to scream, scream, and tries to free herself from their grip. But they hold on to her, walk with her, back and forth, relentlessly, and try to force her jaws open to pour that awful liquid down her throat. She must escape before it's too late but their grip immobilizes her and she screams:

"Papa, help me!"

Andras wipes away her tears with tiny kisses. "Yes, my lovely little girl, my one and only girl, I brought you nougats and caramels. I'll always bring you nougats and caramels, you know that, don't you? You are my one and only girl . . ."

and they walk into a fashionable restaurant in Budapest. It's the Kakuk, the one which the Prince of Wales liked best when he visited the nightspots in Budapest. The headwaiter greets them effusively, calls Papa "Your Honor" and her "Honorable Young Lady." The waiter expects to get a big tip and smiles slyly, baring his yellow teeth. He may suspect that the elegant handsome elderly gentleman, with silvery hair and sideburns and an ivory-handled cane hanging from his arm, has come to dine with his

428

young mistress, she thinks mischievously, and looks adoringly at Andras. Gypsy musicians stroll over to their table. Andras gives each of them a banknote and one of the Gypsies brings his violin close to her ear and plays softly *the one and only girl* and all the Gypsies now play the same tune

she stiffens. The Gypsies have abruptly turned into weird creatures dressed in striped rags, their heads shaven, who stand behind a huge arched wrought-iron gate and go on fiddling, their arms thin as pipes. She recognizes the *Rákóczy March* and refuses to go through the gate. She is pushed, then dragged, and before she is pulled to the other side she looks up.

She sees Gothic-style wrought-iron letters on top of the arch.

ARBEIT MACHT FREI, she reads out loud and she is on the other side of the gate.

A pall of loneliness grips her, a devastating terror at being left alone in the universe, cast out or sucked in but terribly alone. She falters and tears flow down her cheeks. One of the musicians cackles, "Stupid, why do you cry? We welcome you with music!"

"Mamma," she screams from the depths of her being, "Mamma."

Her right arm is numb. Someone gets hold of it. They manipulate her, push her around, they make her sit down, they press in on her, move, move, just like getting in or out of a cattle car. Enough, enough! It hurts, I can't stand it, it hurts.

"Mamma," she screams, "Mammika!"

The shadow in the corner moves. It is Rachel. "Help me Mamma, take me with you. Don't leave me here alone. Take me with you." They are far apart from each other, and Rachel reaches out to her. Still they cannot even touch. The people around her make her walk, march

eins zwei drei vier march, walk, march, march.

"Mamma," she wants to scream, "don't leave me. Don't let them take me away from you. Let me go with you. I hurt so much, Mamma. My right arm always hurts. I always hurt. Mamma, Mamma. Help me. Take me away with you. Or stay with me. Just don't leave me alone. Please.

"Then talk to me, Mamma. Say something."

Rachel moves her lips but she cannot hear her. "What did you say, Mamma? tell me. Let me hear your voice, please, Mamma.

Just this once. For the last time, your voice at least, Mamma. I've forgotten the sound of your voice. Mamma, my Mamma. What did you say?"

Someone flicks Rachel's shoulder with a whip and she is gone.

"What did you say, Mamma?" Lisa shrieked.

Ilona turned to Elena Corcescu. "She'll be fine now. I'll take care of her."

8

She stayed in bed for a few days, wafting in and out of segments of time, holding on to an image or a memory in a blur that was pacific till it would begin to clear and then a sharp pain in her head would thrust her back into deep, benign sleep.

One day she thought of snow, of how it froze into a crisp crust over the ground, and of how a little girl had cracked the crust with a toy shovel, diligently digging for tiny sprouts of green in the dark moist earth underneath. She opened her eyes wide. Perhaps such a little girl was in the room, she thought, ready to go out in the brisk March morning to unearth the green from under the frozen snow. . . .

Ilona was in the room, puttering around, pushing a chair under the table, rearranging a few things. Her presence was intrusive, forcing Lisa's blurry memories into painful focus.

"Go away," Lisa muttered.

"I've made coffee," Ilona said.

"No." If only Ilona would go away she could slip back in time where there was no pain. Maybe even the little girl would come back.

Ilona finished drinking her coffee, adjusted the cover on Lisa's bed. She is the present, Lisa thought, Ilona is the present which was piercing her skin, digging into her. If she were tougher, if her skin was not soft, vulnerable to every touch and sensitive to every heartbeat, she would not ache so badly. "Go away, Ilona," she muttered again, "stop meddling——"

"I didn't meddle——"

"Then why don't you? . . . why did you? . . ." The exertion of thinking the thought out was hurting and she closed her eyes.

"Because I cared, that's why," Ilona said quietly. "And because you matter. You matter a lot."

Lisa looked reproachfully at Ilona. It was no use, she can't keep away the present. She sighed, then said sharply:

"I matter to no one and I owe you nothing!" The effort she made to sound sharp momentarily blunted her pain: it compensated for, or deflected from, something. She couldn't tell.

"But I expect nothing!" Ilona said.

"I don't believe you!" Again, the sharp retort blunted her pain. Yes, something was happening inside her. The present was almost tolerable when she acted tough. "You meddled in my plans and I am not grateful——"

"Good. One shouldn't be grateful for ordinary human decency."

"Did you think you evened scores?" Lisa taunted her.

"No. I simply did what I had to do when I found you unconscious on the bed. I ached when I saw you——"

"What do you know of aches? . . ."

"I do, Lisa," she said almost in a whisper. "I too love."

"But that's not the only pain I have, don't you understand?" She suddenly screamed at Ilona: "I bleed all over. I bleed for lack of love, for lack of family, I bleed for lack of everything! I bleed as a result of atrocities committed against me . . . I wanted to die, damn you, so as not to live in pain for the rest of my life! That's why I wanted to die—to be free of pain! Because nothing, you hear, nothing can cure this pain——"

Jolted, she sat up. Power cures what nothing else can cure, she suddenly remembered all at once, and her mouth tightened. Why hadn't she thought of this solution before?

And if she did not ache, what she did would be of little consequence; she would not feel—it was as simple as that.

Yes, the time had come for Lisa Engler to be good to herself and find a cure that would prevent all future aches.

Curing time has come, as dear Himy would say.

9

". . . if you are ready to forget our last tiff, I am ready to work for you," Lisa told Yankel Schwartz. "Didn't you advise me to join the elite early in the game?"

"Yes, well. Hm," he muttered still gawking at her. His Adam's apple speedily slid up and down several times. He watched her smoke a cigarette and he thought she was too thin and pale, aloof, but still pretty. Even prettier in her aloofness. Her eyes were wider, greener and full of sensuousness.

"I am delighted that you came to see me," he said. "Yes, by all means, let's forget our last tiff. I am not one to hold grudges."

Pound your fist now, comrade secretary, Yankel thought. I promised to deliver the little darling of the soon-to-be-extinct bourgeoisie, and here she is! But you, comrade secretary, you better learn manners and the art of finessing and timing. You can't browbeat a Lisa Engler into submission. Not yet. You want a middle-class damsel as a trophy, comrade secretary? Then learn to play and dance to her tune for a while.

The thought of the forthcoming victory, bludgeoning the party secretary with Negrescu wit and skill, pleasantly tickled Yankel's imagination. Didn't that peasant secretary know that he, Ion Negrescu, had literary clout which meant power, influence? The Negrescu editorials in *Scanteia,* the official Party newspaper, or the articles in the local *Viata Libera* could make or break a person. It was business, good business, to enlist the likes of Lisa Engler, Negrescu would pontificate. You must know how business deals are made *Mister Secretary*, how capital is accumulated; haven't you read your Marx lately, *Mister Secretary?* Negrescu would ask with a cutting edge to his voice. Sure, the sign was still on top of the Engler business building, that gangster Naftuli Kahn was operating there, and people could still read THE HOUSE OF ENGLER AND SONS when they walked on the Grand Corso. But it won't be for long now, Negrescu guarantees. You want those capitalist symbols, the Engler business and the sign, repudiated and abjured? Fine! Then let me handle it my own way, *Mister Secretary* (Yankel would thump his foot or pound the table like the secretary) and don't interfere in my affairs or the only members you'll have left will be yokels as uncouth and uneducated as yourself, you shitty horse's ass.

"I am not one to hold grudges," Yankel repeated to Lisa, his chest heaving with pride, "not if good relations replace old conflicts." He looked at her for a small sign of approval or recognition but she did not bat an eyelash. "I'm glad you'll work for me. After you join the DPB I'll sponsor your membership in the Romanian Communist Party. It takes six to eight months for an application to be approved. Trial period etcetera etcetera . . . But with *my* connections I'll get it for you in two, three months. At the end of May you'll be a full-fledged Party member, I guarantee." He chuckled. *"Then* we'll celebrate, right?"

Lisa stared straight at Yankel. Yes, by that time the cure should be well on its way. No more a bleeding heart, right colonel? she thought. A star replacing a heart though the star was on the epaulettes. But the answer was the star. A star meant power and power was the ultimate antidote to pain. It wiped out all other feelings. Star time had come.

"What will my work be?" she asked.

"You'll be my right hand, what do you say?" He still would have liked some expression of appreciation and waited for an instant. But she only nodded, seriously. "You made the smart decision to change jobs at this time," he then said. "I wonder why it took you so long to switch." And why did she still intrigue him? he mused. After all, another man had been between her legs first. She was no more Lisa Engler, lily-white virgin. Yashenko had

434

been shipped out two months before, yet she was still mourning him, he thought bristling. She was always so terribly loyal, the romantic little fool. It still rankled and harassed his memory, her "you can't kiss me, I am Mano's sweetheart."

Through a glimmer of insight he now perceived, at last, that all he wanted from her was to even the score: revenge that rejection. For in fact he was never infatuated with her, not even in the days when he was fueled by the thought that if he'd become Lisa Engler's boyfriend his standing in the clique would be enhanced; that it would prove he was as good as Mano. Or now the Rusky bastard, for instance. Unless he could fuck her once to rehabilitate his bruised ego, that evening's rejection would always stand between him and his self-esteem. So let her become a full-fledged Party member quickly; her wings will be clipped and she'll dance to the tune of Yankel Schwartz, that is, Ion Negrescu. One fuck, that's all.

"As to the job," he said, bringing himself back into the present, "you'll find it quite stimulating, I am sure. You'll be, to begin with, assistant to the chief." His smile was jubilant. "And that's me, the district executive chairman of the People's Literary Association."

It was not stimulating, the new job, merely different. The change made her edgy, at first, till she settled into a sensible, efficient routine. She considered the job elementary, as it had to do with reading, writing, and arithmetic. Mostly arithmetic, for in the end it was all about keeping scores: who incurred minuses or pluses and whose turn it was to be reduced to zero. She scanned daily *Scanteia, Romania Libera,* and *Viata Libera,* newspapers from which she selected items of interest for Yankel to comment on, or to criticize, in his articles and editorials. Once a week she went with him to Party meetings and took notes. Slowly, she began attending to details Yankel was too busy to take care of personally. His major task was to finish writing the play in which the National People's Literary Association now showed interest. Yankel often spoke of the profound social impact the play was expected to have on the Romanian people.

"It may turn the tide, topple thrones," he said to Lisa. "Beaumarchais and Ion Negrescu, why not; *The Barber of Seville* and . . . ah, but I mustn't yet give away the title. . . ."

As the weeks went by, DPB and Party members recognized her on the street and waved their hands, "*Salut,* Lisa." Office doors promptly opened to her. When she went shopping, merchants charged her below the official ceiling price.

"They are circumspect and guarded," she told Ilona one evening. "There is a certain mood . . . even among my friends. As if I am an outsider."

"Not an outsider." Ilona hesitated. ". . . just a big shot."

"Ridiculous!"

"Well, aren't you?"

"No!" But she knew Ilona was right and it irritated her. "I am one of many, working for the government." Why should she be on the defensive again, she thought, or account for her acts?

"You are not just anybody," Ilona said. "You are——"

"I am taking care of myself. I don't hurt, and they envy me."

"No. They feel you let them down."

Lisa laughed. "What's Hecuba to me that I should weep for her . . . Never mind. I owe them nothing."

"You've said it to me, once before. I let it pass then. Now I'll speak."

Let her speak, Lisa thought, whatever Ilona would say would not pierce her. She lit a cigarette, the harsh Nationale she had bought in the state tobacco shop. There was milder tobacco to be had, but it was loose and she had not yet learned the knack of rolling cigarettes. She watched Party members hand-roll cigarettes; still, each time she had tried to do it the cigarette fell apart.

No, whatever Ilona had to say would not influence her. Lisa had earned a tiny star and it was not bad at all. Bleeding hearts were messy affairs. She promised herself to find a cure and she discovered such a thing as painless aches. It worked. Each time she felt pain she thought of the star, and the pain subsided.

"The day I met you," Ilona was saying, "I remembered the girl with the silver bike. I was ashamed and afraid. The *goyim* always expected a bloodbath, instead——"

"We sang old lullabies, anti-Semitic songs, and got drunk . . ."

"Yes. And I was in love with a Jew; my *mea culpa* was spurned——"

"What did you expect," Lisa erupted, "the other cheek?"

"No. Just a chance to atone; to be given the opportunity to show that I meant it . . . But I don't want to speak about myself now. It's you. You turned your back, not your cheek, on your friends. You've let us down——"

"Ah, you prefer vulnerable people——"

"You don't even listen. It's not that, don't you see? It's that you caved in. You resisted and resisted, and in the end you caved in. All of us knew Yankel was after you. When you told him off you spoke for all of us. You shone in your friends' eyes. Just as you shone when you fell in love with Leonid though everyone warned you against a happy ending. But you did what was in your heart, you were not afraid. You could have had the whole army of survivors march behind your banner."

"You're a fool. What banner?"

"The banner of integrity. I wish I could make you understand . . . You showed us it was possible to love and dream in spite of all that had happened. That there was hope."

"I repeat," Lisa said quietly, "I owe you nothing."

"Oh yes, you do. We all owe each other something. Wasn't this one of the lessons of the war? That each of us is part of the whole? That the deed of one affects us all?" She paused, then added: "You also owe something to me personally——"

"To you? Why do *I* owe *you*?"

"Because you helped me become unhooked from bigotry. By becoming unhooked, my perceptions changed. Morally, you should bear responsibility for that change and live up to what you preached. Because you cannot simply say 'to hell with it.' What you've once stood for——"

"Has made you feel less rotten, is that it?"

Ilona paused again, then glared at Lisa. "You think that by being nasty you can avoid the issue?"

"No, damn it! I don't have to avoid any issues because, as far as I am concerned, there are no issues. I am not interested in issues anymore. What is good for Lisa Engler, that is all which interests me."

She stubbed the cigarette in an ashtray, then quickly lit another one. Each drag reinforced the belief that her skin was tough, impenetrable. That in fact she felt nothing anymore because her skin had become a hide, her new shell. She thought of doors opening before her, of heads bowing. Then she said:

"As to who owes whom, it is you who owe me something!"

"Mother of God," Ilona asked, "will I ever be forgiven?"

"Maybe and maybe not," Lisa said lightly. "Maybe never and maybe it is just as well. It's your problem, not mine. A *goyish* problem really, not a Jewish one . . . But the problem will keep you on your toes. It may do you good in the long run. You are right though: we are connected with each other, in space, time, form."

The Matrushka doll was still in a drawer, wrapped in paper. She ought to take it out, she thought, let it breathe.

"*You* wanted to talk," Lisa said. "All right. Then let's be candid with each other. Listen: if, as you say, I opened your eyes, you are now better off than you were before. For this alone you owe me thanks. But more important, you owe me an enormous apology for bringing me back into a stinking world from which I wanted to escape. So you saved a Jew from dying. What more do you want? A dispensation, or a medal, reading, 'Ilona von Tokay de Györ Hayduczy saved a Jew and is henceforth entitled to go around preaching morality and decency'? Do that, if you wish. Crusading may give you your kicks. But don't go around bellyaching about *my* refusal to join the crusade and to carry banners. That day, after I came to, I told you I ached badly, that I wanted out and that you had no business meddling."

She took a deep breath, then lit another cigarette. These thoughts must have been ripening in her for some time without her being aware of them. She had the opportunity to sort it out right now. Apparently she had been so busy with the job, Lisa mused, and with trying to make good her own promise to "take care of Lisa Engler" that she had little time to think. Maybe she hadn't really wanted to think. And now Ilona.

Paradoxically, Lisa really liked Ilona, a *goy* bent on atoning and seeking absolution. Ilona did atone, Lisa thought, but in no way should she receive absolution. As an individual, yes; as a symbolic *goy*, no. Never. The difficulty was to keep the symbol and the reality separate.

"Courtesy of Ilona von Tokay de Györ Hayduczy, I am here now," Lisa continued, "though it was against my will. It takes some adjusting, believe me. But in addition, you want me to carry on as before, see rainbows on the horizon and wave banners. Be what my friends expect me to be, so they can take heart when they fall short of their own expectations. Let Lisa be just as she was: trusting, always trusting. Sue Naftuli and justice will triumph. Oops! not yet. All right, then let Lisa go somewhere else: the land of her dreams. Oops! someone else has a priority . . ."

She stopped, looked at Ilona, who seemed ready to burst into tears.

"You've talked of banners," Lisa said, glad that Ilona was not weeping. "Sure, I've carried them for a while and I am proud that I did *only* because I met Leonid. But where did it get us, the banners? It got me to work for Yankel and it took my man to the Dombas. . . ."

Lisa watched the bluish smoke from her cigarette curl up in the air. Her eyes were smarting from the smell of tobacco, a strange acrid singed odor. Maybe something was smoldering, she thought, and looked around.

"You liked me when I carried banners," she said, after she made sure nothing was on fire, "and so did Chirie Tiplea, I bet. He yelled at me and I said, 'All right, it's so ugly. All I want back are the silver candlesticks.' And Chirie Tiplea now laughs himself sick between my mother's down comforters while wearing my father's silk pajamas. Or how did you like it, Ilona, when I carried banners and Naftuli Kahn thumbed his nose at religious law, at decency, at friendship, at conscience?"

"He got what he deserved. He's in jail, isn't he?"

"Yes, but for the wrong reason. Not because justice triumphed. As to that justice, he would still leer at me from my father's store. Gyuri had refused to prosecute, remember?"

"But the DPB——"

"Ordered Naftuli to vacate the premises of THE HOUSE OF ENGLER AND SONS because he was found guilty of economic sabotage. But his nemesis was power, not lawlessness or your banner. Power. The Party intervened."

"But there was evidence——"

"True, but evidence is meaningless, don't you know? Let me give you a short lesson in what Ion Negrescu calls 'the art of finessing.' The Party doesn't give a damn about evidence. Evidence: a show for simpletons or innocents. What counts is expediency. Listen: the Party instructed the DPB to use the act of economic antisabotage because I made a deal with them. How's that for banners? They wanted to permanently lease from me, legally, mind you, the premises of THE HOUSE OF ENGLER AND SONS. I, on the other hand, wanted Naftuli to pay for his viciousness towards me. Maybe I also wanted to show the snake that there's a limit to evil. You figure it out. At any rate, I leased the premises after Naftuli got charged with economic sabotage. Ordinary justice triumphed through the exercise of naked power."

Naftuli had come to her after the goons of the economic squad had raided the store and found the business replete with glaring illegalities. Naftuli groveled in her office, sweat poured down his face. "Aren't we all Jews, after all?" he asked. "How about it, Lisa?"

"Banners!" Lisa said slowly to Ilona. "It's pointless to carry them. There is only one banner that makes sense to me: an acheless banner whatever its color. I've ached as much in one single year as the whole world has ached in a thousand years. I've had enough, wouldn't you say? I mean, there must be some proportion even to one's pain. Beyond and above an apology, Ilona, you owe me, most of all, understanding. Not recriminations for refusing to carry your silly banners. Have the humility to understand that I am deserving of something safe: an acheless present."

"The JOINT." Ilona was barely audible. "You had a present there——"

"Now it's you who doesn't listen. The motherless children and childless mothers were all me. Me, me. I was one of them, every second——"

"You could have gone away again. To the West. People still do. And if you would have as much as asked me once, I would have gone away with you."

Ilona's eyes lit up and Lisa thought how lovely she looked, her golden hair gleaming under the light. What a fool Sandor had been, Lisa thought, to have gone away without Ilona. Ilona's dream was still alive, perhaps part of it had become reality. Has she become *amchu*?

"We could still go, Lisa. You and I," Ilona whispered.

"Oh, Ilona." What was she trying to do? Pierce her skin again? "It's too late for that. I want no more pain, no more struggle. I only want security. A little power, not much, just a little, will guarantee it."

"It can't guarantee painlessness——"

"Maybe not. But there is a good chance it could cushion pain."

440

"There are options other than the Party . . . Even Leonid had wanted out."

"Yes. And it did not work. It shows you where the power lies, doesn't it." She won't succeed, Lisa thought, Ilona won't succeed. She knew what Ilona was trying to do but she won't succeed. Lisa was an old hand at fashioning weapons against the night.

"Why do you gripe about me and what I'm doing, anyway?" Lisa lashed out. "Have I done anything despicable? No. Have I been asked to do anything that would debase me? No. Why do you fuss so? For trying a new way of life? Whom do I harm? I tried to go with my dreams to the West. It fizzled out. Maybe it will work in the East. There are boats arriving there too . . . on the Volga, or the Black Sea. Odessa is also a port. And what about the rest of the gang? They are all members——"

"Of the DPB," Ilona said. "It was forced on them, you know that. A voluntary application for membership in the Romanian Communist Party is something else, you know that too. But——"

"No more buts."

(but why does it still ache, tell me, leonyushka: what hurts? is it merely naftuli kahn or chirie tiplea or mekkel? or is it the whole stinking system, corrupt, contaminated? cancer-ridden. but it wasn't supposed to hurt anymore. what happened? and how is it in the dombas, leonyushka: is there any green under the snow?)

10

Life went on. It limped sometimes, but no one was the wiser for it: the limping was invisible.

There was a meeting that morning at the DPB headquarters in the Crown Hotel. Yankel attended the meeting with Lisa. An office boy slipped her a note: "Must see you at once, H." It must be important if Himy wanted to see her in a hurry she thought. She stepped out for a breath of fresh air on a little balcony overlooking Main Street and the Grand Corso.

Below, spring was taking root, sending up shoots. The park was greening, a few trees were budding. A pungent smell was in the air, the smoky smell of spring, she thought. Winter's lifeless undergrowth, twigs and branches, was burning on a lawn nearby. She felt faint, slightly nauseous.

". . . elections." The voice of the speaker in the room filtered to her through the half-opened door. "Print ballots at once. The name of the candidate and the name of the party. 'Petru Groza, Democratic Party Bloc,' that's all there is to it. Swamp the town with posters bearing the slogan ONE COUNTRY, ONE PARTY, ONE VOTE. Full speed ahead. Get ready for May 10——"

"Yeah," Yankel's voice cut in, "and EXERCISE YOUR FREEDOM TO VOTE. Not a bad slogan either."

It must be important if Himy wanted to see her at once, she thought again, and her heart began to pump fast.

Leonid had come back!

Someone had made things well again, recycled them and healed the sores of the world. Of course! Stalin was not such a monster, she thought, glancing across the square at his picture in the center of the huge red star, on top of the *kommandatura* building. The bushy mustache and thick eyebrows over deep dark eyes made Stalin look like a velvety uncle. She imagined him cradling little nieces and nephews in his arms, patting the children on their heads. A kind uncle, nice and ordinary. The nice ordinary velvety uncle snapped his fingers, borders opened up, curtains parted and gates swung open. What a magic trick! Let everyone be happy, Stalin the nice velvety uncle decreed, the time has come for people to love each other. Loving time has come.

Leonid, she thought again, he was here, waiting for her. Go, Lisa, run! Stop retching, the smell was the smell of spring. People were burning wood on their lawns, it's the time of the year, why should it upset you?

Spring, spring was in the air. Stalin was a velvety uncle, frontiers had been eradicated, and the people are happy at last.

She always had the need to believe that the world was not as bad as it was said to be.

i study the picture in the newspaper, look at it over and over and i find he looks normal, ordinary. a funny little man with a small mustache. i am puzzled why the mention of this man's name, hitler, is upsetting the grown-ups. they speak of hitler as if he were a monster, an abomination. yet the picture in the newspaper is that of an ordinary man, looking just like any other ordinary man. hitler has no horns or fangs or claws. then why the fuss? i say: hitler is a man, just a man. so he cannot be all that bad. i know, i say, he is a magician and he pretends to be bad so that one day he can fool us by showing us how good he is. that's it. one day he'll do a magic trick, a nice magic trick and he'll make us laugh. he is just a man, so he cannot be bad

The world cannot be as bad as it seems to be, she thinks. There are always magic tricks available.

Yes, Leonid had come back!

He would be in her office, standing with his back to her desk, facing the door through which she would enter. *Golubka*, he would say opening his arms, I have come for you. The nightmare is over, you can touch the contours of familiar things. All is well again, we are together, I love you, and it is forever.

Lisa ran all the way to her office.

Himy sat in a chair, near the window, reading *Viata Libera*.

"What junk!" he said, smacking the paper with his hand. "They should double your salary for reading this nonsense."

He glanced at his wristwatch and stretched the flexible metal band.

"American," he said, letting the band snap back. "The latest model." He played again with the band. "It's Purim today, did you know? It's not marked on the Party calendar," he said smiling, "that's why I came. I am throwing a Purim party. I ask you to join us."

"I have so much work," she said, disappointed. Then she changed her mind: "It's not the work, Himy. I just don't want to go. Please don't ask me to."

"You may change your mind," he said gently, "once I tell you an old friend of yours is here."

(where? i don't see him. oh leonid, i love you so! i miss you. there are no hollows on my pillow, i am all alone. i stay awake nights needing, you. i make love with you, i feel you. you are inside me, i come with you, sometimes before you; still, it's not the same as when we were together)

". . . he arrived this morning. I thought you should learn it from me. It may rattle you to suddenly face Mano."

He patted her cheek. "Now you have time to pull yourself together. He'll fetch you for the party at nine o'clock."

Mano did not wait till nine o'clock. He was outside her office when she finished work.

"Lisa! At last, at last . . ." He smiled and stretched out his hands to her.

She looked at him and thought, yes, at last he has come to Sighet. He was leaning against the building, his left leg bent at the knee to form a triangle with the wall, and she did not answer him, since all she could think of was which side of the triangle was the hypotenuse.

444

They walked on the street, Sighet's yesterday's sweethearts, they walked like two strangers, side by side on parade, aware of being the focus of attention. The onlookers smiled, nodded their heads. The two strangers seemed to know what was expected of them during a parade. Mano strutted a bit and Lisa kept pace, her face wearing the mask of a smile, her eyes unblinking.

They passed the stores of Tibor and of Imre, who hailed the couple, smiling cheerfully:

"See you kids tonight."

Their smiles bothered Lisa. Leonid was gone but Mano had just returned and all is well, after all. What kind of a whorehouse was this, must we all behave like pimps and whores?

But her face retained the mask and unblinking eyes, for she knew the measure of her own whoring. But that was different, of course. Power healed. Yankel yes and Mano no. That was where she took a stand. Let's see now, she thought, was the banner very soiled?

Himy excelled as host that evening. The setup was near-perfect: food and drink and music, the best that money could buy, and Mano and Lisa, the major protagonists on stage ready to perform; and the audience cued in and expectant.

Maybe she was nasty, she thought, bitter and cynical. Maybe her friends really wished something nice would happen to her. Himy would trade his soul to buy her contentment and Ilona would like to see her radiant again, she was convinced of that.

What was wrong with her, why was she angry?

Mano drank freely and the liquor made him exuberant. He chewed American gum and smoked American cigarettes.

"*Looky streeckes*," he said pretentiously, "they are the finest. The judge wouldn't smoke anything else."

He passed the cigarette pack around. Everyone examined the package and admired the red circle under the cellophane wrapping, then sniffed at the cigarettes and read the words MADE IN USA several times. They were impressed. Mano offered them chewing gum while he entertained them with vignettes of university life in Cluj and spoke of his plans.

". . . at least chief engineer at the Hunedeaora electric works. My brother-in-law the judge knows them all: Malaxa and Ausnit, the old power brokers, and the new *tovarishes*. The judge plays poker with them in Sinaia, just like in the old days. . . ."

Forgive me, Himy, she thought, but your party *is* a bore. Your actors are mediocre, the script lacks freshness. Since it is Purim, it may be more appropriate, surely more entertaining, to speak of Esther, the beautiful Jewess, who married Ahasuerus the King of the Persians. Or to speak of her uncle the *macher*, Mordecai, who manipulated Esther into a position of power. And how about Haman the *mashumed*, bent on destroying the Jewish people? Just think, Himy, of the possibilities, of the many connections, of the grand drama which could be played out with flair and imagination.

What were the thoughts of Esther the Queen when Mordecai instructed her to reveal her origins to the King, thus hoping to save the Jews from Haman? Did Esther give up her power willingly, or did she try to hold on to it and talk Mordecai out of his plan, bribe him, perhaps offer him power, too, if he would keep the secret of her Jewishness from the King? Did Mordecai blackmail Esther to relinquish her position of power or did she, perhaps, relinquish it willingly, nobly, without a moment's hesitation or regret, to save her people?

What did Esther feel, knowing she had power over a multitude? Was it the same feeling as having power over a hundred, over ten human beings? How about having power over one single human being? What was the difference? Was there a difference?

Forgive me, dear Himy.

Lisa and Mano sat facing each other, late at night, in her room. The double-breasted navy-blue suit fitted well, the judge's tailor knew styling, Lisa thought. The American cigarettes did not stink like her Nationales. Mano has come up in the world, no doubt about that.

". . . it would have made all the difference," he was saying. "Why didn't you come?"

She looked at him. His hair was straight, jet-black and wiry, as it always had been. There was a smudge on the left lens of his eyeglasses. She lit one of her own cigarettes.

She had nothing to say to Mano, nothing.

"I had stayed in Sighet for months, waiting for you," he continued. "All along my sister kept sending messages. I was the only survivor. She insisted I go enroll at the university at once . . . Why didn't you come to Cluj when I asked you?"

"It was poor timing. I am sorry."

"But why——"

"Please," she said, "no reproaches. We each did what we had to do. Let it go at that."

"No," he said, "I can't. It's important to me. I simply don't understand you. You could have stayed in my sister's house. The judge is somebody, after all. I can't figure out your refusal to come."

It was way into the night, almost dawn. The window was open and a breeze moved strings of beads fringing the chandelier. She looked at the rippling colored glass beads and heard their tinny, echoless sounds.

". . . answer me, Lisa. You must answer me."

Her glance left the ceiling and shifted to his hands. She expected to see him hold three bullets in his palm.

She rubbed her eyes, she was tired.

"All right," she said, "I had run out of steam. It had taken all my strength to come back to Sighet. There was nothing left in me for another journey . . . to your sister's house. If you don't understand that, you understand nothing."

"Would you stop looking at the ceiling," he said. "You should have come, no matter what. . . ."

This person's image had sustained her *then* and *there*, she reminded herself. There must be a few driblets of compassion left in her heart.

"Tell me about yourself," she asked him.

He brightened up.

"I like it in Cluj . . . everyone knows me . . . socially . . . new types . . . campus committees . . . related to a judge. . . ."

His words rippled along with the beads and she hardly heard what he said. He was back, she thought, and she couldn't wait for him to leave. When he'll leave, she'll cry and mourn a girl she once knew who was in love with this boy. Things happened to both of them and then there was nothing left, not even a clear memory of the past.

(go, mano, leave me be. i want to cry over nothing)

". . . yet I always end up with redheads."

"How is she?" Lisa thought he was speaking of his sister.

". . . they even look like you."

(go, go away, mano. soon i'll even cease remembering a boy with a green school cap and a black visor. go while i still know you were the boy i had loved once upon a time)

"You had no right to turn away from me," he said, "you should have left me at least with an illusion . . . They were all redheads, the other girls, believe me."

He reached for her hands, stood up and pulled her to him.

"Maybe I should have been here when you returned. But my sister . . . don't you see?"

"Yes," she said, "I see."

"Lisa, my sweet Lisa. You are mine, you always were. I know. It doesn't matter what the others say. I know. You are my girl, my baby."

The beads tinkled again and Lisa looked up. He took her head in his hands.

"Look at me," he said urgently. "Listen to me, Lisa, please. We can still make it. I am Mano, your Mano. Don't pretend you stopped caring for me. How could you? You were badly hurt when I wasn't here to meet you, I can see that. But now, how about now? You still love me, don't you?"

The anxious look in his eyes, frightened and supplicating, belied the conceited, proud smile on his face. She was overwhelmed and forgot not to ache.

Driblets of compassion swelled to wells of sorrow mourning the dreams she and he had once had. Those dreams were now beyond recall, gone forever, except for their vague silhouette that reminded her she had once desired him more than anything in the world. The inability to recapture, even for an instant, the impact or the taste of that desire wrenched her heart.

"They talk, they always talked," Mano said dabbing away tears in her eyes with his handkerchief. "It's their dirty minds. I don't believe them. They know nothing. They only know how to envy me because you're my girl. They always envied me for being your sweetheart. I am only a runner-up, they now tell me, and they grin. I don't listen to them, I only listen to Himy. He's right. Pay no attention to anyone, he said to me this morning. Just believe what's in your heart."

He embraced her.

448

"What's in my heart is that you belong to me." His breath was on her face and again she noticed the smudge on the lens. "What's in my heart is that you are as pure as you were the day I said good-bye to you on the train platform," he continued, holding her tighter, "the day I was shipped away with the labor force. I promised to come back for you. I am here now to claim my virgin. You are my virgin, aren't you? That other man, he was only to save face, right baby? My virgin didn't sleep with the Rusky."

He had come to Sighet to heal himself! The discovery took her breath away. Yes, he was here to mend his punctured pride, that was all. Rachel alone had understood Mano, she knew all along that he clung to Lisa to bolster his own image and to heal wounds inflicted by a red-haired girl. His sister.

The wells of sorrow dried up abruptly in Lisa's heart and she thought of Esther the Queen who held power over the multitude and of herself who now held power over one single human being, Mano, and that numbers made no difference. Power was power.

She would say to him what he wanted to hear, she thought coolly, and he would be in her power for as long as she wished to have him. All he wanted to hear was *yes*, she was a virgin. That would validate him as a man. He would get excited, aroused and would want to make love to her at once, and in the passion of the long-awaited union an inner dictate would persuade him beyond doubt that he was deflowering her.

It wasn't much at stake, only one word, one little word. The frightened look in his eyes would turn instantly into a flash of victory, and *she* would taste real power.

The melancholy jingles of the glass beads made her look to the ceiling, but the glass beads had changed to six plaster cherubs. Her heart twitched and she gently disengaged herself from his embrace, reached for his coat, held it up to him, and said:

"They told you the truth. I did sleep with the Rusky."

11

Mano left town next morning and Nagake the Gypsy woman came to see Lisa in her office that afternoon.

Nagake was fourteen when she ran away from a wandering troupe of circus Gypsies who had come to Sighet during the summer and had set up their wagons and circus tent in the Bandzalgo Section.

She did not run far: the newly opened Le Jardin was a stone's throw from the circus tent. The young girl joined the batch of whores and was soon billed as the exotic Alhambra Maiden whom a band of Gypsies had stolen from the harems of Cadiz Pasha. In her bag Nagake still carried a tattered piece of yellow paper with many faded stamps on it. "My whore license," she boasted, "renewed regularly." Once her carnal appeal declined, after years of service at Le Jardin, she worked as an usher at the town's summer theater, in the mid-thirties. A few years later she was promoted to main usher. By that time, she had turned into a chubby little figure who bounced between aisles, parterres and the balcony with the agility of an overfed squirrel. She wore colorful fringed shawls, countless bracelets and charms on her wrists and upper arms, painted glass beads around her neck and huge looped earrings that stretched her earlobes. Patches of rouge on her cheeks and kohl on her eyelids highlighted the umber shade of her skin. Her speech at the time whistled through the gap left by a missing front tooth.

When the theater, along with the Orthodox Synagogue, burned down soon after the Jews were deported, Nagake took to fortune-telling. As the Jews began returning to town, she hit on yet another profitable profession: that of a sleuth in search of stolen Jewish property. This calling kept her active and bustling from dawn to dusk. With the speed of a highly trained combat soldier executing a surprise attack on an enemy camp, she barged into the homes of suspected looters. Her sudden raids left the suspects aghast, too startled to prevent her from dashing through rooms, opening closets and pulling out drawers, poking her head under beds and inspecting sheds and outhouses.

"The pair came to me to hear their fortunes," she now told Lisa in a secretive tone. "The tea leaves speak, they sing to me, did you know, my pretty?" She licked her lips and the tip of her tongue, which by force of habit tried to squeeze through the once empty space, was now blocked by a shiny gold tooth. "One of these days Nagake should tell your fortune! Perhaps even teach you a few magic tricks. A few potions, a few amulets, oh what they could do for you!"

Huge looped earrings jingled, her ample breasts swayed, as she heaved herself from the chair and breathed into Lisa's face:

"Some pair, Erzsi Kasznar and Vlad Radescu! Pinching away whatever their greedy eyes saw! They smell of sulfur, did you know?" She lowered herself back into the chair. "The leaves: Erzsi Kasznar's formed two circles and Radescu the lawman's leaves bunched up. Nagake understood the meaning of all this! Not *kosher*, eh? All those signs . . ."

She licked her lips again, jabbed at her breastbone with a knotty finger. "Nagake went to see the pair. Radescu wasn't home, but I peeked in."

An armlet slipped down to her wrist. She pushed it back and slowly twisted into place all her other armlets. The flabby flesh between the armlets puckered.

"You've become a little big shot in this town, my pretty," she said coyly, holding on to her information a bit longer. "My tip-off will cost you nothing, though. Just a good word from you now and then to the big shots that Nagake knows lots of things . . . The tea leaves, they sing to me."

451

She stood up and announced dramatically: "Erzsi Kasznar got your bicycle and Vlad Radescu, district attorney, has your blue room."

The blue room. The room of a much darker and deeper shade of blue than the conventional blue.

The hue Lisa had picked was deep, deep blue, almost navy blue. *Bleu marin doux*, said the color chart. Rachel had given in reluctantly. A sixteen-year-old girl's room should be a cheerful rose, or yellow, whoever heard . . . and friends had come to see the new custom-designed modern furniture. An entire wall unit consisting of built-in book cases, sliding glass panels, drawers and cabinets, and a wardrobe; a glass-topped table; the two sides of the sofa bed sectioned off into shelves to hold her radio and more books. Wide drawers beneath the seat cushions that the visitors pulled out in wonder. "A comforter and a pillow stuck in a drawer, under a seat," they said, "how chic," and ran their fingers over surfaces painted with six coats of lacquer, murmuring, "How gleaming. Still, a navy-blue room for a girl . . . whoever heard. . . ."

12

An inspector from the office of vehicle control went to Erzsi Kasznar's house the following day to check if she had a permit for her bike. She had none, nor a bill of sale, so the inspector took the bike to the police station for identification.

The red netting was torn a bit and there were some scratches on the chrome fenders. But the bike still shone almost as brightly as on the day Lisa had helped Aunt Hannah remove it from the crate.

She brought it into Ilona's room.

"I've recovered the silver bike," she told Ilona. "I pass it on to you. Now it's your turn to keep it shining."

She then went to her room, picked up a book and tried to read. The letters were indistinct, murky, or maybe her eyes did not focus properly. Her arms itched and she rolled up her sleeves.

The hives again! She slammed the book closed, got up and paced around the room scratching and castigating herself. There was no reason to break out in hives. She had no conflict, no qualms as to what to do about the blue room. So why the hives? At last she did not vacillate, as she had vacillated before going to Senator Petrescu and to the Tiplea brothers. This time she was absolutely resolute and knew exactly what it was she had to do about the blue room: nothing, precisely nothing! She will not lift

453

a finger to recover it because she will forget about the blue room! She does not want it! Period.

"So why the hives?"

She had asked the question aloud of the Matrushka doll she held in her hands.

She was mystified.

When did she take the doll out of the drawer? Was she losing her grip on reality, doing things of which she was not aware? Had the Gypsy woman cast a spell on her?

She looked at the Matrushka doll for an answer. For answers.

The doll looked back at Lisa, a serene expression on her painted pretty face and a childish, innocent smile around the dotlike nostrils, the scalloped little mouth and the round red-apple cheeks. Only her eyes, black glass beads rimmed by painted upper and lower lids and painted eyebrows, were intense. A hint of a frown was between the brows.

Lisa was sure the Matrushka doll blinked as she ran her fingers over its smooth, shiny face. She even tried to push two locks of black hair symmetrically parted in the middle of the high forehead, back under a yellow *babushka* knotted into a gay bow under the doll's chin. The head merged with a purple skirt along the natural configuration of the egg-shaped body. On the round, bulging belly an apron with stylized red geraniums and poppies surrounded by green leaves had been painted with exquisite care. The bottom of the egg was leveled off so that the doll could stand on her own.

Twisting the upper and lower sections in opposite directions, Lisa opened the doll. Nested inside was another doll, the exact reduced replica of the first. The second doll looked at Lisa with the same serene expression and the slight hint of a frown.

"You tell me then," Lisa urged the second doll, "why the hives?"

She waited a bit, then twisted the second doll open.

"If you don't tell," she warned the third doll, "I'll put you back in the drawer."

"Are you accepting the trap?" the doll finally asked, in a small voice, "is this your peace?"

"But it's only furniture," Lisa said. "It's ludicrous that I should be concerned with furniture after all that has happened to me."

454

"Is it? And is it *only* furniture or does it stand for something more——"

"Getting my room back is meaningless. It won't change anything in the long run," Lisa cut in.

"Do you think complacency would?"

"I don't know. Maybe. I am trying it——"

"Are you afraid of Radescu?"

"No. He has power and so have I, though I only have a little of it. But I'm not afraid, just tired. I don't want the blue room. For my own sake. I don't want it. Please understand me. I mustn't ache anymore. I want peace, just a little peace, not struggle——"

"Haven't you learned yet that you achieve nothing without a struggle? And that *we* say: 'If you cannot pass, you must pass'?"

"But I don't want the blue room. The harmony of the universe would not be disturbed for a single instant, one way or the other. With or without my blue room, everything would go on, as if nothing happened. Should I want the blue room, I alone would bleed again, no one else. Bleeding hearts make me squeamish. That's why I don't want the blue room."

"Then why the hives?" the third doll asked.

"Let me tell you something," she told the fourth doll patiently. "I don't want to get involved, is that clear? The room is just wood, lifeless matter. Getting it back would resuscitate nothing."

"Are you sure?"

"Yes, of course!" Lisa said and instantly knew the doll did not believe her. "All right, it would resuscitate everything! Everything, you hear?" she shouted, "and it would make me angry. Damn angry!"

"What's wrong with being angry?"

She quickly twisted the fourth doll open.

"Shouting 'foul' would merely fall on deaf ears," she told the fifth doll confidentially. "Anger would open my wounds but it would not rock the boat."

(the boat. *shalom, shalom,* they shout with joy as the boat anchors and passengers disembark)

". . . and I would scheme and dream again." Her eyes were burning. "All my carefully thought-out plans for an acheless ex-

455

istence would blow up in my face. And in my heart. *Then* what would I do?"

"There is no shortcut to living," the doll said, "unless you turn into an emotional *Muselman*."

"I must do nothing." She will pretend she did not hear what the fifth doll just said. "The confrontation——"

She burst into tears. As soon as she pronounced the word she realized how desperately she had wanted it and, at the same time, how afraid she was of it. The confrontation would exorcise or expiate, she was not sure which, old passivities, physical and emotional inertness.

There were many kinds of dying, Leonid had said, and many kinds of living.

"Still," she begged the sixth doll, "let's forget about the blue room. Let's forget what lies beyond the mountains. I am here, not there. What's the difference who has the room. I've bled enough. Let Radescu have the room. Is that too much to ask?"

"Yes!" the seventh doll replied sternly. "You can't let him have it!"

"Why not?"

"Because I am that I am."

The answer stunned her and she felt disoriented. The doll was behaving strangely, her voice was loud, almost splitting Lisa's head.

"I am that I am," the doll thundered, "and that's why the *goyim* put you on the defensive. And you are that you are, and that's why the good people of your town pilfered and thieved. They would not have broken the law, each and every law from *I am the Lord, thy God* to *thou shalt not covet anything that belongs to thy neighbor.* Their crimes are your fault. Did not Plato teach that doing wrong is worse than suffering wrong?"

"Yes," she answered meekly. "The *goyim* became thieves and murderers because I am that I am."

"Good girl! You appreciate what the *goyim* say, namely, that it is all your fault, because at long last you can see as they see: that what is upside down is truly downside up. That sweet is bitter and night is day. Good girl!"

"But——"

"No buts!" The seventh doll wagged a finger at her that had been tucked away in the folds of her pretty skirt. The finger grew

456

into a rod poking at Lisa's heart. "Why can't you be a graceful victim and let it go at that? You still provoke the *goyim* to be bad, can't you see? Or have you forgotten already that Hitler's plan was thwarted by the Allies' victory, nothing else? I assure you, your survival had nothing to do with me! The world held its breath and closed its eyes while you burned. I saw it all, nobody can tell *me* otherwise. If the Allies had won the war six months later none of you would have survived! So go easy, tread lightly! You were supposed to be *vernichted*, remember that! Someday the world will look for another Hitler."

"Now wait a minute!" Lisa yelled at the seventh doll. "You make me angry and I don't give a damn who you are and what you preach! Where were you when I needed you? You don't even make sense! You speak gibberish——"

"I do, eh?" the doll asked nastily, while the rod-finger receded into an arm which she abruptly thrust forward. *"Heilhitler!"* she growled, twisting herself into the eighth doll.

"She tried to confuse me," Lisa said. "I think her name is——"

"She is that she is," the eighth doll quickly replied. "She has no name, didn't you know? Don't let her upset you," the doll advised. "You'll just begin to ache and feel again. You might even own up to what's in your heart, start to struggle and——"

"And there is no shortcut to living and, moreover, I am not going to become an emotional *Muselman*," Lisa rejoined. "Go tell her, tell the nameless one that trap time is over and that I might do strange things, after all, whether she likes it or not! Tell her that I am not guilty and that I am not going to apologize for not having croaked as planned! I know," she told the doll, "if the Jews of Sighet had been more obliging, had had the good grace to conveniently disappear from the face of the earth, Sighet's *goyim* might have named a street after them, perhaps have erected a nice monument to their memory. After all, *Ordnung muss sein,* no? Well, tell the nameless one that I am a live one and that I intend to stay that way!"

"You've become quarrelsome," the eighth doll said, somewhat surprised. "You were practically persuaded to be passive, to let Radescu have your room. It wasn't a bad idea. It still isn't. Why not accommodate, shut your eyes or don't look. Your anger will discombobulate the status quo, the neat little systems, the pleasant homes made pleasanter with Jewish loot. So what? It's cozy the way it is. They'll start hating you all over again if you rock the boat. . . ."

A limitless yearning for Leonid overwhelmed Lisa and she slowly twisted open the eighth doll, who was giving off a peculiar smell.

"Nagake the Gypsy woman said I was smart," she told the next-to-the-last doll, the ninth doll. "Nagake was off the mark. All I want is to breathe clean air and dream. But it stinks, it always stunk here. Smells are all around me. I can't get rid of those smells, no matter what I do. I never know if I smell the spring or the cesspool. Here, everything smells alike."

She looked reflectively at the doll, who seemed to nod her head. Lisa gratefully hugged the little doll to her chest.

"Then you understand," Lisa whispered. "It is so hard to keep my promise to Leonid. How can I be strong and keep on going, even limping, when I remember that *then* and *there,* during selections, I was happy if the SS finger pointed to the other and not to me . . ."

"You will have to sort out these things at your own pace," the doll replied gently.

"I want to mourn in peace, then do something about my dreams; be strong for the love of Leonid——"

"Unravel the truth, no matter where it leads——"

"The smells. The smells prevent me from differentiating. They are lodged in my nostrils, in my ears, my eyes. I smell them all over, all the time——"

"Then examine your own role. Dare to see the system within systems——"

". . . and I am never sure whether I smell jasmine or shit. All smells turn my stomach——"

". . . refuse to be persuaded against your own moral principles. Once you've set that as your goal, you must persevere," the doll continued. "Then you'll stop retching all the time."

Just before Lisa was ready to twist it, the small doll said: "It won't be easy. It takes courage. Do you have it?"

The tenth doll was the replica of the other nine, except for its size: it was that of a thimble. Lisa held it affectionately in the palm of her hand, marveling at the minute details of the flowered apron, the eyes. The longer she admired the miniature Matrushka doll the more convinced she became that the doll's smile had an impish, cocky gleam and its chin, roundly contoured by the *babushka*, was quite pronounced, as if drawn with a heavier brush stroke than the previous dolls. She lifted the doll closer to her eyes. Yes, the chin had a certain defiant line. Then she also noticed that the two locks of hair symmetrically parted in the middle of the forehead, which were black on all the other dolls, were in fact red on the thimble-sized doll.

"Let me tell you something, you stubborn-looking little doll," Lisa said. "Shlomo Kugel's granddaughter any time has as much courage as you have. So there!"

13

A few evenings later a fiacre took Lisa, Olga, Himy and Gyuri to Radescu's house.

The room was brightly lit by a chandelier, accentuating its deep blue tone. The large rug on the floor had a geometric pattern in rich reds, dark blues and hues of yellow, a center medallion design in a soft gold and the outer guard stripes were red.

She recognized some of her books on the shelves. Margaret Mitchell's *Gone with the Wind*, Rostand's *Cyrano de Bergerac*, the Collected Verses of Endre Ady. Every item from her room, paneling and all, had been installed in his house.

She made a move to touch something: a book, a chair, the table. Something.

"Wait," Olga murmured, putting her hand on Lisa's arm, "just a bit longer. Wait."

"How dare you," Radescu ranted, "how dare you even suggest this furniture is not my property. Do you know whom you are addressing?"

"The district attorney." Himy was unruffled. "What you'll be is another question." He pulled out a handkerchief from his pocket and noisily blew his nose. "But really, Mr. Radescu, we didn't come to chat. Let's not waste each other's time." Himy had promised Gyuri, who was staying behind in the fiacre, to keep his emotions in check. "Thank you for having taken such fine care of Miss Engler's room while she was away," he continued pleasantly. "Well, maybe you didn't know she was back in town since last May, or you would have returned her room a long time ago. No matter. Thank you just the same. She is here now."

Himy pointed to Lisa, who stood with Olga near the door.

"Ridiculous!" Radescu snapped. "Whoever heard of a navy-blue room belonging to a girl! It's not hers——"

"And the chandelier, Mr. District Attorney," Lisa interjected. "I see you like to have some of my books around you."

"Utterly outrageous!" he shouted. Radescu was in shirt sleeves, an ascot tied around his neck. He loosened the knot with trembling hands. "Now you have the gall to claim my books——"

"And the Transylvanian rug," Lisa said doggedly.

"How dare you? You . . ."

He choked on the word, coughed, then stared at her contemptuously. He turned abruptly to Olga. "And you, Miss Petrescu, associating with . . . *zsidans!* You, the daughter of the great Senator Petrescu, to be even seen in the company of such scum, . . ."

Olga walked slowly up to him in the center of the room.

". . . Jews . . . filth. Out, out with you! Filth, just like——"

He stopped abruptly. Olga had slapped him across the face with the back of her hand, once on the right side, once on the left, slam bang, the popping of two paper bags filled with air.

Himy stared at Olga.

"The talk is over," he said in a thick voice. "My truck will be here tomorrow to pick up the furniture in this room. The books, the chandelier, the rug, yes, the paneling too! Will six o'clock suit you, Miss Engler?"

She nodded and Radescu began to shout again. "You'll have to prove it! I object! The law . . . you'll all pay for this insolence, you bunch of——"

Himy took off his jacket. Lisa ran out.

"Mr. Chief of Police" she called into the fiacre, "please come in. Quickly. He objects."

"Comrade," Radescu accosted Gyuri, "these people here,

without a warrant, barging in . . . what kind of justice . . . didn't give me time. . . ."

when they came to take papa they didn't even bother to use the
doorknob. they busted the door open and pointed their rifle butts at
papa, the colored plumage of the shakos fluttering as they motioned with their heads and barked, your time has come filthy jew,
you bloodsucking sonafabitch of a jew, vermin lice rot. and rachel
cried out, where are you taking him and why are you taking him? he
has done no wrong, only bedecked the town with magyar flags in
your honor. don't take him away, he has never harmed a soul. he
sings such beautiful songs, old magyar songs and lullabies about
gypsies and fine hussars, and i love him, he is my man, my children's father. why do you take him away from us? where do you
take him? why? he has done nothing wrong, he is what he is, that's
all. he is innocent of any evil but he is guilty of innocence. i am going
with him, here, take me too, i am going with my man
and they kicked mamma and said, we don't want you, bitch, only
want him and kicked her

They pulled Lisa off Radescu. There was a piece of his shirt in
her hands, and his face was scratched. She could see tiny red
spots on his cheeks. She drank a glass of water Olga brought her,
then sat down calmly in an armchair and gripped its shiny lac-
quered arms.

She wondered why everyone in the room stared at her.

She stared back at them, thinking the reason they looked at her
that way was because of the torn piece of material in her hand.
She had no idea why she held it in her hand. To the exclusion of
all else, she was aware only of a great inner tranquility. Then she
became aware of the absence of her anger.

The arms of the chair were cool and smooth to the touch and
she continued brushing her hands over them after she put the
piece of material on top of the table, near the chair.

"The search warrant." Himy handed Gyuri a document. "We
didn't really need it. We merely stepped into the room. Then all
hell broke loose. He insists it's his. . . ."

"But you can prove otherwise," Gyuri asked Lisa. "Isn't that
so?"

462

She smiled and kept sliding her hands up and down the arm of the chair.

"Open that," she told Radescu, pointing to a section in the cabinet. "After you've opened it, I predict it will become a writing surface."

Radescu mopped his face with a towel. His voice rasped as he spoke: "That's a mock drawer. It can't be opened."

"There is a knob. Pull at it," Lisa goaded him. "It may open for your distinguished self."

"It doesn't open. It's a mock drawer!" His face was livid. He turned to Gyuri: "I should know. After all, it's my furniture!"

"Behind what Radescu calls a mock drawer," Lisa quietly told Gyuri, "there are pictures of my family and friends. Several photo albums, in fact. There is also a book bound in red leather."

Her hand stopped stroking the arms of the chair. In her fingers, there was already the feel of the texture of smooth vellum pages, of boldly imprinted gold letters spelling her name on the cover of the book. She got up from the chair.

"It's my diary," she said without anger, sadly. "My diary, locked with a small clasp. There is also stationery in the 'mock drawer,' light blue, bearing my name and address, 32 General Davilla Street. There are letters addressed to me, personal letters from a childhood friend of mine. His name was Mano Dekler. There are . . ."

She walked to the cabinet, pushed a glass panel, slid her hand inside a corner and pressed a tiny button which at once released a panel from the side of the cabinet. Held by an inner bracket at a ninety-degree angle, the panel had now become a writing surface.

". . . no hidden treasures inside." She reached for a packet of letters tied with a blue ribbon. "Only things of value a young girl keeps in her secret desk."

She held up a light blue sheet of writing paper with dark printing on top, then searched among the photos and pulled one out.

"Recognize me?" she asked holding up the letterhead in one hand and a picture of herself in the other. "Do I still look like the girl in the picture, Mr. District Attorney?"

14

There was a letter on her desk the next morning. It was from Drifter.

"It is not often that the *Bricha* reverses its operational procedures," he wrote. "It has never been done, actually. But we'll do it for your brother. I'll do it.

"He is alive, your brother Laszlo is alive.

"Light one candle less every Friday night.

"He is alive, repeat, Laszlo is alive.

"One of these days, within the next three months certainly, Laszlo should be back in Sighet. I'll put him across the border myself, at Sopron. From there, he'll make it on his own.

"He'll tell you how he eluded Strimbely and the Danube.

"I came upon him in Neugamme. He had thought he was the sole Engler survivor. None of the Red Cross lists he had seen carried your name. I explained to Laszlo why: you were liberated by the Red Army.

"He weighed forty-five kilos when the British took Neugamme. Had they come a week later, Laszlo would have been found dead. He hadn't eaten in four weeks.

"He is recovered now, you'll see.

"Lisa, my dear girl Lisa. You are not alone, after all. You never were, but you could not know that.

464

"I think of you in my quiet moments.

"I have learned how to mourn and I have done my mourning. Now I am living. There is no choice. I have work to do and accept my share. It's a man's responsibility.

"That is why I will not go back with Laszlo. Sighet may hold me for too long, at a time when every second counts in the struggle for independence. At this point, the *Bricha* is my bride.

"I am Drifter no more, nor am I Zoltan Feldman.

"I am Zvi Ben Zak.

"I am not a new man; merely a man united within. Zvi Ben Zak is a whole human being, doing what needs be done: rescuing the survivors and fighting to establish a free and independent Jewish state.

"Screw the Nazis! We are going to live on. Our curve is ascending. We are becoming a Jewish nation, united, finally, at last, after two thousand years.

"I weep with pride and sing in sorrow.

"We have defeated the Nazis, mark my words. Only we, the survivors, have dealt the Nazis absolute defeat.

"The price of our becoming—it's too horrendous to even contemplate.

"But we've busted out of the whorehouse."

Himy shouted: "Laszlo the Prince is alive! He'll come back, all will be well, I'll share with him everything I have, except Olga, my Olga. You'll see, Lisa, things will work out. We'll be ready when the Prince returns. What's mine is his, except Olga, my Olga. We'll repair your house, landscape the garden, furnish the rooms, now at once. . . ."

And they cried in each other's arms.

". . . so you see Leonid, I must stay here, after all," she wrote on the unused pages of her diary. Prior to having recovered it, she had gotten into the habit of writing to Leonid while listening to lengthy speeches at meetings. She tore up her notes in the evening, after she reread them.

"Himy is right," she wrote. "I should move into my house before Laszlo's return. Have him come to a home. But the home needs care, without it decay will set in. Once in my home, I will live in my room again, look out its window into the garden,

465

watch a new train with a new schedule chug in the distance across the field. I should put the piano back where it had once been, play *Anitra's Dance* or Chopin's F Minor Nocturne. I should prune the cherry tree.

"Forgive me, my darling, for disappointing you. I've tried hard to cling to our dream, hold on to it and take it intact beyond the mountains. I failed. Events have captured me. Whatever leads I follow, they seem to bring me back to Sighet. I can't escape it.

"I give up. No, I give in. To Sighet.

"And yet only the other night, after I had wrestled with my feelings, I resolved not to cave in. I saw myself pick up the banner again. I was strong that night, unafraid, and certain of the direction of my path. I was ready to battle for what you taught me to believe in. I owned up to what was in my heart.

"But Laszlo, my brother, will be back.

"I cannot go, my love. All I can do is think of us and know it was the best time of my life. All I can do is ask myself whether I told you how much I love you. All I can do is hope that the sweetness of our love will sustain me for the rest of my life.

"Forgive me for staying. I cannot do otherwise.

"Laszlo, my brother, will be back."

She forgot to date the entry. It was April 12, 1946.

"There were two events which occurred three years ago to the day. Surely, Leonyushka, you knew of at least one. Which one, I wonder . . .

"It was three years ago, on a sunny Monday morning they say, when the Jews in the Warsaw ghetto rose up against the Nazis. Come to think of it, weren't they the only people who kept the Nazis at bay longer than the French army resisted the *Wehrmacht?*

"The second event took place far away, on an island with silky sand beaches and azure skies (I've seen pictures of it). It was the opening of a conference that sunny Monday morning. The Allies had convoked it in Bermuda to discuss problems caused by the Nazi persecution of the Jews. The Jews always caused problems, you see. Why not deliberate on the fate of the troublesome Jews under untroubled skies?

"Of the Warsaw uprising I only learned in Auschwitz; obvi-

466

ously the Nazis and Magyars suppressed the news. Yesterday Olga showed me a 1943 English newspaper clipping the senator has among his documents (he is writing his memoirs). That is how I learned of the Bermuda conference which began the same day as the Warsaw uprising. Strange coincidence, don't you think Leonid? Is there a connection between the two events?

"Although by now it doesn't matter. But it aches. It aches with unfathomable pain. It is not the kind of grief which knocks you out; it is a grief which sobers you up. It's frightful, the white, cool rage. Oh Leonyushka, why didn't someone *do* something? Surely something could have been done, something should have been done! Human beings were put in ovens and all that was done to fight the plague was a convocation of a conference on the sunny beaches of Bermuda. SOMEONE SHOULD HAVE DONE SOMETHING MORE! This much I know. Please tell me, how can I ever think of God or man without a shudder?"

This entry was dated. It was "April 19, 1946."

"April 21, 1946.
"Nothing has changed, not really. On the surface much is different: terminology, theory, men espousing and enforcing them. The principle, though, moving the new breed of comrades is the same: greed for power.

"Systems within systems, blind and deaf to obvious connections.

"Nothing has changed, not really.

"The king is dead. Long live the king.

"Tears are a waste."

"April 24, 1946.
"I walk on Main Street and don't see the big sign. THE HOUSE OF ENGLER AND SONS is gone. I walk by the store and hardly recognize the old place. Inside, workers are hammering and sawing, putting up new fixtures, dividing the place into sections. They are building a new type of business where THE HOUSE OF ENGLER AND SONS once was: the first state-owned cooperative store will be built on my father's premises.

"Let me tell you something, Leonyushka: I am relieved not to see the sign anymore. It reminds me no more of what was. . . ."

467

"April 27, 1946.

"The walls have been paneled, a new floor laid in my room. Himy wants to restore the kitchen too, at least put in a stove. I wouldn't agree to that, not yet.

"It's all settled, then. I shall move to my room. It shall become my nest. No, a grave. Perhaps just a pit. It shall hold me, close me in. I'll be rooted as behooves a Communist Party member, which I shall become soon. The bright promising star they call me, one of Ion Negrescu's protégées, the young intellectual in his youth cadres. That's me, Leonyushka.

"I've learned to limp well. There is hardly a difference between walking straight and limping.

"Only you and I know."

"May 2, 1946.

"Remember the day you had put on a civilian suit you secretly had made by the tailor, who had just returned from Dachau? You stood before me wearing a civilian suit instead of your uniform, a shirt and tie instead of your tunic, even handsomer than my Papa had been. What a happy smile was on your face! 'I knew you'd want to see me like this,' you said.

"Have I told you how much I love you? How could I? It would take a lifetime."

"May 8, 1946.

"It's past midnight. There was another night like this one, Leonyushka, when I could not sleep. That night was a year ago, after I was liberated, and I had wished for total recall. I have it.

"Now, a year later to the night, I am in my blue room.

"I have moved back into my house today.

"I have touched familiar contours but the chill in me stays.

"I wish to absorb again the meaning of this night, as I have absorbed the one a year ago, remember it forever. The density of my feelings, the leaden heaviness of an imminent, uncertain rite of passage.

"And the vast emptiness.

"As if nothing ever was.

"Except you

"and the world.

"Who shall slay my dragon?

"The piano is in my room. The ivory on two keys in the upper register, a g and an e, is missing. The pedal is broken, the soundboard cracked. After playing the first few bars of Chopin's F Minor Nocturne, I had to stop: I forgot the rest. All I remember is how to play *Für Elise*. But the piano is off-key.

"The cherry tree alone is healthy, full of blossoms. The rest of the garden is dead or dying.

"The moment of greatest peril. . . ."

She fell asleep in the middle of the sentence. It was left incomplete.

15

There were myriads of cockchafers in town that spring. The large brown beetles swarmed around the opulent crowns of chestnut trees lining the streets and dropped onto a carpet of fallen white chestnut blossoms around the trunks. Children raked through the petals with their fingers to catch beetles for a flying contest.

The facade of every building on Main Street was plastered with posters. Every store window displayed Petru Groza's picture. The posters carried Yankel's slogan EXERCISE YOUR FREEDOM: VOTE. It had become a household cliché, the slogan, creeping into casual conversation like crabgrass on a neglected lawn. Everyone hummed the *Internationale,* and each day brought new jokes about Stalin's pipe, and Truman's spectacles.

There were rumors that the Salzburg music festival would reopen in the summer.

On May 13 Yankel was back in Sighet from Bucharest where he had been during the last month. He brought galley proofs of his play and

". . . news hot off the unofficial press, so to speak. The rotten Magyars are at it again. They instigate, provoke with Hun perfidy. They'll never be genuine socialists, less so communists."

He paused, anticipating a barrage of questions from Lisa.

"Entre nous," he continued when the questions were not forthcoming, *"entre nous,* I'll tell you what will happen: the shutters will be lowered before the month is up, clamped down for good. The borders sealed off, like this." He interlocked his fingers, rounded out his palms then pressed them slowly together. "Like this," he repeated. The air escaped between his fingers with a gentle hiss. "No more crossings . . ."

"What happened? Why the——"

"Ah, this perks you up, doesn't it?" he teased her in a friendly manner, "well, the lousy Magyars, always the lousy Magyars. This time, it's the Hungarian Renaissance Party, a bunch of subversives, decadent reactionaries, counterrevolutionaries. Slimy imperialist fascists subsidized by capitalists."

He stopped the flow of words though he could have gone on orating a while longer. He had no need to prove how adept he had become in the art of diatribes and tirades. He had proven it up there in Bucharest. The higher-ups were impressed with Negrescu's eloquence, his dramatic use of words and speechcraft. And, of course, his writing.

"We allowed the Renaissance sons of bitches to smuggle out of the country certain elements too tacky for us to handle," he said businesslike, "like the Szálasi crowd. We closed our eyes when the Renaissance scum trafficked with the Szálasi scum. Let the West be saddled with them, what? Divide and conquer, who said that? But the Renaissance hooligans merged with the Szálasi gangsters and went berserk. The swine killed a high-ranking comrade."

He shuffled a few papers on his desk, cleared his throat. "The high-ranking comrade was a Soviet citizen. I can't tell you more," he said. "Top secret . . ."

Her face impassive, she said, "In that case . . ."

"Yes. At any rate, now nobody will be able to get through. Finished, done with! Tightest security. Within a month, every centimeter of the border will be patrolled. We'll comb the frontiers with a fine comb, catch the lice and squash them. . . ."

He had involuntarily laced his fingers again, touching and

pushing apart his palms in rhythm with his Adam's apple that was rapidly pumping up and down. He spread his fingers, put his hands on top of the desk and waited till he had fully regained his calm.

"A few things happened around here while I was away," he said casually. "How is our friend Mano?"

"He sends his regards."

He noted the dullness in her voice. Yankel laughed. He knew from Imre that the reunion was a good-bye. Very well. He would not twist the strings, it may still spoil the whole scheme. Women are more emotional than men. Who said that? A little more patience, a little more finessing and he wouldn't have to pluck the plum: it would fall in his lap. The time was near, only one more week.

Her Communist Party membership would take effect in one week. One more week and the old score would be settled!

"All right," he said. He cleared his throat. "Listen: the Party had planned to have elections on May 10, the former Romanian Independence Day. It had to be postponed for a few months because there are still pockets of resistance in rural areas. We must get to the peasantry. We'll blanket the entire country with more pamphlets and leaflets. Vigorous propaganda, effective slogans and actions are called for. We have a great task before us. We must show the West that the entire Romanian nation voted freely *yes* to socialism. And we must get the people to the polls! During the preelection noise and flurry, the closing of borders will barely be noticed. By the time the nation votes us in officially, it will be too late for anyone to slip through the net."

He looked at her thoughtfully.

"Congratulations," he said. "I heard you did a good job on Radescu. He deserved it. Gyuri is prosecuting him. Now *I* have an assignment for you. I am sure you'll do it equally well."

He reached in a desk drawer for a set of galley proofs.

"This is my play," he said. "Its world premiere will be in Bucharest on June 8. Does the date mean anything to you?"

"June 8, 1930," she said promptly, "the day King Carol took the royal oath after his return from exile."

"Yes. Till his abdication, June 8 was a big national holiday. There is a connection between my play and this date. We would like to use the date as a rallying cry. The day of the father's return should also become that of his son's departure. Of course it won't be June 8, 1946. We'll settle for June 8, 1947. Or thereabouts."

"King Mihai is a figurehead——"

"Not quite, and that's the point. He's becoming obstreperous. An embarrassment to the Party. Any form of monarchy in a socialist state is incongruous. Yet the people are loyal to Mihai. Therefore, he must be discredited before we pack him off into exile. A call for his abdication should come from the grass roots. We'll utilize the press, radio, the arts, to hammer the message home: King Mihai, like his father the former King Carol, is corrupt. To redeem the country, Mihai must go just as Carol went. That's where my play may become a political turning point. Remember, I told you——"

"Yes. You and Beaumarchais."

"That's right. Although in my play the action occurs in a mythical kingdom, with a mythical king, courtesan and villain as its main characters, it's an obvious dramatization of Carol's banishment by the Romanian people who rose up against him. And the reason for the revolt——"

"It was the Vienna award to Hungary that made Carol flee," she reminded him, "and his disastrous policies that led him to an alliance with the Axis. The king didn't flee because of a socialist *coup*——"

"That's not the point. The point is he fled. The flight occurred over five years ago. People have short memories. All they remember is that Carol fled. My play will now tell them why he fled."

"You are very clever, Ion."

"Thank you. I see you get the plot. You are right: the king, in my play, flees because the masses chase him out. The working class brings an end to the monarchy and all the evil it implies."

"Is that what the play is about?"

"Yes. Of course, I've constructed a complex framework for the main idea: there is court intrigue, romance. But essentially the play deals with the sources of corruption and decadence that infected the ruling palace clique. I point out where the rot comes from: the king, his mistress and a cabal of seven bankers shamelessly exploiting the workers. And how finally social revolution, led by dedicated idealists, brings an end to the people's abject poverty and ignorance. The last scene in the play, I predict, will be a blockbuster. Just visualize: the king's apartment. From far away comes the tramp of marching feet. Then the tune of the *Internationale* clearly emerges. The king, his mistress, and the chief banker now rush in and feverishly begin to pack into trunks the crown jewels, priceless ancient Romanian heirlooms, gold plates and gold goblets, gold and silver bullion, in other words treasures which belong to the Romanian people. While the criminals thus prepare to flee, the royal train pulls in to smuggle them out."

"Do they escape?"

"Of course not! That's precisely the point. In reality, Carol succeeded and fled in a train crammed with treasures. He and his Magda Lupescu, née Miriam Wolff. But in the play the villains are caught in the nick of time, tried by the people's tribunal, the king divested of his power and the bunch of capitalists——"

"Have you ever given a thought, Ion, to what you could do with the real scene?"

"What do you mean?"

"Just visualize: the royal train speeds with the villains and the loot towards the border. Meanwhile the king's escape has been discovered. The train is stopped at the border. Police search the train. They search and search. Where is the king? One of the policemen barges into a small compartment. 'How dare you?' Magda cries out in indignation from a tub in which she's taking a bubble bath, 'can't you see I am taking a bath? Don't you have any manners?' 'My apologies, lady,' the policeman mutters, embarrassed by his uncavalier behavior but slightly intoxicated by whiffs of perfume emanating from the mountain of soap bubbles. 'Pardon!' The policeman closes the door of the bath compartment and Carol emerges from under the soap bubbles just in time to catch his breath."

"You are making fun of me——"

"Why should I? In fact, isn't that what really did happen? You could have the policeman, unable to contain himself at the sight of Magda's pink shoulder, make a dive for her into the tub only to discover she was sitting on Carol. . . ."

"Really, Lisa!" He smiled briefly. "Let's be serious, all right? Where was I?"

"The villains are dragged before the people's tribunal——"

"Yes. Exactly. The audience will learn that the king can be divested of his power before he steals Romania's wealth. As our little Mihai surely would do, given more time. Like father like son. And the message is that the people are the real rulers. That they must, and should, get rid of the palace clique. That——"

"It's so basic what you say. So . . ."

"Precisely."

"I see your point. What's my assignment?"

"I'll get to that too. But first I want to make you understand that any allusion to characters living or dead is purely coincidental, as they say. When it comes to creativity, everything goes."

"Ion," she said, "go on with it. The assignment."

He handed her the galley proofs.

"Read the play during the rest of the afternoon. Then draft a review. It will be your first piece to appear in the local paper, under your name. Not bad for a beginner, don't you think?"

He wished she would have acknowledged the distinction with more than a blink of her eyes. He had thought writing a review under her name would please her.

"Write of the parallel between then and now," he said. "Hammer at the parallel between father and son. Allude to their Hohenzollern family tie which by itself would be sufficient to justify Mihai's dethronement. Exhort, exhort! Make them see the moral imperative, bring the message to the people of Sighet. Unless we are voted in, the capitalist pigs will run away with the country. Make it good and strong. My play, *The Seven-Headed Dragon King*, deserves it. And you'll go places, I guarantee it."

Alone in his office, Yankel was uneasy. Something was nagging inside him, sharp little teeth gnawing at his guts, and his anxiety made him sweat. He told himself over and over that he had done everything he could to get her off the hook. That was why he had proposed that instead of reading a self-criticism as required by each Party candidate, she write a review of his play.

How could he have guessed that he was about to be hoisted by his own petard? that the Party wouldn't accept the bargain?

Stop nagging at yourself, Negrescu. Your future is with the Party. Relax.

475

But in the next room she is soon going to realize that one of the chief villains in the play is the capitalist. There, in the next room the girl is discovering that my capitalist villain is drawn after her father, Andras Engler.

I can't help it; but I don't like the way I feel.

I shall also have to tell her that to validate her membership in the Party, she must first read her self-criticism at a meeting of the full membership.

He wiped his forehead. One thing at a time, he told himself, he'll handle one thing at a time.

No, he was not a heartless man and knew it would be hell for her to repudiate her family by praising a play that condemned her own father. He knew that from his own experience, remembering his own momentary hesitation at the forked road. Yet it was different with him: he had always wanted out, to prove himself to be as good as the next fellow. Better. She, on the other hand, had always seemed to have a firm sense of herself and was satisfied to be just Lisa Engler.

It will be tough for Lisa Engler. Precisely because the Andras Englers have vanished. The testing of Lisa Engler in the new world was necessary, of course. He understood that. It was the degree of testing that bothered him.

But she must be tested, go through the rite to demonstrate her fitness. Of course it's a tough business, just like the Bar Mitzvah or the scarring and ordeal by fire in certain tribes.

I am sorry, Lisa. You cannot escape your initiation.

But you'll do your part, I know. You are a strong girl.

He had sincerely tried to help her.

He was not a heartless man. Merely a practical man. That was what he told the comrades earlier this morning, at the committee's executive session: "Comrades, she's proven herself. She's given us the Engler premises, removed the sign. Works hard and for long hours at her desk. She'll write a fine review endorsing *The Seven-Headed Dragon King*. Isn't that proof enough of her loyalty?" And the grinning secretary: "Are you getting soft on her?" "What do you mean, soft?" Yankel wanted to know. "I mean, your kind always sticks together," the secretary retorted, a nasty look in his eyes. Yankel had shot up as if bitten by a tarantula. That's what that son of a bitch secretary wanted, Yankel suddenly realized, to see Negrescu lose his temper. Yankel knew why the secretary was pissed off: Radescu, the secretary's crony and protégé, was in deep trouble. Gyuri was putting Radescu through the wringer, accusing him of flagrant stealing, of withholding evidence, of indulging in bourgeois tastes. The secretary had also promised Radescu the post in Bucharest and instead Ion Negrescu would become the next assistant to the minister of education! The promotion had been confirmed. One more official signature. After June 8.

No wonder the secretary was out to get Negrescu.

But Negrescu kept a lid on his temper.

"The Engler article praising my play should be sufficient proof of her loyalty," he again told the committee members. "Once the town's people see the play, and they shall see it after June 8, they will instantly recognize that Mordecai Gold the capitalist is Andras Engler, her father. Let's be realists, comrades: overdoing is as bad as underdoing. Let's put the final stamp on her membership card and be done with it!"

He looked at the implacable men sitting around the table.

"We are wasting too much time on personal matters," Yankel said half reproachfully. "After all, she is no stranger to us and she is just a girl. Do men like us need this unimportant girl's last drop of blood?"

"Yes!" the secretary screeched, pounding his hand on the table in his usual obnoxious manner. "Yes, yes, if there is the danger that in that last drop of blood there may be a capitalist corpuscle!"

"Let's forgo the rite," Yankel went on, as if he did not hear the secretary's last remark, although the use of the word "corpuscle" shook him up a bit, for he had thought that the illiterate clod, the secretary, wasn't even aware that there were more than two syllable words. "Must she read her self-criticism before an open meeting? And why must she change her name?"

Yankel's damp shirt stuck to his back. He had exhausted himself pleading on her behalf. He had never veered from the Party line and he had never questioned its methods. But this last Party rite was too much, even for Ion Negrescu. It was the Bar Mitzvah *and* the ordeal by fire.

"Why change her name," he asked again. "Too much——"

"Too much?" the secretary yelled. "Was it too much for Yankel Schwartz to change his name to Ion Negrescu? Who is this Lisa Engler anyway? Just a girl, as you've said, an insignificant girl. From capitalist stock. So why shouldn't she change her name? It's a strange name, I can't make heads or tails out of it. I never liked it. It always baffled me. It's a slippery name. Sometimes it sounds like the name of the great Engels. How dare Engler sound like Engels? Did you know the word for *'angel'* in German is *Engel?* How do you like that? Does it mean that Engler is an *Engel?* A little sweet religious symbol. On the other hand, did you think of 'angles' when you heard the name Engler? Profit angles, ha? Or angling in capitalist filthy water like an angler? The name Engler is loaded with hidden meaning, I tell you. I don't like it! Instead of this capitalist-religious hodgepodge I want to hear a good, clear socialist name. No innuendos. Something like *pescar,* a fisherman. Let her be Pescariu! Any objection?"

Yankel looked around. The men around the table had a hard, leathery look, determined knitted brows. Gyuri nodded in agreement with the secretary.

"If you think it's too much, Negrescu-Schwartz, how about letting her off your review? Let someone else write it, if you are so deeply concerned about her feelings. . . ."

Yankel had opened his mouth to say "Done," when he suddenly sensed the secretary's trap: Negrescu's sentimentality makes him unfit for the high post in Bucharest, the secretary would inform the central committee, but Vlad Radescu . . .

"All right, comrade secretary," Yankel then said with dignity, "you'll have your way."

Now I know how a pinned butterfly under glass feels, Yankel thought.

"But I shall appoint her as chairman of the district People's Literary Association when I vacate the post to assume a new one in the ministry in Bucharest," he informed the secretary, then stalked out the room.

Yankel looked at his wristwatch broodingly. He would give her another half hour, then face her.

He must stop being anxious.

478

The play's the thing, who said that? Was it Hamlet? Maybe . . . The point is, *his* play was done, everyone liked it up there in Bucharest. Relax, Negrescu, relax.

Andras Engler was a petit-bourgeois merchant, typical of his class. Yankel did not have to invent such characters.

Again Yankel wondered about rumors he heard many years ago. It was his father, Reb Schwartz, who was supposed to have married Rachel Dankenberg because old man Haskell Dankenberg wanted a pious, learned man to marry his sister. But Rachel had married Andras Engler.

What would have happened if Rachel had married his father? Would Reb Schwartz have become the cosmopolitan, urbane, wealthy merchant rather than the small-time shopkeeper with the big reputation of a great *Talmud-hacham?*

Would Lisa have been his sister?

Andras Engler's kind smile had always irritated Yankel. The self-contained gentleman in perfectly tailored suits, the enormous gold chain swinging across his chest, the elegant ivory cane hanging from his arm, never failed to set Yankel's teeth on edge. And the smoothly brushed sideburns.

How Lisa used to cling to him!

Andras Engler was a perfect model for Mordecai Gold, the chief banker in his play, who as secret adviser to the king, cunningly manipulated and exploited the working class.

There must be no compromise in a matter of artistic integrity, he reminded himself.

I am sorry, Lisa. I really am. Artistic truth must prevail.

Take the title of the play, for instance: *The Seven-Headed Dragon King.* It was an unmistakable reference to the ancient folktale every boy and girl learned in the first grade. That was precisely why he had chosen the title. Instant identification. Bloodsucking dragon reads king and its ugly seven heads reads the cabal of seven bankers led by Mordecai Gold. And Princess Teodora reads the country, pure and beautiful, who must be saved from the jaws of the dragon.

The *plebs* would not fail to get the message: the dragon king and its seven heads must be extirpated.

He looked at his watch. By now she knew.

The name of the game was power, he reminded himself. The

secretary was after him. A swarm of locusts would fight for Yankel's post when he vacated it. But he had settled at least *that*. Lisa would get his post. He was not a heartless man.

Once in Bucharest, Ion Negrescu would remember the secretary's insolence, boorishness and stupidity.

One thing at a time.

First he would mollify Lisa concerning the Andras-Mordecai characterization. Then explain to her the need for the change of name.

His Adam's apple moved fast, fast.

Finally he stepped into her office.

She sat at her desk, smoking.

"Tell me what you think of the play," Yankel asked tensely.

She returned the galley proofs to him.

"And Reb Schwartz was worried what was to become of you," she said. Her voice was controlled, calm, just a whit too subdued, hardly any intimation of emotion. "You'll become an acclaimed playwright, that's what you'll become. Ion Negrescu, the incredible, fantastic playwright. . . ."

Where was the flood of recriminations, of tears? Did he worry needlessly? Yankel wondered. Could it be that she failed to see the similarity?

"Then the review? . . ." he asked tentatively.

"What about it?"

"You understand, of course, there is nothing personal in the play. Merely examining reality under an artistic microscope. . . ."

"Certainly."

"But the review . . ." He was confused. Did she really fail to see the similarity? "When will you draft the review? We have less than a month before June 8."

"I know," she said. "As to the review, it should do justice to the spirit of the play. I cannot simply throw it together any which way. I must agonize over every word, every meaning. I must make it worthy of your play."

"Take your time," he said, sighing with relief. She either missed the point entirely or she was getting used to Party blinders. It was more likely the latter, he thought. "And the rewards——"

480

"Rewards?"

"Yes. There are rewards for you, as soon as you become an official Party member."

"When will that be?"

"A week from today. But first you'll read a certain statement at the general membership meeting. That's tomorrow evening."

"What statement?"

"Nothing to it. Don't worry."

"Worry? Who is worried?"

"I am. I mean, I am not and neither should you be. A mere formality. The usual Party language. It will be over before you know it. It's a short statement, takes only three minutes. I've timed it. And nobody listens anyhow. They'll only look at you, won't even hear what you say," he babbled, then opened a folder he brought along with him and gave her a typed sheet. "Here, see for yourself. The usual Party language. Although I've tried to have you exempted from reading it. Ask Gyuri how I tried. . . ."

"THE HOUSE OF ENGLER AND SONS belonged to my father, Andras Engler," she began to read. "He was a member of the petit-bourgeois class, a wealthy merchant. He was, in other words, a capitalist . . . The capitalist system corrupts . . . erects class barriers . . . This we must not permit to happen . . . values of my class . . . I repudiate . . . hereby reject and renounce . . . I turn to you, comrades . . . emancipate myself from the shackles of my class . . . Accept me in your ranks . . . to become a productive member of the working class . . . build a new society through the Party. Should you accept me in your ranks, I wish to change my name to Elisabeta Pescariu."

Yankel was watching her read, trying to anticipate her reaction. She folded the paper and the thin sound of her fingers creasing it went through him like the point of a needle.

She placed the folded sheet of paper on the desk, put her hands in her lap and looked directly at him, almost serenely.

As she had read the statement, very slowly, she began to feel light, lighter, almost weightless, as if each word she read had entered into her and removed blood, muscles, cartilage, bones, from her insides, cleansed her out thoroughly, leaving her with such a degree of detachment from her boundless rage and pain that she could, at last, master her own emotions with absolute ease. She could, at long last, think with perfect lucidity of what she must do.

"I wasn't going to tell you till after you delivered the self-criticism," Yankel was saying, "but . . . why hold back good news from you."

"Then wait," she said. "I am in no hurry."

"I've tried, you know, I've really tried. I've bucked them all . . . All right, now the good news. A little reward. You deserve it."

"I deserve nothing."

"Oh yes, you do. It's important to me. Listen to this: as of September, I shall take on a post in the national government. Ministry of education and cultural activities. My position here will be filled in by *my* appointee. Guess whom I've appointed?"

"I haven't got the vaguest idea."

"You, of course! No, don't thank me. I've tried to help you all along, believe me. You don't have to be grateful to me. I promised you would go places. Well?"

"You were right," she said, "I am going places."

"Yes. I did it because . . ."

He stopped. He cannot love his own sister. That's an abomination, worst then pederasty, worse than any perversity known to man.

"I did it because you and I are Jews," he said softly, "and we must stick together. Won't you have dinner with me tonight?"

"Oh," she said gently, "I can't. I am having dinner with Olga and Himy tonight. Tomorrow, though. I'll be free then."

Olga understood at once. She and Himy were holding hands. Olga has changed, Lisa thought, she has changed to a woman. To Himy's woman. Olga was glowing, her skin was clear, no rouge or eye makeup. Her long blond hair was pulled back and tied with a grosgrain ribbon. She was so beautiful, Lisa thought. What about children, Olga and Himy's children?

Olga understood and agreed with Lisa. It was Himy who tried to change her mind.

"Sleep on it, Lisa. It's not as if you have no choice. That should make a difference. . . ."

Lisa shook her head.

"But the Prince," Himy said, "he may be here any day."

"She is ready now," Olga said. "Now; not tomorrow, or after-tomorrow. Now."

"I'll fix that bastard Schwartz! I'll get him to direct his play in Siberia . . . or in the Lubianka . . . As to the change of name, you won't have to do it Lisa. I'll see to it. I have connections——"

"Himy." Lisa did not want to disturb her own balance. "Please don't be angry. Or sad. The time has come. Welcome it."

The minutes went by in silence.

"If that's what you want," he said at last. "Go to your house now. Pack. Give me two hours. I'll get the necessary papers and an official Jeep. I'll drive you to Sopron. There——"

"No, Himy. Not to Sopron. Only to Máteyszalka. Just see me out of Romania. From Máteyszalka I must do it on my own."

16

It took her less then a half hour to pack. One dress, a change of underwear, an extra pair of shoes, a few toiletries. Her eyes fell on Plato's *Dialogues.* She reached for it, then changed her mind and left it where it was, on the side shelf of the blue sofa bed.

She wrapped her mother's four-branched silver candelabrum in a towel and gently put it into the open valise. She stared at the bulky package for a while, then picked it up from the valise as gently as she had put it there. She unwrapped the candelabrum and placed it on top of the piano. Then she stared at the candelabrum standing there. She saw scratches on the lid of the piano. She rewrapped the candelabrum in the towel and slowly put it back into the valise.

She released the button to her secret desk, removed several photographs from albums and stacked the pictures neatly next to the candelabrum. She opened her diary and read the last unfinished sentence she had written: "The moment of greatest peril . . .

". . . comes when injustice fails to make one angry; when one does not know how to mourn; when memory becomes a vast aridity; when one is found wanting in wishing for dreams because one has forgotten how to dream; and when dying before one's time does not seem to be a crime." She finished the sentence and closed the diary in the desk.

The Matrushka doll was in the drawer. She took it out, twisted open each top. All ten dolls were there. She fitted the dolls back into one another, rolled the egg-shaped Matrushka doll in another towel, then held it to her chest.

She cradled the Matrushka doll in her arms, cradled and rocked the soft little bundle. She began to cry, a barely audible sigh, a gentle hush, it could have been a lullaby. . . .

It was good to cry *then* and *there.* It was overdue, that kind of crying. It was the beginning of my mourning and I knew I should rejoice. But I cried.

I cried for so many things, past and future, for I knew *then* and *there* that no one can slay my dragon except me and that as long as I stayed in the whorehouse I would never have the courage to take on the dragon. If I stayed, I knew I would forget names and faces and feelings, and I would become an expert at snapping fingers. I knew if I stayed I would never breathe clean air, the smell or the stench would always cling to my nostrils and I would never be certain whether I smelled jasmine or burnt flesh, and that was why I would not stay.

I cried because I knew the batch of letters from Mano I left behind in my secret desk was part of my youth and that it was gone, done with. I had grown up.

I cried because I knew that searching for clear-cut answers is less important than recognizing right from wrong, good from bad, and I cried because I knew such a task was almost impossible to accomplish. I cried because I knew I would have to learn to compromise, but I also knew that without Rachel's moral integrity a compromise could turn into a sellout and I was not certain whether I'd always have the strength to keep from selling out. I cried because I knew it would be difficult to make my own decisions and bear responsibility for them. I cried because I was letting go of my dependency, ceasing to be someone's little sister . . .

I cried because I knew I would always wonder if there is green under the snow in the Dombas; dream that perhaps someday, somewhere . . . And yes, I cried because I knew Leonid would always be in my heart as the old lady had told me in the delousing room in Auschwitz, that first day *then* and *there* when naked and shivering and my hair shorn, frightened and alone among masses of other naked bodies, all I was left with was a certificate in dark green covers. It was my baccalaureate diploma and I pressed it to my heart, clung to it as if it were my Mamma and Papa, and then an SS snatched it away from me and I was left alone in the world, naked and exposed. The SS threw the baccalaureate diploma on a pile of rubbish in the middle of the room, oh how it hurt to see it there, and as the rubbish was carted away and with it my baccalaureate diploma I began to scream, scream, my baccalaureate diploma, it's mine, that's all I have left, don't take away the last vestige of myself, please, that's all I have left from I am that I am, I screamed and screamed and nobody heard me

then this old lady came to me, maybe she was not as old as I was young, the lady came to me and said, "my child, don't you cry now, hush; listen: nobody can take that away from you. It will be in your mind forever what you have learned," and she gently tapped my forehead.

And so I cried with the Matrushka doll in my arms because I knew that Leonid would be forever in my heart. But I also cried because I knew it would not be the same as really being with him, and I cried because that was the way it had to be;

because I was leaving Sighet, the deceptive citadel of safety, I was leaving my natal town for good, never to see it again, and

I cried because I knew someday I would understand Sighet for what it truly was: the mountains, the river, the Grand Corso, the Malom Kert, not caring one way or the other, neutral: stone and soil. Green sprouting every spring, whether I am there or not, whether a little girl digs with her shovel under the snow or not.

I cried because the house was repaired, and I would never live in it again; strangers will look out my window while I shall have to start from scratch to build a new house for myself somewhere;

I cried because I took the candelabrum along, though I did not want to, for I was afraid its silver might eclipse reality again, yet I had to take it along for Mamma had lit the Sabbath candles in it and I am a Jew.

I cried because Himy was so good to me, not always for the sake of my brother Laszlo, but simply because Himy was a kind man with a big heart, and I cried because there were not enough

Ilonas and Elena Corcescus in the world to counterbalance those who make us suffer so much.

I cried because I did not know if I would see my brother Laszlo again; but I knew I had no choice except to do what I was doing: leave everything behind, for I would rather die than reject my name and disown Papa.

And I cried because I remembered that two years ago to the day, there were forty empty cattle cars in the freight yard, waiting under the clear blue sky to take the Jews of Sighet to Auschwitz.

Then I began my mourning. . . .

I mourned my brother Miklos who was murdered by the Nazis one winter morning in a frozen forest in Germany;

and I mourned and I cried for Mamma and Papa whom the Nazis had burned in the ovens in Auschwitz while the world closed its eyes.

In the Jeep with Himy, driving towards Máteyszalka, I cried because I was scared.

But I knew that in spite of it all I would go on, screw the Nazis, we have defeated them. I shall go on, yes, go through Sopron again, go far to see the blue skies of our Homeland, and see other mountains, other oceans.

I cried because I knew I had survived but I was not sure I was free.